"Coben again keeps the reader off-balance with innovative story lines and diabolical bad guys." —*People*

"Mr. Coben's plotting skills are in vigorous form, and he has devised a cleverly intricate scheme surrounding Tara's disappearance." —*The New York Times*

"This crackling spellbinder will . . . keep you mesmerized from beginning . . . to head-spinning, unexpected end. . . . Coben's two previous novels, *Gone for Good* and *Tell No One*—both complicated, compelling, peopled with well-drawn characters, and full of fast action—set admirers' expectations at unreasonable heights. But like Houdini's ever more daring escapes, Coben meets the challenge and then breathtakingly beats it; this book is even better." —*Forbes*

"A killer opening line. . . . Coben turns his hairpin plot inside out. . . . The book has plenty of speed as Coben pushes the pedal to the metal. The pages fly by."
—*The Orlando Sentinel*

"Harlan Coben really moves. His writing zips along, zigging here, zagging there, never settling anywhere long enough to allow self-reflection, which sounds like a stellar road map for a summer read. And stellar is what his latest thriller, *No Second Chance,* proves to be . . . full of clever feints and hairpin narrative turns."
—*The Dallas Morning News*

"Every time you think Harlan Coben couldn't get any better at uncoiling a whip snake of a page-turner, he comes along with a new novel that somehow surpasses its predecessor. That's again the case with *No Second Chance.*" —*San Francisco Chronicle*

continued . . .

Also by Harlan Coben

HARLAN COBEN

no second chance

A SIGNET BOOK

SIGNET
Published by New American Library, a division of
Penguin Group (USA) Inc., 375 Hudson Street,
New York, New York 10014, USA
Penguin Group (Canada), 10 Alcorn Avenue, Toronto,
Ontario M4V 3B2, Canada (a division of Pearson Penguin Canada Inc.)
Penguin Books Ltd., 80 Strand, London WC2R 0RL, England
Penguin Ireland, 25 St. Stephen's Green, Dublin 2,
Ireland (a division of Penguin Books Ltd.)
Penguin Group (Australia), 250 Camberwell Road, Camberwell, Victoria 3124,
Australia (a division of Pearson Australia Group Pty. Ltd.)
Penguin Books India Pvt. Ltd., 11 Community Centre, Panchsheel Park,
New Delhi - 110 017, India
Penguin Broup (NZ), cnr Airborne and Rosedale Roads, Albany,
Auckland 1310, New Zealand (a division of Pearson New Zealand Ltd.)
Penguin Books (South Africa) (Pty.) Ltd., 24 Sturdee Avenue,
Rosebank, Johannesburg 2196, South Africa

Penguin Books Ltd, Registered Offices: 80 Strand, London WC2R 0RL, England

Published by Signet, an imprint of New American Library, a division of
Penguin Group (USA) Inc. Previously published in a Dutton edition.

First Signet Printing, May 2004
10 9 8 7 6 5 4 3

PUBLISHER'S NOTE
This is a work of fiction. Names, characters, places, and incidents either are the
product of the author's imagination or are used fictitiously, and any resem-
blance to actual persons, living or dead, business establishments, events, or lo-
cales is entirely coincidental.
    The publisher does not have any control over and does not assume any re-
sponsibility for author or third-party Web sites or their content.

In loving memory of my mother-in-law,
Nancy Armstrong

And in celebration of her grandchildren:

Thomas, Katharine, McCallum, Reilly, Charlotte, Dovey,
Benjamin, Will, Ana, Eve, Mary, Sam, Caleb, and Annie

chapter 1

When the first bullet hit my chest, I thought of my daughter.

At least, that is what I want to believe. I lost consciousness pretty fast. And, if you want to get technical about it, I don't even remember being shot. I know that I lost a lot of blood. I know that a second bullet skimmed the top of my head, though I was probably already out by then. I know that my heart stopped. But I still like to think that as I lay dying, I thought of Tara.

FYI: I saw no bright light or tunnel. Or if I did, I don't remember that either.

Tara, my daughter, is only six months old. She was lying in her crib. I wonder if the gunfire frightened her. It must have. She probably began to cry. I wonder if the familiar albeit grating sound of her cries somehow sliced through haze, if on some level I actually heard her. But again I have no memory of it.

What I do remember, however, was the moment Tara was born. I remember Monica—that's Tara's mother—bearing down for one last push. I remember the head appearing. I was the first to see my daughter. We all know about life's forks in the road. We all know about opening one door and closing another, life cycles, the changes in seasons. But the moment your child is born …

it's beyond surreal. You have walked through a *Star Trek*–like portal, a full-fledged reality transformer. Everything is different. You are different, a simple element hit with a startling catalyst and metamorphosed into one far more complex. Your world is gone; it shrinks down to the dimensions of—in this case, anyway—a six-pound fifteen-ounce mass.

Fatherhood confuses me. Yes, I know that with only six months on the job, I am an amateur. My best friend, Lenny, has four kids. A girl and three boys. His oldest, Marianne, is ten, his youngest just turned one. With his face permanently set on happily harried and the floor of his SUV permanently stained with congealed fast food, Lenny reminds me that I know nothing yet. I agree. But when I get seriously lost or afraid in the realm of raising a child, I look at the helpless bundle in the crib and she looks up at me and I wonder what I would not do to protect her. I would lay down my life in a second. And truth be told, if push came to shove, I would lay down yours too.

So I like to think that as the two bullets pierced my body, as I collapsed onto the linoleum of my kitchen floor with a half-eaten granola bar clutched in my hand, as I lay immobile in a spreading puddle of my own blood, and yes, even as my heart stopped beating, that I still tried to do something to protect my daughter.

I came to in the dark.

I had no idea where I was at first, but then I heard the beeping coming from my right. A familiar sound. I did not move. I merely listened to the beeps. My brain felt as if it'd been marinated in molasses. The first impulse to break through was a primitive one: thirst. I craved water. I had never known a throat could feel so dry. I tried to call out, but my tongue had been dry-caked to the bottom of my mouth.

A figure entered the room. When I tried to sit up, hot pain ripped like a knife down my neck. My head fell back. And again, there was darkness.

When I awoke again, it was daytime. Harsh streaks of sunlight slashed through the venetian blinds. I blinked through them. Part of me wanted to raise my hand and block the rays, but exhaustion would not let the command travel. My throat was still impossibly parched.

I heard a movement and suddenly there was someone standing over me. I looked up and saw a nurse. The perspective, so different from the one I was used to, threw me. Nothing felt right. I was supposed to be the one standing looking down, not the other way around. A white hat—one of those small, harshly triangular numbers—sat like a bird's nest on the nurse's head. I've spent a great deal of my life working in a wide variety of hospitals, but I'm not sure I've ever seen a hat like that outside of TV or the movies. The nurse was heavyset and black.

"Dr. Seidman?"

Her voice was warm maple syrup. I managed a very slight nod.

The nurse must have read minds because she already had a cup of water in her hand. She put the straw between my lips and I sucked greedily.

"Slow down," she said gently.

I was going to ask where I was, but that seemed pretty obvious. I opened my mouth to find out what had happened, but again she was one step ahead of me.

"I'll go get the doctor," she said, heading for the door. "You just relax now."

I croaked, "My family . . ."

"I'll be right back. Try not to worry."

*   *   *

I let my eyes wander about the room. My vision had that medicated, shower-curtain haze. Still, there were enough stimuli getting through to make certain deductions. I was in a typical hospital room. That much was obvious. There was a drip bag and IV pump on my left, the tube snaking down to my arm. The fluorescent bulbs buzzed almost, but not quite, imperceptibly. A small TV on a swinging arm jutted out from the upper right-hand corner.

A few feet past the foot of the bed, there was a large glass window. I squinted but could not see through it. Still, I was probably being monitored. That meant I was in an ICU. That meant that whatever was wrong with me was something pretty bad.

The top of my skull itched, and I could feel a pull at my hair. Bandaged, I bet. I tried to check myself out, but my head really did not want to cooperate. Dull pain quietly boomed inside me, though I couldn't tell from where it originated. My limbs felt heavy, my chest encased in lead.

"Dr. Seidman?"

I flicked my eyes toward the door. A tiny woman in surgical scrubs complete with the shower cap stepped into the room. The top of the mask was untied and dangled down her neck. I am thirty-four years old. She looked about the same.

"I'm Dr. Heller," she said, stepping closer. "Ruth Heller." Giving me her first name. Professional courtesy, no doubt. Ruth Heller gave me a probing stare. I tried to focus. My brain was still sluggish, but I could feel it sputtering to life. "You are at St. Elizabeth Hospital," she said in a properly grave voice.

The door behind her opened and a man stepped inside. It was hard to see him clearly through the shower-curtain haze, but I don't think I knew him. The man crossed his arms and leaned against the wall with practiced casualness. Not a doctor, I thought. You work with them long enough, you can tell.

Dr. Heller gave the man a cursory glance and then she turned her full attention back to me.

"What happened?" I asked.

"You were shot," she said. Then added: "Twice."

She let that hang for a moment. I glanced toward the man against the wall. He hadn't moved. I opened my mouth to say something, but Ruth Heller pressed on. "One bullet grazed the top of your head. The bullet literally scraped off your scalp, which, as you probably know, is incredibly rich with blood."

Yes, I knew. Serious scalp wounds bled like beheadings. Okay, I thought, that explained the itch on top of my head. When Ruth Heller hesitated, I prompted her. "And the second bullet?"

Heller let out a breath. "That one was a bit more complicated."

I waited.

"The bullet entered your chest and nicked the pericardial sac. That caused a large supply of blood to leak into the space between your heart and the sac. The EMTs had trouble locating your vital signs. We had to crack your chest—"

"Doc?" the leaning man interrupted—and for a moment, I thought he was talking to me. Ruth Heller stopped, clearly annoyed. The man peeled himself off the wall. "Can you do the details later? Time is of the essence here."

She gave him a scowl, but there wasn't much behind it. "I'll stay here and observe," she said to the man, "if that's not a problem."

Dr. Heller faded back and now the man loomed over me. His head was too big for his shoulders so that you feared his neck would collapse from the weight of it. His hair was crew cut all around, except in the front, where it hung down in a Caesar line above his eyes. A soul patch, an ugly smear of growth, sat on his chin like a burrowing insect. All in all, he looked like a member of a boy band gone to serious seed. He smiled down at me, but there was no warmth behind it. "I'm Detective Bob Regan of the Kasselton Police Department," he said. "I know you're confused right now."

"My family—" I began.

"I'll get to that," he interrupted. "But right now, I need to ask you some questions, okay? Before we get into the details of what happened."

He waited for a response. I tried my best to clear the cobwebs and said, "Okay."

"What's the last thing you remember?"

I scanned my memory banks. I remembered waking up that morning, getting dressed. I remembered looking in on Tara. I remembered turning the knob on her black-n-white mobile, a gift from a colleague who insisted it would help stimulate a baby's brain or something. The mobile hadn't moved or bleated out its tinny song. The batteries were dead. I'd made a mental note to put in new ones. I headed downstairs after that.

"Eating a granola bar," I said.

Regan nodded as if he'd expected this answer. "You were in the kitchen?"

"Yes. By the sink."

"And then?"

I tried harder, but nothing came. I shook my head. "I woke up once before. At night. I was here, I think."

"Nothing else?"

I reached out again but to no avail. "No, nothing."

Regan flipped out a pad. "Like the doc here told you,

you were shot twice. You have no recollection of seeing a gun or hearing a shot or anything like that?"

"No."

"That's understandable, I guess. You were in a bad way, Marc. The EMTs thought you were a goner."

My throat felt dry again. "Where are Tara and Monica?"

"Stay with me, Marc." Regan was staring down at the pad, not at me. I felt the dread begin to press down on my chest. "Did you hear a window break?"

I felt groggy. I tried to read the label on the drip bag to see what they were numbing me with. No go. Pain medication, at the very least. Probably morphine in the IV pump. I tried to fight through the effects. "No," I said.

"You're sure? We found a broken window near the rear of the house. It may have been how the perpetrator gained entry."

"I don't remember a window breaking," I said. "Do you know who—"

Regan cut me off. "Not yet, no. That's why I'm here asking these questions. To find out who did this." He looked up from his pad. "Do you have any enemies?"

Did he really just ask me that? I tried to sit up, tried to gain some sort of angle on him, but there was no way that was going to happen. I did not like being the patient, on the wrong end of the bed, if you will. They say doctors make the worst patients. This sudden role reversal is probably why.

"I want to know about my wife and daughter."

"I understand that," Regan said, and something in his tone ran a cold finger across my heart. "But you can't afford the distraction, Marc. Not right yet. You want to be helpful, right? Then you need to stay with me here." He went back to the pad. "Now, what about enemies?"

Arguing with him any further seemed futile or even harmful, so I grudgingly acquiesced. "Someone who would shoot me?"

"Yes."

"No, no one."

"And your wife?" His eyes settled hard on me. A favorite image of Monica—her face lighting up when we first saw Raymondkill Falls, the way she threw her arms around me in mock fear as the water crashed around us—rose like an apparition. "Did she have enemies?"

I looked at him. "Monica?"

Ruth Heller stepped forward. "I think that might be enough for now."

"What happened to Monica?" I asked.

Dr. Heller met up with Detective Regan, standing shoulder to shoulder. Both looked at me. Heller started to protest again, but I stopped her.

"Don't give me this protect-the-patient crap," I tried to shout, fear and fury battling against whatever had put my brain in this fuzz. "Tell me what happened to my wife."

"She's dead," Detective Regan said. Just like that. Dead. My wife. Monica. It was as if I hadn't heard him. The word couldn't reach me.

"When the police broke into your home, you had both been shot. They were able to save you. But it was too late for your wife. I'm sorry."

There was another quick flash now—Monica at Martha's Vineyard, on the beach, tan bathing suit, that black hair whipping across those cheekbones, giving me the razor-sharp smile. I blinked it away. "And Tara?"

"Your daughter," Regan began with a quick throat clear. He looked at his pad again, but I don't think he planned on writing anything down. "She was home that morning, correct? I mean, at the time of the incident?"

"Yes, of course. Where is she?"

Regan closed the pad with a snap. "She was not at the scene when we arrived."

My lungs turned to stone. "I don't understand."

"We originally hoped that maybe she was in the care of a family member or friend. A baby-sitter even, but . . ." His voice faded.

"Are you telling me you don't know where Tara is?"

There was no hesitation this time. "Yes, that's correct."

It felt as if a giant hand were pushing down on my chest. I squeezed my eyes shut and fell back. "How long?" I asked.

"Has she been missing?"

"Yes."

Dr. Heller started speaking too quickly. "You have to understand. You were very seriously injured. We were not optimistic you would survive. You were on a respirator. A lung collapsed. You also contracted sepsis. You're a doctor, so I know I don't have to explain to you how serious that is. We tried to slow down the meds, help you wake up—"

"How long?" I asked again.

She and Regan exchanged another glance, and then Heller said something that ripped the air out of me all over again. "You've been out for twelve days."

chapter 2

"**We're doing all** we can," Regan said in a voice that sounded too rehearsed, as if he'd been standing over my bed while I was unconscious, working on his delivery. "As I told you, we were not sure we had a missing child at first. We lost valuable time there, but we've recovered now. Tara's photo has been sent out to every police station, airport, tollbooth plaza, bus and train station—anything like that within a hundred-mile radius. We've run background profiles on similar abduction cases, see if we can find a pattern or a suspect."

"Twelve days," I repeated.

"We have a trace on your various phones—home, business, cell—"

"Why?"

"In case someone calls in a ransom demand," he said.

"Have there been any calls?"

"Not yet, no."

My head dropped back to the pillow. Twelve days. I'd been lying in this bed for twelve days while my baby girl was . . . I pushed the thought away.

Regan scratched at his beard. "Do you remember what Tara was wearing that morning?"

I did. I had developed something of a morning routine—wake up early, tiptoe toward Tara's crib, stare down. A baby is not all joy. I know that. I know that there are moments of mind-numbing boredom. I know that there are nights when her screams work on my nerve endings like a cheese grater. I don't want to glorify life with an infant. But I liked my new morning routine. Looking down at Tara's tiny form fortified me somehow. More than that, this act was, I guess, a form of rapture. Some people find rapture in a house of worship. Me—and yeah, I know how corny this sounds—I found rapture in that crib.

"A pink one-piece with black penguins," I said. "Monica got it at Baby Gap."

He jotted it down. "And Monica?"

"What about her?"

His face was back in the pad. "What was she wearing?"

"Jeans," I said, remembering the way they slid over Monica's hips, "and a red blouse."

Regan jotted some more.

I said, "Are there—I mean, do you have any leads?"

"We're still investigating all avenues."

"That's not what I asked."

Regan just looked at me. There was too much weight in that stare.

My daughter. Out there. Alone. For twelve days. I thought of her eyes, the warm light only a parent sees, and I said something stupid. "She's alive."

Regan tilted his head like a puppy hearing a new sound.

"Don't give up," I said.

"We won't." He continued with the curious look.

"It's just that . . . are you a parent, Detective Regan?"

"Two girls," he said.

"It's stupid, but I'd know." The same way I knew the world would never be the same when Tara was born. "I'd know," I said again.

He did not reply. I realized that what I was saying—
especially coming from a man who scoffs at notions of
ESP or the supernatural—was ridiculous. I knew that
this "sense" merely came from want. You want to believe so badly that your brain rearranges what it sees.
But I clung to it anyway. Right or wrong, it felt like a
lifeline.

"We'll need some more information from you,"
Regan said. "About you, your wife, friends, finances—"

"Later." It was Dr. Heller again. She moved forward
as if to block me from his gaze. Her voice was firm. "He
needs to rest."

"No, now," I said to her, upping the firm-o-meter a
notch past hers. "We need to find my daughter."

Monica had been buried at the Portman family plot
on her father's estate. I missed her funeral, of course. I
don't know how I felt about that, but then again, my
feelings for my wife, in those stark moments when I was
honest with myself, have always been muddled. Monica
had that beauty of privilege, what with the too-fine
cheekbones, straight silk black hair, and that country
club lockjaw that both annoyed and aroused. Our marriage was an old-fashioned one—shotgun. Okay, that's
an exaggeration. Monica was pregnant. I was fence-
sitting. The upcoming arrival tilted me into the matri-
monial pasture.

I heard the funeral details from Carson Portman,
Monica's uncle and the only member of her family who
kept in touch with us. Monica had loved him dearly.
Carson sat at my hospital bedside with his hands folded
in his lap. He looked very much like your favorite college professor—the thick-lensed spectacles, the nearly
shedding tweed coat, and the overgrown shock of Al-
bert Einstein–meets–Don King hair. But his brown eyes

glistened as he told me in his sad baritone that Edgar, Monica's father, had made sure that my wife's funeral was a "small, tasteful affair."

Of that, I had no doubt. The small part, at least.

Over the next few days I had my share of visitors at the hospital. My mother—everyone called her Honey—exploded into my room every morning as if fuel propelled. She wore Reebok sneakers of pure white. Her sweatsuit was blue with gold trim, as if she coached the St. Louis Rams. Her hair, though neatly coiffed, had the brittle of too many colorings, and there was the whiff of a last cigarette about her. Mom's makeup did little to disguise the anguish of losing her only grandchild. She had amazing energy, staying by my bedside day after day and managing to exude a steady stream of hysteria. This was good. It was as though she was, in part, being hysterical for me, and thus, in a strange way, her eruptions kept me calm.

Despite the room's nearly supernova heat—and my constant protestations—Mom would put an extra blanket over me when I was asleep. I woke up one time—my body drenched in sweat, naturally—to hear my mother telling the black nurse with the formal hat about my previous stay at St. Elizabeth's when I was only seven.

"He had salmonella," Honey stated in a conspiratorial whisper that was only slightly louder than a bullhorn. "You never smelled diarrhea like that. It was just pouring out of him. His stench practically seeped into the wallpaper."

"He ain't all roses now either," the nurse replied.

The two women shared a laugh.

On Day Two of my recovery, Mom was standing over my bed when I awoke.

"Remember this?" she said.

She was holding a stuffed Oscar the Grouch someone

had given me during that salmonella stay. The green had faded to a light mint. She looked at the nurse. "This is Marc's Oscar," she explained.

"Mom," I said.

She turned her attention back to me. The mascara was a little too heavy today, crinkling into the wrinkle lines. "Oscar kept you company back then, remember? He helped you get better."

I rolled and then closed my eyes. A memory came to me. I had gotten the salmonella from raw eggs. My father used to add them into milkshakes for the protein. I remember the way pure terror had gripped me when I'd first learned that I would have to stay in the hospital overnight. My father, who had recently ruptured his Achilles tendon playing tennis, was in a cast and constant pain. But he saw my fear, and as always, he made the sacrifice. He worked all that day at the plant and spent all night in a chair by my hospital bed. I stayed at St. Elizabeth's for ten days. My father slept in that chair every night of them.

Mom suddenly turned away, and I could see she was remembering the same thing. The nurse quickly excused herself. I put a hand on my mother's back. She didn't move, but I could feel her shudder. She stared down at the faded Oscar in her hands. I slowly took it from her.

"Thank you," I said.

Mom wiped her eyes. Dad, I knew, would not come to the hospital this time, and while I am sure my mother had told him what had happened, there was no way to know if he even understood. My father had had his first stroke when he was forty-one years old—one year after staying those nights with me at the hospital. I was eight at the time.

I also have a younger sister, Stacy, who is either a "substance abuser" (for the more politically correct) or "crack-head" (for the more accurate). I sometimes look at old pictures from before my dad's stroke, the ones with the young, confident family of four and the shaggy dog and the well-groomed lawn and the basketball hoop and the coal-overloaded, lighter fluid–saturated barbecue. I look for hints of the future in my sister's front teeth–missing smile, her shadow self perhaps, a sense of foreboding. But I see none. We still have the house, but it's like a sagging movie prop. Dad is still alive, but when he fell, everything shattered Humpty-Dumpty style. Especially Stacy.

Stacy had not visited or even called, but nothing she does surprises me anymore.

My mother finally turned to face me. I gripped the faded Oscar a little tighter as a thought struck me anew: It was just us again. Dad was pretty much a vegetable. Stacy was hollowed out, gone. I reached out and took Mom's hand, feeling both the warmth and the more recent thickening of her skin. We stayed like that until the door opened. The same nurse leaned into the room.

Mom straightened up and said, "Marc also played with dolls."

"Action figures," I said, quick on the correction. "They were action figures, not dolls."

My best friend, Lenny, and his wife, Cheryl, also stopped by the hospital every day. Lenny Marcus is a big-time trial lawyer, though he also handles my small-time stuff like the time I fought a speeding ticket and the closing on our house. When he graduated and began working for the county prosecutor, friends and opponents quickly dubbed Lenny "the Bulldog" because of his aggressive courtroom behavior. Somewhere along the line, it was decided that the name was too mild for Lenny, so now they called him "Cujo." I've known Lenny since elementary school. I'm the godfather of his son Kevin. And Lenny is Tara's godfather.

I haven't slept much. I lie at night and stare at the ceiling and count the beeps and listen to the hospital night sounds and try very much not to let my mind wander to my little daughter and the endless array of possibilities. I am not always successful. The mind, I have learned, is indeed a dark, snake-infested pit.

Detective Regan visited later with a possible lead.

"Tell me about your sister," he began.

"Why?" I said too quickly. Before he could elaborate, I held up my hand to stop him. I understood. My sister was an addict. Where drugs roamed, so too did a certain criminal element. "Were we robbed?" I asked.

"We don't think so. Nothing seems to be missing, but the place was tossed."

"Tossed?"

"Someone made a mess. Any thoughts on why?"

"No."

"So tell me about your sister."

"You have Stacy's record?" I asked.

"We do."

"I'm not sure what I can add."

"You two are estranged, correct?"

Estranged. Did that apply to Stacy and me? "I love her," I said slowly.

"And when was the last time you saw her?"

"Six months ago."

"When Tara was born?"

"Yes."

"Where?"

"Where did I see her?"

"Yes."

"Stacy came to the hospital," I said.

"To see her niece?"

"Yes."

"What happened during that visit?"

"Stacy was high. She wanted to hold the baby."

"You refused?"

"That's right."

"Did she get angry?"

"She barely reacted. My sister is pretty flat when she's stoned."

"But you threw her out?"

"I told her she couldn't be a part of Tara's life until she was clean."

"I see," he said. "You were hoping that would force her back into rehab?"

I might have chuckled. "No, not really."

"I'm not sure I understand."

I wondered how to put this. I thought of the smile in the family photo, the one of her without the front teeth. "We've threatened Stacy with worse," I said. "The truth is that my sister won't quit. The drugs are part of her."

"So you hold out no hope for recovery?"

There was no way I was about to voice that. "I didn't trust her with my daughter," I said. "Let's leave it at that."

Regan headed over to the window and looked out. "When did you move into your current residence?"

"Monica and I bought the house four months ago."

"Not far from where you both grew up, no?"

"That's right."

"Had you two known each other long?"

I was puzzled by the line of questioning. "No."

"Even though you grew up in the same town?"

"We traveled in different circles."

"I see," he said. "And just so I have it straight, you bought your house four months ago and you hadn't seen your sister in six months, correct?"

"Correct."

"So your sister has never visited you at your current residence?"

"That's right."

Regan turned to me. "We found a set of Stacy's fingerprints at your house."

I said nothing.

"You don't seem surprised, Marc."

"Stacy is an addict. I don't think she's capable of shooting me and kidnapping my daughter, but I've underestimated how low she could sink before. Did you check her apartment?"

"No one has seen her since you were shot," he said.

I closed my eyes.

"We don't think your sister could pull off something like this by herself," he went on. "She might have had an accomplice—a boyfriend, a dealer, someone who knew your wife was from a wealthy family. Do you have any thoughts?"

"No," I said. "So, what, you think this whole thing was a kidnapping plot?"

Regan started clawing at his soul patch again. Then he gave a small shrug.

"But they tried to kill us both," I went on. "How do you collect ransom from dead parents?"

"They could have been so doped up that they made a mistake," he said. "Or maybe they thought they could extort money from Tara's grandfather."

"So why haven't they yet?"

Regan did not reply. But I knew the answer. The heat, especially after the shooting, would be too much for crack-heads. Crack-heads don't handle conflict well. It is one of the reasons they snort or shoot themselves up in the first place—to escape, to fade away, to avoid, to dive down into the white. The media would be all over this case. The police would be making inquiries. Crack-heads would freak under that kind of pressure. They would flee, abandon everything.

And they would get rid of all the evidence.

But the ransom demand came two days later.

Now that I had regained consciousness, my recovery from the gunshot wounds was proceeding with surprising smoothness. It could be that I was focused on getting better or that lying in a quasicatatonic state for twelve days had given my injuries time to heal. Or it could be that I was suffering from a pain way beyond what the physical could inflict. I would think of Tara and the fear of the unknown would stop my breath. I would think of Monica, of her lying dead, and steel claws would shred me from within.

I wanted out.

My body still ached, but I pressed Ruth Heller to release me. Noting that I was proving the adage about doctors making the worst patients, she reluctantly gave me the okay to go home. We agreed that a physical therapist would come by every day. A nurse would pop by periodically, just to be on the safe side.

On the morning of my departure from St. Elizabeth, my mother was at the house—the former crime scene—getting it "ready" for me, whatever that meant. Oddly enough, I wasn't afraid to go back there. A house is mortar and brick. I didn't think the sight of it alone would move me, but maybe I was just blocking.

Lenny helped me pack and get dressed. He is tall and wiry with a face darkened by a Homer Simpson five-o'clock shadow that pops up six minutes after he shaves. As a child Lenny wore Coke-bottle glasses and too-thick corduroy, even in the summer. His curly hair had a habit of getting outgrown to the point where he'd start resembling a stray poodle. Now he keeps the curls religiously close cropped. He had laser eye surgery two years ago, so the glasses are gone. His suits lean toward the upscale side.

"You sure you won't stay with us?" Lenny said.

"You have four kids," I reminded him.

"Oh yeah, right." He paused. "Can I stay with you?"

I tried to smile.

"Seriously," Lenny said, "you shouldn't be alone in that house."

"I'll be fine."

"Cheryl cooked you some dinners. She put them in the freezer."

"That was nice of her."

"She's still the world's most god-awful cook," Lenny said.

"I didn't say I was going to eat them."

Lenny looked away, busying himself with the already packed bag. I watched him. We have known each other a long time, since Mrs. Roberts's first-grade class, so it probably did not surprise him when I said, "You want to tell me what's up?"

He'd been waiting for the opening and thus quickly exploited it. "Look, I'm your lawyer, right?"

"Right."

"So I want to give you some legal advice."

"I'm listening."

"I should have said something earlier. But I knew you wouldn't listen. Now, well, now it's a different story, I think."

"Lenny?"

"Yeah?"

"What are you talking about?"

Despite his physical enhancements, I still saw Lenny as a kid. It made it hard to take his advice too seriously. Don't get me wrong. I knew that he was smart. I had celebrated with him when he got his acceptance to Princeton and then Columbia Law. We took the SATs together and were in the same AP chemistry class our junior year. But the Lenny I saw was the one I desperately cruised with on muggy Friday and Saturday nights. We used his dad's wood-paneled station wagon—not exactly a "babe trawler"—and tried to hit the parties. We were always let in but never really welcome, members of that high school majority I call the Great Unseen. We would stand in corners, holding a beer, bopping our heads to the music, trying hard to be noticed. We never were. Most nights we ended up eating a grilled cheese at the Heritage Diner or, better, at the soccer field behind Benjamin Franklin Middle School, lying on our backs, checking out the stars. It was easier to talk, even with your best friend, when you were looking at the stars.

"Okay," Lenny said, overgesturing as was his custom, "it's like this: I don't want you talking to the cops anymore without my being present."

I frowned. "For real?"

"Maybe it's nothing, but I've seen cases like this. Not *like* this, but you know what I mean. The first suspect is always family."

"Meaning my sister."

"No, meaning close family. Or clos*er* family, if possible."

"Are you saying the police suspect me?"

"I don't know. I really don't." He paused but not for very long. "Okay, yeah, probably."

"But I was shot, remember? My kid was the one taken."

"Right, and that cuts both ways."

"How do you figure that?"

"As the days pass, they're going to start suspecting you more and more."

"Why?" I asked.

"I don't know. That's just how it works. Look, the FBI handles kidnappings. You know that, right? Once a child is gone twenty-four hours, they assume it's interstate and the case is theirs."

"So?"

"So for the first, what, ten days or so, they had a ton of agents here. They monitored your phones and waited for the ransom call, that kinda thing. But the other day, they pretty much pulled up stakes. That's normal, of course. They can't wait indefinitely, so they scale back to an agent or two. And their thinking shifted too. Tara became less a possible kidnapping-for-ransom and more a straight-on abduction. But my guess is, they still have the taps on the phones. I haven't asked yet, but I will. They'll claim they're leaving them there in case a ransom demand is eventually made. But they'll also be hoping to hear you say something incriminating."

"So?"

"So be careful," Lenny said. "Remember that your phones—home, biz, cell—are probably tapped."

"And again I ask: So? I didn't do anything."

"Didn't do . . . ?" Lenny waved his hands as if preparing to take flight. "Look, just be careful is all. This might be hard for you to believe, but—and try not to gasp when I say this—the police have been known to twist and distort evidence."

"You're confusing me. Are you saying I'm a suspect simply because I'm the father and husband?"

"Yes," Lenny said. "And no."

"Well, okay, thanks—that clears it up."

A phone next to my bed rang. I was on the wrong side of the room. "You mind?" I said.

Lenny picked it up. "Dr. Seidman's room." His face clouded over as he listened. He spat out the words

"Hold on," and handed the phone to me, as if it might have germs. I gave him a puzzled look and said, "Hello?"

"Hello, Marc. This is Edgar Portman."

Monica's father. That explained Lenny's reaction. Edgar's voice was, as always, way too formal. Some people weigh their words. A select few, like my father-in-law, take each one and put it on a scale before letting it leave their mouths.

I was momentarily taken aback. "Hello, Edgar," I said stupidly. "How are you?"

"I'm fine, thank you. I feel remiss, of course, for not having called you earlier. I understood from Carson that you were busy recuperating from your wounds. I felt it best if I let you be."

"Thoughtful," I said with nary a whiff of sarcasm.

"Yes, well, I understand you're being released today."

"That's right."

Edgar cleared his throat, which seemed out of character for him. "I was wondering if perhaps you could stop by the house."

The house. Meaning his. "Today?"

"As soon as possible, yes. And alone please."

There was silence. Lenny gave me a puzzled look.

"Is something wrong, Edgar?" I asked.

"I have a car waiting downstairs, Marc. We'll talk more when you arrive."

And then, before I could say another word, he was gone.

The car, a black Lincoln Town Car, was indeed waiting.

Lenny wheeled me outside. I was familiar with this area, of course. I had grown up scant miles from St. Elizabeth. When I was five years old, my father had rushed me to the emergency room here (twelve stitches) and when I was seven, well, you already know too much about my salmonella visit. I'd gone to medical school and done my residency at what was then called Columbia Presbyterian in New York, but I returned to St. Elizabeth for a fellowship in ophthalmology for reconstruction.

Yes, I am a plastic surgeon, but not in the way you think. I do the occasional nose job, but you won't find me working with sacks of silicone or any of that. Not that I'm judging. It just isn't what I do.

I work in pediatric reconstructive surgery with my former medical school classmate, a fireball from the Bronx named Zia Leroux. We work for a group called One World WrapAid. Actually, Zia and I founded it. We take care of children, mostly overseas, who suffer deformities either through birth, poverty, or conflict. We travel a lot. I have worked on facial smashes in Sierra Leone, on cleft palates in Upper Mongolia, on Crouzon's in Cambodia, on burn victims in the Bronx. Like most people in my field, I've done extensive training. I've studied ENT—ears, nose, and throat—with a year of reconstructive, plastics, oral, and, as I mentioned above, ophthalmology. Zia's training history is similar, though she's stronger with the maxillofacial.

You may think of us as do-gooders. You'd be wrong. I had a choice. I could do boob jobs or tuck back the skin of those who were already too beautiful—or I could help wounded, poverty-stricken children. I chose the latter, not so much to help the disadvantaged, but alas, because that is where the cool cases lie. Most reconstructive surgeons are, at heart, puzzle lovers. We're weird. We get jazzed on circus-sideshow congenital anomalies and huge tumors. You know those medical textbooks that have hideous facial deformities that you have to dare yourself to look at? Zia and I love that stuff. We get off on repairing it—taking what's shattered and making it whole—even more.

The fresh air tickled my lungs. The sun shone as if it were the first day, mocking my gloom. I tilted my face toward the warmth and let it soothe me. Monica used to like to do that. She claimed that it "destressed" her. The lines in her face would disappear as if the rays were gentle masseurs. I kept my eyes closed. Lenny waited in silence, giving me time.

I have always thought of myself as an overly sensitive man. I cry too easily at dumb movies. My emotions are easily manipulated. But with my father, I never cried. And now, with this terrible blow, I felt—I don't know—beyond tears. A classic defense mechanism, I assumed. I had to push forward. It's not so different from my business: When cracks appear, I patch them up before they become full-fledged fissures.

Lenny was still fuming from the phone call. "Any idea what that old bastard wants?"

"Not a one."

He was quiet a moment. I know what he was thinking. Lenny blamed Edgar for his father's death. His old man had been a middle manager at ProNess Foods, one of Edgar's holdings. He had slaved for the company twenty-six years and had just turned fifty-two years old when Edgar orchestrated a major merger. Lenny's father lost his job. I remember seeing Mr. Marcus sitting slump shouldered at the kitchen table, meticulously stuffing his résumé into envelopes. He never found work and died two years later of a heart attack. Nothing could convince Lenny that the two events were unrelated.

He said, "You sure you don't want me to come?"

"Nah, I'll be all right."

"Got your cell?"

I showed it to him.

"Call me if you need anything."

I thanked him and let him walk away. The driver opened the door. I winced my way in. The drive was not far. Kasselton, New Jersey. My hometown. We passed the split-levels of the sixties, the expanded ranches of the seventies, the aluminum sidings of the eighties, the McMansions of the nineties. Eventually the trees grew denser. The houses sat farther back from the road, protected by the lush foliage, away from the great unwashed who might happen by. We were nearing old wealth now, that exclusive land that always smelled of autumn and woodsmoke.

The Portman family had first settled in this thicket immediately following the Civil War. Like most of suburban Jersey, this had been farmland. Great-great-grandfather Portman slowly sold off acreage and made a fortune. They still had sixteen acres, making their lot one of the largest in the area. As we climbed the drive, my eyes drifted left—toward the family burial plot.

I could see a small mound of fresh dirt.

"Stop the car," I said.

"Sorry, Dr. Seidman," the driver replied, "but I was told to bring you right up to the main house."

I was about to protest but thought better of it. I waited until the car stopped by the front door. I got out and headed back down the drive. I heard the driver say, "Dr. Seidman?" I kept going. He called after me again. I ignored him. Despite the lack of rain, the grass was a green usually reserved for rain forests. The rose garden was in full bloom, an explosion of color.

I tried to hurry on, but my skin still felt as if it might rip. I slowed. This was only my third visit inside the Portman family estate—I had seen it from the outside dozens of times in my youth—and I had never visited the family plot. In fact, like most rational people, I did my best to avoid it. The idea of burying your kin in your backyard like a family pet . . . it was one of those things that rich people do that we regular folk could never quite grasp. Or would want to.

The fence around the plot was maybe two feet high and blindingly white. I wondered if it'd been freshly painted for the occasion. I stepped over the superfluous gate and walked past the modest gravestones, keeping my eye on the dirt mound. When I reached the spot, a shudder tore through me. I looked down.

Yep, a recently dug grave. No stone yet. The marker on it, printed up in wedding-invitation calligraphy, read simply: OUR MONICA.

I stood there and blinked. Monica. My wild-eyed beauty. Our relationship had been turbulent—a classic case of too much passion in the beginning and not enough near the end. I don't know why that happens. Monica was different, no question. At first that crackle, that excitement, had been a draw. Later, the mood swings simply made me weary. I didn't have the patience to dig deeper.

As I looked down at the pile of dirt, a painful memory jabbed at me. Two nights before the attack, Monica had been crying when I came to the bedroom. It was not the first time. Not even close. Playing my part in the stage show that was our lives, I asked her what was wrong, but my heart was not in it. I used to ask with more concern. Monica never replied. I would try to hold her. She would go rigid. After a while the nonresponsiveness got tiresome, taking on a boy-who-cried-wolf aspect that eventually frosts the heart. Living with a depressive is like that. You can't care all the time. At some point, you have to start to resent.

At least, that was what I told myself.

But this time, there was something different: Monica did indeed reply to me. Not a long reply. One line, actually. "You don't love me," she said. That was it. There was no pity in her voice. "You don't love me." And while I managed to utter the necessary protestations, I wondered if maybe she was right.

I closed my eyes and let it all wash over me. Things had been bad, but for the past six months anyway, there had been an escape for us, a calm and warm center in our daughter. I glanced at the sky now, blinked again, and then looked back down at the dirt that covered my volatile wife. "Monica," I said out loud. And then I made my wife one last vow.

I swore on her grave that I would find Tara.

A servant or butler or associate or whatever the current term was led me down the corridor and into the library. The décor was understated though unequivocally rich—finished dark floors with simple Oriental carpets, old-Americana furniture that was solid rather than ornate. Despite his wealth and large plot of land Edgar was not one for show wealth. The term *nouveau riche* was to him profane, unspeakable.

Dressed in a blue cashmere blazer, Edgar rose from behind his expansive oak desk. There was a feather quill pen on the top—his great-grandfather's, if I recall—and two bronze busts, one of Washington and one of Jefferson. I was surprised to see Uncle Carson sitting there too. When he'd visited me in the hospital, I had been too frail to embrace. Carson made up for that now. He pulled me close. I held on to him in silence. He, too, smelled of autumn and woodsmoke.

There were no photographs in the room—no family-vacation snapshots, no school portraits, no shot of the man and his missus decked out at a charity formal. In fact, I do not think I had ever seen a photograph anywhere in the house.

Carson said, "How are you feeling, Marc?"

I told him that I was as well as could be expected and turned toward my father-in-law. Edgar did not come around the desk. We did not embrace. We did not, in fact, even shake hands. He gestured toward the chair in front of the desk.

I did not know Edgar very well. We had only met three times. I do not know how much money he has, but even out of these dwellings, even on a city street or at a bus depot, hell, even naked, you could tell that the Portmans were from money. Monica had the bearing too, the one ingrained over generations, the one that cannot be taught, the one that may literally be genetic. Monica's choice to live in our relatively modest dwelling was probably a form of rebellion.

She had hated her father.

I was not a big fan of his either, probably because I had met his type before. Edgar thinks himself a pull-up-by-the-bootstraps sort, but he himself earned his money the old-fashioned way: He inherited it. I don't know many superwealthy people, but I noticed that the more things were handed to you on a silver platter, the more you complain about welfare mothers and government handouts. It is bizarre. Edgar belongs to that unique class of the entitled who have deluded themselves into believing that they somehow earned their status through hard work. We all live with self-justification, of course, and if you have never fended for yourself, if you live in luxury and have done nothing to deserve it, well, that is going to compound your insecurities, I guess. But it shouldn't make you such a prig, to boot.

I sat. Edgar followed suit. Carson remained standing.

I stared at Edgar. He had the plump of the well fed. His face was all soft edges. The normal ruddy on his cheeks, so far from anything rawbone, was gone now. He laced his fingers and rested them on his paunch. He looked, I was somewhat surprised to see, devastated, drawn, and sapless.

I say *surprised*, because Edgar always struck me as pure id, a person whose own pain and pleasure trumped all others', who believed those who inhabited the space around him were little more than window dressing for his own bemusement. Edgar had now lost two children. His son, Eddie the Fourth, had died while speeding under the influence ten years ago. According to Monica, Eddie veered across the double yellow line and plowed into the semi on purpose. For some reason, she blamed her father. She blamed him for a lot of things.

There is also Monica's mother. She "rests" a lot. She takes "extended vacations." In short, she is in and out of institutions. Both times we met, my mother-in-law was propped up for some social affair, well dressed and powdered, lovely and too pale, a vacancy in her eyes, a slur in her speech, a sway in her stance.

Except for Uncle Carson, Monica had been estranged from her family. As you might imagine, I hardly minded.

"You wanted to see me?" I said.

"Yes, Marc. Yes, I did."

I waited.

Edgar put his hands on his desk. "Did you love my daughter?"

I was caught off guard, but I still said, "Very much," with no hesitation.

He seemed to see the lie. I worked hard to keep my gaze steady. "She still wasn't happy, you know."

"I'm not sure you can blame me for that," I said.

He nodded slowly. "Fair point."

But my own pass-the-buck defense didn't really work on me. Edgar's words were a fresh body blow. The guilt came roaring back.

"Did you know that she was seeing a psychiatrist?" Edgar asked.

I turned toward Carson first, then back to Edgar. "No."

"She didn't want anyone to know."

"How did you find out?"

Edgar did not reply. He stared down at his hands. Then he said: "I want to show you something."

I sneaked another look at Uncle Carson. His jaw was set. I thought I saw a tremble. I turned back to Edgar. "Okay."

Edgar opened his desk drawer, reached in, and pulled out a plastic bag. He raised it into view, gripping the bag at the corner between his forefinger and thumb. It took a moment, but when I realized what I was looking at, my eyes went wide.

Edgar saw my reaction. "You recognize it then?"

I couldn't speak at first. I glanced over at Carson. His eyes were red. I looked back at Edgar and nodded numbly. Inside the plastic bag was a small swatch of clothing, maybe three inches by three inches. The pattern was one I had seen two weeks ago, moments before being shot.

Pink with black penguins.

My voice was barely a hush. "Where did you get this?"

Edgar handed me a large brown envelope, the kind with bubble wrap on the inside. This too was protected in plastic. I turned it around. Edgar's name and address had been printed on a white label. There was no return address. The postmark read New York City.

"It came in today's mail," Edgar said. He gestured to the swatch. "Is it Tara's?"

I think I said yes.

"There's more," Edgar said. He reached into the drawer again. "I took the liberty of putting everything in plastic bags. In case the authorities need to test it."

Again he handed me what looked like a Ziploc bag. Smaller this time. There were hairs inside. Little wisps of hair. With mounting dread, I realized what I was looking at. My breath stopped.

Baby hair.

From far away, I heard Edgar ask, "Are they hers?"

I closed my eyes and tried to picture Tara in the crib. The image of my daughter, I was horrified to realize, was already fading in the mind's eye. How could that be? I could no longer tell if I was seeing memory or something I conjured up to replace what I was already forgetting. Damn it. Tears pressed against my eyelids. I tried to bring back the feel of my daughter's soft scalp, the way my finger would trace the top.

"Marc?"

"They could be," I said, opening my eyes. "There's no way for me to know for sure."

"Something else," Edgar said. He handed me another plastic bag. Gingerly, I put down the bag with her hair on the desk. I took the new bag. There was a sheet of white paper in it. A note from some kind of laser printer.

If you contact the authorities, we disappear. You will never know what happened to her. We will be watching. We will know. We have a man on the inside. Your calls are being monitored. Do not discuss this over the phone. We know that you, Grandpa, are rich. We want two million dollars. We want you,

Daddy, to deliver the ransom. You, Grandpa, will get the money ready. We are enclosing a cell phone. It is untraceable. But if you dial out or use it in any way, we will know. We will disappear and you will never see the child again. Get the money ready. Give it to Daddy. Daddy, keep the money and phone near you. Go home and wait. We will call and tell you what to do. Deviate from what we ask, and you will never see your daughter again. There will be no second chance.

The syntax was odd, to put it mildly. I read the note three times and then I looked up at Edgar and Carson. A funny calm spread over me. Yes, this was terrifying, but receiving this note . . . it was also a relief. Something had finally happened. We could act now. We could get Tara back. There was hope.

Edgar stood and headed toward the corner of the room. He opened a closet door and pulled out a gym bag with a Nike logo on it. Without preamble, he said, "It's all here."

He dropped the bag onto my lap. I stared down at it. "Two million dollars?"

"The bills are not sequential, but we have a list of all the serial numbers, just in case."

I looked at Carson and then back at Edgar. "You don't think we should contact the FBI?"

"Not really, no." Edgar perched himself on the lid of the desk, folding his arms across his chest. He smelled of barbershop bay rum, but I could sense something more primitive, more rancid, that lay just beneath. Up close, his eyes had the dark rings of exhaustion. "It's your decision, Marc. You're the father. We'll respect whatever you do. But as you know, I have had some dealings with the federal authorities. Perhaps my views are colored by my own sense of their incompetence, or perhaps I am biased because I've witnessed the degree to which they are ruled by personal agendas. If it were my daughter, I'd rather trust my own judgment than theirs."

I was not sure what to say or do. Edgar took care of that. He clapped his hands once and then gestured toward the door.

"The note says that you should go home and wait. I think it's best if we obey."

chapter 3

The same driver was there. I slid into the backseat, the Nike bag pressed against my chest. My emotions rocketed between abject fear and the strangest tinge of elation. I could get my daughter back. I could blow it all.

But first things first: Should I tell the police?

I tried to calm myself, to look at it coldly, at a distance, weigh the pros and cons. That was impossible, of course. I am a doctor. I have made life-altering decisions before. I know that the best way to do that is to remove the baggage, the ardent excess, from the equation. But my daughter's life was at stake. My own daughter. To echo what I said in the beginning: my world.

The house Monica and I bought is literally around the corner from the house I grew up in and where my parents still reside. I am ambivalent about that. I really don't like living so close to my parents, but I dislike the guilt of abandoning them even more. My compromise: Live near them and then travel a lot.

Lenny and Cheryl live four blocks away, near the Kasselton Mall, in the house where Cheryl's parents had raised her. Cheryl's parents moved to Florida six years ago. They keep a condo up here in neighboring Roseland so they can visit their grandchildren and escape the molten-lava summers of the Sunshine State.

I don't particularly like living in Kasselton. The town has changed very little over the past thirty years. In our youth, we scoffed at our parents, their materialism, their seemingly aimless values. Now we are our parents. We have simply replaced them, pushed Mom and Dad into whatever retirement village would have them. And our children have replaced us. But Maury's Luncheonette is still on Kasselton Avenue. The fire department is still mostly volunteer. The Little League still plays at Northland Field. The high-tension wires are still too close to my old elementary school. The woods behind the Brenners' house on Rockmont Terrace is still a place where kids hang out and smoke. The high school still gets between five and eight national merit finalists a year, though when I was younger the list was more Jewish while today it tilts toward the Asian community.

We turned right on Monroe Avenue and drove past the split-level where I was raised. With its white paint and black shutters, with its kitchen, living room, and dining room up three steps on the left and its den and garage entrance two steps down on the right, our house, though a bit more threadbare than most, was pretty much indistinguishable from the other cookie-cutters on the block. What did make it stand out, the only thing really, was the wheelchair ramp. We put it in after my dad's third stroke when I was twelve years old. My friends and I liked to skateboard down it. We built a jump out of plywood and cinder blocks and put it at the bottom.

The nurse's car was in the driveway. She comes in during the days. We don't have someone full-time. My father has been confined to a wheelchair for more than two decades now. He cannot speak. His mouth has an ugly down-hook curve on the left side of it. Half his body is totally paralyzed and the other half is not that much better.

When the driver made the turn at Darby Terrace, I saw that my house—our house—looked the same as it had a few weeks before. I didn't know what I'd expected. Yellow crime-scene tape maybe. Or a big bloodstain. But there was nothing hinting at what had occurred two weeks earlier.

When I'd bought the house, it'd been in foreclosure. For thirty-six years the Levinsky family had lived there, but no one really knew them. Mrs. Levinsky had been a seemingly sweet woman with a facial tic. Mr. Levinsky was an ogre who always yelled at her out on the lawn. He scared us. One time, we saw Mrs. Levinsky run out of the house in a nightgown, Mr. Levinsky chasing her with a shovel. Kids cut through every yard but theirs. When I was fresh out of college, rumors surfaced that he had abused his daughter, Dina, a sad-eyed, stringy-haired waif I'd gone to school with since the first grade. Looking back on it, I must have been in a dozen classes with Dina Levinsky and I don't remember ever hearing her speak above a whisper and only then when forced to by well-meaning teachers. I never reached out to Dina. I don't know what I could have done, but I still wished that I'd tried.

Sometime during that year out of college, when the rumors of Dina's abuse began to take root, the Levinskys had up and moved away. No one knew where. The bank took over the house and began to rent it out. Monica and I made an offer a few weeks before Tara was born.

Months later, when we first settled in, I'd stay awake at night and listen for—I don't know—sounds of some sort, for signs of the house's past, of the unhappiness within. I would try to figure out which bedroom had been Dina's and try to imagine what it'd been like for her, what it was like now, but there were no clues here.

As I said earlier, a house is mortar and brick. Nothing more.

Two strange cars were parked in front of my house. My mother was standing by the front door. When I got out, she rushed me like in those newscasts of returning POWs. She hugged me hard, and I got a whiff of too much perfume. I was still holding the Nike bag with the money, so it was hard for me to reciprocate.

Over my mother's shoulder, Detective Bob Regan stepped out of my house. Next to him stood a large black man with a gleaming shaved head and designer sunglasses. My mother whispered, "They've been waiting for you."

I nodded and moved toward them. Regan cupped a hand over his eyes, but only for effect. The sun was not that strong. The black man remained stonelike.

"Where have you been?" Regan asked. When I didn't reply right away, he added, "You left the hospital more than an hour ago."

I thought about the cell phone in my pocket. I thought about the bag of money in my hand. For now, I'd go for the semitruth. "I visited my wife's grave," I said.

"We need to talk, Marc."

"Step inside," I said.

We all moved back into the house. I stopped in the foyer. Monica's body had been found less than ten feet from where I now stood. Still in the entranceway, my eyes scanned the walls, looking for any telltale sign of violence. There was only one. I found it fairly quickly. Above the Behrens lithograph near the stairwell, a bullet hole—one created from the only bullet that had not hit either Monica or me—had been spackled over. The spackle was too white for the wall. It would need a coat of paint.

I stared at it for a long moment. I heard a throat being cleared. It snapped me out of it. My mother rubbed my back and then headed to the kitchen. I showed Regan and his buddy to the living room. They took the two chairs. I took the couch. Monica and I hadn't truly decorated yet. The chairs dated back to my college dorm and looked it. The couch had come from Monica's apartment, a too-formal hand-me-down that looked like something kept in storage at Versailles. It was heavy and stiff and, even in its heyday, had had very little padding.

"This is Special Agent Lloyd Tickner," Regan began, motioning toward the black man. "He's with the FBI."

Tickner nodded. I nodded back.

Regan tried to smile at me. "Good to see you're feeling better," he began.

"I'm not," I said.

He looked puzzled.

"I won't be better until I have my daughter back."

"Right, of course. About that. We have a few follow-up questions, if you don't mind."

I let them know I didn't.

Regan coughed into his fist, buying himself time. "You have to understand something. We need to ask these questions. I don't necessarily like it. I'm sure you don't either, but these questions need to be asked. You understand?"

I didn't really, but this was no time to encourage elaboration. "Go ahead," I said.

"What can you can tell us about your marriage?"

A warning light flashed across my cortex. "What does my marriage have to do with anything?"

Regan shrugged. Tickner remained still. "We're just trying to put some pieces together, that's all."

"My marriage has nothing to do with any of this."

"I'm sure you're right, but look, Marc, the truth is, the trail is getting cold here. Every day that passes hurts us. We need to explore every avenue."

"The only avenue I'm interested in is the one that leads to my daughter."

"We understand that. That's the main focus of our investigation. Finding out what happened to your daughter. And you too. Let's not forget that someone tried to kill you too—am I right?"

"I guess."

"But, see, we can't just ignore these other issues."

"What other issues?"

"Your marriage, for example."

"What about it?"

"When you got married, Monica was already pregnant, right?"

"What does that . . . ?" I stopped myself. I wanted to attack with both barrels, but Lenny's words roared back at me. Don't talk to the cops without him present. I should call him. I knew that. But something about their tone and posture . . . if I stopped now and said I wanted to call my lawyer, it would make me look guilty. I had nothing to hide. Why feed into their suspicions? It would only distract them. Of course, I also knew that this was how they worked, how the police played the game, but I'm a doctor. Worse, a surgeon. We often make the mistake of thinking we're smarter than everyone else.

I went with honesty. "Yes, she was pregnant. So?"

"You're a plastic surgeon, correct?"

The change of subjects threw me. "That's right."

"You and your partner travel overseas and repair cleft palates, serious facial trauma, burns, that kind of thing?"

"Something like that, yes."

"You travel a lot then?"

"A fair amount," I said.

"In fact," Regan said, "in the two years before your marriage, isn't it fair to say that you were probably out of the country more than you were in it?"

"Possibly," I said. I squirmed against the padless cushion. "Could you tell me what the relevance of any of this is?"

Regan gave me his most disarming smile. "We're just trying to get a complete picture here."

"Picture of what?"

"Your work partner"—he checked his notes—"a Ms. Zia Leroux."

"Dr. Leroux," I corrected.

"Dr. Leroux, yes, thank you. Where is she now?"

"Cambodia."

"She's performing surgery on deformed children over there?"

"Yes."

Regan tilted his head, feigning confusion. "Weren't you originally scheduled to take that trip?"

"A long time ago."

"How long ago?"

"I'm not sure I follow."

"How long ago did you take yourself off the schedule?"

"I don't know," I said. "Eight, nine months ago maybe."

"And so Dr. Leroux went instead, correct?"

"Yes, that's correct. And the point of that is . . . ?"

He wouldn't bite. "You like your job, don't you, Marc?"

"Yes."

"You like traveling overseas? Doing this commendable work?"

"Sure."

Regan scratched his head too dramatically, pretending in the most obvious way to be bewildered. "So if you like the traveling, why did you cancel and let Dr. Leroux go in your place?"

Now I saw where he was heading. "I was cutting back," I said.

"On travel, you mean."

"Yes."

"Why?"

"Because I had other obligations."

"Those obligations being a wife and daughter—am I correct?"

I sat up and met his eye. "Point," I said. "Is there a point to all this?"

Regan settled back. The silent Tickner did likewise. "Just trying to get a complete picture, that's all."

"You said that already."

"Yeah, hold on, give me a second here." Regan flipped through the pages of his notebook. "Jeans and a red blouse."

"What?"

"Your wife." He pointed at his notes. "You said that she was wearing jeans and a red blouse that morning."

More images of Monica flooded me. I tried to stem the tide. "So?"

"When we found her body," Regan said, "she was naked."

The tremors began in my heart. They spread down my arms, tingling my fingers.

"You didn't know?"

I swallowed. "Was she ... ?" My voice died in my throat.

"No," Regan said. "Not a mark on her, other than the bullet holes." He did that help-me-understand head-tilt again. "We found her dead in this very room. Did she often parade in here with no clothes on?"

"I told you." Overload. I tried to process this new data, keep up with him. "She was wearing jeans and a red blouse."

"So she was dressed already?"

I remembered the sound of the shower. I remembered her coming out, throwing her hair back, lying on the bed, working the jeans over the hips. "Yes."

"Definitely?"

"Definitely."

"We've been through the whole house. We can't find a red blouse. Jeans, sure. She had several pairs. But no red blouse. Don't you think that's odd?"

"Wait a second," I said. "Her clothes weren't near her body?"

"Nope."

This made no sense. "I'll look in her closet, then," I said.

"We already did that, but sure, go ahead. Of course, I'd still like to know how clothes she was wearing ended up back in her closet, wouldn't you?"

I had no answer.

"Do you own a gun, Dr. Seidman?"

Another subject shift. I tried to keep up, but my head was spinning. "Yes."

"What kind?"

"A Smith and Wesson thirty-eight. It belonged to my father."

"Where do you keep it?"

"There's a compartment in the bedroom closet. It's on the top shelf in a lockbox."

Regan reached behind him and pulled out the metal lockbox. "This it?"

"Yes."

"Open it."

He tossed it to me. I caught it. The gray-blue metal was cold. But more than that, it felt shockingly light. I moved the wheels to the right combination and flipped it open. I poked through the legal documents—the car title, the deed on the house, the property survey—but that was just to get my bearings. I knew right away. The gun was gone.

"You and your wife were both shot with a thirty-eight," Regan said. "And yours seems to be missing."

I kept my eyes on the box, as if I expected the weapon to suddenly materialize in it. I tried to put it together, but nothing was coming to me.

"Any idea where the gun is?"

I shook my head.

"And something else strange," Regan said.

I looked up at him.

"You and Monica were shot with *different* thirty-eights."

"Excuse me?"

He nodded. "Yeah, I found it hard to believe too. I made ballistics check it twice. You and your wife were shot with two different guns, both thirty-eights—and yours seems to be missing." Regan shrugged theatrically. "Help me understand, Marc."

I looked at their faces. I didn't like what I saw. Lenny's warning came back to me again, firmer this time. "I want to call my lawyer," I said.

"You sure?"

"Yes."

"Go ahead."

My mother had been standing by the kitchen door, wringing her hands. How much had she heard? Judging by her face, too much. Mom looked at me expectantly. I nodded, and she went to call Lenny. I folded my arms, but that didn't feel right. I tapped my foot. Tickner took off the sunglasses. He met my eye and spoke for the first time.

"What's in the bag?" he asked me.

I just looked at him.

"That gym bag you been groping." Tickner's voice, belying his tough looks, had a nerdy cadence to it, a quasiwhine quality. "What's in it?"

This had all been a mistake. I should have listened to Lenny. I should have called him right away. Now I was not sure how to reply. In the background, I heard my mother urging Lenny to hurry. I was sifting through a response that might work as a semitruthful stall—none were convincing—when a sound ripped my attention away.

The cell phone, the one the kidnappers had sent to my father-in-law, began to ring.

chapter 4

Tickner and Regan waited for me to answer.

I excused myself, rising before they had a chance to react. My hand fumbled with the phone as I hurried outside. The sun hit me full in the face. I blinked and looked down at the keypad. The phone's answer button was located in a different spot from mine. Across the street, two girls donning brightly hued helmets were riding neon bikes. Ribbon strips of pink cascaded out of the handlebars of one.

When I was little, this neighborhood sheltered more than a dozen kids my age. We used to meet up after school. I don't remember what games we played—we were never organized enough for, say, a real game of baseball or anything like that—but they all involved hiding and chasing and some form of feigned (or borderline-real) violence. Childhood in suburbia is purportedly a time of innocence, but how many of those days ended in tears for at least one kid? We would argue, shift alliances, make declarations of friendship and war, and like some short-term memory case, it was all forgotten the next day. A clean slate every afternoon. New coalitions forged. A new kid running home in tears.

My thumb finally touched down on the right button.

I pressed it and brought the phone to my ear, all in one move. My heart thumped against my rib cage. I cleared my throat and, feeling like a total idiot, I simply said, "Hello?"

"Answer yes or no." The voice had the robotic hum of one of those customer-care phone systems, the ones that tell you to press one for service, press two to check the status of an order. "Do you have the money?"

"Yes."

"You know the Garden State Plaza?"

"In Paramus," I said.

"In exactly two hours from now, I want you parked at the north lot. That's near Nordstrom's. Section Nine. Someone will approach your car."

"But—"

"If you're not alone, we disappear. If you're being followed, we disappear. If I smell a cop, we disappear. There will be no second chances. Do you understand?"

"Yes, but when—"

Click.

I let my hand drop to my side. Numbness seeped in. I did not fight it. The little girls across the street were quarreling now. I couldn't hear the specifics, but the word *my* popped up a lot, that simple syllable accentuated and drawn out. An SUV sped around the corner. I watched it as though from above. The brakes shrieked. The driver-side door was open before the car had come to a complete stop.

It was Lenny. He took one look at me and picked up his pace. "Marc?"

"You were right." I nodded toward the house. Regan was standing by the door now. "They think I'm involved."

Lenny's face darkened. His eyes narrowed, his pupils shrinking to pinpoints. In sports, you call it putting on your "game face." Lenny was becoming Cujo. He stared at Regan as if deciding which limb to chew off. "You talked to them?"

"A little."

Lenny jerked his gaze toward me. "Didn't you tell them you wanted counsel?"

"Not at first."

"Damn it, Marc, I told you—"

"I got a ransom demand."

That made Lenny pull up. I checked my watch. Paramus was a forty-minute ride. With traffic, it could take as much as an hour. I had time, but not much. I started filling him in. Lenny gave Regan another glare and led me farther away from the house. We stopped at the curb, those familiar cloud gray stones that lie on property lines like sets of teeth, and then, like two children, we squatted deep and sat on them. Our knees were at our chins. I could see Lenny's skin between the argyle sock and tapered cuff. Squatting like this was uncomfortable as hell. The sun was in our eyes. We both looked off rather than at each other, again just like in our youths. It made it easier to spill it all out.

I spoke quickly. Midway through my recap, Regan began to move toward us. Lenny turned to him and shouted, "Your balls."

Regan stopped. "What?"

"Are you arresting my client?"

"No."

Lenny pointed toward Regan's crotch. "Then I'm going to have them bronzed and hanging from my rearview mirror, if you take another step."

Regan straightened his spine. "We have some questions for your client."

"Tough. Go abuse the rights of someone with a lesser lawyer."

Lenny made a dismissive gesture and nodded at me to continue. Regan did not look happy, but he took two steps back. I glanced at my watch again. Only five minutes had passed since the ransom call. I finished up while Lenny kept the laser glare aimed at Regan.

"You want my opinion?" he said.

"Yes."

Still glaring. "I think you should tell them."

"You sure?"

"Hell, no."

"Would you?" I said. "I mean, if it was one of your kids?"

Lenny gave it a few seconds. "I can't put myself in your place, if that's what you mean. But yeah, I think I would. I play the odds. The odds are better when you tell the cops. Doesn't mean it works out every time, but they're experts at this. We're not." Lenny put his elbows on his knees and rested his chin in his hands—a pose from his youth. "That's the opinion of Lenny the Friend," he went on. "Lenny the Friend would encourage you to tell them."

"And Lenny the Lawyer?" I asked.

"He would be more insistent. He would strongly urge you to come forward."

"Why?"

"If you go off with two million dollars and it vanishes—even if you get Tara back—their suspicions will be, to put it mildly, aroused."

"I don't care about that. I just want Tara back."

"Understood. Or should I say, Lenny the Friend understands."

Now it was Lenny's turn to check his watch. My insides felt hollow, scooped out canoe-style. I could almost hear the tick-tick. It was maddening. I tried again to do the rational thing, to list the pros on the right, the cons on the left, and then add them up. But the tick-tick would not stop.

Lenny had talked about playing the odds. I don't gamble. I'm not a risk taker. Across the street one of the little girls shouted, "I'm telling!" She stormed down the street. The other girl laughed at her and got back on her bike. I felt my eyes well up. I wished like hell Monica were here. I shouldn't be making this decision alone. She should be in on this, too.

I looked back at the front door. Regan and Tickner were both outside now. Regan had his arms folded across his chest, bouncing on the balls of his feet. Tickner did not move, his face the same placid pool. Were these men I could trust with my daughter's life? Would they put Tara first, or as Edgar had suggested, would they follow some unseen agenda?

The tick-tick grew louder, more insistent.

Someone had murdered my wife. Someone had taken my child. For the past few days, I had asked myself why—why us?—trying again to stay rational and not allowing myself extended forays in the deep end of the pity pool. But no answer came. I could see no motive and maybe that was most frightening of all. Maybe there was no reason. Maybe it was just pure bad luck.

Lenny stared straight ahead and waited. Tick, tick, tick.

"Let's tell them," I said.

Their reaction surprised me. They panicked.

Regan and Tickner tried to hide it, of course, but their body language was suddenly all wrong—the flutter in the eyes, the tightness at the corners of their mouths, the unduly modulated, FM-soft-rock timbre in their tones. The time frame was simply too close for them. Tickner quickly dialed up the FBI specialist on kidnapping negotiations to enlist his help. He cupped his hand around the mouthpiece while he spoke into it. Regan got hold of his police colleagues in Paramus.

When Tickner hung up, he said to me, "We'll get people to cover the mall. Discreetly, of course. We're going to try to get men in cars near every exit and on Route Seventeen in both directions. We'll have people inside the mall by all the entrances. But I want you to listen to me closely, Dr. Seidman. Our expert tells us that we should try to stall him. Maybe we can get the kidnapper to postpone—"

"No," I said.

"They won't just run away," Tickner said. "They want the money."

"My daughter has been with them for almost three weeks," I said. "I'm not putting this off."

He nodded, not liking it, trying to keep up with the placid. "Then I want to put a man in the car with you."

"No."

"He can duck down in the back."

"No," I said again.

Tickner tried another avenue. "Or better yet—we've done this before—we tell the kidnapper that you can't drive. Hell, you're just out of the hospital. We have one of our men drive instead. We say it's your cousin."

I frowned and looked at Regan. "Didn't you say you thought my sister might be involved?"

"It's possible, yes."

"Don't you think she'd know if this guy was a cousin or not?"

Tickner and Regan both hesitated and then nodded in unison. "Good point," Regan said.

Lenny and I exchanged a glance. These were the professionals I was trusting with Tara's life. The thought was not comforting. I started for the door.

Tickner put a hand on my shoulder. "Where are you going?"

"Where the hell do you think?"

"Sit down, Dr. Seidman."

"No time," I countered. "I have to start heading up there. There could be traffic."

"We can clear the traffic."

"Oh, and that won't look suspicious," I said.

"I highly doubt he's going to follow you from here."

I spun on him. "And you'd be willing to risk your child's life on that?"

He paused just long enough.

"You don't get it," I went on, in his face now. "I don't care about the money or if they get away. I just want my daughter back."

"We understand that," Tickner said, "but there is something you're forgetting."

"What?"

"Please," he said. "Sit down."

"Look, do me a favor, okay? Just let me stand. I'm a doctor. I know the delivering-bad-news drill as well as anyone. Don't try to play me."

Tickner held his palms up and said, "Fair enough." He proceeded to take a long, lingering breath. Stall tactic. I was not in the mood.

"So what is it?" I said.

"Whoever did this," he began, "they shot you. They killed your wife."

"I understand that."

"No, I don't think you do. Think about it a second. We can't just let you go in on your own. Whoever did this tried to end your life. They shot you twice and left you for dead."

"Marc," Regan said, moving closer, "we threw some wild theories at you before. The problem is, that's all they are. Theories. We don't know what these guys are really after. Maybe this is just a simple kidnapping, but if it is, it's not like any we've seen before." His interrogation face was gone now, replaced with an aw-shucks, eyebrow-raised attempt at openness. "What we do know with certainty is that they tried to kill you. You don't try to kill the parents, if you're just after ransom."

"Maybe they planned on getting the money from my father-in-law," I said.

"Then why did they wait so long?"

I had no answer.

"Maybe," Tickner went on, "this isn't about kidnapping at all. At least, not at first. Maybe that's become a sideline. Maybe you and your wife were the targets all along. And maybe they want to finish the job."

"You think this is a setup?"

"It's a strong possibility, yes."

"So what are you advising?"

Tickner took that one. "Don't go alone. Buy us some time so we can prepare properly. Let them call you back."

I looked at Lenny. He saw it and nodded. "That's not possible," Lenny said.

Tickner turned at him hard. "With all due respect, your client is in grave danger here."

"So is my daughter," I said. Simple words. This decision was a no-brainer when you kept it simple. I pulled away and started toward my car. "Keep your people at a distance."

chapter 5

There was no traffic, so I made it to the mall with plenty of time to spare. I turned the engine off and sat back. I glanced around. I figured that the feds and cops were probably still on me, but I couldn't see them. That was a good thing, I guess.

Now what?

No idea. I waited some more. I fiddled with the radio, but nothing caught my attention. I turned on the CD player/tape deck. When Donald Fagan of Steely Dan began singing "Black Cow," I felt a slight jerk. I had not listened to this particular tape since, what, my college days. Why did Monica have it? And then, with a renewed pang, I realized that Monica had been the last to use this car, that this may have been the last song she ever heard.

I watched the shoppers prepare for mall entry. I concentrated on the young mothers: the way they flipped open the back door of the minivan; the way they unfolded the baby strollers midair with a magician's flourish; the way they struggled to release their offspring from safety seats that reminded me of Buzz Aldrin's on *Apollo 11*; the way the mothers skirted forward, heads high, smartly pressing the remote control that slid the minivan door to a close.

The mothers, all of them, looked so blasé. Their children were with them. Their safety, what with the five-star side-collision rating and NASA-sleek car seats, was a given. And here I sat with a bag of ransom money, hoping to get my daughter back. The thin line. I wanted to roll down the window and shout out a warning.

We were getting close to drop time. The sun beat down on my windshield. I reached for my sunglasses but then thought better of it. I don't know why. Would putting on my sunglasses somehow make the kidnapper uneasy? No, I don't think so. Or maybe it would. Better to just leave them off. Take no chances.

My shoulders bunched up. I kept trying to look around without, for some odd reason, looking conspicuous about it. Whenever someone parked near me or walked anywhere in the vicinity of my car, my stomach tightened and I wondered: Was Tara nearby?

We were at the two-hour mark now. I wanted this over. The next few minutes would decide everything. I knew that. Calm. I needed to stay calm. Tickner's warning reverberated in my head. Would someone simply walk up to my car and blow my brains out?

It was, I realized, a very real possibility.

When the cell phone rang, I started forward. I brought it to my ear and barked a too-quick hello.

The robotic voice said, "Pull out by the west exit."

I was confused. "Which way is west?"

"Follow the signs for Route Four. Take the overpass. We're watching. If someone follows, we disappear. Keep the phone near your ear."

I obeyed with gusto; my right hand pressed the phone against my ear to the point where I started losing circulation. My left hand gripped the wheel as if preparing to tear it off.

"Get on Route Four heading west."

I took the right turn and jug-handled onto the high-way. I looked in my rearview mirror to see if anyone was following me. Hard to tell.

The robotic voice said, "You'll see a strip mall."

"There's a million strip malls," I said.

"It's on the right, next to a store selling baby cribs. In front of the Paramus Road exit."

I saw it. "Okay."

"Pull in there. You'll see a driveway on the left. Take it to the back and kill the engine. Have the money ready for me."

I understood immediately why the kidnapper had picked this spot. There was only one way in. The stores were all for rent, except for the baby-crib place. That was on the far right. In other words, it was self-contained and directly off a highway. There was no way anyone could come around back or even slow down without being noticed.

I hope the feds understood that.

When I reached the back of the building, I saw a man standing by a van. He wore a red-and-black flannel shirt with black jeans, dark sunglasses, and a Yankee baseball cap. I tried to find something distinct, but the word that came to mind was *average*. Average height, average build. The only thing was his nose. Even from this distance I could see it was misshapen, like an ex-boxer's. But was that real or some kind of disguise? I didn't know.

I checked out the van. There was a sign for B & T ELECTRICIANS of Ridgewood, New Jersey. No phone number or address. The license plate was from New Jersey. I memorized it.

The man raised a cell phone to his lips walkie-talkie style, and I heard the mechanical voice say, "I'm going to approach. Pass the money through the window. Do not get out of the car. Do not say a word to me. When we're safely away with the money, I'll call and tell you where to pick up your daughter."

The man in red flannel and black jeans lowered the phone and approached. His shirt was untucked. Did he have a gun? I couldn't tell. And even if he did, what could I do about it now? I hit the button to open the windows. They didn't budge. The key needed to be turned. The man was getting closer. The Yankee cap was pulled down until the brim touched the sunglasses. I reached for the key and gave it a tiny twist. The lights on the dashboard sprung to life. I pressed the button again. The window slid down.

Again I tried to find something about the man that was distinct. His walk was slightly off balance, as though maybe he'd had a drink or two, but he didn't look nervous. His face was unshaven and patchy. His hands were dirty. His black jeans were ripped in the right knee. His sneakers, canvas high-tops from Converse, had seen better days.

When the man was only two steps from the car, I pushed the bag up to the window and braced myself. I held my breath. Without breaking stride, the man took the money and swirled toward the van. He hurried his step now. The van's back doors opened and he leapt in, the door immediately closing behind him. It was as if the van had swallowed him whole.

The driver gunned the engine. The van sped off and now, for the first time, I realized that there was a back entrance onto a side road. The van shot down it and was gone.

I was alone.

I stayed where I was and waited for the cell phone to ring. My heart pounded. My shirt was drenched in sweat. No other car traveled back here. The pavement was cracked. Cardboard boxes jutted out of the garbage Dumpster. Broken bottles littered the ground. My eyes stared hard at the ground, trying to make out the words on faded beer labels.

Fifteen minutes passed.

I kept picturing my reunion with my daughter, how I would find her and pick her up and cradle her and hush her with gentle sounds. The cell phone. The cell phone was supposed to ring. That was part of what I was picturing. The phone ringing, the robotic voice giving me instructions. Those were parts one and two. Why wasn't the damn phone cooperating?

A Buick Le Sabre pulled into the lot, keeping a decent distance away from me. I did not recognize the driver, but Tickner was in the passenger seat. Our eyes met. I tried to read something in his expression, but he was still pure stoic.

I stared now at the cell phone, not daring to look away. The tick-tick was back, this time slow and thudding.

Ten more minutes passed before the phone grudgingly issued its tinny song. I had it to my ear before the sound had a chance to travel.

"Hello?" I said.

Nothing.

Tickner watched me closely. He gave me a slight nod, though I had no idea why. His driver still had both hands on the wheel at ten and two o'clock.

"Hello?" I tried again.

The robotic voice said, "I warned you about contacting the cops."

Ice flooded my veins.

"No second chance."

And then the phone went dead.

chapter 6

There was no escape.

I longed for the numb. I longed for the comatose state of the hospital. I longed for that IV bag and the free flow of anesthetics. My skin had been torn off. My nerve endings were exposed now. I could feel everything.

Fear and helplessness overwhelmed me. The fear locked me in a room, while the helplessness—the awful knowing that I had blown it and could do nothing to alleviate my child's pain—wrapped me in a straitjacket and turned out the lights. I may very well have been losing my mind.

Days passed in a syrupy haze. Most of the time I sat by the phone—by several phones, actually. My home phone, my cell phone, and the kidnapper's cell phone. I bought a charger for the kidnapper's cell, so I could keep it working. I stayed on the couch. The phones sat on my right. I tried to look away, to watch television even, because I remembered that old saying about a watched kettle never boiling. I still stole glances at those damn phones, fearing that they might somehow flee, willing them to ring.

I tried to mine that supernatural father-daughter connection again, the one that had insisted earlier that Tara was still alive. The pulse was still there, I thought (or at least, made myself believe), beating faintly, the connection now tenuous at best.

"No second chance . . ."

To add to my guilt, I had dreamed last night of a woman other than Monica—my old love, Rachel. It was one of those time-and-reality-warp dreams, the ones where the world is totally alien and even contradictory and yet you don't question any of it. Rachel and I were together. We had never broken up yet we had been apart all these years. I was still thirty-four, but she hadn't aged since the day she left me. Tara was still my daughter in the dream—she had, in fact, never been kidnapped—but somehow she was also Rachel's, though Rachel wasn't the mother. You've probably had dreams like this. Nothing really makes sense, but you don't challenge what you see. When I woke up, the dream faded into smoke the way dreams always do. I was left with an aftertaste and a longing that pulled with unexpected force.

My mother hung around too much. She had just plopped another tray of food in front of me. I ignored it, and for the millionth time, Mom repeated her mantra: "You have to keep up your strength for Tara."

"Right, Mom, strength is the key here. Maybe if I do enough bench presses, that'll bring her back."

Mom shook her head, refusing to rise to the bait. It was a cruel thing to say. She was hurting too. Her granddaughter was missing and her son was in horrific shape. I watched her sigh and head back to the kitchen. I didn't apologize.

Tickner and Regan visited frequently. They reminded me of Shakespeare's sound and fury signifying nothing. They told me about all the technological wonders that were being utilized in the quest to find Tara—stuff involving DNA and latent prints and security cameras and airports and tollbooths and train stations and trac-

ers and surveillance and labs. They trotted out the tried-
and-true cop clichés like "no stone unturned" and
"every possible avenue." I nodded at them. They had
me look at mug shots, but the bagman in flannel was not
in any of the books.

"We ran a trace on B and T Electricians," Regan told
me that first night. "The company exists, but they use
magnetic signs, the kind you can just peel off a truck.
Someone stole one two months ago. They never thought
it was worth reporting."

"What about the license plate?" I asked.

"The number you gave us doesn't exist."

"How can that be?"

"They used two old license plates," Regan explained.
"See, what they do is, they cut the license plates in half
and then they weld the left half of one with the right
half of the other."

I just stared at him.

"There is something of a bright side to that," Regan
added.

"Oh?"

"It means we're dealing with professionals. They
knew that if you contacted us, we'd be set up at the mall.
They found a drop spot that we couldn't get to without
being seen. They have us tracking down useless leads
with the fake sign and welded license plates. Like I said,
they're pros."

"And that's good because . . . ?"

"Pros usually aren't bloodthirsty."

"So what are they doing?"

"Our theory," Regan said, "is that they're softening
you up, so they can ask for more money."

Softening me up. It was working.

My father-in-law called after the ransom fiasco. I
could hear the disappointment in Edgar's voice. I don't

want to sound unkind here—Edgar was the one who provided the money and made it clear he would do so again—but the disappointment sounded more aimed at me, at the fact that I had not taken his advice about not contacting the police, than at the final outcome.

Of course, he was right about that. I had messed up big time.

I tried to participate in the investigation, but the police were far from encouraging. In the movies the authorities cooperate and share information with the victim. I naturally asked Tickner and Regan a lot of questions about the case. They didn't answer. They never discussed specifics with me. They treated my interrogatories with near disdain. I wanted to know, for example, more about how my wife was found, about why she'd been naked. They stonewalled.

Lenny was at the house a lot. He had trouble meeting my eye because he, too, blamed himself for encouraging me to come forward. The faces of Regan and Tickner fluctuated between guilt because everything had gone so wrong and guilt of another kind, like maybe I, the grieving husband and father, had been behind this from the get-go. They wanted to know about my shaky marriage to Monica. They wanted to know about my missing gun. It was exactly as Lenny had predicted. The more time passed, the more the authorities aimed their sights on the only available suspect.

Yours truly.

After we hit the one-week mark, the police and FBI presence started fading. Tickner and Regan no longer came by very much. They checked their watches more often. They excused themselves for phone calls involving other cases. I understood that, of course. There had been no new leads. Things were quieting down. Part of me welcomed the respite.

And then, on the ninth day, everything changed.

At ten o'clock, I began to get undressed and ready for bed. I was alone. I love my family and friends, but they began to realize that I needed some time by myself. They had all left before dinner. I ordered delivery from Hunan Garden and, per Mom's earlier instructions, ate for strength.

I looked at the bedside alarm clock. That's how I knew that the time was exactly 10:18 P.M. I glanced at the window, just a casual land sweep. In the dark, I almost missed it—nothing consciously registered anyway—but something snagged my gaze. I stopped and looked again.

There, standing on my walk like a stone, staring at my house, was a woman. I assume that she was staring. I did not know for certain. Her face was lost in the shadows. She had long hair—that much I could see in the silhouette—and she wore a long coat. Her hands were jammed into her pockets.

She just stood there.

I was not sure what to make of it. We were in the news, of course. Reporters stopped by at all hours. I looked up and down the street. No cars, no news vans, nothing. She had come on foot. Again that was not unusual. I live in a suburban neighborhood. People take walks all the time, usually with a dog or spouse or both, but it was hardly earth-shattering for a woman to be walking alone.

Then why had she stopped?

Morbid curiosity, I figured.

She looked tall from here, but that was pretty much a guess. I wondered what to do. An uneasy feeling slithered up my back. I grabbed my sweatshirt and threw it over my pajama top. Ditto with a pair of sweatpants and the bottoms. I looked out the window again. The woman stiffened.

She had seen me.

The woman turned and began to hurry away. My chest felt tight. I tried to open the window. It was stuck. I hit the sides to loosen it and tried again. It grudgingly gave me an inch. I lowered my mouth to the opening.

"Wait!"

She picked up the pace.

"Please, hold up a second."

She broke into a run. Damn. I turned away and sprinted after her toward the door. I had no idea where my slippers were and there was no time for shoes. I ran outside. The grass tickled my feet. I sprinted in the direction she had gone. I tried to follow, but I lost her.

When I got back inside my house, I called Regan and told him what had happened. It sounded stupid even as I said it. A woman had been standing in front of my house. Big deal. Regan, too, sounded thoroughly unimpressed. I convinced myself that it was nothing, just a nosy neighbor. I climbed back into bed, flipped off the television, and eventually I closed my eyes.

The night, however, was not over.

It was four in the morning when my phone rang. I was in the state I now refer to as sleep. I never fall into true slumber anymore. I hang above it with my eyes shut. The nights struggle by like the days. The separation between the two is the flimsiest of curtains. At night, my body manages to rest, but my mind refuses to shut down.

With my eyes closed, I was replaying the morning of the attack for the umpteenth time, hoping to stir a new memory. I started where I am now: in the bedroom. I remembered my alarm clock going off. Lenny and I were going to play racquetball that morning. We'd started playing every Wednesday about a year before, and so far, we had progressed to the point where our games had improved from "pitiful" to "almost remedial." Monica was awake and in the shower. I was scheduled for surgery at 11:00 A.M. I got up and looked in on Tara. I headed back to the bedroom. Monica was out of the shower now and putting on her jeans. I went down to the kitchen, still in my pajamas, opened the cabinet to the right of the Westinghouse refrigerator, chose the raspberry granola bar over the blueberry (I had actually told this detail to Regan recently, as if it might be relevant), and bent over the sink while I ate. . . .

Bam, that was it. Nothing until the hospital.

The phone rang a second time. My eyes opened.

My hand found the phone. I picked it up and said, "Hello?"

"It's Detective Regan. I'm with Agent Tickner. We'll be over in two minutes."

I swallowed. "What is it?"

"Two minutes."

He hung up.

I got out of bed. I glanced out the window, half expecting to see that woman again. No one was there. My jeans from yesterday were crumpled on the floor. I slid them on. I pulled a sweatshirt over my head and made my way down the stairs. I opened the front door and peered out. A police car turned the corner. Regan was driving. Tickner was in the passenger seat. I don't think that I had ever seen them arrive in the same vehicle.

This, I knew, would not be good news.

The two men stepped out of the car. Nausea swept over me. I had prepared myself for this visit since the ransom had gone wrong. I'd even gone so far as to rehearse in my mind how it would all happen—how they would deliver the hammer blow and how I would nod and thank them and excuse myself. I practiced my reaction. I knew precisely how it would all go down.

But now, as I watched Regan and Tickner head toward me, those defenses fled. Panic set in. My body began to shiver. I could barely stand. My knees wobbled, and I leaned against the doorframe. The two men moved in step. I was reminded of an old war movie, the scene where the officers come to the mother's house with solemn faces. I shook my head, wishing them away.

When they reached the door, the two men pushed inside.

"We have something to show you," Regan said.

I turned and followed. Regan flicked on a lamp, but it didn't provide much light. Tickner moved to the couch. He opened his laptop computer. The monitor sprang to life, bathing him in an LCD blue.

"We had a break," Regan explained.

I moved closer.

"Your father-in-law gave us a list of the serial numbers on the ransom bills, remember?"

"Yes."

"One of those bills was used at a bank yesterday afternoon. Agent Tickner is bringing up a video feed right now."

"From the bank?" I asked.

"Yes. We downloaded the video onto his laptop. Twelve hours ago, someone brought a hundred-dollar bill to this bank in order to get smaller notes. We want you to take a look at the video."

I sat next to Tickner. He pressed a button. The video started up immediately. I expected black-and-white or poor, grainy quality. This feed had neither. The angle was shot from above in almost too-brilliant color. A bald man was talking to a teller. There was no sound.

"I don't recognize him," I said.

"Wait."

The bald man said something to the teller. They appeared to be sharing a good-natured chuckle. He picked up a slip of paper and waved a good-bye. The teller gave a small wave back. The next person in line approached the booth. I heard myself groan.

It was my sister, Stacy.

The numb I had longed for suddenly flooded me. I don't know why. Perhaps because two polar emotions pulled at me simultaneously. One, dread. My own sister had done this. My own sister, whom I loved dearly, had betrayed me. But, two, hope—we now had hope. We had a lead. And if it was Stacy, I could not believe that she would harm Tara.

"Is that your sister?" Regan asked, pointing his finger at her image.

"Yes." I looked at him. "Where was this taken?"

"The Catskills," he said. "A town called—"

"Montague," I finished for him.

Tickner and Regan looked at each other. "How do you know that?"

But I was already heading for the door. "I know where she is."

chapter 7

My grandfather had loved to hunt. I always found this strange because he was such a gentle, soft-spoken soul. He never talked about his passion. He didn't hang deer heads over the fireplace mantel. He did not keep trophy pictures or souvenir antlers or whatever else hunters liked to do with carcasses. He did not hunt with friends or family members. Hunting was a solitary activity for my grandfather; he did not explain, defend, or share it with others.

In 1956, Grandpa purchased a small cabin in the hunting woods of Montague, New York. The cost, or so I am told, was under three thousand dollars. I doubt that it would fetch much more today. There was only one bedroom. The structure managed to be rustic without any of the charm associated with that term. It was almost impossible to find—the dirt road stopped two hundred yards before the cabin. You had to hike along a root-infested trail the rest of the way.

When he died four years ago, my grandmother inherited it. At least, that is what I assumed. No one really thought about it much. My grandparents had retired to Florida almost a decade before. My grandmother was in the murky throes of Alzheimer's now. The old cabin, I guessed, was part of her estate. In terms of taxes and whatever expenses, it was probably deep in arrears.

When we were children, my sister and I spent one weekend each summer with our grandparents at the cabin. I did not like it. Nature to me was boredom occasionally broken up by an onslaught of mosquito bites. There was no TV. We went to bed too early and in too much darkness. During the day, the deep silence was too often shattered by the charming echo of shotgun blasts. We spent most of our time taking walks, an activity I find tedious to this very day. One year, my mother packed me only khaki-colored clothes. I spent two days terrified that a hunter would mistake me for a deer.

Stacy, on the other hand, found solace out there. Even as a young child, she seemed to revel in the escape from our suburban rat maze of school and extracurricular activities, of sports teams and popularity. She would wander for hours. She would pick leaves off the trees and collect inchworms in a jar. She would shuffle her feet across carpets of fallen pine needles.

I explained about the cabin to Tickner and Regan as we sped up Route 87. Tickner radioed the police department in Montague. I still remembered how to find the cabin, but describing it was harder. I did my best. Regan kept his foot on the gas pedal. It was four thirty in the morning. There was no traffic and no need for the siren. We reached Exit 16 on the New York Thruway and sped past the Woodbury Common Outlet Center.

The woods were a blur. We were not far now. I told him where to turn off. The car wound up and down back roads that had not changed one iota in the past three decades.

Fifteen minutes later, we were there.

*　　*　　*

Stacy.

My sister had never been very attractive. That may have been part of her problem. Yes, that sounds like nonsense. It is silly, really. But I lay it out for you anyway. No one asked Stacy to any prom. Boys never called. She had very few friends. Of course, there are many adolescents with such hardships. Adolescence is always a war; no one gets out unscathed. And yes, my father's illness was a tremendous burden on us. But that doesn't explain it.

In the end, after all the theories and psychoanalyzing, after all the combing through her childhood traumas, I think what went wrong with my sister was more basic. She had some kind of chemical imbalance in her brain. Too much of one compound flowing here, not enough of another flowing there. We did not recognize the warning signs soon enough. Stacy was depressed in an era when such behavior was mistaken for sullen. Or maybe, yet again, I use this sort of convoluted rationale to justify my own indifference to her. Stacy was just my weird younger sister. I had my own problems, thank you very much. I had the selfishness of a teenager, a truly redundant description if ever I've heard one.

Either way, be the origins of my sister's unhappiness physiological, psychological, or the deluxe combo plan, Stacy's destructive journey was over.

My little sister was dead.

We found her on the floor, curled up in a tight fetal position. That was how she had slept when she was a child, her knees up to her chest, her chin tucked. But even though there was not a mark on her, I could see that she was not sleeping. I bent down. Stacy's eyes were open. She stared straight at me, unblinking, questioning. She still looked so very lost. That wasn't supposed to be. Death was supposed to bring solitude. Death was supposed to bring the peace she had found so elusive in life. Why, I wondered, did Stacy still look so damn lost?

A hypodermic needle lay on the floor by her side, her companion in death as in life. Drugs, of course. Intentional or otherwise, I did not yet know. I had no time to dwell on it either. The police fanned out. I wrested my eyes away from her.

Tara.

The place was a mess. Raccoons had found their way in and made a little home for themselves. The couch where my grandfather had taken his naps, always with his arms folded, was torn up. The stuffing had bled onto the floor. Springs popped up looking for someone to stab. The entire place smelled like urine and dead animals.

I stopped and listened for the sound of a crying baby. There was none. Nothing in here. Only one other room. I dived into the bedroom behind a policeman. The room was dark. I hit the light switch. Nothing happened. Flashlights sliced through the black like saber swords. My eyes scanned the room. When I saw it, I nearly cried out.

There was a playpen.

It was one of those modern Pack 'N Plays with the mesh sides that fold up for easy transport. Monica and I have one. I don't know anyone with a baby who doesn't. The product tag dangled off the side. It had to be new.

Tears came to my eyes. The flashlight cut past the Pack 'N Play, giving it a strobe-light effect. It appeared to be empty. My heart sank. I ran over anyway, in case the light had caused an optical illusion, in case Tara was nestled so sweetly that she—I don't know—barely made a bump.

But there was only a blanket inside.

A soft voice—a voice from a whispery, inescapable nightmare—floated across the room: "Oh Christ."

I swiveled my head toward the sound. The voice came again, weaker this time. "In here," a policeman said. "In the closet."

Tickner and Regan were already there. They both looked inside. Even in the dim glow, I saw their faces lose color.

My feet stumbled forward. I crossed the room, nearly falling, grabbing the closet doorknob at the last moment to regain my balance. I looked through the doorway and saw it. And then, as I looked down at the frayed fabric, I could actually feel my insides implode and crumble into ash.

There, lying on the floor, torn and discarded, was a pink one-piece outfit with black penguins.

eighteen months later

chapter 8

Lydia saw the widow sitting alone at Starbucks.

The widow was on a stool seat, gazing absently at the gentle trickle of pedestrians. Her coffee was near the window, the steam forming a circle on the glass. Lydia watched her for a moment. The devastation was still there—the battle-scarred, thousand-yard stare, the posture of the defeated, the hair with no sheen, the shake in the hands.

Lydia ordered a grande skim latte with an extra shot of espresso. The *barista*, a too-skinny black-clad youth with a goatee, gave her the shot "on the house." Men, even ones this young, did stuff like that for Lydia. She lowered her sunglasses and thanked him. He nearly wet himself.

Lydia moved toward the condiment table, knowing he was checking out her ass. Again she was used to it. She added a packet of Equal to her drink. The Starbucks was fairly empty—there were plenty of seats—but Lydia slid up on the stool immediately next to the widow. Sensing her, the widow started out of her reverie.

"Wendy?" Lydia said.

Wendy Burnet, the widow, turned toward the soft voice.

"I'm very sorry for your loss," Lydia said.

Lydia smiled at her. She had, she knew, a warm smile. She wore a tailored gray suit on her petite, tight frame. The skirt was slit fairly high. Business sexy. Her eyes had that shiny-wet thing going, her nose small and slightly upturned. Her hair was auburn ringlets, but she could— and often did—change that.

Wendy Burnet stared just long enough for Lydia to wonder if she'd been recognized. Lydia had seen that stare plenty of times before, that unsure I-know-you-from-somewhere expression, even though she had not been on TV since she turned thirteen. Some people would even comment, "Hey, you know who you look like?" but Lydia—she had been billed as Larissa Dane back then—would shrug it away.

But alas, this hesitation was not like that. Wendy Burnet was still shell-shocked from the horrible death of her beloved. It simply took her a while to register and assimilate unfamiliar data. She was probably wondering how to react, if she should pretend she knew Lydia or not.

After another few seconds, Wendy Burnet went for the noncommittal. "Thank you."

"Poor Jimmy," Lydia followed up. "Such an awful way to go."

Wendy fumbled for the paper coffee cup and downed a healthy sip. Lydia checked out the little boxes on the side of the cup and saw that the Widow Wendy had ordered a grande latte too, though she'd chosen half decaf and soy milk. Lydia slid a little closer to her.

"You don't know who I am, do you?"

Wendy gave her a weak got-me smile. "I'm sorry."

"No need to be. I don't think we ever met."

Wendy waited for Lydia to introduce herself. When she didn't, Wendy said, "You knew my husband then?"

"Oh yes."

"Are you in the insurance business too?"

"No, I'm afraid not."

Wendy frowned. Lydia sipped her beverage. The awkwardness grew, at least for Wendy. Lydia was fine with it. When it became too much, Wendy rose to leave.

"Well," she said, "it was nice meeting you."

"I . . ." Lydia began, hesitating until she was sure that she had Wendy's full attention. "I was the last person to see Jimmy alive."

Wendy froze. Lydia took another sip and closed her eyes. "Nice and strong," she said, gesturing toward the cup. "I love the coffee here, don't you?"

"Did you say . . . ?"

"Please," Lydia said with a small sweep of her arm. "Have a seat so I can explain properly."

Wendy glanced over at the *baristas*. They were busy gesticulating and whining about what they thought was the great world conspiracy that kept them from the most amazing of lives. Wendy slid back onto the stool. For a few moments, Lydia just stared at her. Wendy tried to hold her gaze.

"You see," Lydia began, offering up a fresh, warm smile and tilting her head to the side, "I'm the one who killed your husband."

Wendy's face went pale. "That isn't funny."

"True, yes, I'd have to agree with you on that, Wendy. But then again humor was not really my aim. Would you like to hear a joke instead? I'm on one of those joke e-mail lists. Most are duds, but every once in a while, they send a howler."

Wendy sat stunned. "Who the hell are you?"

"Calm down a second, Wendy."

"I want to know—"

"Shhh." Lydia put her finger to Wendy's lip with too much tenderness. "Let me explain, okay?"

Wendy's lips trembled. Lydia kept her finger there for a few more seconds.

"You're confused. I understand that. Let me clarify a few things for you. First off, yes, I'm the one who put the bullet in Jimmy's head. But Heshy"—Lydia pointed out the window in the direction of an enormous man with a misshapen head—"he did the earlier damage. Personally, by the time I shot Jimmy, well, I think I might have been doing him a favor."

Wendy just stared.

"You want to know why, am I right? Of course, you do. But deep down inside, Wendy, I think you know. We're women of the world, aren't we? We know our men."

Wendy said nothing.

"Wendy, do you know what I'm talking about?"

"No."

"Sure you do, but I'll say it anyway. Jimmy, your dearly departed husband, owed a great deal of money to some very unpleasant people. As of today, the amount is just under two hundred thousand dollars." Lydia smiled. "Wendy, you're not going to pretend you know nothing about your husband's gambling woes, are you?"

Wendy had trouble forming the words in her mouth. "I don't understand. . . ."

"I hope your confusion has nothing to do with my gender."

"What?"

"That would be really narrow and sexist on your part, don't you think? This is the twenty-first century. Women can be whatever they want."

"You"—Wendy stopped, tried again—"you murdered my husband?"

"Do you watch much television, Wendy?"

"What?"

"Television. You see, on television, whenever someone like your husband owes money to someone like me, well, what happens?"

Lydia stopped as if she really expected her to answer. Wendy finally said, "I don't know."

"Sure you do, but again I'll answer for you. The someone-like-me—okay, usually the *male* someone-like-me—is sent to threaten him. Then maybe my cohort Heshy out there would beat him up or break his legs, something like that. But they never kill the guy. That's one of those TV-bad-guy rules. 'You can't collect from a dead man.' You've heard that, haven't you, Wendy?"

She waited. Wendy finally said, "I guess."

"But, see, that's wrong. Let's take Jimmy, for example. Your husband had a disease. Gambling. Am I right? It cost you everything, didn't it? The insurance business. That had been your father's. Jimmy took it over for him. It's gone now. Wiped out. The bank was ready to foreclose on your house. You and the kids barely had enough money for groceries. And still Jimmy didn't stop." Lydia shook her head. "Men. Am I right?"

There were tears in Wendy's eyes. Her voice, when she was able to speak, was so weak. "So you killed him?"

Lydia looked up, shaking her head gently. "I'm really not explaining this well, am I?" She lowered her gaze and tried again. "Have you ever heard the expression that you can't squeeze blood from a stone?"

Again Lydia waited for an answer. Wendy finally nodded. Lydia seemed pleased.

"Well, that's the case here. With Jimmy, I mean. I could have Heshy out there work him over—Heshy is good at that—but what good would that do? Jimmy didn't have the money. He would never be able to get his hands on that kind of cash." Lydia sat a little straighter and put out her hands. "Now, Wendy, I want you to think like a businessman—check that, a business*person*. We don't have to be raving feminists, but I think we should at least keep ourselves on equal footing."

Lydia gave Wendy another smile. Wendy cringed.

"Okay, so what am I—as a wise business*person*— what am I supposed to do? I can't let the debt go unpaid, of course. In my line of work, that's professional suicide. Someone owes my employer money, they have to pay. No way around that. The problem here is, Jimmy doesn't have a cent to his name but"—Lydia stopped and widened her smile—"but he does have a wife and three kids. And he used to be in the insurance business. Do you see where I'm going with this, Wendy?"

Wendy was afraid to breathe.

"Oh, I think you do, but again I'll say it for you. Insurance. More specifically, *life* insurance. Jimmy had a policy. He didn't admit it right away, but eventually, well, Heshy can be persuasive." Wendy's eyes drifted toward the window. Lydia saw the shiver and hid a smile. "Jimmy told us he had two policies, in fact, with a total payout of nearly a million dollars."

"So you"—Wendy was struggling to comprehend— "you killed Jimmy for the insurance money?"

Lydia snapped her fingers. "You go, girlfriend."

Wendy opened her mouth but nothing came out.

"And, Wendy? Let me make this crystal clear. Jimmy's debts don't die with him. We both know that. The bank still wants you to pay the mortgage—am I right? The credit card companies don't stop mounting the interest." Lydia shrugged her small shoulders, palms to the sky. "Why should my employer be any different?"

"You can't be serious."

"Your first insurance check should come in about a week. By that time, your husband's debt will be two hundred eighty thousand dollars. I'll expect a check for that amount on that day."

"But the bills he left alone—"

"Shhh." Again Lydia silenced her with a finger to her lips. Her voice dropped to an intimate whisper. "That doesn't really concern me, Wendy. I have given you the rare opportunity to get out from under. Declare bankruptcy, if you must. You live in a ritzy area. Move out. Have Jack—that's your eleven-year-old, correct?"

Wendy jolted at the sound of her son's name.

"Well, no summer camp for Jack this year. Have him get a job after school. Whatever. None of that concerns me. You, Wendy, will pay what you owe, and that will be the end of this. You will never see or hear from me again. If you don't pay, however, well, take a good look at Heshy over there." She paused, letting Wendy do just that. It had the desired effect.

"We'll kill little Jack first. Then, two days later, we'll kill Lila. If you report this conversation to the police, we'll kill Jack and Lila and Darlene. All three, in age order. And then, after you bury your children—please listen, Wendy, because this is key—I'll still make you pay."

Wendy couldn't speak.

Lydia followed up a deep, caffeinated sip with an "Ahh" of satisfaction. "Dee-lightful," she said, rising from her seat. "I really enjoyed our little girl chat, Wendy. We should get together again soon. Say, your house at noon on Friday the sixteenth?"

Wendy kept her head down.

"Do you understand?"

"Yes."

"What are you going to do?"

"I'm going to pay the debt," Wendy said.

Lydia smiled at her. "Again, my sincerest condolences."

Lydia headed outside and breathed in the fresh air. She looked behind her. Wendy Burnet had not moved. Lydia waved good-bye and met up with Heshy. He was nearly six six. She was five one. He weighed 275 pounds. She was 105. He had a head like a misshapen pumpkin. Her features seemed to have been made in the Orient out of porcelain.

"Problems?" Heshy asked.

"Please," she said with a dismissive wave. "On to more profitable ventures. Did you find our man?"

"Yes."

"And the package is already out?"

"Sure, Lydia."

"Very good." She frowned, felt a gnawing.

"What's wrong?" he asked.

"I have a funny feeling, that's all."

"You want to back out?"

Lydia smiled at him. "Not on your life, Pooh Bear."

"Then what do you want to do?"

She thought about it. "Let's just see how Dr. Seidman reacts."

chapter 9

"Don't drink any more apple juice," Cheryl told her two-year-old, Conner.

I stood on the sidelines with my arms folded. It was a bit nippy, the frosty, damp chill of late New Jersey autumn, so I pulled the hood of my sweatshirt over my Yankee cap. I also had on a pair of Ray-Bans. Sunglasses and hood. I looked very much like the police sketch of the Unabomber.

We were at a soccer game for eight-year-old boys. Lenny was the head coach. He needed an assistant and recruited me because, I assume, I am the only one who knows even less about soccer than he does. Still our team was winning. I think the score was about eighty-three to two, but I am not certain.

"Why can't I have more juice?" Conner asked.

"Because," Cheryl answered with the patience of a mother, "apple juice gives you diarrhea."

"It does?"

"Yes."

To my right, Lenny drowned the kids in a steady stream of encouragement. "You're the best, Ricky." "Way to go, Petey." "Now *that's* what I call hustle, Davey." He always added a *y* to the end of their names.

And yes, it is annoying. Once, in a pitch of overexcitement, he called me Marky. Once.

"Uncle Marc?"

I feel a tug at my leg. I look down at Conner, who is twenty-six months old. "What's up, pal?"

"Apple juice gives me a diarrhea."

"Good to know," I said.

"Uncle Marc?"

"Yeah?"

Conner gave me his gravest look. "Diarrhea," he said, "is not my friend."

I glanced at Cheryl. She smothered a smile, but I saw the concern there too. I looked back at Conner. "Words to live by, kid."

Conner nodded, pleased by my response. I love him. He breaks my heart and brings me joy in equal measure and at exactly the same time. Twenty-six months old. Two months older than Tara. I watch his development with awe and a longing that could heat a furnace.

He turned back to his mother. Littered about Cheryl was the product of her mommy-as-packmule harvest. There were Minute Maid juice boxes and Nutri-Grain bars. There were Pampers Baby-Dry diapers (as opposed to Baby-Wet?) and Huggies wipes containing aloe vera for the discriminating buttock. There were angled baby bottles from Evenflo. There were cinnamon Teddy Grahams and well-scrubbed baby carrots and sectioned oranges and cut-up grapes (sliced the long way so as to make them chokeproof) and cubes of what I hoped was cheese, all hermetically sealed in their own Ziploc bags.

Lenny, the head coach, was yelling out key, game-winning strategy to our players. When we are on offense, he tells them to "Score!" When we are on defense, he advises them to "Stop him!" And then sometimes, like right now, he offers keen insight into the subtleties of the game:

"Kick the ball!"

Lenny glanced at me after he'd shouted that for the fourth time in a row. I gave him a thumbs-up and way-to-go nod. He wanted to give me the finger, but there were too many underage witnesses. I refolded my arms and squinted at the field. The kids were geared up like the pros. They wore cleats. Their socks were pulled up over their shin guards. Most wore that black grease under their eyes, even though there was nary a hint of sunshine. Two even had those breathing strip–bandages across their noses. I watched Kevin, my godson, try, per his father's instructions, to kick the ball. And then it hit me like a body blow.

I staggered back.

That was how it always happened. I will be watching the game or I'll be having dinner with friends or I'll be working on a patient or listening to a song on the radio. I'll be doing something normal, average, feeling pretty decent, and then, wham, I get blindsided.

My eyes welled up. That never used to happen to me before the murder and kidnapping. I am a doctor. I know how to play poised in both my professional and personal life. But now I wear sunglasses all the time like some self-important B-movie star. Cheryl looked up at me and again I saw the concern. I straightened and forced a smile. Cheryl was becoming beautiful. That happened sometimes. Motherhood agreed with certain women. It gave their physical appearance a wonder and richness that borders on the celestial.

I don't want to give you the wrong impression. I don't spend every day crying. I still live my life. I am be-reaved, sure, but not all the time. I am not paralyzed. I work, though I haven't yet had the courage to travel overseas. I keep thinking that I need to stay close by, in case there is a new development. That kind of thinking is, I know, not rational and perhaps even delusional. But I am still not ready.

What gets me—what gives me that surprise *wham*— is the way grief seems to relish in catching you unawares. Grief, when spotted, can be, if not handled, somewhat manipulated, finessed, concealed. But grief likes to hide behind bushes. It enjoys leaping out of nowhere, startling you, mocking you, stripping away your pretense of normalcy. Grief lulls you to sleep, thus making that blindside hit all the more jarring.

"Uncle Marc?"

It was Conner again. He talked pretty well for a kid his age. I wondered what Tara's voice would have sounded like, and behind my sunglasses, my eyes closed. Sensing something, Cheryl reached out to pull him away. I shook her off. "What is it, pal?"

"What about poop?"

"What about it?"

He looked up and closed one eye in concentration. "Is poop my friend?"

Hell of a question. "I don't know, pal. What do you think?"

Conner considered his own query so hard it appeared as if he might explode. Finally he replied, "It's more my friend than diarrhea."

I nodded sagely. Our team scored another goal. Lenny shot his fists into the air and shouted, "Yes!" He nearly cartwheeled out to congratulate Craig (or should I say Craigy), the goal scorer. The players followed him. There was much high-fiving. I didn't join in. My job, I figured, was to be the quiet partner to Lenny's histrionics, the Tonto to his Lone Ranger, the Abbott to his Costello, the Rowan to his Martin, the Captain to his Tennille. Balance.

I watched the parents on the sidelines. The mothers became clusters. They talked about their kids, about their child's achievements and extracurricular activities, and no one listened much because other people's children are boring. The fathers offered more variety. Some videotaped. Some yelled encouragement. Some rode their kids in a way that borders on the unhealthy. Some gabbed on cell phones and constantly fiddled with handheld electronics of one kind or another, experiencing a bit of the bends after spending all week immersed in their work.

Why did I go to the police?

I have been told countless times since that terrible day that I am not to blame for what happened. On one level, I realize that my actions may have changed nothing. In all likelihood, they had never intended to let Tara come home. She might even have been dead before the first ransom call. Her death may have been accidental. Maybe they just panicked or were strung out. Who knows? I certainly don't.

And, ah, there's the rub.

I cannot, of course, be certain that I am not responsible. Basic science: For every action, there is a reaction.

I do not dream about Tara—or if I do, the gods are generous enough to not let me remember. That is probably giving them too much credit. Let me rephrase. I may not dream about Tara specifically, but I do dream about the white van with the mix-and-match license plate and the stolen magnetic sign. In the dreams I hear a noise, muffled, but I'm pretty sure it is the sound of a baby crying. Tara, I know now, was in the van, but in my dream, I don't go toward the sound. My legs are buried deep in that nightmare muck. I can't move. When I finally wake up, I cannot help but ponder the obvious. Was Tara that close to me? And more important: Had I been a little braver, could I have saved her then and there?

The referee, a lanky high school boy with a good-natured grin, blew the whistle and waved his hands over his head. Game over. Lenny shouted, "Woo, yeah!" The eight-year-olds stared at one another, confused. One asked a teammate, "Who won?" and the teammate shrugged. They lined up, Stanley Cup hockey style, for the postgame handshakes.

Cheryl stood up and put a hand on my back. "Great win, Coach."

"Yeah, I carry this team," I said.

She smiled. The boys started rambling back toward us. I congratulated them with my stoic nod. Craig's mother had brought a fifty-pack of Dunkin' Donuts Munchkins in a box with a Halloween design. Dave's mom had boxes of something called Yoo-Hoo, a perverse excuse for chocolate milk that tastes like chalk. I popped a Munchkin in my mouth and skipped the washdown. Cheryl asked, "What flavor was that?"

I shrugged. "They come in different flavors?" I watched the parents interact with their children and felt tremendously out of place. Lenny came toward me.

"Great win, wasn't it?"

"Yeah," I said. "We're the balls."

He gestured for us to step away. I complied. When we were out of earshot, Lenny said, "Monica's estate is almost wrapped up. It shouldn't be too much longer now."

I said, "Uh-huh," because I didn't really care.

"I also have your will drawn up. You need to sign it."

Neither Monica nor I had made up a will. For years, Lenny had warned me about that. You need to put in writing who gets your money, he'd remind me, who is going to raise your daughter, who is going to care for your parents, yadda, yadda, yadda. But we didn't listen.

We were going to live forever. Last wills and testaments were for, well, the dead.

Lenny changed subjects on the fly. "You want to come back to the house for a game of foosball?"

Foosball, for those of you who lack a basic education, is that tabletop bar game with the soccer-type men skewered on sticks. "I'm already champion of the world," I reminded him.

"That was yesterday."

"Can't a man revel in his title for little while? I'm not yet ready to let go of the feeling."

"Understood." Lenny headed back to his family. I watched his daughter, Marianne, corner him. She was gesturing like mad. Lenny slumped his shoulders, took out his wallet, peeled out a bill. Marianne took it, kissed him on the cheek, ran off. Lenny watched her disappear, shaking his head. There was a smile on his face. I turned away.

The worst part—or should I say the best part—was that I have hope.

Here was what we found that night at Grandpa's cabin: my sister's corpse, hairs belonging to Tara in the Pack 'N Play (DNA confirmed), and a pink one-piece with black penguins that matched Tara's.

Here was what we did not find and, in fact, still have not found: the ransom money, the identity, if any, of Stacy's accomplices—and Tara.

That's right. We never found my daughter.

The forest is big and sprawling, I know. The grave would be small and easily hidden. There could be rocks over it. An animal might have found it and dragged the contents deeper into the thicket. The contents could be miles from my grandfather's cabin. They could be somewhere else entirely.

Or—though I keep this thought to myself—maybe there is no grave at all.

So you see, the hope is there. Like grief, hope hides and pounces and taunts and never leaves. I am not sure which of the two is the crueler mistress.

The police and FBI theorize that my sister acted in conjunction with some very bad people. While no one is quite sure if their original intention was kidnapping or robbery, most everyone agrees that someone panicked. Maybe they thought that Monica and I would not be home. Maybe they thought that they would just have to contend with a baby-sitter. Whatever, they saw us, and acting in some drugged or crazed state, someone fired a shot. Then someone else fired a shot, ergo the ballistic tests showing Monica and I were shot by different .38s. They then kidnapped the baby. Eventually they double-crossed Stacy and killed her with an overdose of heroin.

I keep saying "they" because the authorities also believe that Stacy had at least two accomplices. One would be the professional, the cool head who knew how to work the drop and weld the license plates and disappear without a trace. The other accomplice would be the "panicker," if you will, the one who shot us and probably caused the death of Tara.

Some, of course, don't buy that theory. Some believe that there was only one accomplice—the cool professional—and that the one who panicked was Stacy. She, this theory goes, was the one who fired the first bullet, probably at me since I don't remember any shots, and then the professional killed Monica to cover the mistake. This theory is backed up by one of the few leads we had following that night in the cabin: a drug dealer who, in some bizarre plea bargain on another charge, told authorities that Stacy had purchased a gun from him, a .38, a week before the murder-kidnapping. This theory is further backed up by the fact that the only unexplained hairs and fingerprints found at the murder scene were Stacy's. While the cool pro would know to wear gloves and be careful, a drugged-out accomplice would probably not.

Still others do not embrace that theory either, which is why certain members of the police department and FBI cling to and support a more obvious third scenario: I was the mastermind.

The theory goes something like this: first caveat, the husband is always suspect number one. Second, my Smith & Wesson .38 is still missing. They press me on this question all the time. I wish I had an answer. Third, I never wanted a child. Tara's birth forced me into a loveless marriage. They believe that they have evidence that I was considering divorce (something that yes, I did indeed contemplate) and so I planned the whole thing, top to bottom. I invited my sister over to my house and perhaps enlisted her help so that she would take the fall. I have the ransom money hidden away. I killed and buried my own daughter.

Awful, yes, but I am past anger. I am past exhaustion. I am not sure where I am anymore.

The main problem with their hypothesis is, of course, that it is hard to finesse my being left for dead. Did I kill Stacy? Did she shoot me? Or—drum roll here—is there a third possibility out there, a blending of the two different theories into one? Some believe that yes, I was behind it, but I had another accomplice besides Stacy. That accomplice killed Stacy, perhaps against my wishes, perhaps as part of my grand scheme to deflect my guilt and avenge my own shooting. Or something like that.

And round and round we go.

In sum, when you cut through it all, they—and I—have nothing. No ransom money. No idea who did it. No idea why. And most important: no small corpse.

That is where we are today—a year and a half after the abduction. The file is still technically open, but Regan and Tickner have moved on to new cases. I haven't heard a word from either in nearly six months. The media gnawed on us for a few weeks, but with nothing new to feed on, they too slithered toward juicier troughs.

The Dunkin' Donuts Munchkins were gone. Everyone started heading to a parking lot overloaded with minivans. After the game we coaches take our budding athletes to Schrafft's Ice Cream Parlor, a tradition in our town. Every coach in every other league in every other age group follows the same tradition. The place was packed. Nothing like an ice cream cone in the autumn frost to burrow the chill into the bone.

I stood with my Cookies-n-Cream cone and surveyed the scene. Children and fathers. It was getting to be too much for me. I checked my watch. Time for me to leave anyway. I met Lenny's eye and motioned that I was going. He mouthed the words *Your will* at me. In case I didn't get the drift, he even made a signing motion with his hand. I waved that I understood. I got back into my car and flipped on the radio.

For a long while, I sat there and watched the flow of families. I kept my eyes on the fathers mostly. I gauged their reactions to this most domestic of activities, hoping to see a flicker of doubt, something in the eyes that might comfort me. But I didn't.

I'm not sure how long I stayed like that. Not more than ten minutes, I suppose. An old favorite by James Taylor came on the radio. It brought me back. I smiled, started up the car, and made my way toward the hospital.

An hour later, I was scrubbing up to perform surgery on an eight-year-old boy with—to use terminology familiar to both layman and professional—a facial smash. Zia Leroux, my medical partner, was there.

I'm not sure why I first chose to be a plastic surgeon. It was neither the siren song of easy dollars nor the ideal of helping my fellowman. I had wanted to be a surgeon pretty much from the get-go, but I saw myself more in the vascular or cardiac fields. Life's turns come in funny ways though. During my second year of residency, the cardiac surgeon who ran our rotation was— what's the phrase?—a total prick. On the other hand, the doctor in charge of the cosmetic surgery, Liam Reese, was incredible. Dr. Reese had that enviable have-it-all feel to him, that combination of good looks, calm confidence, and internal warmth that naturally drew people. You wanted to please him. You wanted to be like him.

Dr. Reese became my mentor. He showed how reconstructive surgery was creative, a Humpty-Dumpty process that forced you to find new ways to put back together what had been destroyed. The bones in the face and skull are the most complex stretch of skeletal landscape in the human body. We who repair them are artists. We are jazz musicians. If you talk to orthopedic or thoracic surgeons, they can be pretty specific about their procedures. Our work—reconstruction—is never exactly the same. We improvise. Dr. Reese taught me that. He appealed to my inner technoweenie with talk of microsurgery and bone grafts and synthetic skin. I remember visiting him in Scarsdale. His wife was long legged and beautiful. His daughter was school valedictorian. His son was captain of the basketball team and the nicest kid I've ever met. At the age of forty-nine Dr. Reese was killed in a car crash on Route 684 heading to Connecticut. Somebody might find something poignant in that, but that person wouldn't be me.

When I was finishing up residency, I landed a one-year fellowship to train in oral surgery overseas. I didn't apply to be a do-gooder; I applied because it sounded pretty cool. This trip would be, I hoped, my version of backpacking through Europe. It was not. Things went wrong right away. We got caught up in a civil war in Sierra Leone. I handled wounds so horrible, so unfathomable, that it was hard to believe the human mind could conjure up the necessary cruelty to inflict them. But even in the midst of this destruction, I felt a strange exhilaration. I don't try to figure out why. Like I said before, this stuff gets me jazzed. Maybe part of it was the satisfaction of helping people truly in need. Or maybe I was drawn to this work the same way some are drawn to extreme sports because they need the risk of death to feel whole.

When I came back, Zia and I set up One World, and we were on our way. I love what I do. Perhaps our work is like an extreme sport, but it also has a very—pardon the pun—human face. I like that. I love my patients and yet I love the calculating distance, the necessary coldness, of what I do. I care about my patients so much, but then they are gone—intense love mixed with fleeting commitment.

Today's patient presented us with a rather complicated challenge. My patron saint—the patron saint of many in reconstructive surgery—is the French researcher René LeFort. LeFort tossed cadavers off a tavern roof onto their skulls to see the natural pattern of fracture lines in the face. I bet this impressed the ladies. Today we name certain fractures for him—more specifically, LeFort type I, LeFort type II, LeFort type III. Zia and I checked the films again. The Water view gave us the best look, but the Caldwell and lateral backed it up.

Simply put, the fracture line on this eight-year-old was a LeFort type III, causing a complete separation of the facial bones and the cranium. I could pretty much rip off the boy's face like a mask if I wanted to.

"Car accident?" I asked.

Zia nodded. "Father was drunk."

"Don't tell me. He's fine, right?"

"He even remembered to put on his own seat belt."

"But not his son's."

"Too much trouble. What with him being tired from raising a glass so many times."

Zia and I started our life's journey in two very different places. Like the Stories' classic seventies song "Brother Louie," Zia is black as the night while I am whiter than white (my skin tone, as described by Zia: "underwater fish belly"). I was born at Beth Israel Hospital in Newark and grew up on the suburban streets of Kasselton, New Jersey. Zia was born in a mud hut in a village outside of Port-au-Prince, Haiti. Sometime during the reign of Papa Doc, her parents became political prisoners. No one knows too many details. Her father was executed. Her mother, when released, was damaged goods. She grabbed her daughter and escaped on what might liberally be dubbed a raft. Three passengers died on the journey. Zia and her mother survived. They made their way to the Bronx, where they took up residence in the basement of a beauty parlor. The two spent their days quietly sweeping hair. The hair, it seemed to Zia, was inescapable. It was on her clothes, clinging to her skin, in her throat, in her lungs. She lived forever with that feeling that a stray strand was in her mouth and she couldn't quite pull it out. To this day, when Zia gets nervous, her fingers play with her tongue, as though trying to pluck out a memento of her past.

When the surgery was over, Zia and I collapsed onto

a bench. Zia untied her surgical mask and let it fall to her chest.

"Piece of cake," she said.

"Amen," I agreed. "How did your date go last night?"

"It sucked," she said. "And I don't mean that literally."

"Sorry."

"Men are such scum."

"Don't I know it."

"I'm getting so desperate," she said, "I'm thinking of sleeping with you again."

"Gasp," I said. "Woman, have you no standards?"

Her smile was blinding, the bright white against the dark skin. She was a shade under six feet tall with smooth muscles and cheekbones so high and sharp you feared they might pierce her skin. "When are you going to start dating?" she asked.

"I date."

"I mean, long enough to have a sexual encounter."

"Not all women are easy as you, Zia."

"Sad," she said, giving my arm a playful punch.

Zia and I slept together once—and we both knew that it would never happen again. It was how we met. We hooked up during my first year of medical school. Yep, a one-night stand. I have had my fair share of one-night stands, but only two have been memorable. The first led to disaster. The second—this one—led to a relationship I will cherish forever.

It was eight o'clock at night by the time we got out of our scrubs. We took Zia's car, a tiny thing called a BMW Mini, to the Stop & Shop on Northwood Avenue and picked up some groceries. Zia chatted without letup as we wheeled carts down the aisles. I liked when Zia talked. It gave me energy. At the deli counter Zia pulled a call number. She looked at the specials board and frowned.

"What?" I said.

"Boar's Head ham on sale."

"What about it?"

"Boar's Head," she repeated. "What marketing genius came up with that name? 'Say, I have an idea. Let's name our premium cold cuts after the most disgusting animal imaginable. No, check that. Let's name it after its head.' "

"You always order it," I said.

She thought about it. "Yeah, I guess."

We moved to the checkout line. Zia put her stuff up front. I placed the divider down and unloaded my cart. A portly cashier began to ring up her items.

"You hungry?" she asked me.

I shrugged. "Guess I could go for a couple of slices at Garbo's."

"Let's do it." Zia's eyes drifted over my shoulder and then jerked to a stop. She squinted and something crossed her face. "Marc?"

"Yeah."

She waved it off. "Nah, can't be."

"What?"

Still staring over my shoulder, Zia gestured with her chin. I turned slowly, and when I saw her, I felt it in my chest.

"I've only seen her in pictures," Zia said, "but isn't that . . . ?"

I managed a nod.

It was Rachel.

The world closed in around me. It shouldn't feel this way. I knew that. We had broken up years ago. Now, after all this time, I should be smiling. I should feel something wistful, a passing nostalgia, a poignant remembrance of a time when I was young and naïve. But no, that was not what was going on here. Rachel stood ten yards away and it all flooded back. What I felt was a still-too-powerful yearning, a longing that tore through me, that made both the love and heartbreak feel fresh and alive.

"You okay?" Zia said.

Another nod.

Are you one of those who believe that we all have one true soul mate—one and only one preordained love? There, across three Stop & Shop checkout lanes and under a sign reading EXPRESS LANE—15 ITEMS OR LESS, stood mine.

Zia said, "I thought she got married."

"She did," I said.

"No ring." Then Zia punched my arm. "Oooh, this is exciting, isn't it?"

"Yeah," I said. "Exhilaration city."

Zia snapped her fingers. "Hey, you know what this is like? That crappy old album you used to play. The song about meeting the old lover in the grocery store. What's the name of it?"

The first time I'd seen Rachel, when I was a lad of nineteen years, the effect was relatively gentle. There was no big boom. I'm not even sure that I found her overly attractive. But as I'd soon learn, I like a woman whose looks grow on you. You start off thinking, Okay, she's pretty decent looking, and then, a few days later, maybe it's something she says or the way she tilts her head when she says it, but then, wham, it's like getting hit by a bus.

It felt like that again now. Rachel had changed but not by much. The years had made that sneaky beauty harden maybe, more brittle and angled. She was thinner. Her dark blue-black hair was pulled back and tied into a ponytail. Most men like the hair down. I've always liked it tied back, the openness and exposure of it,

I guess, especially with Rachel's cheekbones and neck. She wore jeans and a gray blouse. Her hazel eyes were down, her head bent in that pose of concentration I knew so well. She had not seen me yet.

" 'Same Old Lang Syne,' " Zia said.

"What?"

"The song about the lovers in the grocery store. By Dan Somebody. That's the title. 'Same Old Lang Syne.' " Then she added: "I think that's the title."

Rachel reached into her wallet and plucked out a twenty. She began to hand it to the cashier. Her gaze lifted—and that was when she saw me.

I can't say exactly what crossed her face. She did not look surprised. Our eyes met, but I did not see joy there. Fear, perhaps. Maybe resignation. I don't know. I also don't know how long we both stood there like that.

"Maybe I should move away from you," Zia whispered.

"Huh?"

"If she thinks you're with a chick this hot, she'll conclude that she has no chance."

I think I smiled.

"Marc?"

"Yeah."

"The way you're standing like that. Gaping like a total whack job. It's a little scary."

"Thanks."

I felt her hand push on my back. "Go over and say hello."

My feet started moving, though I don't remember the brain issuing any commands. Rachel let the cashier bag her groceries. She stepped toward me and tried to smile. Her smile had always been spectacular, the kind that makes you think of poetry and spring showers, a dazzler that can change your day. This smile, however, was not like that. It was tighter. It was pained. And I wondered if she was holding back or if she could no longer smile like she used to, if something had dimmed the wattage permanently.

We stopped a yard away from each other, neither sure if the proper protocol called for a hug, a kiss, a handshake. So we did none of the above. I stood there and felt the hurt everywhere.

"Hi," I said.

"Good to see you still have all the smooth lines," Rachel replied.

I feigned a rakish grin. "Hey, baby, what's your sign?"

"Better," she said.

"Come here often?"

"Good. Now say, 'Haven't we met before?' "

"Nah." I arched an eyebrow. "No way I'd forget meeting a foxy lady like you."

We both laughed. We were both trying too hard. We both knew it.

"You look good," I said.

"So do you."

Brief silence.

"Okay," I said, "I'm out of uncomfortable clichés and forced banter."

"Whew," Rachel said.

"Why are you here?"

"I'm buying food."

"No, I mean—"

"I know what you meant," she interrupted. "My mother moved into a condo development in West Orange."

A few of the strands had escaped her ponytail and fell across her face. It took all my willpower to stop from pushing them away.

Rachel glanced away and then back at me. "I heard about your wife and daughter," she said. "I'm sorry."

"Thank you."

"I wanted to call or write but . . ."

"I heard you got married," I said.

She wiggled the fingers on her left hand. "Not anymore."

"And that you were an agent with the FBI."

Rachel put her hand back down. "Also not anymore."

More silence. Again I don't know how long we stood there. The cashier had moved on to the next shopper. Zia came up behind us. She cleared her throat and jammed her hand toward Rachel. "Hi, I'm Zia Leroux," she said.

"Rachel Mills."

"Good to meet you, Rachel. I'm Marc's practice partner." Then, thinking about it, she added: "We're just friends."

"Zia," I said.

"Oh, right, sorry. Look, Rachel, I'd love to stay and chat, but I have to run." She jerked her thumb toward the exit to emphasize the point. "You two talk. Marc, I'll meet you back here later. Great meeting you, Rachel."

"Same here."

Zia rushed off. I shrugged. "She's a great doctor."

"I bet she is." Rachel took hold of her cart. "I have someone waiting in the car, Marc. It was good seeing you."

"You too." But surely, with all I'd lost, I must have learned something, right? I couldn't just let her go. I cleared my throat and said, "Maybe we should get together."

"I'm still living in Washington. I head back tomorrow."

Silence. My insides turned to jelly. My breathing was shallow.

"Good-bye, Marc," Rachel said. But those hazel eyes were wet.

"Don't go yet."

I tried to keep the pleading out of my voice, but I don't think I was successful. Rachel looked at me, and she saw everything. "What do you want me to say here, Marc?"

"That you want to get together too."

"That's all?"

I shook my head. "You know that's not all."

"I'm not twenty-one anymore."

"Neither am I."

"The girl you loved is dead and gone."

"No," I said. "She's right in front of me."

"You don't know me anymore."

"So let's get reacquainted. I'm not in a rush."

"Just like that?"

I tried to smile. "Yeah."

"I live in Washington. You live in New Jersey."

"So I'll move," I said.

But even before the impetuous words came out, even before Rachel made that face, I could recognize my own false bravado. I couldn't just leave my parents or dump my business with Zia or—or abandon my ghosts. Somewhere between my lips and her ears the sentiment crashed and burned.

Rachel turned to leave then. She did not say goodbye again. I watched her push the cart toward the door. I saw the door automatically swing open with an electric grunt. I saw Rachel, the love of my life, disappear again without so much as a backward glance. I stayed still. I did not follow her. I felt my heart tumble and shatter, but I did nothing to stop her.

Maybe I hadn't learned anything, after all.

chapter 10

I drank.

I am not a big drinker—pot had been my elixir of choice during my younger days—but I found an old bottle of gin in a cabinet over the sink. There was tonic in the fridge. I have an automatic icemaker in the freezer. You do the math.

I still lived in the old Levinsky house. It is much too big for me, but I don't have the heart to let it go. It feels like a portal now, a lifeline (albeit a fragile one) to my daughter. Yes, I know how that sounds, but selling it now would be like closing a door on her. I can't do that.

Zia wanted to stay with me, but I begged off. She did not push it. I thought about the corny Dan Fogelberg (not Dan Somebody) song where the old lovers talk until their tongues get tired. I thought about Bogie questioning the gods who would allow Ingrid Bergman into his, of all possible, gin joints. Bogie drank after she left. It seemed to help him. Maybe it would help me too.

The fact that Rachel could still pack this kind of wallop annoyed the hell out of me. It was stupid and childish really. Rachel and I had first met during summer break between my sophomore and junior years of college. She was from Middlebury, Vermont, and supposedly a distant cousin of Lenny's wife, Cheryl, though no one could ascertain the exact relationship. That summer—the summer of all summers—Rachel stayed with Cheryl's family because Rachel's folks were going through a nasty divorce. We were introduced, and like I said before, it took some time for the bus to smack into me. Maybe that's what made it all the more potent when it did.

We began to date. We doubled a lot with Lenny and Cheryl. The four of us spent every weekend at Lenny's summerhouse on the Jersey shore. It was indeed a glorious summer, the kind of summer everyone should experience at least once in a lifetime.

If this were a movie, we'd be cueing up the montage music. I went to Tufts University while Rachel was starting out at Boston College. First scene of the montage, well, they'd probably have us on a boat on the Charles, me paddling, Rachel holding a parasol, her smile tentative, then mocking. She'd splash me and then I'd splash her and then the boat would tip. It never happened, but you get the point. Next maybe there would be a picnic scene on campus, a shot of us studying in the library, our bodies entwined on a couch, me staring mesmerized as Rachel reads from her textbook, her glasses on, absentmindedly tucking a hair behind her ear. The montage would probably close on two bodies tussling under a white satin sheet, even though no college student uses satin sheets. Still, I'm thinking cinematic here.

I was in love.

During one Christmas break, we visited Rachel's grandmother, a card-carrying yenta from the old school, in a nursing home. The old woman took both our hands in hers and declared us *beshert,* which is a Yiddish word that means predestined or fated.

So what happened?

Our ending was not an uncommon one. We were

young, I guess. During my senior year, Rachel decided that she wanted to spend a semester in Florence. I was twenty-two. I got pissed off, and while she was away, I slept with another woman—a one-night stand with a featureless coed from Babson. It meant absolutely nothing. I understand that makes it no better, but maybe it should. I don't know.

Anyway, someone at the party told someone else and eventually it got back to Rachel. She called me from Italy and broke it off, just like that, which I saw as something of an overreaction. Like I said, we were young. At first, I was too proud (read: too stupid) to beg and then, when I started soaking in the repercussions, I called and wrote letters and sent flowers. Rachel never responded. It was over. We were done.

I stood and stumbled to my desk. I fished out the key I had taped under the credenza and unlocked the bottom drawer. I lifted off the files and found my secret stash underneath. No, not drugs. The past. Rachel things. I found the familiar photo and pulled it into view. Lenny and Cheryl still have this picture in their den, which had, understandably enough, angered Monica to no end. It was a photograph of the four of us—Lenny, Cheryl, Rachel, and me—at a formal during my senior year. Rachel is wearing a spaghetti-strap black dress and the thought of the way it clung to her shoulders still takes my breath away.

A long time ago.

I've moved on, of course. Per my life plan, I went to medical school. I always knew that I wanted to be a doctor. Most doctors I know will tell you the same. It is rarely a decision you come to late.

And I dated too. I even had other one-night stands (remember Zia?), but—and this is going to sound pitiful— even after all these years, I never go through a day without thinking, at least fleetingly, about Rachel. Yes, I know that I've romanticized the romance, if you will, completely out of proportion. Had I not made that stupid blunder, I would probably not be living in some blissful alternative universe, still entwined on the couch with my beloved. As Lenny once pointed out in a moment of naked honesty, if my relationship with Rachel had been that great, it surely could have survived this most hackneyed of speed bumps.

Am I saying that I never loved my wife? No. At least, I think the answer is no. Monica was beautiful—right away beautiful, nothing slow about the way her looks hit you—and passionate and surprising. She was also wealthy and glamorous. I tried not to compare—that is a terrible way to live your life—but I could not help but love Monica in my smaller, less bright, post-Rachel world. Given time, the same might have happened had I stayed with Rachel, but that's using logic, and in matters of the heart, logic need not apply.

Over the years, Cheryl grudgingly kept me informed on what Rachel was up to. Rachel, I'd learned, had gone into law enforcement and become a federal agent in Washington. I can't say I was totally surprised. Three years ago, Cheryl told me that Rachel had gotten married to an older guy, a senior fed. Even after all this time—Rachel and I had been broken up eleven years by then—I felt my insides cave in. I realized with a heavy thud just how badly I'd messed up. I'd always assumed somehow that Rachel and I were biding our time, living in some sort of suspended animation, until we inevitably came to our senses and got back together. Now she had married someone else.

Cheryl saw my face and has never again spoken to me about Rachel.

I stared at the picture and heard the familiar SUV

pull up. No surprise there. I did not bother walking to the door. Lenny had a key. He never knocked anyway. He'd know where I was. I put away the photograph as Lenny entered the room carrying two enormous, brightly clad paper cups.

Lenny held up the Slurpees from 7-Eleven. "Cherry or cola?"

"Cherry."

He handed it to me. I waited.

"Zia called Cheryl," he said in way of explanation.

I had figured that. "I don't want to talk about it," I said.

Lenny hopped onto the couch. "Me neither." He reached into his pocket and took out a thick sheaf of papers. "The will and the final stuff on Monica's estate. Read it whenever." He picked up the remote control and began to flip. "Don't you have any porno?"

"No, sorry."

Lenny shrugged and settled on a college basketball game on ESPN. We watched a few minutes in silence. I broke it.

"Why didn't you tell me Rachel was divorced?"

Lenny grimaced in pain and raised his palm as if stopping traffic.

"What?" I said.

"Brain freeze." He rode it out. "I always drink these things too fast."

"Why didn't you tell me?"

"I thought we weren't going to talk about it."

I looked at him.

"It's not that simple, Marc."

"What's not?"

"Rachel has been through some tough times."

"So have I," I said.

Lenny watched the game a little too closely.

"What happened to her, Lenny?"

"It's not my place." He shook his head. "You haven't even seen her in, what, fifteen years?"

Fourteen actually. "Something like that."

His eyes scanned the room and rested on a photograph of Monica and Tara. He looked away and sipped his Slurpee. "Have to stop living in the past, my friend."

We both settled back and pretended to watch the game. Stop living in the past, he'd said. I looked at the photograph of Tara and wondered if Lenny was talking about more than Rachel.

Edgar Portman picked up the leather dog leash. He jingled the end. Bruno, his champion bull mastiff, clattered toward the sound at full speed. Bruno had won a Best in Breed at the Westminster Dog Show six years ago. Many believed that he had what it took to earn Best in Show. Edgar chose instead to retire Bruno. A show dog is never home. Edgar wanted Bruno with him.

People disappointed Edgar. Dogs never.

Bruno stuck out his tongue and wagged his tail. Edgar clipped the leash onto the collar. They would go for an hour. Edgar looked down at his desk. There, on the shiny veneer, sat a cardboard package, identical to the one he had received eighteen months earlier. Bruno whimpered. Edgar wondered if it was a whimper of impatience or if he could sense his master's dread. Maybe both.

Either way, Edgar needed air.

The package from eighteen months ago had undergone every possible forensic test. The police had learned nothing. Edgar was relatively certain, based on that past experience, that the incompetents in law enforcement would find nothing again. Eighteen months ago, Marc had not listened to him. That mistake, Edgar hoped, would not be repeated.

He started for the door. Bruno led the way. The air felt good. He stepped outside and sucked in a deep breath. It did not change his outlook, but it helped. Edgar and Bruno started down the familiar route, but something made Edgar veer to the right. The family plot. He saw it every day, so often that he no longer saw it, so to speak. He never visited the stones. But today, suddenly, he felt drawn. Bruno, surprised by the deviation in his routine, grudgingly followed.

Edgar stepped over the small fence. His leg throbbed. Old age. These walks were getting more difficult. He had begun using a walking stick a lot of the time—he had purchased one purportedly used by Dashiell Hammett during a TB stint—but for some reason, Edgar never took it with him when he was with Bruno. It felt wrong somehow.

Bruno hesitated and then leapt the fence. They both stood in front of the two most recent headstones. Edgar tried not to ponder about life and death, about wealth and its relativity to happiness. That sort of lint picking was best left to others. He realized now that he had probably not been a very good father. He had learned, however, from his father, who learned from his. And in the end, perhaps his aloofness had saved him. Had he loved his children fully, had he been deeply involved in their lives, he doubted that he could have survived their deaths.

The dog began to whimper again. Edgar looked down at his companion, deep into his eyes. "Time to go, boy," he said softly. The front door of the house opened. Edgar turned and spotted his brother, Carson, rushing toward him. Edgar saw the look on his brother's face.

"My God," Carson called out.

"I assume you saw the package."

"Yes, of course. Did you call Marc?"

"No."

"Good," Carson said. "It's a hoax. It has to be."

Edgar did not reply.

"You don't agree?" Carson said.

"I don't know."

"You can't possibly think that she's still alive."

Edgar gave the leash a gentle tug. "Best to wait for the tests to come back," he said. "Then we'll know for certain."

I like to work night hours. I always have. I am lucky in my career choice. I love my job. It is never a chore or drudgery or something I do simply to put food on the table. I disappear into my work. Like a troubled athlete, I forget everything when I'm playing my game. I enter the zone. I am at my best.

This night, however—three nights after seeing Rachel—I was off duty. I sat alone in my den and flipped stations. I, like most males of our species, hit the remote too frequently. I can watch several hours of nothing. Last year, Lenny and Cheryl got me a DVD player, explaining to me that my VCR was heading the way of the eight-track. I checked the clock on it now. A few minutes after nine. I could pop in a DVD and still get to bed by eleven.

I had just removed the rental DVD from its box and was about to stick it into the machine—they do not have a remote that does that yet—when I heard a dog bark. I rose. A new family had moved in two houses down. They had four or five young kids, something like that. Hard to say when a family has that many. They seem to blur into one another. I had not introduced myself yet, but I had seen in their yard an Irish wolfhound, who was approximately the size of a Ford Explorer. The bark, I believed, was his.

I pushed the curtain aside. I looked out the window, and for some reason—a reason I cannot properly articulate—I was not surprised by what I saw.

The woman stood in the exact same spot where I had seen her eighteen months earlier. The long coat, the long hair, the hands in the pockets—all the same.

I was afraid to let her out of my sight, but then again, I did not want her to see me. I dropped to my knees and slid to the side of the window, supersleuth-style. With my back and cheek pressed against the wall, I considered my options.

First off, I was now not watching her. That meant she could leave and I wouldn't notice. Hmm, not good. I had to risk a look. That was the first thing.

I turned my head and sneaked a peek. Still there. The woman was still out front, but she had moved a few steps closer to my front door. I had no idea what that meant exactly. So now what? How about going to the door and confronting her? That seemed a pretty good move. If she ran, well, I guess that I would have pursued.

I risked another glimpse, just a quick head turn, and when I did, I realized that the woman was staring directly at my window. I fell back. Damn. She'd seen me. No way around it. My hands grabbed the bottom of the window, readying to open it, but she had already started hurrying up the block.

Oh no, not this time.

I was wearing surgical scrubs—every doctor I know has a few pairs for loungewear use—and I was barefoot. I sprinted to the door and threw it open. The woman was almost to the top of the block. When she saw me at the door, she stopped the hurry-walk and broke into an all-out run.

I gave chase. To hell with my feet. Part of me felt ridiculous. I am not the fastest fellow on two legs. I am probably not even the fastest on one leg—and here I was running down a strange woman because she was standing in front of my house. I don't know what I hoped to find here. The woman was probably taking a walk, and I had spooked her. She would probably call the police. I could see their reaction. Bad enough I killed my own family and got away with it. Now I was chasing strange women around my neighborhood.

I did not stop.

The woman turned right onto Phelps Road. She had a big lead. I pumped my arms and willed my legs to pick up the pace. The pebbles on the sidewalk dug into the soles of my feet. I tried to stay on grass. She was out of view now, and I was out of shape. I had gone maybe a hundred yards and I could already hear the wheeze in my breath. My nose started running.

I reached the end of my street and made the right.

But there was no one.

The road was long and straight and well enough lit. In other words, she should still be visible. For some dumb reason I looked the other way too, behind me. But the woman was not there either. I ran the route she'd taken. I looked down Morningside Drive, but there was no sign of her.

The woman was gone.

But how?

She could not have been that fast. Carl Lewis was not that fast. I stopped, put my hands on my knees, sucked in some very necessary oxygen. Think. Okay, could she live in one of these houses? Perhaps. And if she did, so what? That meant that she was taking a walk in her own neighborhood. She had seen something that had struck her as curious. She stopped to take a look.

Like she did eighteen months ago?

Okay, first off, we don't know if it was the same woman.

So two women stopped in front of your house in the exact same spot and stood like statues?

It was possible. Or maybe it was the same woman. Maybe she liked looking at houses. Maybe she was into architecture or something.

Oh yes, the ever-desirable architecture of the seventies suburban split-level. And if her visit was totally innocent, why did she run away?

I don't know, Marc, but maybe—and this is just a stab in the dark—maybe because some lunatic chased her?

I shook the voice away and started running again, looking for I-don't-know-what. But when I passed the Zuckers' house, I came to a halt.

Was that possible?

The woman had simply disappeared. I had checked both exit roads. She was not on either one of them. So that meant, A, she lived in one of the houses, B, she was hiding.

Or C, she had taken the Zucker path in the woods.

When I was a kid, we sometimes used to cut through the Zuckers' backyard. There was a path to the middle school fields. It was not easy to find, and Old Lady Zucker really didn't like us going through her lawn. She would never say anything, but she would stand by the window, her beehive hair glazed like a Krispy Kreme, and glare us down. After a while, we stopped using the path and took the long way.

I looked left and right. No sign of her.

Could the woman know about the path?

I sprinted into the blackness of the Zuckers' backyard. I half expected Old Lady Zucker to be at her kitchen window, glaring at me, but she had moved out to Scottsdale years ago. I don't know who lived here anymore. I didn't even know if the path was still there.

It was black-hole dark in the yard. No lights were on

in the house. I tried to remember where exactly the path was. Actually, that took no time. You remember stuff like that. It's automatic. I ran toward it and something whacked me in the head. I felt the thud and fell on my back.

My head swam. I looked up. In the faint moonlight, I could see a swing set. One of those fancy wooden ones. It hadn't been there in my childhood, and in the dark, I hadn't seen it. I felt woozy, but time was key here. I leapt to my feet with too much bravado, reeling back.

The path was still there.

I headed along it as fast as I could. Branches whipped my face. I did not care. I stumbled on a root. I did not care. The Zucker path was not long, maybe forty, fifty feet. It opened into a big clearing of soccer fields and baseball diamonds. I was still making good enough time. If she had taken this route, I would be able to spot her in the recreational expanse.

I could see the smoky haze from the fluorescent lights drifting down from the field's parking lots. I burst out into the opening and quickly scanned my surroundings. I saw several sets of soccer posts and one chain-link backstop.

But no woman.

Damn.

I had lost her. Again. My heart fell. I don't know. I mean, when you thought about it, what was the point? This whole thing was stupid, really. I looked down at my feet. They hurt like hell. I felt a trickle of what was probably blood on my right sole. I felt like an idiot. A defeated idiot, at that. I started to turn away. . . .

Hold the phone.

In the distance, under the lights of the parking lot, there was a car. One solitary car, all by its lonesome. I nodded to myself and followed my thoughts. Let's say that the car belonged to the woman. Why not? If it doesn't, well, nothing lost, nothing gained. But if it did, if she had parked here, it made sense. She parks, she goes through the woods, she stands in front of my house. Why she would do any of this, I had no idea. But for right now, I decided to go with it.

Okay, if that was the case—if that was her car—then I could conclude that she had not yet departed. No flies on me. So what had happened here? She's spotted, she runs, she starts heading down the path. . . .

. . . and she realizes that I might follow.

I almost snapped my fingers. The mystery woman would know that I had grown up in this neighborhood and thus might remember the path. And if I did, if I somehow put together (as I had) that she would use the path, then I would spot her in the opening. So what would she do?

I thought about it and the answer came pretty quickly.

She would hide in the woods along the path.

The mystery woman was probably watching me at this very moment.

Yes, I know that this argument barely reached the level of flimsy conjecture. But it felt right. Very right. So what to do? I gave a heavy sigh and said out loud, "Damn." I slumped my shoulders as though deflated, trying hard not to oversell this, and started trudging back through the path to the Zucker place. I lowered my head, my eyes swerving left and right. I walked delicately, my ears alert, straining to hear a rustle of some sort.

The night remained silent.

I reached the end of the path and kept walking as if I were heading home. When I was deep in the thicket of darkness, I dropped to the ground. I commando-crawled back under the swing set toward the path's opening. I stopped and waited.

I don't know how long I stayed there. Probably not more than two or three minutes. I was about to give up when I heard the noise. I was still on my stomach, my head raised. The silhouette rose and started down the path.

I scrambled to my feet, trying to stay quiet, but that was a major no-go. The woman spun toward the sound, spotting me.

"Wait," I shouted. "I just want to talk to you."

But she had already darted back into the woods. Off the path, the woods were thick and, yep, it was plenty dark. I could lose her easily. I was not about to risk that. Not again. Maybe I couldn't *see* her, but I could still *hear* her.

I jumped into the thicket and almost immediately hit a tree. I saw stars. Man, that had been a dumb move. I stopped now and listened.

Silence.

She had stopped. She was hiding again. So now what?

She had to be nearby. I considered my options and then thought, Ah, the hell with it. Remembering where I had last heard a noise, I leapt at the spot, spread-eagle, my hands and legs stretched to the max so that my body would cover as much territory as possible. I landed on a shrub.

But my left hand touched something else.

She tried to crawl away, but my fingers closed tight around her ankle. She kicked at me with her free leg. I held on like a dog digging his teeth in.

"Let go of me!" she shouted.

I did not recognize the voice. I did not let go of her ankle.

"What the—let go of me!"

No. I got some leverage and pulled her toward me. It was still too dark, but my eyes were beginning to adjust.

I gave another tug. She rolled onto her back. We were close enough now. I was finally able to see her face.

It took a few moments to register. The memory was an old one, for one thing. The face, or what I could see of it, had changed. She looked different. What gave it away, what helped me recognize her, was the way her hair had fallen in front of her face during our tussle. That was almost more familiar than the features—the vulnerability of the pose, the way she now avoided eye contact. And of course, living in that house, that house I had always so closely associated with her, had kept her image in the forefront of my memory banks.

The woman pushed her hair to the side and looked up at me. I fell back to school days, the brick building barely two hundred yards from where we now lay. Now maybe it made some sort of sense. The mystery woman had been standing in front of the house where she used to live.

The mystery woman was Dina Levinsky.

chapter 11

We sat at the kitchen table. I made tea, a Tazo blend of Chinese green I'd bought at Starbucks. It was supposed to soothe. We'd see. I handed Dina a cup.

"Thank you, Marc."

I nodded and sat across from her. I had known Dina my whole life. I knew her in the way only a kid can know another kid, the way only elementary school classmates know each other, even—bear with me here—even though I don't think we ever really spoke to one another.

We all have a Dina Levinsky in our past. She was the class victim, the girl so much an outcast, so often teased and abused, you wonder how she stayed sane. I never picked on her, but I stood on the sidelines plenty of times. Even if I didn't reside in her childhood home, Dina Levinsky would still live in me. She lives in you too. Quick: Who was the most picked-on kid in your elementary school? Right, exactly, you remember. You remember their first and last name and what they looked like. You remember watching them walk home alone or sitting in the cafeteria in silence. Whatever, you remember. Dina Levinsky stays with you.

"I hear you're a doctor now," Dina said to me.

"Yes. And you?"

"A graphic designer and artist. I have a show in the Village next month."

"Paintings?"

She hesitated. "Yes."

"You were always a good artist," I said.

She cocked her head, surprised. "You noticed?"

There was a brief pause. Then I found myself saying, "I should have done something."

Dina smiled. "No, I should have."

She looked good. No, she had not grown into a beauty like those ugly-duckling swans you see in the movies. First off, Dina had never been ugly. She had been plain. Maybe she still was. Her features were still too narrow, but they worked better on an adult face. Her hair, so drippy in her youth, had body now.

"Do you remember Cindy McGovern?" she asked me.

"Sure."

"She tortured me more than anyone."

"I remember."

"Well, this is funny. I had an exhibit a few years back at a gallery in midtown—and Cindy shows up. She comes up to me and gives me a big hug and kiss. She wants to talk about old times, you know, like 'Remember how dorky Mr. Lewis was?' She's all smiles and I swear, Marc, she didn't remember what she'd been like. She wasn't pretending either. She just totally blocked out how she'd treated me. I find that sometimes."

"Find what?"

Dina raised the cup with two hands. "No one remembers being the bully." She hunched over, her eyes darted about the room. I wondered about my own remembrance. Had I just been on the sidelines—or was that, too, some sort of revisionist history?

"This is so messed up," Dina said.

"Being back in this house?"

"Yeah." She put down the cup. "I guess you want an explanation."

I waited.

Her eyes started darting again. "You want to hear something bizarre?"

"Sure."

"This is where I used to sit. I mean, when I was a kid. We had a rectangular table too. I always sat in the same spot. When I came in here now, I don't know, I just naturally gravitated to this chair. I guess—I guess that's part of the reason why I was here tonight."

"I'm not sure I understand."

"This house," she said. "It still has a pull on me. A hold." She leaned forward. Her eyes met mine for the first time. "You've heard the rumors, haven't you? About my father and what happened here."

"Yes."

"They're true," she said.

I forced myself not to wince. I had no idea what to say. I thought about the hell of school. I tried to add on to that the hell of this house. It was unfathomable.

"He's dead now. My father, I mean. He died six years ago."

I blinked and looked away.

"I'm okay, Marc. Really. I was in therapy—well, I mean, I still am. Do you know Dr. Radio?"

"No."

"That's his real name. Stanley Radio. He's pretty famous for the Radio Technique. I've been with him for years. I'm much better. I'm over the self-destructive tendencies. I'm past feeling worthless. It's funny though. I got over it. No, I mean it. Most victims of abuse have commitment and sex issues. I never did. I'm able to be intimate, no problem. I'm married now. My husband is a great guy. It's not happily-ever-after, but it's pretty damn good."

"I'm glad," I said, because I had no idea what else to say.

She smiled again. "Are you superstitious, Marc?"

"No."

"Me neither. Except, I don't know, when I read about your wife and daughter, I started to wonder. About this house. Bad karma and all that. Your wife was so lovely."

"You knew Monica?"

"We'd met."

"When?"

Dina did not reply right away. "Are you familiar with the term *trigger*?"

I remembered it from my medical school rotations. "You mean, in terms of psychiatry?"

"Yes. You see, when I read about what happened here, it was a trigger. Like with an alcoholic or anorexic. You're never fully cured. Something happens—a trigger—and you fall back into bad patterns. I started biting my nails. I started doing physical harm to myself. It was like—it was like I had to face down this house. I had to confront the past in order to defeat it."

"And that's what you were doing tonight?"

"Yes."

"And when I spotted you eighteen months ago?"

"Same thing."

I sat back. "How often do you stop by?"

"Once every couple of months, I guess. I park at the school lot and come through the Zucker path. But there's more to it than that."

"More to what?"

"My visits. See, this house still holds my secrets. I mean that literally."

"I'm not following."

"I keep trying to work up the courage to knock on the door again, but I can't do it. And now I'm inside, in this kitchen, and I'm okay." She tried to smile, as if to prove the point. "But I still don't know if I can do it."

"Do what?" I asked.

"I'm babbling." Dina started scratching the back of her hand, hard and fast, digging her nails in and nearly breaking skin. I wanted to reach out to her, but it felt too forced. "I wrote it all down. In a journal. What happened to me. It's still here."

"In the house?"

She nodded. "I hid it."

"The police went through here after the murder. They searched this place pretty good."

"They didn't find it," she said. "I'm sure of it. And even if they did, it's just an old journal. There'd be no reason for them to disturb it. Part of me wants it to stay put. It's over and done with it—you know what I mean? Let sleeping dogs lie. But another part wants to let it out into the light. Like it's a vampire and the sunshine will kill it."

"Where is it?" I asked.

"In the basement. You have to stand on the dryer to get to it. It's behind one of the ducts in the crawl space." She glanced at the clock. She looked at me and hugged herself. "It's getting late."

"Are you okay?"

The eyes were darting again. Her breathing was suddenly uneven. "I don't know how much longer I can stay here."

"Do you want to look for your journal?"

"I don't know."

"Do you want me to get it for you?"

She shook her head hard. "No." She stood, gulping air now. "I better go now."

"You can always come back, Dina. Anytime you want."

But she wasn't listening. She was in full panic mode and heading for the door.

"Dina?"

She suddenly spun toward me. "Did you love her?"

"What?"

"Monica. Did you love her? Or was there someone else?"

"What are you talking about?"

Her face drained of color. She stared at me now, backing away, petrified. "You know who shot you, don't you, Marc?"

I opened my mouth, but nothing came out. By the time I found my voice, Dina had turned away.

"I'm sorry. I have to go."

"Wait."

She flung the door open and ran out. I stood by the window and watched her scurry back up toward Phelps Road. This time, I chose not to follow.

Instead, I turned and with her words—*"You know who shot you, don't you, Marc?"*—still reverberating in my ears, I sprinted to the basement door.

All right, let me explain something here. I was not going down into the dingy, unfinished subdwelling to invade Dina's privacy. I did not pretend to know what was best for her, what might salve her horrendous pain. Many of my psychiatry colleagues would disagree, but sometimes I wonder if the past is better left buried. I don't have the answer, of course, and as my psychiatry colleagues would remind me, I don't ask them for their take on the best way to handle a cleft palate. So in the end, all I know for certain is that it is not my place to decide for Dina.

And I was not going in the basement out of curiosity about her past either. I had no interest in reading the details of Dina's torment. In fact, I actively did not want to know them. To speak selfishly, I was creeped out plenty just knowing such horrors had occurred in the place I call home. It was already enough in my face, thank you very much. I needed to hear or read no more.

So what exactly was I after?

I hit the light switch. A bare bulb came on. I was putting the pieces together even as I started to descend. Dina had said several curious things. Putting aside the most dramatic for a moment, I was starting to pick up on the more subtle ones. It was a night of spontaneous behavior on my part. I decided to let the trend continue.

First off, I remembered how Dina, when she was still the mystery woman on the sidewalk, had taken a step toward the door. I know now, as Dina herself had told me, that she'd been "trying to work up the courage to knock on the door again."

Again.

Knock on the door *again*.

The obvious implication was that Dina had, on at least one other occasion, worked up the courage to knock on my door.

Second, Dina had told me that she had "met" Monica. I could not imagine how. Yes, Monica, too, had grown up in this town, but from all I knew of her, she might as well have grown up in a different, more opulent era. The Portman estate was on the opposite end of our rather sprawling suburb. Monica had started boarding school at a young age. No one in town knew her. I remember seeing her once at the Colony movie theater over the summer of my sophomore year in high school. I had stared. She had studiously ignored me. Monica had that whole remote-beauty thing down pat by then. When I met her years later—she actually came on to me—the flattery turned my head. Monica had seemed so fabulous at a distance.

So how, I wondered now, had my wealthy, remote, beautiful wife met poor, drab Dina Levinsky? The most likely answer, when you consider the "again" comment, was that Dina had knocked on the door and Monica had answered. They met then. They probably talked. Dina probably told Monica about the hidden journal.

"You know who shot you, don't you, Marc?"

No, Dina. But I plan on finding out.

I had reached the cement floor. Boxes that I would never throw away and never open were piled everywhere. I noticed, perhaps for the first time, that there were paint splatters on the floor. A large variety of hues. They'd probably been here since Dina's time, a reminder of her sole escape.

The washer and dryer were in the corner on the left. I moved slowly toward them in the shadowy light. I tiptoed, actually, as though I were afraid of waking Dina's sleeping dogs. Stupid really. As I said before, I am not superstitious, and even if I were, even if I believed in evil spirits and the like, there was no reason to fear angering them. My wife was dead and my daughter was missing—what else could they do to me? In fact, I should disturb them, make them act, hope they let me know what really happened to my family, to Tara.

There it was again. Tara. Everything circled back to her eventually. I don't know how she fitted into all this. I don't know how her kidnapping was connected to Dina Levinsky. It probably wasn't. But I was not turning back.

You see, Monica never mentioned meeting Dina Levinsky.

I found that odd. True, I am building this ridiculous

theory on pure foam. But if Dina had indeed knocked on the door, if Monica had indeed opened it, you would think that my wife would have mentioned it to me at some point. She knew that Dina Levinsky had gone to school with me. Why keep her visit—or the fact that they had met—a secret?

I hopped up on the dryer. I had to both crouch and look above me. Dust city. Spiderwebs were everywhere. I saw the duct and reached up. I felt around. It was difficult. There was a web of pipes, and my arm was having trouble fitting between them. It would have been much easier for a young girl with thin arms.

Eventually I worked my hand through the copper. I slid my fingertips to the right and pushed up. Nothing. My hand crawled a few more inches over and pushed again. Something gave way.

I pulled up my sleeve and twisted my arm in another inch or two. Two pipes pressed against my skin, but they gave enough. I was able to reach into the crawl space. I felt around, found something, pulled it into view.

The journal.

It was a classic school notebook with the familiar black marble cover. I opened and paged through it. The handwriting was minuscule. It reminded me of that guy in the mall who writes names on a grain of rice. Dina's immaculate penmanship—belying, no doubt, the content—started at the very top of the sheet and ran all the way to the bottom. There were no left or right margins. Dina had used both sides of every sheet.

I did not read it. Again that was not what I had come down for. I reached back up and put the journal back in its place. I don't know how this would set me with the gods—if just touching it would unleash a King Tut–like curse—but again I didn't care very much either.

I felt around again. I knew. I don't know how, but I

just knew. Eventually my hand hit something else. My heart thumped. It felt smooth. Leather. I pulled it into view. Some dust followed. I blinked the particles out of my eyes.

It was Monica's DayRunner.

I remembered when she bought it at some chic boutique in New York. Something to organize her life, she'd told me. It'd had the customary calendar and datebook. When had we bought it? I wasn't sure. Maybe eight, nine months before she died. I tried to remember the last time I'd seen it. Nothing came to me.

I jammed the leather planner between my knees and put the ceiling panel back in place. I grabbed the datebook and climbed down from the dryer. I considered waiting until I got upstairs into better light, but, uh-uh, no way. The datebook had a zipper. Despite the dust it opened smoothly.

A CD fell out and landed on the floor.

It glittered in the low light like a jewel. I picked it up by the edges. There was no label on it. Memorex had manufactured it. CD-R, it said, 80 MINUTES.

What the hell is this?

One way to find out. I hurried upstairs and booted up my computer.

chapter 12

When I put the disk into the CD drive, the following screen appeared:

Password: _ _ _ _ _ _
MVD
Newark, NJ

Six-digit password. I typed in her birthday. No go. I tried Tara's birthday. No go. I put in our anniversary and then my birthday. I tried the code for our ATM. Nothing worked.

I sat back. So now what?

I debated calling Detective Regan. By now it was closing in on midnight, and even if I could reach him, what exactly would I say? "Hi, I found a CD hidden in my basement—rush over"? No. Hysterics would not work here. Better to show calm, to feign rationality. Patience was key. Think it through. I could call Regan in the morning. Nothing he could or would do tonight anyway. Sleep on it.

Fine, but I was not about to give up quite yet. I logged on to the Internet and brought up a search engine. I typed in MVD in Newark. A listing popped up.

"MVD—Most Valuable Detection."

Detection?

There was a link to a Web site. I clicked it, and the MVD Web site came up. My eyes did a quick scan. MVD was a "group of professional private investigators" who "provided confidential services." They offered on-line background checks for less than a hundred dollars. Their ads exclaimed, "Find out if that new boyfriend has a criminal record!" and "Where is your old sweetheart? Maybe she's still pining for you!" Stuff like that. They also did more "intense, discreet investigations" for those who required such things. They were, per the top banner, a "full-service investigative entity."

So, I asked myself, what had Monica needed investigated?

I picked up the phone and dialed MVD's 800 number. A machine picked up—no surprise considering the hour—and told me how much they appreciated my call and that their office opened at nine in the morning. Okay. I'd call back then.

I hung up the phone and pressed the e: drive's eject button. The CD slid into view. I lifted up by the edges and checked for, I don't know, clues, I guess. Nothing new. Time to think here. It seemed pretty clear that Monica had hired MVD to investigate something and that this CD contained whatever it was she wanted investigated. Not exactly a brilliant deduction on my part, but it was a start.

Let's go back then. Fact is, I had no idea what Monica wanted investigated or why or any of that. But if I was right, if this CD did indeed belong to Monica, if she had hired a private investigator for whatever reason, it would naturally follow that she would have had to pay MVD for said services.

I nodded. Okay, a better start.

But—and here is where confusion immediately set

in—the police had thoroughly combed through our bank accounts and financial records. They had scrutinized every transaction, every Visa purchase, every written check, every ATM withdrawal. Had they seen one to MVD? If so, they decided not to tell me. Of course, I had not been a potted plant here. My daughter was gone. I, too, had examined those financial statements. There was nothing to any detective agency nor were there any cash withdrawals out of the ordinary.

So what did that mean?

Maybe this CD was old.

That was a possibility. I don't think any of us checked transactions going back more than six months before the attack. Maybe her relationship with Most Valuable Detection predated that. I could probably check through the old statements.

But I wasn't buying it.

This CD was not old. I was fairly certain of that. And it didn't matter much anyway. Time frame, when I thought about it, was irrelevant. Recent or otherwise, the key questions remained: Why would Monica hire a private investigator? What was password protected on that damn CD? Why had she hidden it in that creepy space in the basement? What, if anything, did Dina Levinsky have to do with any of this? And most important, did it have anything to do with the attack—or was this all a big exercise in wishful thinking on my part?

I looked out the window. The street was clear and silent. Suburbia sleeps. No more answers would come tonight. In the morning, I would take my father for our weekly walk and then I would call MVD and maybe even Regan.

I climbed into bed and waited for sleep.

* · * *

The phone next to Edgar Portman's bed rang at four thirty in the morning. Edgar jerked awake, pulled out in middream, and fumbled with the phone.

"What?" he barked.

"You said to call as soon as I knew."

Edgar rubbed his face. "You have the results."

"I do."

"And?"

"It's a match."

Edgar closed his eyes. "How certain are you?"

"It's preliminary. If I were taking it to court, I'd need a few more weeks to line up all the arrows. But that would just be following proper protocol."

Edgar could not stop shaking. He thanked the man, put the phone back in its cradle, and began to prepare.

chapter 13

At six the next morning, I left my house and walked down the block. Using a key I've had since college, I unlocked the door and slipped into my childhood home.

The years had not been a friend to this dwelling, but then again, it hadn't been featured in *House and Garden* (except maybe as one of their "before" photos) to begin with. We'd replaced the shag carpet four years ago—the blue-white speck had been so faded and threadbare, it practically replaced itself—and went with close-cropped office gray so that my father's wheelchair could move with ease. Other than that, nothing had been changed. The overvarnished side tables still held Lladró porcelain knickknacks from a long-ago trip to Spain. Holiday Inn–like oils of violins and fruit—none of us are the least bit musical or, uh, fruity—still adorned the white-painted wood paneling.

There were photos on the fireplace mantel. I always stopped and looked at the ones of my sister, Stacy. I don't know what I was looking for. Or maybe I do. I was searching for clues, for foreshadowing. I was searching for any hint that this young, fragile, damaged woman would one day buy a gun off the street, shoot me, harm my daughter.

"Marc?" It was Mom. She knew what I was doing. "Come help me, okay?"

I nodded and headed toward the back bedroom. Dad slept on the ground floor now—easier than trying to get up the stairs with a wheelchair. We dressed him, which was a bit like dressing wet sand. My father lolls from side to side. His weight has a tendency toward sudden shifts. My mother and I were used to that, but it doesn't make the task less arduous.

When my mother kissed me good-bye, the faint and familiar whiff of breath mint and cigarette smoke came off her. I had urged her to quit. She kept promising, but I knew that it would never happen. I noticed how loose the skin on her neck was getting, her gold chains almost embedded in their folds. She leaned down and kissed my father on the cheek, holding her lips to him a few seconds too long.

"Be careful," she told us. Then again, that was what she always told us.

We began our journey. I pushed Dad past the train station. We live in a commuter town. Mostly men but yes, women, too, were lined up in long coats, briefcase in one hand, coffee cup in the other. This might sound odd, but even before 9/11, these people were heroes to me. They board that damn train five times a week. They take it to Hoboken and switch to the PATH. That train takes them into New York City. Some will head up to Thirty-third Street and change to hit midtown. Others will take it to the financial center, now that it's opened up again. They make the everyday sacrifice, stifling their own wants and dreams in order to provide for those they love.

I could be doing cosmetic plastic surgery and making a mint. My parents would be able to afford better care for my dad. They could move someplace nice, get that full-time nurse, find a place that could cater more to their needs. But I don't do that. I don't help them by taking the more traveled route because, frankly, working such a job would bore me. So I choose to do something more exciting, something I love to do. For that, people think I'm the heroic one, that I am the one making the sacrifice. Here's the truth. The person who works with the poor? They are usually more selfish. We are not willing to sacrifice our needs. Working a job that provides for our families is not enough for us. Supporting those we love is secondary. We need personal satisfaction, even if our own family is made to do without. Those suits I now watch numbingly board the NJ Transit train? They often hate where they are going and what they are doing, but they do it anyway. They do it to take care of their families, to provide a better life for their spouses, their children, and maybe, just maybe, their aging and ill parents.

So, really, which one of us is to be admired?

Dad and I followed the same route every Thursday. We took the path around the park behind the library. The park was chockful—and you'll notice a suburban theme here—of soccer fields. How much quality real estate was tied up in this supposedly second-tier foreign sport? My father seemed comforted by the playground, by the sights and sounds of children at play. We stopped and took deep breaths. I glanced to my left. Several healthy women jogged by clad in your finest sheer-clingy Lycra. Dad seemed very still. I smiled. Maybe Dad's liking this spot had nothing to do with soccer.

I no longer remember what my father used to be like. When I try to think back that far, my memories are snapshots, flashes—a man's deep laugh, a little boy clinging to his bicep, dangling off the ground. That was pretty much it. I remember that I loved him deeply, and I guess that has always been enough.

After his second stroke sixteen years ago, Dad's speech became extremely labored. He'd get stuck mid-sentence. He'd drop words. He'd go silent for hours and sometimes days. You'd forget that he was there. No one really knew for sure if he understood, if he had classic "expressive aphasia"—you understand but you can't really communicate—or something even more sinister.

But on a hot June day during my senior year of high school, my father suddenly reached out and grabbed hold of my sleeve with an eagle-talon grip. I'd been heading out to a party at the time. Lenny was waiting for me by the door. My father's surprisingly strong grasp stopped me cold. I looked down. His face was pure white, the tendons of his neck taut, and more than anything, what I saw was naked fear. That look on his face haunted my sleep for years afterward. I slid into the chair next to him, his hand still clutching my arm.

"Dad?"

"I understand," he pleaded. His grip on my sleeve tightened. "Please." Every word was a struggle. "I still understand."

That was all he said. But it was enough. What I took it to mean was this: "Even though I can't speak or respond, I comprehend. Please don't shut me out." For a while, the doctors agreed. He had expressive aphasia. Then he had another stroke, and the doctors became less sure of what he did and did not understand. I don't know if I apply my own version of Pascal's Wager here—if he understands me, then I should talk to him, if he doesn't, what's the harm?—but I figure that I owe him that. So I talk to him. I tell him everything. And right now, I was telling him about Dina Levinsky's visit—"Do you re-member her, Dad?"—and the hidden CD.

Dad's face was locked, immobile, the left side of his mouth turned down in an angry slash-hook. I often wished that he and I never had that "I understand" conversation. I don't know which is worse: to be beyond comprehension, or to understand how trapped you really are. Or maybe I do know.

I was making the second turn, the one by the new skateboard run, when I spotted my former father-in-law. Edgar Portman sat on a bench, splendid in his casual best, his legs crossed, his pants crease sharp enough to slice tomatoes. After the shootings, Edgar and I tried to keep up a relationship that had never existed when his daughter was alive. We had hired a detective agency together—Edgar, of course, knew the best—but they came up with nothing. After a while, Edgar and I both grew weary of the pretense. The only bond between us was one that conjured up the worst moment of my life.

Edgar's being here could, of course, have been a coincidence. We live in the same town. It would only be natural to bump into one another from time to time. But that wasn't the case. I knew that. Edgar was not one for casual park visits. He was here for me.

Our eyes met, and I wasn't sure I liked what I saw. I wheeled the chair toward the bench. Edgar kept his eyes on me, never glancing down at my father. I might as well have been pushing a shopping cart.

"Your mother told me I'd find you here," Edgar said.

I stopped a few feet away from him. "What's up?"

"Sit with me."

I set my father's chair on my left. I lowered the brake. My father stared straight out. His head lolled toward his right shoulder, the way it does when he gets tired. I turned and faced Edgar. He uncrossed his legs.

"I've been wondering how to tell you this," he began.

I gave him a little space. He looked off. "Edgar?"

"Hmm."

"Just tell me."

He nodded, appreciating my directness. Edgar was that kind of man. Without preamble, he said, "I got another ransom demand."

I reeled back. I don't know what I had expected to hear—maybe that Tara had been found dead—but what he was saying . . . I couldn't quite comprehend it. I was about to ask a follow-up question when I saw that he now had a satchel in his lap. He opened it and pulled something into view. It was in a plastic bag—just like the last time we went through this. I squinted. He handed it to me. Something ballooned in my chest. I blinked and looked at the bag.

Hairs. There were hairs inside it.

"This is their proof," Edgar said.

I could not speak. I just looked at the hairs. I laid the bag gently on my lap.

"They understood that we would be skeptical," Edgar said.

"Who understood?"

"The kidnappers. They said they'd give us a few days. I immediately brought the hairs to a DNA laboratory."

I looked up at him and then back at the hairs.

"The preliminary results came in two hours ago," Edgar said. "Nothing they could use in court, but it's still pretty conclusive. The hairs match the ones sent to us a year and a half ago." He stopped and swallowed. "The hairs belong to Tara."

I heard the words. I didn't understand them. For some reason, I shook my head no. "Maybe they just saved them from before. . . ."

"No. They have aging tests too. Those hairs came from a child around two years old."

I guess that I knew that already. I could look and see that these were not my daughter's wispy baby hairs. She wouldn't have them anymore. Her hair would have darkened and thickened. . . .

Edgar handed me a note. Still in a fog, I took it from him. The font was the same as from the note we'd gotten eighteen months before. The top line over the fold said:

WANT ONE LAST CHANCE?

I felt the thud deep in my chest. Edgar's voice seemed suddenly far away. "I probably should have told you immediately, but it seemed an obvious hoax. Carson and I didn't want to get your hopes up unnecessarily. I have friends. They were able to rush through the DNA results. We still had hairs from the last mailing." He put a hand on my shoulder. I did not move.

"She's alive, Marc. I don't know how or where, but Tara is alive."

My eyes stayed on the hairs. Tara. They belonged to Tara. The sheen, that golden wheat hue. I petted them through the plastic. I wanted to reach inside the bag, to touch my daughter, but I thought my heart would burst.

"They want another two million dollars. The note warns us again about calling the police—they claim to have an inside source. They sent another cell phone for you. I have the money in the car. We have another twenty-four hours maybe. That was the window they gave us for the DNA testing. You'll have to be ready."

I finally read the note. Then I looked over at my father in his wheelchair. He still stared straight ahead.

Edgar said, "I know you think I'm rich. I am, I guess. But not like you'd think. I'm leveraged and . . ."

I turned toward him. His eyes were wide. His hands shook.

"What I mean to say is that I don't really have that many liquid assets left. I'm not made of money. This is it."

"I'm surprised you're doing this at all," I said.

The words, I could see immediately, wounded him. I wanted to take them back, but for some reason I didn't. I let my eyes drift back toward my father. Dad's face remained frozen, but—I looked closer—there was a tear on his cheek. That didn't mean anything. Dad has teared up before, usually with no apparent provocation. I did not take this as any kind of sign.

And then, I don't know why, I followed his gaze. I looked across the soccer field, past the goalposts, past two women with Baby Joggers, all the way to the street nearly a hundred yards away. My stomach dropped. There, standing on the sidewalk, looking back at me with his hands in his pockets, was a man wearing a flannel shirt and black jeans and a Yankee cap.

I couldn't say for sure that it was the same man from the ransom drop. Red-and-black flannel is hardly an uncommon pattern. And maybe it was my imagination—I was pretty far away—but I think he was smiling at me. I felt my whole body jerk.

Edgar said, "Marc?"

I barely heard him. I rose and kept my eyes up. At first, the man in the flannel stayed perfectly still. I ran toward him.

"Marc?"

But I knew that it was no mistake. You don't forget. You close your eyes and you still see him. He never leaves you. You wish for moments like this. I knew that. And I knew what wishes could bring. But I ran straight toward him. Because there was no mistake. I knew who it was.

When I was still a good distance away, the man lifted his hand and waved to me. I kept moving, but I could already see that it was futile. I was only halfway across the park when a white van drove up. The man in flannel snapped a salute in my direction before disappearing into the back.

The van was out of sight before I reached the street.

chapter 14

Time started playing games with me. Going in and out. Speeding up and slowing down. In focus and suddenly blurred. But that did not last long. I let the surgeon side of me take over. He, Marc the Doctor, knew how to compartmentalize. I have always found this easier to do at work than in my personal life. The skill—to partition, to separate, to detach—has never translated. At work, I am able to take my emotional excess and channel it, allow it to converge into a constructive focus. I have never been successful at doing this at home.

But this crisis had forced a change. Compartmentalizing wasn't a question of desire as much as survival. To get emotional, to allow myself to wallow in doubt or consider the implications of a child missing for eighteen months . . . it would paralyze me. That was probably what the kidnappers wanted. They wanted me to come apart. But I work well under pressure. I am at my best. I know that. I had to do that now. The walls came up. I could look at the situation rationally.

First thing: No, I would not contact the police this time.

But that did not mean I had to wait around helplessly.

By the time Edgar handed me the duffel bag stuffed with money, I had an idea.

* * *

I called Cheryl and Lenny's house. There was no answer. I checked my watch. Eight fifteen in the morning. I didn't have Cheryl's cell phone number, but it would be better to do this in person anyway.

I drove over to Willard Elementary School and arrived at eight twenty-five. I parked behind a line of SUVs and minivans and got out. This elementary school, like so many others, has the bricks, the cement back steps, the one level, the architectural design made shapeless by the many additions. Some additions try to blend in, but then there are the others, usually built between 1968 and 1975, that were faux-sleek with blue glass and odd tiling. They looked like postapocalyptic greenhouses.

Kids scrambled around the playground as they always do. The difference was, the parents now stayed and watched. They chatted with one another, and when the bell rang, they made sure that their charges were safely ensconced inside the brick or sleek blue glass before departing. I hated to see the fear in the eyes of the parents. But I understood it. The day you become a parent, fear becomes your constant companion. It never lets you go. My life was Exhibit A in the why.

Cheryl's blue Chevy Suburban pulled into the drop-off line. I started toward her. She was unharnessing Justin from his car seat when she spotted me. Justin gave her a dutiful kiss, an act he takes for granted, which, I guess, is how it should be, and then he ran off. Cheryl watched him as though afraid he could vanish on the short concrete trek. Kids can never understand that fear, but that's okay. Hard enough to be a kid without having that weight on you.

"Hey," Cheryl said to me.

I said hi back. Then: "I need something."

"What?"

"Rachel's phone number."

Cheryl was already back at the driver-side door. "Get in."

"My car is parked over there."

"I'll bring you back. Swim practice ran late. I've got to get Marianne to school."

She had already started the car. I hopped up into the front passenger seat. I turned and smiled at Marianne. She wore headphones and quick-fingered her Game Boy Advance. She gave me an absentminded wave, barely glancing up. Her hair was still wet. Conner was in the child seat next to her. The car reeked of chlorine, but I found the smell oddly comforting. Lenny, I know, cleans out the car religiously, but you can't possibly keep up. There were French fries in the crevice between the seats. Crumbs of unknown origin clung to the upholstery. On the floor by my feet lay a potpourri of school notices and children's artwork that had been subjected to onslaughts of rain boots. I sat on a small action figure, the kind that McDonald's gives away with their Happy Meals. A CD case reading NOW THAT'S WHAT I CALL MUSIC 14 sat between us, providing listeners with the latest from Britney and Christina and Generic Boy Band. The windows in the back were smeared with greasy fingerprints.

The kids were only allowed to play with the Game Boy in the car, never in the house. They were never, under any circumstance, allowed to watch a PG-13 movie. I asked Lenny about how he and Cheryl went about deciding such matters and he responded, "It's not the rules themselves, but the fact that there are rules." I think I know what he meant.

Cheryl kept her eyes on the road. "It's not my nature to pry."

"But you want to know my intentions."

"I guess."

"And if I don't want to tell you?"

"Maybe," she said, "it's better if you don't."

"Trust me here, Cheryl. I need the number."

She flipped on her signal light. "Rachel is still my closest friend."

"Okay."

"It took her a long time to get over you." She hesitated.

"And vice versa."

"Exactly. Look, I'm not saying this right. It's just . . . there are some things you need to know."

"Like?"

She kept her eyes on the road, two hands on the wheel. "You asked Lenny why we never told you she got divorced."

"Yes."

Cheryl glanced in the rearview mirror, not at the road, but at her daughter. Marianne seemed wrapped up in her game. "She didn't get divorced. Her husband is dead."

Cheryl glided to a stop in front of the middle school. Marianne took off the headphones and slid out. She did not bother with the dutiful kiss, but she did say goodbye. Cheryl put the car back in drive.

"I'm sorry to hear that," I said, because that was what people said under these circumstances. I almost added, because the mind works in very strange and even macabre ways: Hey, Rachel and I have something else in common.

And then, as if Cheryl could read these thoughts, she said, "He was shot."

This eerie parallel sat between us for several seconds. I stayed quiet.

"I don't know the details," she quickly added. "He was

with the FBI too. Rachel was one of the highest-ranking women in the bureau at the time. She resigned after he died. She stopped taking my calls. It hasn't been good for her since." Cheryl pulled up to my car and stopped. "I'm telling you this because I want you to understand. A lot of years have passed since college. Rachel isn't the same person you loved all those years ago."

I kept my tone steady. "I just need her phone number."

Without another word, Cheryl grabbed a pen from the visor, uncapped it with her teeth, and jotted the number on a Dunkin' Donuts napkin.

"Thanks," I said.

She barely nodded as I got out.

I did not hesitate. I had my cell phone. I slipped into my car and dialed the number. Rachel answered with a tentative hello. My words were simple enough.

"I need your help."

chapter 15

Five hours later, Rachel's train pulled into Newark Station.

I couldn't help but think of all those old movies where trains separate lovers, steam billowing from beneath, the conductor calling a last warning, the whistle sounding, the chug-chug as the wheels begin to move, one lover hanging out and waving, the other running along the platform. I don't know why I thought of this. The Newark train station is about as romantic as a pile of hippo dung with head lice. The train approached with nary a whisper and nothing you'd want to see or smell wafted in the air.

But when Rachel stepped off, I still felt the hum in my chest. She was dressed in faded blue jeans and a red turtleneck. Her overnight bag dangled from one shoulder, and she hoisted it up as she stepped down. For a moment, I just stared. I'd just turned thirty-six years old. Rachel was thirty-five. We had not been together since our very early twenties. We had lived our entire adult lives apart. Odd when you think of it that way. I told you before about our breakup. I try to unearth the whys, but maybe it is that simple. We were kids. Kids do dumb things. Kids don't understand repercussions, don't think long term. Kids don't understand that the hum may never really leave your chest.

Yet today, when I realized that I needed help, I thought first of Rachel. And she had come.

She moved toward me with no hesitation. "You okay?"

"Fine."

"Did they call?"

"Not yet."

She nodded and started walking down the platform. Her tone was no nonsense. She, too, had slipped into her role as a professional. "Tell me more about the DNA test."

"I don't know anything else."

"So it's not definitive?"

"Not court-evidence definitive, no, but they seem pretty sure."

Rachel shifted her bag from her right shoulder to her left. I tried to keep up with her pace. "We have to make some tough decisions, Marc. You ready for that?"

"Yes."

"First off, are you certain that you don't want to contact the cops or FBI?"

"The note said they had an inside source."

"That's probably bull," she said.

We walked a few more steps.

"I contacted the authorities last time," I said.

"Doesn't mean it was the wrong move."

"But it certainly wasn't the right one."

She made a yes-no gesture with her head. "You don't know what happened last time. Maybe they spotted the tail. Maybe they watched your house. But most likely, they never intended to give her back. You understand that?"

"Yes."

"But you still want them left out."

"It's why I called you."

She nodded and finally stopped, waiting for me to signal which way. I pointed to the right. She started up again. "Another thing," she said.

"What?"

"We can't let them dictate the tempo this time. We have to insist on assurances that Tara is alive."

"They'll say the hairs prove it."

"And we'll say the tests were inconclusive."

"You think they'll buy that?"

"I don't know. Probably not." She kept walking, the cut of her jaw held high. "But this is what I mean by tough decisions. That flannel-shirt guy in the park? That's about head games. They want to intimidate and weaken you. They want you to follow blindly again. Tara is your child. If you want to just hand over the money again, that's up to you. But I wouldn't advise it. They vanished before. There's no reason to think they won't again."

We entered the parking garage. I handed the attendant my ticket. "So what do you suggest?" I asked her.

"A few things. First, we have to demand an exchange. No 'Here's the money, call us later.' We get your daughter when they get the money."

"And if they don't agree?"

She looked at me with those eyes. "Tough decisions. You understand?"

I nodded.

"I also want a total electronic surveillance hookup, so I can stay with you. I want to strap on a fiber-optic camera and see what this guy looks like, if possible. We don't have manpower, but there are still things we can do."

"Suppose they catch on?"

"Suppose they run away again?" she countered. "We're taking chances here no matter what we do. I'm trying to learn from what happened the first time. There are no guarantees. I'm simply trying to improve our odds."

The car arrived. We slid in and started up McCarter Highway. Rachel suddenly grew very quiet. The years again melted away. I knew this posture. I had seen it before.

"What else?" I said.

"Nothing."

"Rachel."

Something in my tone made her look away. "There are some things you should know."

I waited.

"I called Cheryl," she said. "I know she filled you in on most of it. You understand that I'm not a fed anymore."

"Yes."

"There's a limit to what I can do."

"I understand that." She sat back. The posture was still there. "What else?"

"You need a reality check here, Marc."

We pulled to a red light. I turned and looked at her—really looked at her—for the first time. The eyes still had that hazel with gold flakes. I know the years had been tough, but it didn't show in the eyes.

"The odds that Tara is still alive are minuscule," she said.

"But the DNA test," I countered.

"I'll handle that later."

"Handle it?"

"Later," she said again.

"What the hell does that mean? It's a match. Edgar said the final confirmation is a formality."

"Later," she repeated with steel in her voice. "Right

now we might as well assume that she's alive. We should go through with the ransom drop-off as if there is a healthy child on the other end. But somewhere along the line, I need you to understand that this could be an elaborate con."

"How do you figure?"

"That's not relevant."

"Like hell it isn't. Are you saying, what, they faked a DNA test?"

"I doubt it." Then she added, "But it's a possibility."

"How? There was a match between the two sets of hairs."

"The hairs matched each other."

"Yes."

"But," she said, "how do you know the first set of hairs—the ones you got a year and a half ago—belonged to Tara?"

It took a few moments for the meaning to reach me.

"Did you ever run a test on the first set, see if the DNA matched yours?" she asked.

"Why would we?"

"So for all you know, the original kidnappers sent you the hairs of another kid."

I tried to shake my head clear. "But they had a snippet of her clothes," I said. "The pink with black penguins. How do you explain that?"

"You don't think the Gap sold more than one of those? Look, I don't know what the story is yet, so let's not get bogged down in hypotheticals. Let's just concentrate on what we can do here and now."

I sat back. We fell into silence. I wondered if I had made the right move by calling her. There was so much excess baggage here. But at the end of the day, I trusted her. We needed to maintain the professional, to keep compartmentalizing.

"I just want my daughter back," I said.

Rachel nodded, opened her mouth as if to say something, and then grew silent again. And that was when the ransom call came in.

chapter 16

Lydia liked to stare at old photographs.

She did not know why. They offered her little comfort. The nostalgia factor was, at best, limited. Heshy never looked back. For reasons that she could never properly articulate, Lydia did.

This particular photograph had been taken when Lydia was eight years old. It was a black-and-white still from the beloved classic TV sitcom *Family Laughs*. The show ran for seven years—in Lydia's case, from the age of six until just near her thirteenth birthday. *Family Laughs* starred ex–movie hunk Clive Wilkins as the widowed father of three adorable children: twin boys, Tod and Rod, who were eleven when the series began, and an adorable pixie of a little sister named, cutely enough, Trixie, played by the irrepressible Larissa Dane. Yes, the show was at least three steps beyond precious. Old repeats of *Family Laughs* still run on TV Land.

Every once in a while, the *E! True Hollywood Story* runs a piece on the old cast of *Family Laughs*. Clive Wilkins died from pancreatic cancer two years after the show ended. The narrator would note that Clive was "just like a father on the set," which, Lydia knew, was a load of crap. The guy drank and smelled liked tobacco. When she hugged him for the cameras, it took all her considerable young acting skills not to gag from the stench.

Jarad and Stan Frank, the real-life identical twins who played Tod and Rod, had been trying to get a music career going since the show's cancellation. On *Family Laughs*, they had a groovy garage band with a repertoire of songs written by others, instruments played by others, and voices so echoed and distorted by synthesizers that even Jarad and Stan, who could not hold a key if it was tattooed onto their palms, started to believe that they were genuine musical artistes. The twins were both nearing forty now, both clearly clients of the Hair Club, both deluding themselves that, even though they claimed to be "tired of the fame," they were one break away from the return to stardom.

But the true draw here, the gripping enigma of the *Family Laughs* saga, involved the fate of the adorable "Pixie named Trixie," Larissa Dane. Here is what is known about her: During the show's final season, Larissa's parents got divorced and fought bitterly over her earnings. Her dad ended up blowing his brains out. Her mother remarried a con artist who disappeared with the money. Like most child actors, Larissa Dane became an immediate has-been. Rumors of promiscuity and drug abuse swirled, though—this being before the nostalgia craze—no one really cared enough to be interested. She overdosed and nearly died when she was just fifteen. She was sent to a sanatorium of some sort and seemingly dropped off the face of the earth. No one really knows what became of her. Many believe that she died from a second drug overdose.

But of course, she had not.

Heshy said, "You ready to make the call, Lydia?"

She did not answer right away. Lydia moved to the next photograph. Another shot from *Family Laughs*,

this time Season 5, Episode 112. Little Trixie wore a cast
on her arm. Tod wanted to draw a guitar on it. Father
didn't really approve. Tod protested, "But, Dad, I promise only to draw it, not play it!" The laugh track howled.
Young Larissa didn't understand the joke. Grown-up
Lydia didn't either. What she did remember, however,
was how she had broken her arm that day. Typical kid
stuff really. She was horsing around and fell down the
stairs. The pain was tremendous, but they needed to get
this show in the can. With that in mind, the studio doctor shot her up with Lord-knows-what and two hack
screenwriters incorporated the injury into the script.
She was barely conscious when they filmed.

But please, do not start up the violins.

Lydia had read Danny Partridge's book. She had listened to the whining of Willis on *Diff'rent Strokes*. She
had heard all about the plight of the child star, the
abuse, the stolen money, the long hours. She had seen all
the talk shows, heard all the complaints, seen all the
crocodile tears from her colleagues—and their dishon-
esty sickened her.

Here was the truth about the child star dilemma. No,
it's not the abuse, though when Lydia was young and
foolish enough to believe a shrink could help, he kept
telling her how she must be "blocking," that she had in
all likelihood been molested by one of the show's pro-
ducers. And no, don't blame parental neglect for what
child stars become. Or, in reverse, parental pushing. It's
not the lack of friends, the long hours, the poor social-
ization skills, the stream of studio tutors. No, it is none
of that.

It is, quite simply, the loss of the spotlight.

Period. The rest are excuses because no one wants to
admit that they are that shallow. Lydia began working
on the show when she was six. She had few memories

that dated back before then. All she remembers, thus, is being a star. A star is special. A star is royalty. A star is the closest thing on earth to a god. And for Lydia, there had never been anything else. We teach our children that they are special, but Lydia lived it. Everyone thought she was adorable. Everyone thought she was the perfect daughter, loving and kind and yet properly sassy. People stared at her with a bizarre longing. People wanted to be near her, to know about her life, spend time with her, touch the hem of her cloak.

And then, one day, poof—all gone.

Fame is more addictive than crack. Adults who lose fame—one-hit wonders, for example—usually tailspin into depression, though they try to act like they're above it. They don't want to admit the truth. Their whole life is a lie, a desperate scramble for another dose of that most potent of drugs. Fame.

Those adults had a mere sip of the nectar before it was snatched away. But for a child star, that nectar is mother's milk. It's all they've ever known. They can't comprehend that it's fleeting, that it won't last. You can't explain that to a child. You can't prepare them for the inevitable. Lydia had never known anything but adulation. And then, pretty much overnight, the spotlight went out. She was, for the first time in her life, alone in the dark.

That was what screws you up.

Lydia recognized that now. Heshy had helped her. He had gotten her off the junk once and for all. She had hurt herself, had been a slut, had snorted and shot up more narcotics than one could imagine. She did none of these things to escape. She did them to lash out, to hurt something or someone. Her mistake, she realized in rehab after a truly horrific and violent incident, was that she was hurting *herself*. Fame raises you up. It makes others lesser. So why on earth was she hurting the one who should be on top? Instead, why not hurt the pitiful masses, those who had worshipped her, who had given her such heady power, who had turned on her? Why harm the superior species, the one who'd been worthy of all this praise?

"Lydia?"

"Hmm."

"I think we should call now."

She turned to Heshy. They had met in the loony bin, and right away, it was as if their mutual misery could reach out and embrace. Heshy had rescued her when two orderlies had pinned her down. At the time, he had merely pushed them off her. The orderlies threatened them, and they both promised not to say anything. But Heshy understood how to bide his time. He waited. Two weeks later, he ran over one of the goons with a stolen car. While the goon lay wounded, Heshy backed up over his head and then, positioning the tire near the base of the neck, hit the accelerator. A month later, the second goon—the lead orderly—was found in his home. Four of his fingers had been ripped off. Not cut or sliced, but twisted. The ME could tell by the rotation tears. The fingers had been rotated around and around until the tendons and bone finally snapped. Lydia still had one of the fingers somewhere in the basement.

Ten years ago, they ran off together and changed their names. They altered their appearances just enough. They both started over, avenging angels, damaged but superior, above the riffraff. She didn't hurt anymore. Or at least, when she did, she found an outlet.

They had three residences. Heshy purportedly lived in the Bronx. She had a place in Queens. They both had working addresses and working phones. But that was all for show. Business offices, if you will. Neither of them wanted anyone to know that they were, in fact, a team, connected, lovers. Lydia, using an alias, had bought this bright yellow house four years ago. It had two bedrooms and one and a half baths. The kitchen, where Heshy now sat, was airy and happy. They were on a lake in the tippy north corner of Morris County, New Jersey. It was peaceful here. They loved the sunsets.

Lydia kept staring at the pictures of "Pixie Trixie." She tried to remember what she'd felt like back then. The memories were pretty much gone. Heshy stood behind her now and waited with his usual patience. There were those who would claim that she and Heshy were cold-blooded killers. That, Lydia quickly realized, was pretty much a misnomer, another Hollywood creation. Like the wonderfulness of Pixie Trixie. No one enters this violent business merely because it is profitable. There are easier ways to make a living. You may act like a professional. You may keep your emotions in check. You may even delude yourself into thinking it's just another day at the office, but when you look at it honestly, the reason you walk on this wrong side of the line is because you enjoy it. Lydia understood that. Hurting someone, killing someone, fading or turning out the light in a person's eyes . . . no, she did not need that. She did not crave it as she had the spotlight. But yes, no question, there was that pleasant jolt, that unmistakable thrill, a lessening of her own pain.

"Lydia?"

"I'm on it, Pooh Bear." She picked up the cell phone with the stolen number and the scramble. She turned and faced Heshy. He was hideous, but she didn't see that. He nodded at her. She flipped on the voice changer and dialed the number.

When Lydia heard Marc Seidman's voice, she said, "Shall we try this again?"

chapter 17

Before I answered the phone, Rachel put her hand over mine. "This is a negotiation," she said. "Fear and intimidation are tools in that. You have to stay strong. If they intend to let her go, they will be flexible."

I swallowed and flicked on the phone. I said hello.

"Shall we try this again?"

The voice had the same robotic hum. I felt a tick in my blood. I closed my eyes and said, "No."

"Pardon me?"

"I want assurances that Tara is alive."

"You received hair samples, did you not?"

"Yes."

"And?"

I looked over at Rachel. She nodded. "The match was inconclusive."

"Fine," the voice said. "I might as well hang up now."

"Wait," I said.

"Yes?"

"You drove off last time."

"So we did."

"How do I know you won't do that again?"

"Did you call the police this time?"

"No."

"Then you have nothing to worry about. Here is what I want you to do."

"It's not going to work like that," I said.

"What?"

I could feel my body begin to quake. "We make a swap. You don't get the money until I get my daughter."

"You're not in any position to bargain."

"I get my daughter," I said, my words coming out slowly, dead weights. "You get your money."

"It's not going to work like that."

"Yes," I said, trying to force bravado into my voice. "This ends here and now. I don't want you running away again and then coming back for more. So we make an exchange and end this."

"Dr. Seidman?"

"I'm here."

"I want you to listen to me carefully."

The silence was too long, straining my nerves.

"If I hang up now, I won't call back for another eighteen months."

I closed my eyes and hung on.

"Think about the repercussions for a moment. Aren't you wondering where your daughter has been? Aren't you wondering what will become of her? If I hang up, you won't know anything for another eighteen months."

It felt like a steel belt was being tightened around my chest. I couldn't breathe. I looked at Rachel. She stared back steadily, urging me to stay strong.

"How old would she be then, Dr. Seidman? I mean, if we keep her alive."

"Please."

"Are you ready to listen?"

I squeezed my eyes shut. "I'm just asking for assurances."

"We sent you the hair samples."

"I bring the money. You bring my daughter. You get the money when I see her."

"Are you trying to dictate terms, Dr. Seidman?"

The robotic voice had a funny lilt now.

"I don't care who you are," I said. "I don't care why you did any of this. I just want my daughter back."

"Then you'll make the drop exactly as I tell you."

"No," I said. "Not without assurances."

"Dr. Seidman?"

"Yes."

"Good-bye."

And then the phone went dead.

chapter 18

Sanity is a thin string. Mine snapped.

No, I did not scream. Just the opposite. I grew impossibly calm. I pulled the phone away from my ear and looked at it as if it'd just materialized there and I had no idea what it was.

"Marc?"

I looked at Rachel. "They hung up."

"They'll call back," she said.

I shook my head. "They said not for another eighteen months."

Rachel studied my face. "Marc?"

"Yes?"

"I need you to listen to me closely."

I waited.

"You did the right thing here."

"Thanks. Now I feel better."

"I've had experience with this. If Tara is still alive and if they have any intention of giving her back, they'll give on this issue. The only reason not to make this exchange is because they don't want to—or can't."

Can't. The tiny part of my brain that remained rational understood that. I reminded myself of my training. Compartmentalize. "So now what?"

"We get ready just as we planned before. I have

enough equipment with me. We'll wire you up. If they call back, we'll be ready."

I nodded dumbly. "Okay."

"Meanwhile, is there anything else we can do here? Did you recognize the voice at all? Do you remember anything new about the man in flannel, about the van, anything?"

"No," I said.

"On the phone, you mentioned finding a CD in your basement."

"Yes." I quickly told her the story about the disk and the label reading MVD. She took out a pad and jotted down notes.

"Do you have the disk with you?"

"No."

"Doesn't matter," she said. "We're in Newark now. We might as well see what we can learn from this MVD."

chapter 19

Lydia lifted the Sig-Sauer P226 into the air.

"I don't like how that went," she said.

"You made the right move," Heshy said. "We cut out now. This is over."

She stared at the weapon. She wanted very much to pull the trigger.

"Lydia?"

"I heard you."

"We were doing this because it was simple."

"Simple?"

"Yes. We thought that it would be easy money."

"Lots of money."

"True," he said.

"We can't just walk away."

Heshy saw the wetness in her eyes. This was not about the money. He knew that. "He's tortured either way," he said.

"I know."

"Think about what you just did to him," Heshy said. "If he never hears from us again, he will spend the rest of his life wondering, blaming himself."

She smiled. "Are you trying to turn me on?"

Lydia moved onto Heshy's lap, curled into him like a kitten. He wrapped his giant arms around her and for a moment, Lydia calmed. She felt safe and quiet. She closed her eyes. She loved the feeling. And she knew—as did he—that it would never last. That it would never be enough.

"Heshy?"

"Yes."

"I want to get that money."

"I know you do."

"And then, I think, it would be best if he died."

Heshy pulled her close. "Then that's what will happen."

chapter 20

I don't know what I expected from the offices of Most Valuable Detection. A pebbled-glass door à la Sam Spade or Philip Marlowe maybe. A soiled building of faded brick. A walk-up, for sure. A buxom secretary with a bad dye job.

But the office of Most Valuable Detection had none of that. The building was shiny and bright, part of the "urban renewal" program of Newark. I keep hearing about Newark's renaissance, but I don't see it. Yes, there are several beautiful office buildings—like this one—and a stunning Performing Arts Center conveniently located so that those who can afford to attend (read: those who don't live in Newark) can get to it without, well, driving through the city. But these sleek edifices are flowers among the weeds, scant stars in an otherwise black sky. They do not change the basic color. They do not blend or bleed. They remain removed. Their sterile beauty is not contagious.

We stepped off the elevator. I still held the bag with two million dollars in it. It felt weird in my hand. There were three headphone-clad receptionists behind a wall of glass. Their desk was high. We stated our names into an intercom. Rachel showed an ID that listed her as a retired FBI agent. We were buzzed in.

Rachel pushed open the door. I trailed behind her. I felt empty, but I was functioning. The horror of what had happened—the hang-up—was so great that I had pushed beyond paralysis to a strange state of focus. Again I compare all this to the surgery room. I enter that room, I cross that gateway, and I shed the world. I had a patient once, a six-year-old boy, who was getting a fairly routine cleft palate repair. While on the table, his vitals dropped suddenly. His heart stopped. I didn't panic. I fell into a state of focus, not unlike this one. The boy pulled through.

Still flashing the ID, Rachel explained that we wanted to see someone in charge. The receptionist smiled and nodded in that way people do when they aren't listening. She never took off the headphones. Her fingers pressed some buttons. Another woman appeared. She led us down the corridor and into a private office.

For a moment, I couldn't tell if we were in the presence of a man or a woman. The bronze nameplate on the desk read Conrad Dorfman. Conclusion: a man. He rose theatrically. He was too slim in a blue suit with *Guys and Dolls*–wide pinstripes, tapered at the waist so that the bottom of the jacket flared out almost enough to be mistaken for a skirt. His fingers were thin like a pianist's, his hair slicked down like Julie Andrews's in *Victor/Victoria*, and his face had a blotchy smoothness I usually associate with a cosmetic foundation.

"Please," he said in a voice with too much affect. "My name is Conrad Dorfman. I'm the executive vice president of MVD." We shook his hand. He held our hands a second too long, putting the free hand over the shake and peering intently into our eyes. Conrad invited us to sit. We did. He asked us if we'd enjoy a cup of tea. Rachel, taking the lead, said that we would.

There were a few more minutes of chitchat. Conrad

asked Rachel questions about her time with the FBI. Rachel was vague. She implied that she, too, worked in the private detection biz and was thus his colleague and worthy of professional courtesy. I said nothing, letting her work. There was a knock on the door. The woman who had escorted us down the corridor opened the door and wheeled in a silver tea cart. Conrad began to pour. Rachel got to the point.

"We were hoping you could help us," Rachel said. "Dr. Seidman's wife was a client of yours."

Conrad Dorfman concentrated on the tea. He used one of those screen-door sifters that seemed all the rage nowadays. He shook out some leaves and slowly poured.

"You folks provided her with a CD that's password protected. We need to get into it."

Conrad handed a cup of tea to Rachel first, then me. He settled back and took a deep sip. "I'm sorry," he said. "I can't help you. The password is set by the client on their own."

"The client is dead."

Conrad Dorfman did not blink. "That really doesn't change anything."

"Her husband here is next of kin. That makes the CD his."

"I wouldn't know," Conrad said. "I don't practice estate law. But we have no control over any of that. As I said before, the client sets the password. We may have given her the CD—I really can't confirm or deny that at this stage—but we would have no idea what numbers or letters she programmed in for the password."

Rachel waited a beat. She stared at Conrad Dorfman. He stared back but dropped his eyes first. He picked up his tea and took another sip. "Can we find out why she came to you in the first place?"

"Without a court order? No, I don't think so."

"Your CD," she said. "There's a back entry."

"Excuse me?"

"Every company has one," Rachel said. "The info isn't lost forever. Your company programs in its own password so that you folks can get on the CD."

"I don't know what you're talking about."

"I used to be an FBI agent, Mr. Dorfman."

"So?"

"So I know these things. Please don't insult my intelligence."

"That was not my intent, Ms. Mills. But I simply can't help."

I looked at Rachel. She seemed to be weighing her options. "I still have friends, Mr. Dorfman. In the department. We can ask questions. We can poke around. The feds don't much like private eyes. You know that. I don't want trouble. I just want to know what's on the CD."

Dorfman put down his cup. He strummed his fingers. There was a knock, and the same woman opened the door. She beckoned Conrad Dorfman. He rose, again too theatrically, and practically leapt across the floor. "Excuse me a moment."

When he left the office, I looked at Rachel. She wouldn't turn toward me. "Rachel?"

"Let's just see how it plays out, Marc."

But there really wasn't much more to play. Conrad came back into the office. He crossed the room and stood over Rachel, waiting for her to look up. She wouldn't give him the satisfaction.

"Our president, Malcolm Deward, is a former federal agent himself. Did you know that?"

Rachel said nothing.

"He made some calls while we chatted." Conrad

waited. "Ms. Mills?" Rachel finally looked up. "Your threats are impotent. You have no friends at the agency. Mr. Deward, alas, does. Get out of my office. Now."

chapter 21

I said, "What the hell was that all about?"

"I told you before. I'm not an agent anymore."

"What happened, Rachel?"

She kept her eyes forward. "You haven't been a part of my life in a long time."

There was nothing to add. Rachel drove now. I held on to the cell phone, again willing it to ring. When we arrived back at my house, dusk had settled in. We went inside. I debated calling Tickner or Regan, but what good would that do now?

"We need to get that DNA checked," Rachel said. "My theory might sound implausible, but does the idea of your daughter being held all this time sound any more so?"

So I called Edgar. I told him that I wanted to run some additional tests on the hair. He said that would be fine. I hung up without telling him that I had already endangered the drop by enlisting the help of a former FBI agent. The less said on that, the better. Rachel called someone she knew to pick up the samples from Edgar, as well as a blood sample from me. He ran a private lab, she said. We would know something within twenty-four to forty-eight hours, which would probably be, in terms of a ransom demand, too late.

I settled into a chair in the den. Rachel sat on the floor. She opened her bag and pulled out wires and electronic contraptions of all sorts. Being a surgeon makes me pretty good with my hands, but when it comes to high-tech gizmos, I'm totally lost. She carefully spread the contents of the bag across the carpet, giving this action her full attention. Again I was reminded of the way she'd do the same thing with textbooks when we were in college. She reached into the bag and pulled out a razor.

"The bag of money?" she said.

I handed it to her. "What are you going to do?"

She opened it. The money was in packs of hundred-dollar bills. She grabbed a wad and slowly slipped the money out, not breaking the band around it. She cut the bills like they were a deck of cards.

"What are you doing?" I asked.

"I'm going to cut a hole."

"In the actual currency?"

"Yup."

She did it with the straight razor. She dug out a circle about the perimeter of a silver dollar, maybe a quarter inch thick. She scanned the floor, found a black device that was about the same size, fit it into the bills. Then she put the wrapping back on it. The device was totally hidden in the middle of the money wad.

"A Q-Logger," she said in way of explanation. "It's a GPS device."

"You say so."

"GPS stands for Global Positioning System. Put simply, it will track the money. I'll put one in the lining of the bag too, but most criminals know about that. They usually dump the cash into a bag of their own. But with all this money, they won't have time right away to search through every pack."

"How small do those things come?"

"The Q-Loggers?"

"Yes."

"They can make them even thinner, but the problem is the power source. You need a battery. That's where we lose out. I need something that can travel at least eight miles. This will do it."

"And where does it go to?"

"You mean where do I keep track of the movements?"

"Yes."

"Most of the time it goes to a laptop, but this is state of the art." Rachel lifted a device into the air, one I see too often in the world of medicine. In fact, I think I'm the only doctor on the planet without one.

"A Palm Pilot?"

"Designed with a special tracking screen. I'll have it on me if I have to move." She went back to work.

"What's all the other stuff?" I asked.

"Surveillance equipment. I don't know how much I'll be able to use, but I'd like to put a Q-Logger in your shoe. I want to get a camera on the car. I'd like to see if I can hook up some fiber optics on you, but that could be riskier." She started to organize her equipment, lost in the activity. Her eyes were down when she spoke again. "Something else I want to explain to you."

I leaned forward.

"Do you remember when my parents got divorced?" she asked.

"Yeah, sure." It had been when we first met.

"Close as we were, we never talked about it."

"I always got the impression you didn't want to."

"I didn't," she said too quickly.

And, I thought, neither had I. I was selfish. We were

supposedly in love for two years—and yet I never so much as nudged her to open up about her parents' divorce. It was more than an "impression" that made me hold my tongue. I knew something dark and unhappy lay there. I did not want to poke at it, disturb it, have it possibly turn its attention in my direction.

"It was my father's fault."

I almost said something really stupid like "It's never anyone's fault" or "There are two sides to every story," but a flyby of good sense kept my tongue in check. Rachel still hadn't looked up. "My father destroyed my mother. Crushed her soul. Do you know how?"

"No."

"He cheated on her."

She lifted her head and held my gaze. I did not look away. "It was a destructive cycle," she said. "He'd cheat, he'd get caught, he'd swear he'd never do it again. But he always did. It wormed into my mother, ate away at her." Rachel swallowed, turned back to her high-tech toys. "So when I was away in Italy and I heard you'd been with someone else . . ."

I thought of a million different things to say, but they were all meaningless. Frankly, so was what she was telling me. It explained a lot, I guess, but it was the ultimate too-little-too-late. I stayed where I was, not moving from the chair.

"I overreacted," she said.

"We were young."

"I just wanted . . . I should have told you about this back then."

She was reaching out. I started to say something, but I pulled up short. Too much. Just all too much. It had been six hours since the ransom call. The seconds tick-ticked, a deep, painful pounding in the well of my chest.

I jumped when the phone rang, but it was my regular

line, not the kidnapper's cell. I picked it up. It was Lenny.

"What's wrong?" he said without preamble.

I looked at Rachel. She shook her head. I nodded back that I understood. "Nothing," I said.

"Your mom told me you saw Edgar in the park."

"Don't worry."

"That old bastard will screw you—you know that."

There was no reasoning with Lenny when it came to Edgar Portman. He also might be right. "I know."

There was brief silence.

"You called Rachel," he said.

"Yes."

"Why?"

"Nothing important."

There was another pause. Then Lenny said, "You're lying to me, right?"

"Like a Vegas toupee."

"Yeah, okay. Hey, we still on for racquetball tomorrow morning?"

"I better cancel."

"No problem. Marc?"

"Yeah."

"If you need me . . ."

"Thanks, Lenny."

I hung up. Rachel was busy with her electronic gizmos. The words she had said were gone now, dissipated smoke. She looked up and saw something in my face.

"Marc?"

I didn't speak.

"If your daughter is alive, we'll bring her home. I promise."

And for the first time, I was not sure that I believed her.

chapter 22

Special Agent Tickner stared down at the report.

The Seidman murder-kidnapping had been beyond back burner. The FBI had realigned its priorities in recent years. Terrorism was number one on the most wanted list. Numbers two through ten were, well, terrorism. The Seidman case had only involved him when it became a kidnapping issue. Despite what you see on television, the local police are usually anxious to have the FBI involved. The feds have the resources and the know-how. Calling them too late can cost a life. Regan had been smart enough not to wait.

But once the kidnapping issue was—and he hated to use this term for it—"resolved," Tickner's job (unofficially at least) was to back off and leave it to the locals. He still thought about it a lot—you don't forget the sight of a baby's clothing in a cabin like that—but in his mind, the case had been inactive.

Until five minutes ago.

He read the brief report for the third time. He wasn't trying to put it together. Not yet. This was too weird for that. What he was trying to do, what he hoped to accomplish, was to find some kind of angle, some sort of handle he could grip. Nothing came to him.

Rachel Mills. How the hell did she fit into this?

A young subordinate—Tickner couldn't remember if his name was Kelly or Fitzgerald, something Irish like that—stood in front of the desk, hands not sure what to do. Tickner leaned back in the chair and crossed his legs. He tapped the pen against his lower lip.

"There has to be a connection between them," he told Sean or Patrick.

"She claimed to be a private detective."

"Is she licensed?"

"No, sir."

Tickner shook his head. "There's more to it than that. Check phone records, find some friends, whatever. Trace it down for me."

"Yes, sir."

"Call that detective agency. The MVD. Tell them I'm on my way."

"Yes, sir."

The Irish kid left. Tickner stared off. He and Rachel had gone through training together at Quantico. They'd both had the same mentor. Tickner thought about what to do here. While he didn't always trust the locals, he liked Regan. The guy was just off enough to be an asset. He picked up the phone and dialed Regan's cell.

"Detective Regan."

"Long time, no speak."

"Ah, Federal Agent Tickner. You still wearing the sunglasses?"

"You still stroking that soul patch—uh, among other things?"

"Yes. And maybe."

Tickner could hear sitar music in the background. "You busy?"

"Not at all. I was just meditating."

"Like Phil Jackson?"

"Exactly. Except I don't have all those pesky championship rings. You should join me sometime."

"Yeah, I'll put that on my list of must-dos."

"It would relax you, Agent Tickner. I hear tremendous strain in your voice." Then: "I assume that there was a reason for this call?"

"Remember our favorite case?"

There was a funny pause. "Yes."

"How long has it been since we had something new?"

"I don't think we ever had anything new."

"Well, we may now."

"I'm listening."

"We just got a strange call from an ex–FBI agent. Guy named Deward. He's a private dick in Newark now."

"So?"

"It seems our friend Dr. Seidman paid his office a visit today. And he had someone very special with him."

Lydia dyed her hair black—the better to blend in with the night.

The plan, as it were, was simple.

"We confirm that he has the money," she told Heshy. "Then I kill him."

"You sure?"

"Positive. And the beauty of it is, the murder will automatically get tied to the original shooting." Lydia smiled at him. "Even if something goes wrong, nothing ties back to us."

"Lydia?"

"Something the matter?"

Heshy shrugged his giant shoulders. "Don't you think it would be better if I kill him?"

"I'm the better shot, Pooh Bear."

"But"—he hesitated, shrugged again—"I don't need a weapon."

"You're trying to protect me," she said.

He said nothing.

"That's sweet." And it was. But one of the reasons she wanted to do it herself was to protect Heshy. He was the vulnerable one here. Lydia never worried about getting caught. Part of it was classic overconfidence. Dumb people get caught, not those who were careful. But more than that, she knew if she did get nabbed, they'd never convict her. Forget her still girl-next-door looks, though that would undoubtedly be an asset. What no prosecutor would ever overcome would be the weepy Oprahization of her case. Lydia would remind them of her "tragic" past. She would claim abuses in many forms. She would cry on the talk shows. She would talk about the plight of the child star, of the calamity of being forced into the world of Pixie Trixie. She would look adorably victimized and innocent. And the public—not to mention the jury—would lap it up.

"I think it's best this way," she told him. "If he sees you approach, well, he is apt to run. But if he catches sight of li'l ol' me . . ." Lydia let her voice die out with a small shrug.

Heshy nodded. She was right. This should be cake. She stroked his face and handed him the car keys.

"Does Pavel understand his part?" Lydia asked.

"He does. He'll meet us there. And yes, he'll be wearing the flannel shirt."

"Then we might as well start on our way," she said. "I'll call Dr. Seidman."

Heshy used the remote to unlock the car doors.

"Oh," she said, "I have to check something before we go."

Lydia opened the back door. The child was fast asleep in the car seat. She checked the straps and made sure that they were secure. "I better sit in the back, Pooh Bear," she said. "Just in case a little someone wakes up."

Heshy angled his way into the driver's seat. Lydia took out the phone and voice changer and dialed the number.

chapter 23

We ordered a pizza, which I think was a mistake. Late-night pizzas are college. It was yet another not-so-subtle reminder of the past. I kept staring at the mobile phone, wishing it to ring. Rachel was quiet, but that was okay. We had always been good with silence. That, too, was weird. In many ways, we were falling back, picking up where we'd left off. But in many more ways, we were strangers with a tenuous, awkward connection.

What was odd was that my memories were suddenly hazy. I'd thought that once I saw her again, they'd head straight to the surface. But few specifics came to me. It was more a feeling, an emotion, like the way I remembered the ruddy cold of New England. I don't know why I couldn't remember. And I wasn't sure what it meant.

Rachel's brow creased as she toyed with the electronic equipment. She took a bite of pizza and said, "Not as good as Tony's."

"That place was awful."

"A little greasy," she agreed.

"A little? Didn't the large come with a coupon for a free angioplasty?"

"Well, there was that sludge-through-the-veins feel to it."

We looked at each other.

"Rachel?"

"Yeah."

"Suppose they don't call."

"Then they don't have her, Marc."

I let that settle in. I thought about Lenny's son, Conner, the things he could say and do, and I tried to apply it to the baby I'd last laid eyes on in her crib. It wouldn't compute, but that didn't mean anything. There was hope. I held on to that. If my daughter was dead, if that phone never rang again, the hope would, I know, kill me. But I didn't care. Better to go down this way than try to go the distance.

So I had hope. And I, the cynic, let myself believe the best.

When the cell phone finally did ring, it was nearly ten. I did not even glance over to Rachel and wait for her nod. My finger was on the ANSWER button before the first chirp could die off.

"Hello?"

"Okay," the robotic voice said, "you'll get to see her."

I couldn't breathe. Rachel moved over closer and put her ear near mine.

"Good," I said.

"You have the money?"

"Yes."

"All of it?"

"Yes."

"Then listen closely. Deviate from what I tell you and we disappear. Do you understand?"

"Yes."

"We checked with our police sources. So far, so good. It appears that you haven't contacted the authorities. But we need to make sure. You will drive alone toward the George Washington Bridge. Once there, we will be in range. Use the two-way radio feature on the phone. I will tell you where to go and what to do. You will be searched. If we find any weapons or wires, we will disappear. Do you understand?"

I could feel Rachel's breath quicken.

"When do I see my daughter?"

"When we meet."

"How do I know you won't just take the money?"

"How do you know I'm not going to hang up on you now?"

"I'm on my way," I said. Then I quickly added, "But I won't hand over the money until I see Tara."

"Then we are in agreement. You have an hour. Signal me then."

chapter 24

Conrad Dorfman did not appear happy to be dragged back into the MVD office this late. Tickner didn't care. If Seidman had come here alone, that would be an important lead, no doubt about it. But the fact that Rachel Mills had been here, too, that she was somehow involved, well, let's just say that Tickner's curiosity was more than piqued.

"Did Ms. Mills show you an ID?" he asked.

"Yes," Dorfman replied. "But it was stamped 'Retired.'"

"And she was with Dr. Seidman?"

"Yes."

"They arrived together."

"I think so. I mean, yes, when they came in here, they were together."

Tickner nodded. "What did they want?"

"A password. For a CD-ROM."

"I'm not sure I follow."

"They claimed that they had a CD-ROM we provided to a client. Our CDs are password protected. They wanted us to give them the password."

"Did you?"

Dorfman looked properly shocked. "Of course not. We had a call put in to your agency. They explained to us ... well, they never quite explained to us anything really. They just stressed that we should not cooperate with Agent Mills in any way."

"*Ex*-agent," Tickner said.

How? Tickner wondered. How the hell had Rachel Mills hooked up with Seidman? He had tried to give her the benefit of the doubt. Unlike his fellow agents, he had known her, had seen her in action. She'd been a good agent, maybe even a great one. But now he wondered. He wondered about the timing. He wondered about her being here. He wondered about her flashing her badge and trying to apply pressure.

"Did they tell you how they came by this CD-ROM?"

"They claimed that it belonged to Dr. Seidman's wife."

"Does it?"

"I believe so, yes."

"Are you aware that his wife died more than a year and a half ago, Mr. Dorfman?"

"I know that now."

"But you didn't when they were here?"

"Right."

"Why did Seidman wait eighteen months to ask for the password?"

"He didn't say."

"Did you ask?"

Dorfman shifted in his seat. "No."

Tickner smiled, buddy-to-buddy. "No reason you should," he said, faux-genteel. "Did you give them any information at all?"

"None."

"You didn't tell them why Mrs. Seidman hired your agency in the first place?"

"That's correct."

"Okay, very good." Tickner leaned forward, his elbows on his knees now. He was about to ask another question when his cell phone rang. "Excuse me," he said, reaching into his pocket.

"Is this going to take much longer?" Dorfman asked. "I have plans."

He didn't even bother responding. Rising, he put the phone to his ear. "Tickner."

"It's Agent O'Malley," the young kid said.

"Did you find anything?"

"Oh yeah."

"I'm listening."

"We checked the phone records going back three years. Seidman never called her—at least, not from his house or office—until today."

"Am I about to hear a *but*?"

"You are. But Rachel Mills called him—once."

"When?"

"June two years ago."

Tickner did the math. That would have been about three months before the murder and kidnapping. "Anything else?"

"Something big, I think. I had one of our agents check Rachel's apartment in Falls Church. He's still poking around, but guess what he found in her night table drawer."

"Does this look like a quiz show, O'Ryan?"

"O'Malley."

Tickner rubbed the bridge of his nose. "What did the agent find?"

"A prom photo."

"What?"

"I mean, I don't know if it's from the prom exactly. It's some kind of old formal. Photo's gotta be fifteen, twenty years old. She's wearing her hair in some flip style and she's got one of those flower bands on her arm. What do you call those?"

"A corsage?"

"Right."

"What the hell does this have to do with—"

"The guy in the picture."

"What about him?"

"Our agent is sure. The guy she's with—her date, I mean—is our own Dr. Seidman."

Tickner felt the thrum rush through him. "Keep digging," he said. "Call me when you get more."

"On it."

He hung up the phone. Rachel and Seidman went to a prom together? What the hell was going on? She was from Vermont, if he remembered correctly. Seidman lived in New Jersey. They didn't go to high school together. How about college? They'd have to look into it.

"Something wrong?"

Tickner turned. It was Dorfman. "Let me see if I have this straight, Mr. Dorfman. This CD-ROM belonged to Monica Seidman?"

"That's what we were told, yes."

"Yes or no, Mr. Dorfman."

He cleared his throat. "We believe the answer is yes."

"So she was a client here?"

"Yes, that we've been able to confirm."

"So to sum up, a murder victim was a client of yours."

Silence.

"Her name was in every paper in the state," Tickner went on, giving him the hard stare. "How come you never came forward?"

"We didn't know."

Tickner kept with the hard stare.

"The guy who handled that case is no longer employed by us," he added quickly. "See, he was gone by the time Mrs. Seidman was killed. So no one here put the pieces together."

Defensive. Tickner liked that. He believed him, but he didn't show it. Make the guy anxious to please.

"What was on the CD?"

"Photographs, we think."

"Think?"

"That's usually the case. Not always. We use the CD to store photographs, but there could be some scanned documents too. I really couldn't tell you."

"Why the hell not?"

He put up both hands. "Don't worry. We have a backup. But any file more than a year old is stored in the basement. The office was closed, but when I heard you were interested, I got someone to come in. He's running off the material on the backup CD right now."

"Where?"

"He's on the lower level." Dorfman checked his watch. "He should be done or just about by now. Do you want to go down and see?"

Tickner stood. "Let's rumble."

chapter 25

"There are still things we can do," Rachel said. "This stuff is state of the art. Even if they pat you down, we can get away with it. I have a bulletproof vest that has a pinhole camera right in the center."

"And you don't think they'll find that with a pat-down?"

"Yeah, okay, look, I know you're worried about them finding out, but let's be realistic here. There's an excellent chance this is all a setup. Don't give up the money until you see Tara. Don't get yourself stuck somewhere alone. Don't worry about the Q-Logger—if they're being up front, we'll have Tara before they can search the stacks of money. I know this isn't an easy decision, Marc."

"No, you're right. I played it safe last time. I think we need to take some chances. But the vest is out."

"Okay, here's what we're going to do. I'm going to be in the trunk. They may check the backseat to see if someone is lying there. The trunk will be a safer bet. I'll disconnect the wires back there so when the trunk opens, no lights will come on. I'll try to keep up with you, but I have to stay at a safe distance. Make no mistake here. I'm not Wonder Woman. I might lose you, but remember: Don't look for me. Not even casually.

These guys are probably pretty good. They'll spot that."

"I understand." She was dressed totally in black. I said, "You look like you're going to do a reading in the Village."

"Kumbaya, my Lord. You ready?"

We both heard the car pull up. I looked out the window and felt my panic needle jump. "Damn," I said.

"What?"

"That's Regan, the cop on the case. I haven't seen him in more than a month." I looked at her. Her face was stark white against the black outfit. "Coincidence?"

"No coincidence," she said.

"How the hell did he find out about the ransom?"

She moved back from the window. "He's probably not here for that."

"Then what?"

"My guess would be that they got word of my involvement from MVD."

I frowned. "So?"

"No time to explain. Look, I'm going to go out to the garage and hide. He's going to ask about me. Tell him I went back to D.C. If he presses, tell him I'm an old friend and leave it at that. He's going to want to interrogate you."

"Why?"

But she was already moving away from me. "Just be firm and get him out of there. I'll wait for you by the car."

I didn't like it, but now was not the time. "Okay."

Rachel headed to the garage via the door in the den. I waited until she was out of sight. When Regan hit my front walkway, I opened the door, trying to cut him off at the pass.

Regan smiled. "Were you expecting me?" he asked.

"I heard your car."

He nodded as if I'd said something that required serious analysis. "Do you have a few moments, Dr. Seidman?"

"Actually, it's a bad time."

"Oh." Regan did not break stride. He slid past me and into my front foyer, his eyes taking in everything. "Heading out, are we?"

"What do you want, Detective?"

"Some new information has come to our attention."

I waited for him to say more.

"Don't you want to know what it is?"

"Of course."

Regan had a strange, almost serene look on his face. He looked up at the ceiling, as if he were considering what color to paint it. "Where have you been today?"

"Get out, please."

His eyes were still on the ceiling. "Your hostility surprises me." But he did not look surprised.

"You said you had some new information. If you do, say it. If not, get out. I'm not in the mood to be questioned."

He made a well-well face. "We hear that you visited a private detective agency in Newark today."

"So?"

"So what were you doing there?"

"Tell you what, Detective. I'm going to ask you to leave because I know answering your questions will bring me no closer to finding my daughter."

He looked at me. "You sure about that?"

"Kindly get the hell out of my house. Now."

"Suit yourself." Regan started for the door. When we reached it, he asked, "Where's Rachel Mills?"

"Don't know."

"She's not here?"

"Nope."

"No idea at all where she could be?"

"I think she's on her way back to Washington."

"Hmm. How do you two know each other?"

"Good night, Detective."

"Okay, sure. But one last question."

I stifled a sigh. "You've watched too many episodes of *Columbo*, Detective."

"Indeed I have." He smiled. "But let me ask it anyway."

I spread my hands for him to go ahead.

"Do you know how her husband died?"

"He was shot," I said too quickly, and immediately regretted it. He leaned a little more into my space and kept on me.

"And do you know who shot him?"

I stood without moving.

"Do you, Marc?"

"Good night, Detective."

"She killed him, Marc. A bullet to the head at close range."

"That," I said, "is a load of bull."

"Is it? I mean, are you sure?"

"If she killed him, why isn't she in jail?"

"Good question," Regan said, backing down the walkway. When he reached the end of the walkway, he added, "Maybe you should ask her."

chapter 26

Rachel was in the garage. She looked up at me. She suddenly looked small, I thought. And I saw fear in her face. The car trunk was open. I moved toward the driver-side door.

"What did he want?" she asked.

"What you said."

"He knew about the CD?"

"He knew we'd been at MVD. He didn't say anything about the CD."

I slid into the car. She let it drop. Now was not the time to raise any new issues. We both knew that. But again I questioned my judgment here. My wife had been murdered. So had my sister. Someone had tried very hard to kill me. Stripping it bare, I was trusting a woman I really didn't know. I was trusting her not only with my life, but with my daughter's. How stupid when you think about it. Lenny had been right. It was not so simple. In truth, I had no idea who she was or what she'd become. I had deluded myself into making her something she might not be, and now I wondered what it might cost me.

Her voice cut through my haze. "Marc?"

"What?"

"I still think you should wear the bulletproof vest."

"No."

My tone was firmer than I'd wanted. Or maybe not. Rachel climbed into the trunk and closed it. I put the duffel bag with the money on the seat next to me. I hit the garage-door opener under the sun visor and started the car.

We were on our way.

When Tickner was nine years old, his mother bought him a book of optical illusions. You'd look at a drawing of, say, an old lady with a big nose. You'd look a little longer and then, poof, it appeared now to be a young woman with her head turned. Tickner had loved the book. When he got a little older, he moved on to those Magic Eyes, staring for however long it took for the horsey or whatever to appear in the swirling colors. Sometimes it would take a long time. You'd even start to wonder if there was anything there at all. And then, suddenly, the image surfaced.

That was what was happening here.

There were moments in a case, Tickner knew, that altered everything—just like those old optical illusions. You are viewing one reality and then, with a gentle tilt, reality changes. Nothing is as it appeared.

He had never really bought the conventional theories on the Seidman murder-kidnapping. They all felt too much like reading a book with missing pages.

Over the years, Tickner had not dealt with that many murders. They were, for the most part, left to the local cops. But he knew plenty of homicide investigators. The best ones were always off center, overly theatrical, ridiculously imaginative. Tickner had heard them talk about a point in the case where the victim "reaches out" from the grave. The victim "talks" to them somehow, pointing them toward the killer. Tickner would listen to this nonsense and nod politely. It always sounded like a load of hyperbole, just one of those meaningless things cops say because the general public laps it up.

The printer still whirred. Tickner had seen twelve photos already.

"How many more?" he asked.

Dorfman looked at the computer screen. "Six more."

"Same as these?"

"Pretty much, yeah. I mean, same person."

Tickner stared down at the photographs. Yes, the same person was featured in all of them. They were all in black and white, all taken without the subject knowing, probably from a distance with a zoom lens.

The reach-from-the-grave stuff—it no longer sounded so silly. Monica Seidman had been dead for eighteen months. Her murderer had gone free. And now, with all hope lost, she seemed to have risen from the dead to point a finger. Tickner looked again and tried to understand.

The subject of the pictures, the person Monica Seidman was pointing at, was Rachel Mills.

When you take the eastern spur of the New Jersey Turnpike north, the night skyline of Manhattan beckons. Like most people who see it nearly every day, I used to take it for granted. No more. For a while afterward, I thought I could still see the Towers. It was as though they were bright lights I'd stared at for a long time, so that even when I closed my eyes, their images were still there, imbedded. But like any sunspot, the images eventually began to fade. It is different now. When I drive this route, I still make myself look for them. Even tonight. But sometimes I forget precisely where those towers stood. And that angers me more than I can express.

Out of habit, I took the lower level of the George Washington Bridge. There was no traffic at this hour. I drove through the E-ZPass lane. I had managed to keep myself distracted. I flipped stations between two talk radio shows. One was a sports station where lots of guys named Vinny from Bayside called up and complained about inept coaches and how much better they'd be at the job. The other station featured two beyond-puerile Howard Stern rip-offs who thought it was funny for a college freshman to call his mother and tell her he had testicular cancer. Both were, if not entertaining, mildly distracting.

Rachel was in the trunk, which was totally weird if I thought about it. I reached for the cell phone and flipped on the two-way radio feature. My finger pressed down on the CALL button and almost instantly I heard the robotic voice say, "Take the Henry Hudson north."

I put the phone to mouth, walkie-talkie style. "Okay."

"Tell me the moment you get on the Hudson."

"Right."

I got into the left lane. I knew the way. This area was familiar to me. I had done a fellowship at New York Presbyterian, which resided about ten blocks south. Zia and I had roomed with a cardiac resident named Lester in an Art Deco building at the tail end of Fort Washington Avenue in upper, upper Manhattan. When I lived here, this section of the city was known as the far northern point of Washington Heights. Now I had noticed several realtors redubbing it "Hudson Heights" so as to differentiate it, in both substance and cost, from its lower-class roots.

"Okay, I'm on the Hudson," I said.

"Take your next exit."

"Fort Tryon Park?"

"Yes."

Again I knew it. Fort Tryon floats cloudlike high above the Hudson River. It is a quiet and restful jagged cliff, New Jersey on its west, Riverdale-Bronx on its east. The park is a mishmash of terrains—walkways of harsh stone, fauna from a bygone era, terraces of stone, nooks and crannies of cement and brick, thick brush, rocky slopes, open grass. I had spent plenty of summer days on her green lawns, adorned in shorts and T-shirt, Zia and unread medical books my companions. My favorite time here: summer, right before dark. The orange glow bathing the park is something almost ethereal.

I put on my blinker and glided onto the exit ramp. There were no cars and few lights. The park was closed at night, but the roadway stayed open for through traffic. My car chugged up the steep road and entered what felt like a medieval fortress. The Cloisters, a former quasi-French monastery that was now part of the Metropolitan Museum of Art, held middle ground. It houses a fabulous collection of medieval artifacts. Or so I'm told. I've been in this park a hundred times. I've never been inside the Cloisters.

It was, I thought, a smart place for a ransom drop—dark, quiet, filled with serpentine trails, stone cliffs, sudden drops, thick woods, paved and unpaved walks. You could get lost here. You could hide here for a very long time and never be found.

The robotic voice asked, "Are you there yet?"

"I'm in Fort Tryon, yes."

"Park near the café. Get out and walk up to the circle."

Riding in the trunk was noisy and jarring. Rachel had brought a padded blanket, but there was not much she could do about the noise. A flashlight stayed in her satchel. She had no interest in turning it on. Rachel had never minded the dark.

Sight could be distracting. The dark was a good place to think.

She tried to keep her body loose, riding bumps, and wondered about Marc's behavior right before they left. The cop at the house had, no doubt, said something that shook him. About her? Probably. She wondered what exactly he had said and how she should react.

Didn't matter now. They were on their way. She had to concentrate on the task at hand.

Rachel was falling back into a familiar role. There was a pang here. She missed being with the FBI. She had loved her job. Yes, perhaps it was all she had. It was more than her escape—it was the only thing she really enjoyed doing. Some people pushed through the nine-to-five so they could go home and live their lives. For Rachel, it was the opposite.

After all these years apart, here was something that she and Marc had in common: They'd both found careers they loved. She wondered about that. She wondered if there was a connection, if their careers had become some kind of true-love substitute. Or was that looking at it too deeply?

Marc still had his job. She did not. Did that make her more desperate?

No. His child was gone. Game, set, match.

In the darkness of the trunk, she smeared her face with black makeup, enough to take the shine away. The car started climbing upward. Her gear was packed and ready.

She thought about Hugh Reilly, the son of a bitch.

Her breakup with Marc—and everything after—was his fault. Hugh had been her dearest friend in college. That was what he wanted, he told her. Just to be her friend. No pressure. He understood that she had a boyfriend. Had Rachel been naive or purposefully naïve? Men who want to "just be friends" do so because they hope to be next in line, as though friendship were an on-deck circle, a good place for practice swings before heading to the plate. Hugh had called her in Italy that night with nothing but the best of intentions. "I just think you should know," he said, "as your friend." Right. And then he told her what Marc had done at some stupid frat party.

Yes, enough blaming herself. Enough blaming Marc. Hugh Reilly. If that son of a bitch had just minded his own business, what would her life be like right now? She couldn't say. Ah, but what had her life become? That was easier to answer. She drank too much. She had a bad temper. Her stomach bothered her more than it should. She spent too much time reading *TV Guide*. And let's not forget the pièce de résistance: She had gotten herself ensnared in a self-destructive relationship—and gotten herself out of it in the worst way possible.

The car veered and climbed upward, forcing Rachel to roll back. A moment or two later, the car stopped. Rachel lifted her head. The cruel musings fled.

It was game time.

From the old fort's lookout tower, some two hundred fifty feet above the Hudson River, Heshy had one of the most stunning views of the Jersey Palisades, stretching from the Tappan Zee Bridge on the right to the George Washington Bridge on his left. He actually took the time to appreciate it before he got to the matter at hand.

As though on cue, Seidman took the exit off the Henry Hudson Parkway. No one followed. Heshy kept his eyes on the road. No car slowed. No car sped up. No one was trying to make it look as though they weren't following.

He spun around, lost sight of the car for a brief moment, then spotted it again as it came back into view. He could see Seidman in the driver's seat. No one else was visible. That didn't mean much—someone could be ducking down in the back—but it was a start.

Seidman parked the car. He turned off the engine and opened the door. Heshy lifted the microphone to his mouth.

"Pavel, you ready?"

"Yes."

"He's alone," he said, speaking now for Lydia's benefit. "Proceed."

"Park near the café. Get out and walk up to the circle."

The circle, I knew, was Margaret Corbin Circle. When I reached the clearing, the first thing I spotted, even in the dark, was the bright colors of the children's playground near Fort Washington Avenue at 190th Street. The colors still leapt out. I'd always liked this playground, but tonight the yellows and blues taunted me. I thought of myself as a city boy. When I lived near here, I'd imagined staying in this neighborhood—too sophisticated was I for the vanilla suburbs—and of course, that meant that I would bring my children to this very park. I took that as an omen, but I didn't know of what.

The phone squawked. "There's a subway station on the left."

"Okay."

"Take the stairs down toward the elevator."

I might have suspected this. He would put me on the elevator and then on the A train. It would be difficult, if not impossible, for Rachel to follow me.

"Are you on the stairs?"

"Yes."

"At the bottom, you'll see a gate on the right."

I knew where it was. It led to a smaller park and was locked except for weekends. It had been set aside as something of a small picnic area. There were Ping-Pong tables, though you had to bring your own net and paddles to play. There were benches and eating areas. Kids used it for birthday parties.

The wrought-iron gate, I remember, was always locked.

"I'm there," I said.

"Make sure no one sees you. Push open the gate. Slip through and quickly close it."

I peered inside. The park was black. Distant streetlights reached out and gave the area no more than a dull glow. The duffel bag felt heavy. I adjusted it up my shoulder. I looked behind me now. No one. I looked to my left. The subway elevators were still. I put my hand on the gate door. The padlock had been cut. I gave the area one more quick glance because that was what the robotic voice had told me to do.

No sign of Rachel.

The gate creaked when I pushed it open. The echo ripped through the still night. I slipped through the opening and let the dark swallow me whole.

Rachel felt the car rock as Marc got out.

She made herself wait a full minute, which felt like two hours. When she thought that it was probably safe, Rachel lifted the trunk an inch and peeked out.

She saw no one.

Rachel had a gun with her, a fed-issue Glock .22 40-caliber semiautomatic, and she carried her night-vision goggles, Rigel 3501 military-grade Gen. 2+. The Palm Pilot that could read the Q-Logger transmitter was in her pocket.

She doubted that anyone would see her, but she still

only opened the trunk wide enough so she could roll out. She huddled down low. Her hand reached back and grabbed the semiautomatic and night-vision goggles. Then she quietly closed the trunk.

Field operations had always been her favorite—or at least, the training for them. There had been very few missions that required this sort of cloak-and-dagger reconnaissance. For the most part, stakeouts were high-tech. You had vans and spy planes and fiber optics. You rarely found yourself crawling through the night in black clothes and greasepaint.

She made herself small against the back tire. In the distance, she saw Marc heading up the drive. She put the gun in its holster and strapped the night-vision goggles to her belt. Keeping low, Rachel moved up the grass to higher ground. There was still enough light. She didn't need the goggles yet.

A sliver of moon sliced through the sky. There were no stars tonight. Up ahead, she could see that Marc had the cell phone near his ear. The duffel bag was on his shoulder. Rachel looked around, saw no one. Would the drop take place here? It wasn't a bad place, if you had a planned escape route. She started to think about the possibilities.

Fort Tryon was hilly. The secret would be to try to get higher. She started climbing and was just about to settle in when Marc exited the park.

Damn. She'd have to move again.

Rachel commando-crawled down the hill. The grass was prickly and smelled like hay, the cause being, she assumed, the recent water shortage. She tried to keep her eyes on Marc, but she lost him when he left the park grounds. She took a risk and moved quicker. At the park gate, she ducked behind a stone pillar.

Marc was there. But not for very long.

With the phone back to his ear, Marc veered to the left and vanished down the steps leading to the A train.

Up ahead, Rachel saw a man and a woman walking a dog. They could be part of this—or they could be a man and a woman walking a dog. Marc was still out of sight. No time for debate now. She ducked low at a stone wall.

Leaning her back against it, Rachel made her way toward the stairs.

Tickner thought that Edgar Portman looked like something out of a Noël Coward production. He wore silk pajamas under a red robe that appeared to have been tied with great care. There were velvet slippers on his feet. His brother, Carson, on the other hand, looked properly ruffled. His pajamas were askew. His hair was all over the place. His eyes were bloodshot.

Neither Portman could take his eyes off the photographs from the CD.

"Edgar," Carson said, "let's not jump to conclusions."

"Not jump ... ?" Edgar turned to Tickner. "I gave him money."

"Yes, sir," Tickner said. "A year and a half ago. We know about that."

"No." Edgar tried to make the word snap with impatience, but he didn't have the strength. "I mean, recently. Today, in fact."

Tickner sat up. "How much?"

"Two million dollars. There was another ransom demand."

"Why didn't you contact us?"

"Oh sure." Edgar made a sound that was half chortle, half sneer. "You all did such a wonderful job last time."

Tickner felt the tick in his blood. "Are you saying

that you gave your son-in-law an additional two million dollars?"

"That is precisely what I'm saying."

Carson Portman was still staring at the photographs. Edgar glanced at his brother, then back at Tickner. "Did Marc Seidman kill my daughter?"

Carson stood up. "You know better."

"I'm not asking you, Carson."

Both men looked at Tickner now. Tickner was not having any of it. "You said you met with your son-in-law today?"

If Edgar was upset about his question being ignored, he did not show it. "Early this morning," he said. "At Memorial Park."

"That woman in the pictures." Tickner gestured toward them. "Was she with him?"

"No."

"Has either of you ever seen her before?"

Both Carson and Edgar answered in the negative. Edgar picked up one of the photographs. "My daughter hired a private investigator to take these?"

"Yes."

"I don't understand. Who is she?"

Tickner again ignored his question. "The ransom note came to you, like last time?"

"Yes."

"I'm not sure I follow. How did you know that it wasn't a hoax? How did you know that you were dealing with the real kidnappers?"

Carson took that one. "We did think it was a hoax," he said. "At first, I mean."

"So what changed your mind?"

"They sent hairs again." Carson quickly explained about the tests and about Dr. Seidman's request for additional tests.

"You gave him all the hairs, then?"

"We did, yes," Carson said.

Edgar seemed lost in the photographs again. "This woman," he spat. "Was Seidman involved with her?"

"I can't answer that."

"Why else would my daughter want these pictures taken?"

A mobile phone rang. Tickner excused himself and put the receiver to his ear.

"Bingo," O'Malley said.

"What?"

"We got a hit on Seidman's E-ZPass. He crossed the George Washington Bridge five minutes ago."

The robotic voice told me, "Walk down the path."

There was still enough light to see the first few steps. I started down them. The darkness gathered around, closed in. I started to use my foot to feel my way, like a blind man swinging a cane. I didn't like this. I didn't like this at all. I wondered again about Rachel. Was she near here? I tried to follow the path. It curved to the left. I stumbled on the cobblestone.

"Okay," the voice said. "Stop."

I did so. I could see nothing in front of me. Behind me, the street was a faded glow. On my right was a steep incline. The air had that city-park smell to it, a swirling potpourri of fresh and stale. I listened for some sort of clue, but there was nothing other than the distant humming swish of traffic.

"Put down the money."

"No," I said. "I want to see my daughter."

"Put down the money."

"We had a deal. You show me my daughter, I show you the money."

There was no reply. I could hear the blood roaring in

my ears. The fear was crippling. No, I did not like this. I was too exposed. I checked the path behind me. I could still break into a run and scream like a psycho. This neighborhood was tighter than most in Manhattan. Someone might call the police or try to help.

"Dr. Seidman?"

"Yes?"

And then a flashlight hit my face. I blinked and raised a hand to block my eyes. I squinted, trying to see past it. Someone lowered the flashlight beam. My eyes quickly adjusted, but there was no need. The beam was cut off by a silhouette. There was no mistake. I could see immediately what was being highlighted.

There was a man. I may have even seen flannel—I'm not sure. As I said, it was in silhouette. I couldn't really make out features or colors or design. So that part could have been my imagination. But not the rest. I saw the shapes and outlines clear enough to know.

Standing next to the man, gripping his leg just above the knee, was a small child.

chapter 27

Lydia wished that there was more light. She would very much like to see the look on Dr. Seidman's face right now. Her desire to see his expression had nothing to do with the cruelty that was about to come down. It was curiosity. It was deeper than the slow-to-see-the-car-accident aspect of human nature. Imagine. This man had had his child taken away. For a year and a half, he had been left to wonder about her fate, tossing through sleepless nights, conjuring up horrors best left in the dark abyss of our subconscious.

Now he had seen her.

It would be unnatural *not* to want to see the expression on his face.

Seconds ticked away. She wanted that. She wanted to stretch the tension, pull him beyond what a man could handle, soften him for the final blow.

Lydia took out her Sig-Sauer. She held it to her side. Peering out from behind the bush she judged the distance between her and Seidman at thirty, maybe forty feet. She put the voice changer and phone back to her mouth. She whispered into it. Whisper or scream, it made no difference. The voice changer made it all sound the same.

"Open the money bag."

From her perch, she watched him move like a man in a trance. He did what she asked—now without question. This time, she was the one using the flashlight. She shone it at his face and then dropped the beam to the bag.

Money. She could see the stacks. She nodded to herself. They were good to go.

"Okay," she said. "Leave the money on the ground. Walk slowly down the path. Tara will be waiting for you."

She watched Dr. Seidman drop the bag. He was squinting at the spot where he believed his daughter would be waiting. His movements were stiff, but then again his vision had probably been affected by the lights in his eyes. That again would make it easier.

Lydia wanted a close shot. Two quick bullets to the head, in case he was wearing a flak jacket. She was a good shot. She could probably hit him in the head from here. But she wanted the sure thing. No mistakes. No chance to run.

Seidman moved toward her. He was twenty feet away. Then fifteen. When he was only ten feet away, Lydia raised the pistol and took aim.

If Marc took the subway, Rachel knew that it'd be near impossible to follow him without being spotted.

Rachel hurried toward the stairwell. When she got there, she looked down into the dark. Marc was gone. Damn. She scanned the surroundings. There was a sign for elevators leading down to the A train. On the right was a closed wrought-iron gate. Nothing else.

He had to be in an elevator heading down to the subway.

Now what?

She heard footsteps behind her. With her right hand, Rachel quickly wiped the greasepaint, hoping to make herself look at least semipresentable. With her left hand, she slid the goggles behind her and out of sight.

Two men trotted down the stairs. One caught her eye and smiled. She wiped her face again and smiled back. The men jogged the rest of the way down the steps and turned toward the elevator bank.

Rachel quickly considered her options. Those two men could be her cover. She could follow them down, get into the same elevator, get off with them, maybe even engage them in conversation. Who'd suspect her then? Hopefully Marc's subway car hadn't left yet. If it had . . . well, no use in thinking negative.

Rachel started toward the men when something made her stop. The wrought-iron gate. The one she had seen on her right. It was closed. The sign on it read: OPEN ON WEEKENDS AND MAJOR HOLIDAYS ONLY.

But through the thicket, Rachel saw the beam of a flashlight.

She pulled up. She tried to peer through the fence, but all she could see was the light beam. The brush was too thick. On her left, she heard the ding of an elevator. The doors slid open. The men stepped inside. No time to pull out the Palm Pilot and check the GPS. Besides, the elevator and beam of flashlight were too close. It would be hard to pinpoint the difference.

The man who had smiled at her put his hand against the side, keeping the door open. She wondered what to do.

The flashlight beam went out.

"Are you coming?" the man asked.

She waited for the flashlight beam to come back on. It didn't. She shook her head. "No, thank you."

Rachel quickly broke back up the stairs, trying to find a dark spot. It had to be dark for the goggles to work. The Rigels came with a built-in overlight sensor system

to protect from bright lights, but Rachel still found that
the fewer artificial lights, the better. Street level looked
down over the park. Okay, the positioning was pretty
good, but there was still too much light from the street.

She moved to the side of the stone hut that housed
the elevators. On the left, there was a spot that—if she
pressed herself against the wall—would give her total
darkness. Perfect. The trees and bushes were still too
heavy to get a clear view. But it would have to do.

Her goggles were supposedly lightweight but they
still felt bulky. She should have bought a model you
could just hold up to your face, binocular style. Most
have that feature. This model didn't. You could not just
hold it to up your eyes. You had to strap it on as a mask.
The advantage, however, was obvious: If you attached it
like a mask, you could keep your hands free.

As she pulled them over her head, the flashlight
beam appeared again. Rachel tried to follow it, see
where it was coming from. It seemed to her that it was
a different spot this time. Over on the right now. Closer.

And then, before she could pinpoint it, the beam was
gone.

Her eyes locked on the spot where she thought the
beam had come from. Dark. Very dark now. Still keeping her eyes looking there, she finished getting the
night-vision goggles in place. Night-vision goggles are
not magic. They don't really see in the dark. Night-
vision optics work by intensifying existing light, even
very small amounts. But here, there was pretty much
nothing. That used to be a problem, but now most
brands came with an infrared illuminator standard. The
illuminator cast a beam of infrared light that was not
visible to the human eye.

But it was visible to the night-vision goggles.

Rachel flipped on the illuminator. The night lit up in

full green. She was looking not through a lens, but at a phosphor screen, not unlike the one on your TV set. The eyepiece magnified the picture—you were looking at a picture, not the actual site—and the picture was green because the human eye can differentiate more shades of green than any other phosphor color. Rachel stared.

Got something.

The view was hazy, but it looked to Rachel like a small woman. The woman seemed to be hiding behind a bush. She held something up to her mouth. A phone maybe. Peripheral vision is nearly nonexistent with these goggles, though these claimed to give you a thirty-seven-degree angle. She had to swivel her head to the right, and there, putting down the duffel bag with the two million dollars in it, was Marc.

Marc started walking toward the woman. His steps were short, probably because he was on cobblestones in the dark.

Rachel swiveled her head from the woman, to Marc, back to the woman. Marc was approaching, getting closer. The woman was still crouched in hiding. There was no way Marc could see her. Rachel frowned and wondered what the hell was going on.

Then the woman swung her arm up.

It was hard to see clearly—there were trees and branches in the way—but the woman seemed to be pointing her finger at Marc. They were not far apart anymore. Rachel squinted at the screen attached to her face. And it was then that she realized that the woman was not pointing a finger. The image was too big for a hand.

It was a gun. The woman was pointing a gun at Marc's head.

A shadow crossed over Rachel's vision. She started back, opening her mouth to call out a warning, when a hand like a baseball glove covered her mouth and smothered all sound away.

Tickner and Regan hooked up on the New Jersey Turnpike. Tickner drove. Regan sat next to him and stroked his face.

Tickner shook his head. "Can't believe you still have that soul patch."

"You don't like it?"

"You think you're Enrique Iglesias?"

"Who?"

"Exactly."

"What's wrong with the soul patch?"

"It's like wearing a T-shirt that says, 'I Had a Middle-Age Crisis in 1998.' "

Regan thought about it. "Yeah, okay, fair point. By the way, those sunglasses you always wear. I was wondering if they were FBI issue."

Tickner grinned. "Helps me land the chicks."

"Yeah, those and your stun gun." Regan shifted in the chair. "Lloyd?"

"Uh-huh."

"I'm not sure I get it."

They weren't talking about eyewear or facial hair anymore.

"We don't have all the pieces," Tickner said.

"But we're getting close?"

"Oh yeah."

"Let's go through it then, cool?"

Tickner nodded. "First off, if the DNA lab Edgar Portman used is correct, the child is still alive."

"Which is weird."

"Very. But it explains a lot. Who would be most likely to keep a kidnapped child alive?"

"Her father," Regan said.

"And whose gun mysteriously vanished from the murder scene?"

"Her father's."

Tickner made a gun with his forefinger and thumb, aimed it at Regan, dropped the hammer. "Righto."

"So where has the kid been all this time?" Regan asked.

"Hidden."

"Well, gee, that helps."

"No, think about it. We've been looking at Seidman. We've looked closely. He knows that. So who would be the best person to hide his kid?"

Regan saw where he was going. "The girlfriend we didn't know about."

"More than that, a girlfriend who used to work for the feds. A girlfriend who would know how we work. How to do a ransom drop. How to hide a child. Someone who would know Seidman's sister, Stacy, and be able to enlist her help."

Regan thought about it. "Okay, let's assume I believe all that. They commit this crime. They get two million dollars and the kid. But then what? They bide their time for eighteen months? They decide they need more cash? What?"

"They need to wait to avoid suspicion. Maybe they wanted the wife's estate to clear. Maybe they need another two million dollars to run away—I don't know."

Regan frowned. "We're still trying to finesse away the same point."

"What's that?"

"If Seidman was behind this, how come he was nearly killed? This was no wound-me-so-it-looks-good injury. He was flatlined. The paramedics were sure they had a goner when they first got there. Hell, we quietly called it a double homicide for almost ten days."

Tickner nodded. "It's a problem."

"And more than that, where the hell is he going right now? I mean, crossing the George Washington Bridge. Do you think he decided now was the time to flee with the two million dollars?"

"Could be."

"If you were fleeing, would you use your E-ZPass to pay the toll?"

"No, but he might not know how easy it is to trace."

"Hey, everyone knows how easy it is to trace. You get the bill in the mail. It tells you what time you hit what tollbooth. And even if he was dumb enough to forget that, your federal agent Rachel Whatshername isn't."

"Rachel Mills." Tickner nodded slowly. "Good point, though."

"Thank you."

"So what conclusions can we draw?"

"That we still don't have a clue what the hell is going on," Regan said.

Tickner smiled. "Nice to be in familiar territory."

The cell phone rang. Tickner picked it up. It was O'Malley. "Where are you?" O'Malley asked.

"A mile from the George Washington Bridge," Tickner said.

"Hit the accelerator."

"Why? What's up?"

"NYPD just spotted Seidman's car," O'Malley said. "It's parked at Fort Tryon Park—a mile, maybe mile and a half, from the bridge."

"Know it," Tickner said. "We'll be there in less than five."

Heshy had thought that it was all going a little too smoothly.

He'd watched Dr. Seidman leave his car. He waited.

No one else had come out. He'd started down from the old fort's tower.

That was when he spotted the woman.

He paused, watching her head down toward the subway elevators. Two guys were with her. Nothing suspicious in that. But then, when the woman sprinted back up alone, well, that was when things had changed.

He kept a close eye from then on. When she moved into the darkness, Heshy started creeping toward her.

Heshy knew that his appearance was intimidating. He also knew that much of the circuitry inside of his brain was not wired normally. He didn't much care, which, he assumed, was part of the wiring problem. There were those who would tell you that Heshy was pure evil. He had killed sixteen people in his life, fourteen of them slowly. He had left six men alive who still wished that he hadn't.

Supposedly, people like Heshy did not understand what they were doing. Other people's pain did not reach them. That was not true. His victims' pain was not something distant to him. He knew what pain was like. And he understood love. He loved Lydia. He loved her in ways most people could never fathom. He would kill for her. He would die for her. Many people say that about their loved ones, of course—but how many are willing to put it to the test?

The woman in the dark had binoculars strapped onto her head. Night-vision goggles. Heshy had seen them on the news. Soldiers in battle wore them. Having them did not necessarily mean she was a cop. Most weaponry and military gizmos were available on-line to anyone with the proper dollars. Heshy watched her. Either way, cop or no cop, if the goggles worked, this woman would be a witness to Lydia committing murder.

So she had to be silenced.

He closed in slowly. He wanted to hear if she was talking to anyone, if she had some kind of radio control to other units. But the woman was silent. Good. Maybe she was indeed on her own.

He was about two yards away from her when her body stiffened. The woman gave a little gasp. And Heshy knew that it was time to close her down.

He hurried over, moving with a grace that defied his bulk. He snaked one hand around her face and clasped it over her mouth. His hand was big enough to cover her nose too. Cut off the air supply. With his free hand, he cupped the back of her skull. He pushed his hands together.

And then, with both hands firmly placed on the woman's head, Heshy lifted her all the way off the ground.

chapter 28

A sound made me stop. I turned to my right. I thought that maybe I heard something up there, near the street level. I tried to see, but my eyes were still suffering from the onslaught of the flashlight. The trees also helped cut off my view. I waited, seeing if I heard a follow-up. Nothing. The sound was gone now. It wasn't important anyway. Tara should be waiting for me at the end of this path. Whatever else might go on, that was all that counted.

Focus, I thought again. Tara, end of the path. All else was extraneous.

I started up again, not even glancing behind me to check on the fate of the duffel bag with the two million dollars in it. It, too, was, like everything else but Tara, irrelevant. I tried to conjure up the shadowy image again, the silhouette made by the flashlight. I trudged on. My daughter. She could be right here, scant steps from where I now walked. I had been given a second chance to rescue her. Focus on that. Compartmentalize. Let nothing stop me.

I continued down the path.

While with the Federal Bureau of Investigation, Rachel had been well trained in weapons and hand-to-

hand combat. She had learned much during her four
months at Quantico. She knew that true fighting was
nothing like you saw on TV. You would never, for example, mess around with a high kick to the face. You
would never try anything involving turning your back
on an opponent, spinning, leaping—none of that.

Successful hand-to-hand combat could be broken
down pretty simply. You aimed for the vulnerable spots
on the body. The nose was good—it usually made your
opponent's eyes well up with tears. The eyes, of course.
The throat was good too—anyone who has ever been
struck there knew how it could shut down your will to
fight. The groin, well, obvious. You always hear that. The
groin, however, is a difficult target, probably because a
man is prone to defend it. It's usually better as a decoy
move. Fake there and then go to one of the other more
exposed, vulnerable spots.

There were other areas—the solar plexus, the instep,
the knee. But there was also a problem with all these
techniques. In the movies, a smaller opponent might
beat a larger one. In reality, yes, that can happen, but
when the woman is as small as Rachel and the man as
large as her current attacker, the odds of her coming out
on the winning end are very small. If the attacker knows
what he is doing, very small becomes pretty close to
nonexistent.

The other problem for a woman is that fights never
go as they do in the movies. Think about any physical altercation you may have seen in a bar or at a sporting
event or even on a playground. The battle almost always
ends up in a grapple on the floor. On TV or in a boxing
ring, sure, people stand and hit each other. In real life,
one or the other ducks down and grabs the opponent
and they go down to the ground and wrestle. It didn't
matter how much training you had. If the fight reached

that stage, Rachel would never defeat an opponent this large.

Lastly, while Rachel had practiced and trained and been in simulated dangerous situations—Quantico went so far as to have a "mock town" for these purposes—she had never been involved in a real physical altercation before. She was not ready for the pure panic, the tingly, unpleasant numbness in the legs, the way adrenaline mixed with fear saps your strength.

Rachel could not breathe. She felt the hand on her mouth and, out of her element, reacted wrong. Instead of immediately kicking behind her—trying to take out his knee or stomping down on the instep—Rachel worked on instinct and used both her hands to pry her mouth free. It did not work.

Within seconds, the man had his other hand on the base of her head, holding her skull in a viselike grip. She could feel his fingers dig into her gums, push in her teeth. His hands seemed so powerful that Rachel was sure he could crush her skull like an eggshell. He didn't. Instead he wrenched up. Her neck took the brunt of it. It felt as if her head was being torn off. The hand against her mouth and nostrils effectively cut off her air supply. He lifted more. Her feet fully left the ground. She took hold of his wrists and tried to pull up, tried to lessen the strain on her neck.

But she still could not breathe.

There was a roaring in her ears. Her lungs burned. Her feet kicked out. They landed on him, blows so tiny and impotent he didn't bother to block them. His face was close to her now. She could feel the spit in his breath. Her night-vision goggles had been knocked askew but not all the way off. They blocked her sight.

The pressure in her head was pounding. Trying to remember her training, Rachel dug her nails into the pressure point on his hand beneath the thumb. No effect. She kicked harder. Nothing. She needed a breath. She felt like a fish on the line, flailing, dying. Panic took hold.

Her gun.

She could reach for it. If she could just control herself long enough, to have the courage to release her hand, she could go for her pocket, pull out the weapon, and fire it. It was her only chance. Her brain was going groggy. Consciousness was starting to ebb away.

With her skull seconds away from exploding, Rachel dropped her left hand away. Her neck stretched so taut, she was sure it would snap like a rubber band. Her hand found her holster. Her fingers touched the gun.

But the man saw what she was doing. With Rachel still dangling in the air like a rag doll, he kneed her hard in the kidney. Pain exploded in a flash of red. Her eyes rolled back. But Rachel did not give in. She kept going for the gun. The man had no choice. He put her down.

Air.

Her breathing passage was finally opened. She tried not to gulp it down, but her lungs had other ideas. She couldn't stop.

Her relief, however, was short-lived. With one hand, the man stopped her from pulling out her gun. With the other, he delivered a dartlike blow to her throat. Rachel gagged and went down. The man took hold of her weapon and tossed it away. He dropped hard on top of her. The little wind she had managed to gather was gone now. He straddled her chest and moved his hands toward her throat.

That was when the police car sped past.

The man suddenly sat up. She tried to take advantage, but he was simply too big. He grabbed a cell phone from his pocket and put it to his mouth. In a harsh whisper, he said, "Abort! Cops!"

Rachel tried to move, tried to do something. But there was nothing left. She looked up in time to see the man cock his fist. It started toward her. She tried to turn away. But there was no place to go.

The blow jarred her head back against the cobblestone. And then darkness flooded in.

When Marc walked past her, Lydia stepped out of the bush from behind him with the gun up. She was aiming at the back of the head and had her finger on the trigger. The "Abort! Cops!" call in her earpiece startled her so, she almost pulled the trigger. But her mind worked fast. Seidman was still heading down the path. Lydia saw everything. Saw it clearly. She dumped the gun. No gun on her, no proof of any wrongdoing. The weapon could never be tied to her as long as it was not in her possession. Like most weapons, it was untraceable. She wore gloves, of course, so there would be no fingerprints.

But—her mind was still working fast here—what was there to prevent her from taking the money?

She was just Miss Citizen taking a stroll through the park. She could spot the duffel bag, right? If she was caught with it, well, she was just being a good Samaritan. Given the chance, she would have brought the bag to the police. No crime there. No risk.

Not when you consider that two million dollars was inside it.

Her mind quickly ran through the pros and cons. Simple when you think about it. Take the money. If they caught her with it, so what? There was absolutely nothing to tie her to this crime. She had dumped the gun. She had dumped the cell phone. Sure, someone might find it. But it would not lead to either her or Heshy.

She heard a noise. Marc Seidman, who'd been about fifteen feet in front of her, broke into a sprint. Fine, no problem. Lydia started toward the money. Heshy appeared around the corner. She continued toward him. Without hesitation, Lydia scooped up the bag.

Then Lydia and Heshy headed down the path, fading into the night.

I continued to stumble forward. My eyes were beginning to adjust, but they were still several minutes from being particularly useful. The path slid downward. There were small cobblestones. I tried not to trip. The route grew steeper now, and I let the momentum carry me so that I could move faster without appearing to be running.

On my right, I could see the abrupt slope that overlooked the Bronx. Lights twinkled from way below.

I heard a child's yelp.

I stopped. It was not loud, but the sound was unmistakably that of a small child. I heard rustling. The child yelped again. It was farther away now. The rustling sound was gone, but I could hear the steady slap of footsteps on the pavement. Someone was running. Running with a child. Away from me.

No.

I broke into a sprint. The faraway lights provided enough illumination so that I could stay on the path. Up ahead, I saw the chain-link fence. It had always been locked. When I reached it, I saw that someone had used a bolt cutter on it. I pushed through and was back on the path now. I looked to my left, which led back up to the park.

No one.

Damn, what the hell had gone wrong? I tried to think rationally. Focus. Okay, if I were the one running away,

which way would I go? Simple. I would veer to the right.
The paths were confusing, dark, windy. You could easily
hide in the shrubs. That would be the way to go if one
were a kidnapper. I stopped for only an instant, hoping
to pick up the sounds of a child. I didn't. But I did hear
someone say, "Hey!" with what sounded like genuine
surprise.

I cocked my head. The sound had indeed come from
my right. Good. I sprinted again, searching the horizon
for a flannel shirt. Nothing. I continued down the hill. I
lost my footing and almost tumbled down the hill. From
my time living in this area, I knew the homeless found
sanctuary on the off-path inclines too steep for the casual trekker. They made shelter out of branches and
caves. Every once in a while, you could hear a rustling
too loud for a squirrel. Sometimes a homeless guy
would emerge out of seemingly nowhere—longhaired,
matted beard, the stench coming off him in waves. There
was a spot not far from here where the male street prostitutes plied their trade to the businessmen getting off
the A train. I used to jog by that area during the quiet
of the day. Condom wrappers often littered the walkway.

I kept running, trying to keep my ears open. I hit a
fork in the path. Damn. Again I asked, What way was
the more twisty? I didn't know. I was about to veer right
again when I heard a sound.

Rustling in the bush.

Without thinking, I dived in. There were two men.
One in a business suit. Another, much younger and
dressed in jeans, was on his knees. The business suit
yelled an expletive. I did not back away. Because I had
heard the man's voice before. Seconds ago.

He had been the one who yelled, "Hey."

"Did you see a man and a little girl go by here?"

"Get the hell out—"

I crossed over and slapped him in the face. "Did you see them?"

He looked far more shocked than hurt. He pointed to the left. "They went up that way. He was carrying the kid."

I jumped back on the path. Okay, right. They were heading back up toward the green. If they stayed that route, they would come out not far from where I'd parked. I started running again, pumping my arms. I ran past the male prostitutes sitting on the wall. One of them caught my eye—he had a blue kerchief on his head—nodded, and pointed to stay on the path. I nodded a thanks back. I kept running. In the distance, I could see the lights of the park. And there, crossing in front of the lamppost, I caught a fleeting glimpse of the man in the flannel shirt carrying Tara.

"Stop!" I shouted. "Someone stop him!"

But they were gone.

I swallowed and started up the path, still shouting for help. No one reacted or shouted back. When I reached the outpost where lovers often gazed at the eastern view, I again spotted the flannel shirt. He was jumping over the wall into the woods. I started to follow but when I turned the corner, I heard someone yell, "Freeze!"

I looked behind me. It was a cop. He had his gun drawn.

"Freeze!"

"He has my kid! This way!"

"Dr. Seidman?"

The familiar voice came to my right. It was Regan. What the . . . ? "Look, just follow me."

"Where's the money, Dr. Seidman?"

"You don't understand," I said. "They just jumped over that wall."

"Who did?"

I saw where this was going. Two cops had their guns pointed. Regan was staring at me with his arms crossed. Tickner appeared behind him.

"Let's talk about this, okay?"

Not okay. They wouldn't shoot. Or if they did, I didn't much care. So I started running. They took chase. The cops were younger and no doubt in better shape. But I had something going for me. I was crazed. I jumped the fence and fell down the incline. The cops pursued, but they were moving more gingerly, with normal human care.

"Freeze!" the cop yelled again.

I was breathing too fast to try to yell out more explanation. I wanted them to stay with me—I just didn't want them to catch up.

I curled up my body and rolled down the hill. Dried glass clung to me and got caught up in my hair. The dust kicked up. I stifled a cough. Just as I was picking up speed, my rib cage slammed into the trunk of tree. I could hear the hollow thud. I gasped, the wind almost knocked out of me, but I hung on. Sliding to the side, I reached the path. The cops' flashlights pursued. They were within sight but far enough behind. Fine.

On the path, my eyes swerved right, then left. No sign of the flannel shirt or Tara. I tried again to figure out which way he might run. Nothing came to me. I stopped. The police were coming closer.

"Freeze!" the cop yelled yet again.

Fifty-fifty chance.

I was about to break to my left, to head back into the darkness, when I saw the young man with the blue kerchief, the one who had nodded at me earlier. He shook his head this time and pointed in the direction behind me. "Thank you," I said.

He might have said something in return, but I was already on my way. I cut back up and headed through the same chain-link fence I had pushed through earlier. I heard footsteps, but they were too far away. I looked up and again spotted the flannel shirt. He was standing near the lights of the subway steps. He seemed to be trying to catch his breath.

I ran faster.

So did he.

There was probably fifty yards that separated us. But he had to carry a child. I should be able to close in on him. I started running. The same cop yelled, "Halt!" this time, I guess for the sake of variety. I hoped like hell they didn't decide to shoot.

"He's back on the street!" I shouted. "He has my daughter."

I don't know if they were listening or not. I reached the steps and took them three at a time. I was out of the park again, back on Fort Washington Avenue at Margaret Corbin Circle. I looked ahead at the playground. No movement. I glanced down Fort Washington Avenue and spotted someone running near Mother Cabrini High School, near the chapel.

The mind flashes to odd things. Cabrini Chapel was one of the most surreal stops in all of Manhattan. Zia had dragged me to Mass there once to see without telling why the chapel was something of a tourist spot. I immediately understood the draw. Mother Cabrini died in 1901, but her embalmed body is kept in what looks like a lucite block. That's the altar. The priests conduct mass over her body/table. No, I'm not making that up. The same guy who preserved Lenin in Russia worked on Mother Cabrini. The chapel is open to the public. It even has a gift shop.

My legs felt heavy, but I kept moving. I no longer

heard the police. I quickly glanced behind me. The flashlights were far away.

"Over here!" I shouted. "Near Cabrini High!"

I started sprinting again. I reached the entrance to the chapel. It was locked. There was no sign of flannel shirt anywhere. I looked around, eyes wide, panicked. I had lost them. They were gone.

"This way!" I shouted, hoping that either (or both) the police and Rachel would hear me.

But my heart sank. My chance. My daughter was gone again. I felt the weight on my chest. And that was when I heard the car start up.

My head jerked to the right. I scanned the street and started running. A car started moving. It was about ten yards in front of me. A Honda Accord. I memorized the license plate, even as I knew that would be futile. The driver was still trying to maneuver out of a parking spot. I couldn't see who it was. But I wasn't about to take any chances.

The Honda had just cleared the bumper of the car in front of it and was about start up when I grabbed the driver's-side door handle. Lucky break finally—he hadn't locked the door. No time, I assumed, because he'd been in a rush.

Several things happened in a very short period of time. As I started pulling the door open, I was able to see through the window. It was indeed the flannel-shirt man. He reacted quickly. He grabbed the door and tried to hold it closed. I pulled harder. The door opened a crack. He hit the accelerator.

I tried to run with the car, like you see in the movies. The problem is, cars move faster than people. But I would not let go. You hear those stories about people gaining extraordinary strength in certain circumstances, about average men being able to lift cars off the ground to rescue trapped loved ones. I scoff at those stories. You probably do too.

I am not saying that I lifted a car. But I held on. I wedged my fingers in and wrapped them around the divide between the front door and back. I used both hands and willed my fingers into vises. I would not let go. No matter what.

If I hold on, my daughter lives. If I let go, my daughter dies.

Forget focus. Forget compartmentalizing. This thought, this equation, was as simple as breathing.

The man in the flannel shirt pushed down on the gas. The car was picking up speed now. I kicked my legs off the ground, but there was no place to perch them. They slid down the back door and landed with a clunk. I felt the skin of my ankles being scraped off on the pavement. I tried to regain my footing. No go. The pain was tremendous but inconsequential. I held on.

The status quo, I knew, was working against me. I couldn't hang on much longer, no matter how much I willed it. I had to make a move. I tried to pull myself into the car, but I wasn't strong enough. I hung on and let my arms go straight. I tried hopping up again. My body was horizontal now, parallel to the ground. I extended my body. My right leg reached up and curled around something. The antenna on the top of the car. Would that hold me? I didn't think so. My face was pressed against the backseat window. I saw the little car seat.

It was empty.

Panic seized me again. I felt my hands slipping. We had only driven maybe twenty, thirty yards. With my face against the glass, my nose bouncing against the window, my body and face scraped and battered, I looked at the child in the front seat and a crushing truth pried my hands off the car window.

Again the mind works in odd ways. My first thought was classically doctor: The child should be sitting in the back. The Honda Accord has a passenger-side airbag. No child under the age of twelve should ever sit in the front. Also, small children should be in a proper car seat. That was, in fact, the law. Riding out of a car seat and in the front . . . that was doubly unsafe.

Ridiculous thought. Or maybe natural. Either way, that was not the thought that ripped the fight out of me.

The flannel-shirted man yanked the steering wheel to the right. I heard the tires squeak. The car jerked, and my fingers slipped away. My grip was gone now. I went airborne. My body landed hard, skidding across the pavement like a stone. I could hear the police sirens behind me. They would, I thought, follow the Honda Accord. But it wouldn't matter. I had only gotten a brief glimpse. But it had been enough to know the truth.

The child in the car was not my daughter.

chapter 29

Again I was in a hospital, this time New York Presbyterian—my old stomping grounds. They hadn't yet run X rays, but I was pretty sure they'd find a cracked rib. Nothing you could really do about it other than shoot yourself up with painkillers. It would hurt. That was okay. I was pretty scraped up. There was a gash on my right leg that looked like the work of a shark attack. Skin had been ripped off both elbows. None of that mattered.

Lenny arrived in record time. I wanted him here because I was not really sure how to handle this. At first, I almost convinced myself that I had made a mistake. A child changes, right? I had not seen Tara since she was six months old. A lot of growth occurs in that period. She'd have matured from wee infancy to an older toddler. I'd been hanging on to a moving car, for crying out loud. I had only gotten the briefest of glimpses.

But I knew.

The child in the front seat of the car looked to be a boy. He was probably closer to three years old than two. His skin, his coloring, was simply too pale.

It was not Tara.

I knew that Tickner and Regan had questions. I wanted to cooperate. I also wanted to know how the hell they had found out about the ransom drop. I hadn't seen Rachel yet either. I wondered if she were in the building. I also wondered about the fate of the ransom money, the Honda Accord, the man in the flannel shirt. Had they caught him? Had he kidnapped my daughter originally—or had that first ransom drop been a con job too? If so, how had my sister, Stacy, fitted into it?

In short, I was confused. Enter Lenny aka Cujo.

He burst through the door dressed in baggy khakis and a pink Lacoste shirt. His eyes had that scared, wild look that again brought back memories of our childhood. He pushed past a nurse and approached my bed.

"What the hell happened?"

I was about to give Lenny an overview when he stopped me with a raised finger. He turned to the nurse and asked her to leave. When we were alone he nodded for me to go ahead again. Starting with seeing Edgar in the park, I ran through calling Rachel, her arrival, her preparation with all the electronic gizmos, the ransom calls, the drop, my dive on the car. I backtracked and told him about the CD. Lenny interrupted—he always interrupted—but not as often as usual. I saw something cross his face, and maybe—I don't want to read too much into it here—but maybe he was hurt that I hadn't confided in him. The look didn't last long. Lenny gathered himself a piece at a time.

"Any chance that Edgar has been playing you?" he asked.

"To what end? He's the one who's lost four million dollars."

"Not if he's the one who set it up."

I made a face. "That doesn't make any sense."

Lenny didn't like it, but he didn't have a response either. "So where is Rachel now?"

"She's not here?"

"I don't think so."

"I don't know, then."

We both went quiet a second.

"Maybe she went back to my house," I said.

"Yeah," Lenny said. "Maybe."

There was nary a trace particle of conviction in his voice.

Tickner pushed open the door. His sunglasses sat atop his shaved head, a look I found disconcerting; if he bent his neck and drew a mouth on the lower part of his pate, it would look like a second face. Regan followed in a sort of hip-hop step, or maybe the soul patch was affecting the way I viewed him. Tickner took the lead.

"We know about the ransom demand," he said. "We know your father-in-law gave you another two million dollars. We know that you visited a private detective agency today called MVD and asked about the password to a CD-ROM owned by your late wife. We know that Rachel Mills was with you and that she did not, as you told Detective Regan earlier, return to the Washington, D.C., area. So we can skip all that."

Tickner moved closer. Lenny watched him, ready to pounce. Regan folded his arms and leaned against the wall. "So let's start with the ransom money," Tickner said. "Where is it?"

"I don't know."

"Did someone take it?"

"I don't know."

"What do you mean, you don't know?"

"He told me to put it down."

"Who is 'he'?"

"The kidnapper. Whoever was on the cell phone."

"Where did you put it down?"

"In the park. On the path."

"And then what?"

"He said to start walking forward."

"Did you?"

"Yes."

"And then?"

"That's when I heard a child cry and someone start running. Everything went crazy after that."

"And the money?"

"I told you. I don't know what happened to the money."

"How about Rachel Mills?" Tickner asked. "Where is she?"

"I don't know."

I looked at Lenny, but he was studying Tickner's face now. I waited.

"You lied to us about her returning to Washington, D.C.—isn't that correct?" Tickner asked.

Lenny put a hand on my shoulder. "Let's not start by mischaracterizing my client's statements."

Tickner made a face as if Lenny were a turd that had plopped down from the ceiling. Lenny stared back, unfazed. "You told Detective Regan that Ms. Mills was on her way back to Washington—did you not?"

"I said I didn't know where she was," I corrected him. "I said she *might* have gone back."

"And where was she at the time?"

Lenny said, "Don't answer."

I let him know that it was okay. "She was in the garage."

"Why didn't you tell Detective Regan that?"

"Because we were getting ready for the ransom drop. We didn't want anything slowing us down."

Tickner folded his arms. "I'm not sure I understand."

"Then ask another question," Lenny snapped.

"Why would Rachel Mills be involved in the ransom drop?"

"She's an old friend," I said. "And I knew she'd been a special agent with the FBI."

"Ah," Tickner said. "So you thought maybe her experience could help you here?"

"Yes."

"You didn't call Detective Regan or myself?"

"That's correct."

"Because?"

Lenny took that one. "You know damn well why."

"They told me no cops," I said. "Like last time. I didn't want to risk it again. So I called Rachel."

"I see." Tickner looked back at Regan. Regan looked off as if trying to follow a stray thought. "You chose her because she used to be a federal agent?"

"Yes."

"And because you two were"—Tickner made vague hand gestures—"close."

"A long time ago," I said.

"Not anymore?"

"No. Not anymore."

"Hmm, not anymore," Tickner repeated. "And yet you chose to call her in a matter involving your child's life. Interesting."

"Glad you think so," Lenny said. "By the way, is there a point to any of this?"

Tickner ignored him. "Before today, when was the last time you saw Rachel Mills?"

"What difference does that make?" Lenny said.

"Please just answer my question."

"Not until we know—"

But my hand was on Lenny's arm now. I knew what he was doing. He had automatically snapped into his adversarial pose. I appreciated it, but I wanted to get past this as quickly as possible.

"About a month ago," I said.

"Under what circumstances?"

"I bumped into her at the Stop and Shop on Northwood Avenue."

"Bumped into her?"

"Yes."

"You mean, as in a coincidence? As in not knowing the other was going to be there, out of the blue?"

"Yes."

Tickner turned around and looked at Regan again. Regan kept perfectly still. He wasn't even toying with the soul patch.

"And before that?"

"What before that?"

"Before you 'bumped' "—Tickner's sarcasm spit the word across the room—"into Ms. Mills at the Stop and Shop, when was the last time you'd seen her?"

"Not since college," I said.

Again Tickner spun toward Regan, his face lit up with incredulity. When he turned back, the glasses dropped down to his eyes. He pushed them back up onto his forehead. "Are you telling us, Dr. Seidman, that the only time you've seen Rachel Mills between your college days and today was just that one time at the supermarket?"

"That's exactly what I'm telling you."

For a moment, Tickner seemed at a loss. Lenny looked as if he might have something to add, but he kept himself in check.

"Have you two spoken on the phone?" Tickner asked.

"Before today?"

"Yes."

"No."

"Not ever? You never talked to her on the phone before today? Not even when you were dating?"

Lenny said, "Jesus Christ, what kind of question is that?"

Tickner snapped his head toward Lenny. "You have a problem?"

"Yeah, your questions are moronic."

They started again with the death stares. I broke the silence. "I hadn't spoken to Rachel on the phone since college."

Tickner turned to me. His expression was openly skeptical now. I glanced behind him at Regan. Regan was nodding to himself. While they both looked off balance, I tried to press it. "Did you find the man and child in the Honda Accord?" I asked.

Tickner considered the question a moment. He looked back at Regan, who shrugged a why-not. "We found the car abandoned on Broadway near 145th Street. It'd been stolen a few hours earlier." Tickner took out his notebook but didn't look at it. "When we spotted you at the park, you began yelling about your daughter. Do you believe that she was the child in the car?"

"I thought so at the time."

"But not anymore?"

"No," I said. "It wasn't Tara."

"What made you change your mind?"

"I saw him. The child, I mean."

"It was a he?"

"I think so."

"When did you see him?"

"When I jumped on the car."

Tickner spread his hands. "Why don't you start at the beginning and tell us exactly what happened?"

I told them the same story I'd told Lenny. Regan never moved from the wall. He still hadn't said a word. I found that odd. As I spoke, Tickner seemed to be growing more and more agitated. The skin on his cleanly shaven head tightened, making the sunglasses, which still sat perched on the top of his skull, start sliding forward. He kept readjusting them. I saw the pulse near his temples flutter. His jaw was locked.

When I was done, Tickner said, "You're lying."

Lenny slid between Tickner and my bed. For a moment, I thought that they might come to blows, which, let's face it, would not be good for Lenny. But Lenny never gave an inch. It reminded me of the time in third grade when Tony Merullo picked a fight with me. Lenny had stepped between us then, faced Tony bravely, and gotten clobbered.

Lenny stayed nose-to-nose with the larger man. "What the hell is wrong with you, Agent Tickner?"

"Your client is a liar."

"Gentlemen, this interview is over. Get out."

Tickner bent his neck so that his forehead pressed against Lenny's. "We have proof he's lying."

"Let's see it," Lenny said. Then, "No, wait, forget it. I don't want to see it. Are you arresting my client?"

"No."

"Then get your sorry butt out of this hospital room."

I said, "Lenny."

With one more glare at Tickner to show he wasn't intimidated, Lenny looked back at me.

"Let's finish this now," I said.

"He's trying to hang you for this."

I shrugged because I didn't really care. I think Lenny saw that. He slid away. I nodded for Tickner to do his worst.

"You've seen Rachel before today."

"I told you—"

"If you hadn't seen or spoken to Rachel Mills, how did you know she'd been a federal agent?"

Lenny started to laugh.

Tickner quickly spun toward him. "What are you laughing at?"

"Because, numb-nuts, my wife is friends with Rachel Mills."

That confused him. "What?"

"My wife and I talk to Rachel all the time. We introduced them." Lenny laughed again. "That's your proof?"

"No, that's not my proof," Tickner snapped, defensive now. "Your story about getting this ransom call, about reaching out to an old girlfriend like that. You expect that to fly?"

"Why," I said, "what do you think happened?"

Tickner said nothing.

"You think I did it, right? That this was yet another elaborate scheme to, what, get another two million from my ex-father-in-law?"

Lenny tried to slow me down. "Marc . . ."

"No, let me just say something here." I tried to get Regan into it, but he still looked off, so I locked eyes with Tickner. "Do you really think I staged all this? Why go through all the machinations of having this meeting in the park? How did I know you'd track me down there—hell, I still don't know how you did that. Why would I bother leaping on a car like that? Why wouldn't I have just taken the money and hidden it and come up with a story for Edgar? If I was just running a scam, did I hire this guy with the flannel shirt? Why? Why involve another person or a stolen car? I mean, come on. It makes no sense."

I looked at Regan, who still wasn't biting. "Detective Regan?"

But all he said was "You're not being straight with us, Marc."

"How?" I asked. "How am I not being straight with you?"

"You claim that before today you and Ms. Mills haven't spoken on the phone since college."

"Yes."

"We have phone records, Marc. Three months before your wife was murdered, there was a call from Rachel's house to yours. Do you want to explain that?"

I turned to Lenny for help, but he was staring down at me. This made no sense. "Look," I said, "I have Rachel's cell phone number. Let's call her and find out where she is."

"Do that," Tickner said.

Lenny picked up the hospital phone next to my bed. I gave him the number. I watched him dial it, all the while trying to put it together. The phone rang six times before I heard Rachel's voice tell me she could not answer her phone and that I should leave a message. I did so.

Regan finally peeled himself off the wall. He pulled a chair to the side of my bed and sat. "Marc, what do you know about Rachel Mills?"

"Enough."

"You dated in college?"

"Yes."

"How long?"

"Two years."

Regan spread his arms, all open and wide eyed. "See, Agent Tickner and I still aren't sure why you called her. I mean, okay, you dated a long time ago. But if you haven't been in touch at all"—he shrugged—"why her?"

I thought about how to put this and chose the direct route. "There's still a connection."

Regan nodded as if that explained a lot. "You were aware that she got married?"

"Cheryl—that's Lenny's wife—she told me."

"And you knew her husband was shot?"

"I learned about it today." Then, realizing that it had to be after midnight, "I mean, yesterday."

"Rachel told you?"

"Cheryl told me." Regan's words from his late-night visit to my abode came back to me. "And then you said Rachel shot him."

Regan looked back at Tickner. Tickner said, "Did Ms. Mills mention that to you?"

"What, that she shot her husband?"

"Yes."

"You're kidding, right?"

"You don't believe it, do you?"

Lenny said, "What's the difference what he believes?"

"She confessed," Tickner said.

I looked at Lenny. Lenny looked away. I tried to sit up a little more. "Then why isn't she in jail?"

Something dark crossed Tickner's face. His hands clenched into fists. "She claimed the shooting was accidental."

"And you don't believe that?"

"Her husband was shot in the head at point-blank range."

"So again I ask: Why isn't she in jail?"

"I'm not privy to all the details," Tickner said.

"What does that mean?"

"The local cops handled the case, not us," Tickner explained. "They decided not to pursue it."

I am neither a cop nor a great student of psychology, but even I could see that Tickner was holding something back. I looked at Lenny. His face was emotionless, which, of course, is not at all like Lenny. Tickner took a step away from the bed. Regan filled the void.

"You said you still felt a connection with Rachel?" Regan began.

"Asked and answered," Lenny said.

"Did you still love her?"

Lenny couldn't let that one go without comment. "Are you Ann Landers now, Detective Regan? What the hell does any of this have to do with my client's daughter?"

"Bear with me."

"No, Detective, I will not bear with you. Your questions are nonsense." Again I put my hand on Lenny's shoulder. He turned to me. "They want you to say yes, Marc."

"I know that."

"They're hoping to use Rachel as a motive for killing your wife."

"I know that too," I said. I looked at Regan. I remembered the feeling when I first saw Rachel at the Stop & Shop.

"You still think about her?" Regan asked.

"Yes."

"Does she still think about you?"

Lenny was not about to surrender. "How the hell would he know that?"

"Bob?" I said. It was the first time I had used Regan's first name.

"Yes."

"What are you trying to get at here?"

Regan's voice was low, almost conspiratorial. "Let me ask you one more time: Before the incident at the Stop and Shop, had you seen Rachel Mills since you broke up in college?"

"Jesus Christ," Lenny said.

"No."

"You're sure?"

"Yes."

"No communication at all?"

"They didn't even pass notes during study hall," Lenny said. "I mean, get on with it."

Regan leaned away. "You went to a private detective agency in Newark to ask about a CD-ROM."

"Yes."

"Why today?"

"I'm not sure I understand."

"Your wife has been dead for a year and a half. Why the sudden interest in the CD?"

"I'd just found it."

"When?"

"The day before yesterday. It was hidden in the basement."

"So you had no idea that Monica had hired a private detective?"

It took me a moment to answer. I thought about what I had learned since my beautiful wife's death. She had been seeing a psychiatrist. She had hired a private detective. She had hidden his findings in our basement. I hadn't known about any of it. I thought about my life, my love of work, my wanting to keep traveling. Sure, I loved my daughter. I cooed on command and marveled at the wonder of her. I would die—and kill—to protect her, but in my honest moments, I knew that I had not accepted all the changes and sacrifices she'd brought to my life.

What kind of husband had I been? What kind of father?

"Marc?"

"No," I said softly. "I had no idea she had hired a private investigator."

"Do you have any idea why she did?"

I shook my head. Regan faded back. Tickner pulled out a manila folder.

"What's that?" Lenny said.

"The contents of the CD." Tickner looked at me one more time. "You never saw Rachel, right? Just that time in the supermarket."

I did not bother answering.

Without fanfare, Tickner withdrew a photograph and handed it to me. Lenny snapped on his half-moon reading glasses and stood over my shoulder. He did that thing where you tilt your head up to look down. The photograph was black and white. It was a shot of Valley Hospital in Ridgewood. There was a date stamped on the bottom. The photograph had been taken two months before the shooting.

Lenny frowned. "The lighting is pretty good, but I'm not sure about the overall composition."

Tickner ignored the sarcasm. "That's where you work, is it not, Dr. Seidman?"

"We have an office there, yes."

"We?"

"My partner and I. Zia Leroux."

Tickner nodded. "There's a date stamped on the bottom."

"I can see that."

"Were you in the office on that day?"

"I really don't know. I'd have to check my calendar."

Regan pointed to near the hospital entrance. "Do you see that figure over there?"

I looked harder, but I couldn't make much out. "No, not really."

"Just notice the length of the coat, okay?"

"Okay."

Then Tickner handed me a second glossy. The photographer had used the zoom lens on this one. Same angle. You could see the person in the coat clearly now. She wore sunglasses, but there was no mistake. It was Rachel.

I looked up at Lenny. I saw the surprise on his face too. Tickner pulled out another photo. Then another. They were all taken in front of Valley Hospital. In the eighth one, Rachel entered the building. In the ninth one, taken one hour later, I exited alone. In the tenth, taken six minutes after that, Rachel went out the same doors.

At first, my mind could simply not soak in the implications. I was one big, swirling "Huh?" of bewilderment. There was no time to process. Lenny seemed stunned too, but he recovered first.

"Get out," Lenny said.

"You don't want to explain these photographs first?" I wanted to argue, but I was too dazed.

"Get out," Lenny said again, more forcefully this time. "Get out now."

chapter 30

I sat up in the bed. "Lenny?"

He made sure the door was closed. "Yes," he said. "They think you did it. Check that, they think you and Rachel did it together. You two were having an affair. She killed her husband—I don't know if they think you were involved with that or not—and then you both killed Monica, did who-knows-what with Tara, and came up with this scheme to rip off her father."

"That makes no sense," I said.

Lenny kept quiet.

"I was shot, remember?"

"I know."

"So what, they think I shot myself?"

"I don't know. But you can't talk to them anymore. They have evidence now. You can deny a relationship with Rachel to the skies, but Monica was suspicious enough to hire a private detective. Then, Jesus, think about it. The private detective delivers. He takes those photographs and gives them to Monica. Next thing you know, your wife is dead, your kid is gone, and her father is out two million bucks. Skip ahead a year and a half. Her father is out another two million and you and Rachel are lying about being with one another."

"We're not lying."

Lenny would not look at me.

"What about all I was saying," I tried, "about how no one would go through all this? I could have just taken the ransom money, right? I didn't have to hire that guy with the car and the kid. And what about my sister? Do they think I murdered her too?"

"Those pictures," Lenny said softly.

"I never knew about them."

He could barely look at me, but that didn't stop him from reverting to our youth. "Well, duh."

"No, I mean I don't know anything about them."

"You really haven't seen her except for that time at the supermarket?"

"Of course not. You know all this. I wouldn't hide it from you."

He weighed that statement for too long. "You might hide it from Lenny the Friend."

"No, I wouldn't. But even if I would, there's no way I could keep it from Lenny the Lawyer."

His voice was soft. "You didn't tell either one of us about this ransom drop."

So there it was. "We wanted to keep it contained, Lenny."

"I see." But he didn't. I couldn't blame him. "Another thing. How did you find that CD in the basement?"

"Dina Levinsky came by the house."

"Dina the fruitcake?"

"She's had it rough," I said. "You have no idea."

Lenny waved off my sympathy. "I don't understand. What was she doing at your house?" I filled him in on the story. Lenny started making a face. When I finished, I was the one who said, "What?"

"She told you she was better now? That she was married?"

"Yes."

"That's bull."

I stopped. "How do you know that?"

"I do some legal work for her aunt. Dina Levinsky has been in and out of asylums since she was eighteen. She even served time for aggravated assault a few years back. She's never been married. And I doubt she's ever had an art exhibit."

I did not know what to make of that. I remembered Dina's haunting face, the way the color ebbed away when she said, *"You know who shot you, don't you, Marc?"*

What the hell had she meant by that anyway?

"We need to think this through," Lenny said, rubbing his chin. "I'm going to check with some of my sources, see what I can learn. Call me if anything comes up, okay?"

"Yeah, okay."

"And promise me you won't say another word to them. There is an excellent chance they'll arrest you." He raised a hand before I could protest. "They have enough for an arrest and maybe even an indictment. True, the *t*'s aren't all crossed and the *i*'s aren't all dotted. But think about that Skakel case. They had less there and they convicted him. So if they come back in here, promise me you won't say a word."

I promised because, yet again, the authorities were on the wrong track. Cooperating with them would not help find my daughter. That was the bottom line. Lenny left me alone. I asked him to shut off the lights. He did. But the room did not grow dark. Hospital rooms never get totally dark.

I tried to understand what was happening. Tickner had taken those strange photographs with him. I wished he hadn't. I wanted to take another look because no matter how I laid it out, those pictures of

Rachel at the hospital made no sense. Were they for real? Trick photography was a strong possibility, especially in this digital day and age. Could that be the explanation? Were they phonies, a simple cut-and-paste job? My thoughts veered toward Dina Levinsky again. What had her bizarre visit really been about? Why had she asked if I loved Monica? Why did she think I knew who shot me? I was considering all of this when the door opened.

"Is this the room belonging to the Stud in Scrubs?"

It was Zia. "Hey."

She entered, gestured at my supine position with a sweep of her hand. "This supposed to be your excuse for missing work?"

"I was on call last night, wasn't I?"

"Yep."

"Sorry."

"They woke my ass up instead, interrupting, I might add, a rather erotic dream." Zia pointed with her thumb toward the door. "That big black man down the hall."

"The one with the sunglasses on top of a shaved head?"

"That's him. He a cop?"

"An FBI agent."

"Any chance you can introduce us? Might make up for interrupting my dream."

"I'll try to do that," I said, "before he arrests me."

"After is okay too."

I smiled. Zia sat on the edge of the bed. I told her what had happened. She didn't offer a theory. She didn't throw up a question. She just listened, and I loved her for it.

I was just getting to the part about being a serious suspect when my cell phone started ringing. Both of us, because of our training, were surprised. Cell phones in the hospital were a no-no. I reached it for quickly and brought it to my ear.

"Marc?"

It was Rachel. "Where are you?"

"Following the money."

"What?"

"They did exactly what I thought," she said. "They dumped the bag, but they haven't spotted the Q-Logger in the pack of bills. I'm heading up the Harlem River Drive right now. They're maybe a mile ahead of me."

"We need to talk," I said.

"Did you find Tara?"

"It was a hoax. I saw the kid they had with them. It wasn't my daughter."

There was a pause.

"Rachel?"

"I'm not doing so good, Marc."

"What do you mean?"

"I took a beating. At the park. I'm okay, but I need your help."

"Wait a second. My car is still at the scene. How are you following them?"

"Did you notice a Parks Department van on the circle?"

"Yes."

"I stole it. It's an old van, easy to hot-wire. I figured it wouldn't be missed until the morning."

"They think we did it, Rachel. That we were having an affair or something. They found photos on that CD. You in front of where I work."

Cell-phone-static silence.

"Rachel?"

"Where are you?" she asked.

"I'm at New York Presbyterian Hospital."

"Are you okay?"

"Banged up. But I'm fine, yeah."

"The cops there?"

"The feds too. A guy named Tickner. You know him?"

Her voice was soft. "Yes." Then, "How do you want to play it?"

"What do you mean?"

"Do you want me to keep following them? Or do you want to turn it over to Tickner and Regan?"

I wanted her back here. I wanted to ask her about those photos and the phone call to my house. "I'm not sure it matters," I said. "You were right from the beginning. It was a con job. They must have used someone else's hair."

More static.

"What?" I said.

"You know anything about DNA?" she asked me.

"Not much," I said.

"I don't have time to explain it, but a DNA test goes layer by layer. You start seeing things match up. It takes at least twenty-four hours before we can really say with any degree of certainty that there's a match."

"So?"

"So I just spoke to my lab guy. We've only had about eight hours. But so far, that second set of hairs that Edgar got?"

"What about them?"

"They match yours." I wasn't sure I heard correctly. Rachel made a sound that might have been a sigh. "In other words, he hasn't ruled out that you're the father. Just the opposite, in fact."

I nearly dropped the phone. Zia saw it and moved closer. Again I focused and compartmentalized. Process. Rebuild. I considered my options. Tickner and Regan would never believe me. They would not allow me to go. They'd probably arrest us. At the same time, if

I told them, I might be able to prove our innocence. On the other hand, proving my innocence was irrelevant.

Was there a chance my daughter was still alive?

That was the only question here. If she was, then I had to resort to our original plan. Confiding in the authorities, especially with their fresh suspicions, would not work. Suppose there was, as the ransom note said, a mole? Right now, whoever had picked up that bag of money had no idea that Rachel was on to them. But what would happen if the cops and feds got involved? Would the kidnappers run, panic, do something rash?

There was something else here that I should be considering: Did I still trust Rachel? Those photographs had shaken my faith. I didn't know what to believe anymore. But in the end, I had no choice but to treat those doubts as a distraction. I needed to focus on one goal. Tara. What would give me the best chance of finding out what really happened to her?

"How badly hurt are you?" I asked.

"We can do this, Marc."

"I'm on my way, then."

I hung up and looked at Zia.

"You have to help me get out of here."

Tickner and Regan sat in the doctors' lounge down the hall. A lounge seemed a strange name for this threadbare dwelling with too much light and a rabbit-ear TV set. There was a minifridge in the corner. Tickner had opened it. There were two brown-bag lunches in it, both with names written on them. It reminded him of elementary school.

Tickner collapsed on a couch with absolutely no springs. "I think we should arrest him now."

Regan said nothing.

"You were awfully quiet in there, Bob. Something on your mind?"

Regan started scratching the soul patch. "What Seidman said."

"What about it?"

"Don't you think he had a point?"

"You mean that stuff about him being innocent?"

"Yes."

"No, not really. You buy it?"

"I don't know," Regan said. "I mean, why would he go through all this with the money? He couldn't have known we'd learn about that CD and decide to track him with E-ZPass and find him at Fort Tryon Park. And even if he had, why go through all that? Why jump on a moving car? Christ, he's lucky he wasn't killed. Again. Which brings us back to the original shooting and our original problem. If he and Rachel Mills did this together, why was he nearly killed?" Regan shook his head. "There are too many holes."

"Which we are filling in one by one," Tickner said.

Regan made a yes-no with a head tilt.   ·

"Look at how many we plugged today by learning about Rachel Mills's involvement," Tickner said. "We just need to get her in here and sweat them both."

Regan looked off again.

Tickner shook his head. "What now?"

"The broken window."

"The one at the crime scene?"

"Yeah."

"What about it?"

Regan sat up. "Play along with me, okay? Let's go back to the original murder-kidnapping."

"At the Seidman house?"

"Right."

"Okay, go."

"The window was broken from the outside," Regan said. "That could be how the perp gained entry to the house."

"Or," Tickner added, "Dr. Seidman broke the window to throw us off."

"Or he had an accomplice do it."

"Right."

"But either way, Dr. Seidman would have been in on the broken window, right? If he was involved, I mean."

"Where are you going with this?"

"Just stay with me, Lloyd. We think Seidman was involved. Ergo, Seidman knew that the window had been broken to make it look like, I don't know, a random break-in. Agreed?"

"I guess."

Regan smiled. "Then how come he never mentioned the broken window?"

"What?"

"Read his statement. He remembers eating a granola bar and then—bam—nothing. No sound. No one sneaking up on him. Nothing." Regan spread his hands. "Why doesn't he remember hearing the window break?"

"Because he broke it himself to make it look like an intruder."

"But see, if that's the case, he would have kept the broken window in his story. Think about it. He breaks the window to convince us the perp broke in and shot him. So what would you say if you were him?"

Now Tickner saw where he was heading. "I'd say, 'I heard the window break, I turned, and bam, the bullets hit me.' "

"Exactly. But Seidman did none of that. Why?"

Tickner shrugged. "Maybe he forgot. He was seriously injured."

"Or maybe—just stay with me—maybe he's telling the truth."

The door opened. An exhausted-looking kid in scrubs looked in. He saw the two cops, rolled his eyes, left them alone. Tickner turned back toward Regan. "But wait a second, you've caught yourself in a Catch-22."

"How so?"

"If Seidman didn't do it—if it really was a perp who broke the window—why didn't Seidman hear it?"

"Maybe he doesn't remember. We've seen this a million times. A guy getting shot and hurt that seriously loses some time." Regan smiled, warming up to this theory. "Especially if he saw something that totally shocked him—something he wouldn't want to remember."

"Like his wife being stripped down and killed?"

"Like that," Regan said. "Or maybe something worse."

"What's worse?"

A beeping sound came from the corridor. They could hear the nearby nurse's station. Someone was bitching about a shift time or schedule change.

"We said we're missing something," Regan said slowly. "We've been saying that from the beginning. But maybe it's just the opposite. We've been *adding* something."

Tickner frowned.

"We keep adding Dr. Seidman. Look, we both know the score. In cases like this, the husband is always involved. Not nine times out of ten—ninety-nine times out of a hundred. Every scenario we've devised includes Seidman."

Tickner said, "And you think that's wrong?"

"Listen to me a second. We've had Seidman in our sights from the get-go. His marriage was not idyllic. He got married because his wife was pregnant. We seized on all that. But if their marriage had been friggin' *Ozzie and Harriet*, we'd still say, 'Nah, no one is that happy,' and leap on that. So whatever we've stumbled across, we've tried to fit it into that reality: Seidman had to be involved. So for just a second, let's take him out of the equation. Let's pretend he's innocent."

Tickner shrugged. "Okay, so?"

"Seidman talked about a connection with Rachel Mills. One that's lasted all these years."

"Right."

"He sounded a little obsessed with her."

"A little?"

Regan smiled. "Suppose the feeling was mutual. Check that. Suppose it was more than mutual."

"Okay."

"Now remember. We're assuming Seidman didn't do it. That means he's telling us the truth. About everything. About when he last saw Rachel Mills. About those photographs. You saw his face, Lloyd. Seidman isn't that great an actor. Those pictures shocked him. He didn't know about them."

Tickner frowned. "Hard to say."

"Well, there was something else I noticed about those pictures."

"What?"

"How come that private eye didn't get any pictures of the two of them together? We have her outside the hospital. We have him coming out. We have her going out. But none of them together."

"They were careful."

"How careful? She was hanging outside his place of work. If you're being careful, you don't do that."

"So what's your theory?"

Regan smiled. "Think about it. Rachel had to know Seidman was inside the building. But did he have to know she was outside?"

"Wait a second," Tickner said. A smile started coming to his face. "You think she was stalking him?"

"Maybe."

Tickner nodded. "And—whoa—we're not talking about just any woman here. We're talking about a well-trained federal agent."

"So, one, she would know how to run a professional kidnapping operation," Regan added, raising a finger. He raised another. "Two, she would know how to kill someone and get away with it. Three, she would know how to cover her tracks. Four, she would know Marc's sister, Stacy. Five"—the thumb now—"she'd be able to use her old contacts to find and set the sister up."

"Holy Christ." Tickner looked up. "And what you said before. About seeing something so horrible Seidman doesn't remember."

"How about seeing the love of your life shooting you? Or your wife. Or . . ."

They both stopped.

"Tara," Tickner said. "How does the little girl fit into all this?"

"A way of extorting money?"

Neither one of them liked that. But whatever other answers they came up with, they liked those even less.

"We can add something else," Tickner said.

"What?"

"Seidman's missing thirty-eight."

"What about it?"

"His gun was in a lockbox in his closet," Tickner said. "Only someone close to him would know where it was hidden."

"Or," Regan added, seeing something else now, "maybe Rachel Mills brought her own thirty-eight. Remember that two were used."

"But that raises another question: Why would she need two guns?"

Both men frowned, ran a few new theories through their heads, and came up with a solid conclusion. "We're still missing something," Regan said.

"Yep."

"We need to go back and get some answers."

"Like?"

"Like why did Rachel skate on the murder of her first husband?"

"I can ask around," Tickner said.

"Do that. And let's get a man on Seidman. She has four million dollars now. She might want to eliminate the only guy who can still tie her to this."

chapter 31

Zia found my clothes in the closet. Bloodstains darkened my jeans, so we decided to go with surgical scrubs. She ran down the hall and found me a pair. Wincing from the cracked ribs, I slipped them on and tied the string waist. It would be a slow go. Zia checked to see if the coast was clear. She had a backup plan in case the feds were still watching. Her friend, Dr. David Beck, had been involved in a major federal case a few years ago. He knew Tickner from that. Beck was on call. If it came to it, he was waiting at the end of the hall and would try to slow them down with some sort of reminiscence.

In the end, we didn't need Beck. We simply walked out. No one questioned us. We made our way through the Harkness Pavilion and out into the courtyard north of Fort Washington Avenue. Zia's car was parked in the lot on 165th and Fort Washington. I moved gingerly. I felt sore as hell, but basically all right. Marathon running and heavy lifting would be out, but the pain was controllable and I had full range of motion. Zia had slipped me a bottle of Vioxx, the fifty-milligram big boys. They'd be good because they worked without making you drowsy.

"If anyone asks," she said, "I'll tell them I took public

transportation and that my car is home. You should be okay for a while."

"Thanks," I said. "Actually, can I also trade cell phones?"

"Sure, why?"

"They might try, I don't know, to track me down using mine."

"They can do that?"

"Beats the hell out of me."

She shrugged and dug out her cell. It was a tiny thing, the size of a compact mirror. "You really think Tara is alive?"

"I don't know."

We hurried up the parking garage's cement steps. The stairwell stank, as always, of urine.

"This is insane," she said. "You know that, right?"

"Yeah."

"I got my pager. You need me, you page me."

"I will."

We stopped at the car. Zia handed me the keys.

"What?" I said to her.

"You got a pretty big ego, Marc."

"This your idea of a pep talk?"

"Just don't let it get you hurt or anything," Zia said. "I need you."

I hugged her and slipped into the driver's seat. I started north on the Henry Hudson, dialing Rachel's number. The night was clear and still. The lights from the bridge made the dark water look like a star-filled sky. I heard two rings and then Rachel picked up. She didn't say anything and then I realized why. She probably had Caller ID and didn't recognize the number.

"It's me," I said. "I'm using Zia's phone."

Rachel asked, "Where are you?"

"About to get on the Hudson."

"Keep going north to the Tappan Zee. Cross it and start heading west."

"Where are you now?"

"By that huge Palisades Mall."

"In Nyack," I said.

"Right. Keep in phone touch. We'll find a place to hook up."

"I'm on my way."

Tickner was on his mobile phone, filling in O'Malley. Regan hurried back into the lounge. "Seidman's not in his room."

Tickner looked annoyed. "What do you mean, he's not in his room?"

"How many different ways are there to interpret that, Lloyd?"

"Did he go down to X ray or something?"

"Not according to the nurse," Regan said.

"Damn. The hospital has security cameras, right?"

"Not on every room."

"But they have to cover the exits."

"They must have a dozen exits here. By the time we get the tapes and review them—"

"Yeah, yeah, yeah." Tickner thought about it. He put the phone back to his ear. "O'Malley?"

"I'm here."

"You heard?"

"Yup."

"How long will it take you to get phone logs from both Seidman's hospital room and cell phone?" Tickner asked.

"Immediate calls?"

"It would have to have been in the past fifteen minutes, yeah."

"Give me five."

Tickner pressed the END button. "Where's Seidman's lawyer?"

"I don't know. I think he said he was leaving."

"Maybe we should give him a ring."

"He didn't hit me as the helpful type," Regan said.

"That was before, when we thought his client was a wife-and-baby killer. We're now theorizing that an innocent man's life is in danger." Tickner handed Regan the business card Lenny had given him.

"Worth a shot," Regan said, and began dialing.

I caught up with Rachel just over the north New Jersey–south New York border town of Ramsey. Using our phones we managed to hook up in the parking lot of the Fair Motel on Route 17 in Ramsey, New Jersey. The motel was a no-tell, complete with a sign proudly reading COLOR TV! (as if most motels were still using black and white) where all the letters (and the exclamation point) are a different color, in case you don't know what the word *color* means. I always liked the name. The Fair Motel. We're not great, we're not terrible. We're, well, Fair. Honesty in advertising.

I pulled into the lot. I was scared. I had a million questions for Rachel, but in the end, it all boiled down to different variations of the same thing. I wanted to know about her husband's death, sure, but more than that, I wanted to know about those damn private-eye pictures.

The lot was dark, most of the light coming off the highway. The stolen Parks Department van sat by a Pepsi machine on the far right side. I pulled next to it. I never saw Rachel leave the van, but the next thing I knew she had slid into the passenger seat next to me.

"Start moving," she said.

I turned to confront her, but her face made me pull up short. "Jesus, are you all right?"

"I'm fine."

Her right eye was swollen over like that of a boxer who had gone the distance. There were yellow-purple bruises around her neck. Her face had a giant red mark across both cheeks. I could see scarlet indentations from where her attacker had dug in his fingers. The finger-nails had even broken the skin. I wondered if there was deeper trauma to her face, if whatever blow she took to the eye had been powerful enough to break a bone. I doubted it. A break like that would normally knock someone out of commission. Then again, best-case scenario and these were only surface wounds: It was amazing she was still upright.

"What the hell happened?" I asked.

She had her Palm Pilot out. The screen was dazzlingly bright in the dark of the car. She looked down at it and said, "Take Seventeen south. Hurry, I don't want to get too far behind."

I put the car in reverse, backed up, started down the highway. I reached into my pocket and pulled out the bottle of Vioxx. "These should help deaden the pain."

She pulled off the top. "How many should I take?"

"One."

Her index finger scooped it out. Her eyes never left the Palm Pilot's screen. She swallowed it down and said thanks.

"Tell me what happened," I said.

"You first."

I filled her in as best I could. We stayed on Route 17. We passed the Allendale and Ridgewood exits. The streets were empty. The shops—and, man, there were lots of them, the entire highway pretty much one con-tinuous strip mall—were all closed up. Rachel listened without interrupting. I glanced at her as I drove. She looked in pain.

When I finished, she asked, "Are you sure it wasn't Tara in the car?"

"Yes."

"I called my DNA guy again. The layers are still matching up. I don't get that."

Neither did I. "What happened to you?"

"Somebody jumped me. I was watching you through the night-vision goggles. I saw you put down the money bag and start walking. There was a woman in the bushes. Did you see her?"

"No."

"She had a gun. I think she planned on killing you."

"A woman?"

"Yes."

I wasn't sure how to react to that. "Did you get a good look at her?"

"No. I was about to call out a warning when this monster grabbed me from behind. Strong as hell. He lifted me off my feet by my head. I thought he was going to rip my skull off."

"Jesus."

"Anyway, a cop car drove by. The big guy panicked. He punched me here"—she pointed to the swollen eye—"and it was lights-out. I don't know how long I was lying on the pavement. When I woke up, the cops were all over the place. I was huddled in a corner in the dark. I guess they didn't see me or figured I was a homeless guy sleeping one off. Anyway, I checked the Palm Pilot. I saw the money was on the move."

"Which direction?"

"South, walking near 168th Street. Then suddenly they went still. See, this thing"—she gestured to the screen—"works two ways. I zoom in, I can get as close as a quarter mile. I go out a little farther, like right now, I get more an idea than an exact address. Right now, based on the speed, I figure they're driving about six miles ahead of us still on Route Seventeen."

"But when you first spotted them, they were on 168th Street?"

"Right. Then they start heading downtown fast."

I thought about it. "The subway," I said. "They took the A train from the 168th Street stop."

"That's what I figured. Anyway, I stole the van. I started downtown. I was near the seventies when all of a sudden they started going east. This time it was more stop and go."

"They were stopping for lights. They had a car now."

Rachel nodded. "They sped up on the FDR and Harlem River Drive. I tried to cut across town, but that took too long. I fell behind by five, six miles. Anyway, you know the rest."

We slowed for night construction near the Route 4 interchange. Three lanes became one. I looked at her, at the bruises and the swelling, at the giant handprint on her skin. She looked back at me and didn't say a word. My fingers reached out and caressed her face as gently as I knew how. She closed her eyes, the tenderness seemingly too much, and even in the midst of all this we both knew that it felt right. A stirring, an old one, a dormant one, started deep inside of me. I kept my eyes on that lovely, perfect face. I pushed back her hair. A tear escaped her eye and ran down her cheek. She put her hand on my wrist. I felt the warmth start there and spread.

Part of me—and, yes, I know how this will sound—wanted to forget this quest. The kidnapping had been a hoax. My daughter was gone. My wife was dead. Someone was trying to kill me. It was time to start again, a new chance, a way, this time, to get it right. I wanted to turn the car around and start heading in the other di-

rection. I wanted to drive—keep driving—and never
ask about her dead husband and those pictures on the
CD. I could forget all that. I knew I could. My life was
filled with surgical procedures that altered the surface,
that helped people begin anew, that improved what was
visible and thus what was not. That could be what would
happen here. A simple face-lift. I would make my first
incision the day before that damn frat party, pull the
fourteen-year-old folds across time, close the suture at
now. Stick the two moments together. Nip and tuck.
Make those fourteen years disappear, as though they'd
never happened.

Rachel opened her eyes now and I could see that she
was thinking pretty much the same thing, hoping I'd call
it off and turn around. But of course, that could not be.
We blinked. The construction cleared. Her hand left my
forearm. I risked another glance at Rachel. No, we were
not twenty-one years old anymore, but that didn't matter. I saw that now. I still loved her. Irrational, wrong, stupid, naïve, whatever. I still loved her. Over the years, I
might have convinced myself otherwise, but I had never
stopped. She was still so damn beautiful, so damn perfect, and when I thought of how close she'd just come to
death, those giant hands smothering away her breath,
those niggling doubts began to soften. They wouldn't go
away. Not until I knew the truth. But no matter what the
answers were, they would not consume me.

"Rachel?"

But she suddenly sat up, her eyes back on the Palm
Pilot.

"What is it?" I asked.

"They've stopped," Rachel said. "We'll be on them in
two miles."

chapter 32

Steven Bacard replaced the phone's receiver.

You slip-slide into evil, he thought. You cross the line for just one moment. You cross back. You feel safe. You change things, you believe, for the better. The line is still there. It's still intact. Okay, maybe there's a smudge there now, but you can still see it clearly. And next time you cross, maybe that line smudges a little more. But you have your bearings. No matter what happens to that line, you remember where it is.

Don't you?

There was a mirror above the fully stocked bar in Steven Bacard's office. His interior decorator had insisted that all people of prestige had to have a place to toast their successes. So he had one. He didn't even drink. Steven Bacard stared at his reflection and thought, not for the first time in his life: Average. He had always been average. His grades in school, his SAT and LSAT scores, his law-school ranking, his bar score (he passed it on the third attempt). If life were a game where children choose sides for kickball, he'd be picked in the middle of the pack, after the good athletes and before the really bad ones—in that cusp for those who leave no mark.

Bacard became a lawyer because he believed that

being a JD would give him a level of prestige. It didn't.
No one hired him. He opened up his own pitiful office
near the Paterson courthouse, sharing space with a bail
bondsman. He ambulance-chased, but even as a member of this small-time pack, he couldn't distinguish himself. He managed to marry a woman slightly above his
station, though she reminded him of that as often as she
could.

Where Bacard had indeed been below average—*way*
below average—was in sperm count. Try as he might—
and Dawn, his wife, didn't really like him to try—he
could not impregnate his wife. After four years, they
tried to adopt. Again, Steven Bacard fit into the abyss of
the great unspectacular, which made finding a white
baby—something Dawn truly craved—nearly impossible. He and Dawn traveled to Romania, but the only
children available were too old or born drug addled.

But it was there, overseas in that god-deserted place,
that Steven Bacard finally came up with an idea that,
after thirty-eight years, made him rise above the crowd.

"Problem, Steven?"

The voice startled him. He turned away from his reflection. Lydia stood in the shadows.

"Staring in the mirror like that," Lydia said, adding a
tsk-tsk at the end. "Wasn't that Narcissus's downfall?"

Bacard could not help it. He began to tremble. It
wasn't just Lydia, though, in truth, she often had that effect on him. The phone call had set him on edge. Lydia
popping up like that—that was the clincher. He had no
idea how she'd gotten in or how long she'd been standing there. He wanted to ask what had happened tonight.
He wanted details. But there was no time.

"We do indeed have a problem," Bacard said.

"Tell me."

Her eyes chilled him. They were big and luminous

and beautiful and yet you sensed nothing behind them, only a cold chasm, windows to a house long abandoned.

What Bacard had discovered while in Romania—what had finally helped him rise above the pack—was a way to beat the system. Suddenly, for the first time in his life, Bacard was on a roll. He stopped chasing ambulances. People started looking up to him. He was invited to fund-raisers. He became a sought-after speaker. His wife, Dawn, started to smile at him again and ask him about his day. He even appeared on News 12 New Jersey when the cable station needed a certain kind of legal expert. He stopped, however, when a colleague overseas reminded him of the danger of too much publicity. Besides, he no longer needed to attract clients. They found him, these parents searching for a miracle. The desperate have always done that, like plants stretching through the dark for any sliver of sunlight. And he, Steven Bacard, was that sunlight.

He pointed to the phone. "I just got a call."

"And?"

"The ransom money is bugged," he said.

"We switched bags."

"Not just the bags. There's some kind of device in the money. Between the bills or something."

Lydia's face clouded over. "Your source didn't know about this before?"

"My source didn't know about any of it until just now."

"So what you're telling me," she said slowly, "is that while we stand here the police know exactly where we are?"

"Not the police," he said. "The bug wasn't planted by the cops or the feds."

That seemed to surprise her. Then Lydia nodded. "Dr. Seidman."

"Not exactly. He has a woman named Rachel Mills helping him. She used to be a fed."

Lydia smiled as if this explained something. "And this Rachel Mills—this ex-fed—she's the one who bugged the money?"

"Yes."

"Is she following us right now?"

"No one knows where she is," Bacard said. "No one knows where Seidman is either."

"Hmm," she said.

"The police think this Rachel woman is involved."

Lydia lifted her chin. "Involved in the original kidnapping?"

"And the murder of Monica Seidman."

Lydia liked that. She smiled and Bacard felt a fresh shiver slink down his back. "Was she, Steven?"

He teetered. "I wouldn't know."

"Ignorance is bliss, that it?"

Bacard chose to say nothing.

Lydia said, "Do you have the gun?"

He stiffened. "What?"

"Seidman's gun. Do you have it?"

Bacard did not like this. He felt as if he were sinking. He considered lying, but then he saw those eyes. "Yes."

"Get it," she said. "How about Pavel? Have you heard from him?"

"He's not happy with any of this. He wants to know what's going on."

"We'll call him in the car."

"We?"

"Yes. Now let's hurry, Steven."

"I'm coming with you?"

"Indeed."

"What are you going to do?"

Lydia put her fingers to her lips. "Shh," she said. "I have a plan."

Rachel said, "They're on the move again."

"How long did they stop?" I asked

"Maybe five minutes. They could have met up with someone and transferred the money. Or maybe they were just getting gas. Turn right here."

We pulled up on Centuro Road off Route 3. Giants Stadium loomed in the distance. About a mile up, Rachel pointed out the window. "They were somewhere over there."

The sign read METROVISTA and the parking lot appeared to be a never-ending expanse, disappearing in the distant marsh. MetroVista was a classic New Jersey office complex, built during the great expanse of the eighties. Hundreds of offices, all cold and impersonal, sleek and robotic, with too many tinted windows not letting in enough sunlight. The vapor lights buzzed and you could imagine, if not actually hear, the drone of worker bees.

"They weren't stopping for gas," Rachel muttered.

"So what do we do?"

"Only thing we can," she said. "Let's keep following the money."

Heshy and Lydia headed west toward the Garden State Parkway. Steven Bacard followed in the car behind them. Lydia ripped open the wads of bills. It took her ten minutes to find the tracking device. She dug it out from the money crevice.

She held it up, so Heshy could see it. "Clever," she said.

"Or we're slipping."

"We've never been perfect, Pooh Bear."

Heshy did not reply. Lydia opened the car window. She stuck her hand out and signaled for Bacard to follow them. He waved back that he understood. When they slowed for the toll, Lydia quickly pecked Heshy's cheek and got out of the car. She took the money with her. Heshy was now left alone with just the tracking device. If this Rachel woman still had any juice or if the police got wind of what was happening, they would pull Heshy over. He would toss the tracking device into the street. They would find the device, sure, but they wouldn't be able to prove it had come from his car. And even if they could, so what? They would search Heshy and his car and find nothing. No kid, no ransom note, no ransom money. He was clean.

Lydia hurried over to Steven Bacard's car and slipped into the passenger's side. "You got Pavel on the line?" she asked.

"Yes."

She took the phone. Pavel started screaming in whatever the hell language was native to him. She waited and then told him the meeting place. When Bacard heard the address, his head snapped toward her. She smiled. Pavel, of course, didn't understand the significance of the location, but then again, why should he? He ranted a little more, but eventually Pavel calmed enough to say he'd be there. She hung up the phone.

"You can't be serious," Bacard said to her.

"Shh."

Her plan was simple enough. Lydia and Bacard would race ahead to the meeting spot while Heshy, who had the tracker on him, would stall. When Lydia was set up and fully prepared, she would call Heshy on the cell phone. Then and only then would Heshy go to the meeting spot. He would have the tracking device with him. The woman, this Rachel Mills, would hopefully follow.

She and Bacard arrived in twenty minutes. Lydia spotted a car parked up the block. Pavel's, she figured. A stolen Toyota Celica. Lydia didn't like that. Strange cars parked on streets like these were noticed. She glanced over at Steven Bacard. His face was moon pale. It almost seemed detached, floating. The scent of fear came off him in waves. His fingers gripped the wheel, tense. Bacard didn't have the stomach for this. That would be a liability.

"You can just drop me off," she said.

"I want to know," he began, "what you plan on doing here."

She just looked at him.

"My God."

"Spare me the indignant act."

"No one was supposed to be hurt."

"You mean like Monica Seidman?"

"We had nothing to do with that."

Lydia shook her head. "And the sister, what was her name, Stacy Seidman?"

Bacard opened his mouth as though he might counter. Then he lowered his head. She knew what he had planned on saying. Stacy Seidman had been a drug addict. She was expendable, a waste, a danger, heading for death, whatever justification floated his boat. Men like Bacard needed justification. In his mind, he wasn't selling babies. He really believed that he was helping. And if he made money—lots of money—from it and broke the law, well, he was taking tremendous risks to better lives. Shouldn't he be well compensated?

But Lydia had no interest in digging into his psyche nor comforting it. She had counted the money in the car. He had hired her. Her take was a million dollars. Bacard got the other million. She shouldered the duffel bag with her—and Heshy's—money. She stepped out of the car. Steven Bacard stared straight ahead. He did not refuse the money. He did not call her back and say that he wanted to wash his hands of this. There was a million dollars sitting in the seat next to him. Bacard wanted it. His family had a big house in Alpine now. His kids went to private school. So no, Bacard did not back off. He simply stared ahead and put the car in drive.

When he was gone, Lydia called Pavel with the two-way radio portion of the cell phone. Pavel was hiding behind some shrubs up the block. He still wore the flannel shirt. His walk was a labored lumber. His teeth had suffered under a lifetime of cigarettes and ill care. He had a squashed-from-too-many-fights nose. He was Balkan rough trade. He had seen a lot in his life. Didn't matter, though. When you don't know what's happening, you are in over your head.

"You," he said, spitting the word. "You no tell me."

Pavel was right. She no tell him. In other words, he'd known nothing. His English was beyond broken, which was why he had been the perfect front man for this crime. He'd come over from Kosovo two years ago with a pregnant woman. During the first ransom drop, Pavel had been given specific instructions. He'd been told to wait for a certain car to pull into the lot, to approach the car without speaking to the man, to take a bag from him, to get into the van. Oh, and to confuse matters a little more, they told Pavel to keep a phone in front of his mouth and pretend to talk into it.

That was it.

Pavel had no idea who Marc Seidman was. He had no idea about what was in the bag, about a kidnapping, about a ransom, nothing. He didn't wear his gloves—his fingerprints were not on file in the United States—and he didn't carry ID.

They paid him two thousand dollars and sent him

back to Kosovo. Based on Seidman's rather specific description, the police circulated a sketch of a man who, for all practical purposes, was impossible to find. When they decided to rerun the ransom drop, Pavel was the natural go-to guy. He would dress the same, look the same, play with Seidman's head in case he decided to fight back this time.

Still, Pavel was a realist. He would adapt. He had spent time selling women in Kosovo. White slavery in the guise of strip clubs was a big market over there, though Bacard had come up with another way of using those women. Pavel, no stranger to sudden change, would do what needed to be done. He gave Lydia some attitude, but once she handed him a wad of bills adding up to five thousand dollars, he grew quiet. The fight was out of him. It was only a question of how.

She handed Pavel a gun. He knew how to use it.

Pavel set up near the driveway, keeping his two-way radio channel open. Lydia called Heshy and told them they were ready. Fifteen minutes later, Heshy drove past them. He tossed the tracking device out the car window. Lydia caught it and threw back a kiss. Heshy kept driving. Lydia brought the tracking device into the backyard. She took out her gun and waited.

The night air was starting to give way to the morning dew. That tingle was there, lighting up her veins. Heshy, she knew, was not far away. He wanted to join in, but this was her game. The street was silent. It was 4:00 A.M.

Five minutes later, she heard the car pull up.

chapter 33

Something was very wrong here.

The roads were becoming so familiar I barely noticed them. I was wired, jazzed, the pain in my ribs barely noticeable. Rachel was absorbed in her Palm Pilot. She'd click screens with her little wand, tilt her head, change viewing angles. She dug through the backseat and found Zia's road atlas. With the cap of the Flair pen in her mouth, Rachel started marking up the route, trying to discern a pattern, I guess. Or maybe she was just stalling, so I wouldn't ask the inevitable.

I called her name softly. She flicked her eyes at me and then back to the screen.

"Did you know about that CD-ROM before you got here?" I said.

"No."

"There were photos of you in front of the hospital where I work."

"So you told me."

She clicked the screen again.

"Are the photos real?" I asked.

"Real?"

"I mean, were they digitally altered or something—or were you really in front of my office two years ago?"

Rachel kept her head down, but out of the corner of

my eye, I could see her shoulders slump. "Make a right," she said. "Up here."

We were on Glen Avenue now. This was getting creepy. My old high school was up on the left. They'd refurbished it four years ago, adding a weight room, a swimming pool, and a second gymnasium. The facade had been intentionally scuffed up and aged with ivy, giving the place a proper collegiate feel, reminding the youth of Kasselton what was expected of them.

"Rachel?"

"The pictures are real, Marc."

I nodded to myself. I don't know why. Maybe I was trying to buy myself some time. I was heading into something worse than unchartered waters here. I knew that the answers would alter everything again, make it all go topsy-turvy, just when I hoped to set the world right. "I think I'm owed an explanation," I said.

"You are." She kept her head down on the screen. "But not right now."

"Yeah, right now."

"We need to concentrate on what we're doing."

"Don't hand me that crap. We're just driving here. I can handle two things at the same time."

"Maybe," she said softly, "I can't."

"Rachel, what were you doing in front of that hospital?"

"Whoa."

"Whoa what?"

We were approaching the traffic lights at Kasselton Avenue. Because of the hour, they were blinking yellow and red. I frowned and turned to her. "Which way?"

"Right."

My heart iced. "I don't understand."

"The car has stopped again."

"Where?"

"Unless I'm reading this wrong," Rachel said, and finally she looked up and met my gaze, "they're at your house."

I made the right turn. Rachel no longer needed to direct me. She kept her eyes on the screen. We were less than a mile away now. My parents had taken this route to the hospital on the day I was born. I wondered how many times I'd been on this road since. Weird thought, but the mind goes where it must.

I made the right on Monroe. My parents' house was on the left. The lights were off except, of course, for the lamp downstairs. We had it on a timer. It stayed on from 7:00 P.M. to 5:00 A.M. every day. I'd put in one of those long-life, energy-saving lightbulbs that look like soft-ice-cream swirls. Mom bragged about how long it lasted. She'd read somewhere that keeping a radio on was also a good way to scare away burglars, so she had an old AM radio constantly tuned into a talk station. The problem was, the sound of the radio kept her up at night, so now Mom put the volume so low that a burglar would have to press his ear against it to be warded off.

I started making the turn onto my road, onto Darby Terrace, when Rachel said, "Slow down."

"They moving?"

"No. The signal is still coming from your house."

I looked up the block. I started thinking about it. "They didn't exactly take a direct route here."

She nodded. "I know."

"Maybe they found your Q-Logger," I said.

"That's exactly what I was thinking."

The car inched forward. We were in front of the Citrons' house now, two away from mine. No lights were on—not even a timer lamp. Rachel chewed on her lower lip. We were at the Kadisons' house now, nearing my driveway. It was one of those situations people describe as "too quiet," as if the world had frozen, as if all you saw, even animate objects, was trying to stay still.

"This has to be a setup," she said.

I was just about to ask her what we should do—pull back, park and walk, call the cops for help?—when the first bullet shattered the front windshield. Shards of glass smacked my face. I heard a short scream. Without conscious thought, I ducked my head and raised my forearm. I looked down and saw blood.

"Rachel!"

The second shot zinged so close to my head that I felt it in my hair. The impact hit my seat with a sound like a pillowy wallop. Instincts took over again. But this time it had a mission, a direction of sorts. I hit the accelerator. The car lurched forward.

The human brain is an amazing instrument. No computer can duplicate it. It can process millions of stimuli in hundredths of a second. That was, I guess, what was going on now. I was hunched over in the driver's seat. Someone was taking shots at me. The base part of my brain wanted to flee, but something farther along the evolutionary path realized that there might be a better way.

The thought process took—and this is just a rough estimate—less than a tenth of a second. I had my foot on the accelerator. The tires shrieked. I thought about my house, the familiar setup of it, the direction the bullets had come from. Yes, I know how that sounds. Maybe panic speeds up those brain functions. I don't know, but I realized that if I were the one doing the shooting, if I had been lying in wait for this car to approach, I'd have hidden behind the three shrubs that divide my property from the Christies' next door. The shrubs were big and bushy and right on our driveway.

If I had pulled all the way in, bam, you could have blown us away from the passenger side. When I hesitated, when the shooter had seen that we might back away, he was still in position, though not as good, to take us from the front.

So I looked up, turned the wheel, and aimed the car for those bushes.

A third bullet rang out. It hit something metal, probably the front grille, with a *ka-ping*. I sneaked a glance at Rachel long enough to take a visual snapshot: her head was down, her hand pressed against the side of her head, blood seeping through the fingers. My stomach fell, but my foot stayed on the pedal. I moved my head back and forth, as if that might throw off the shooter's aim.

My headlights illuminated the bushes.

I saw flannel.

Something happened to me. I talked before about sanity being a thin string and that mine had snapped. In that case, I went quiet. This time, a mix of rage and dread roared through my body. I pressed the pedal harder, almost through the floor. I heard a yell of surprise. The man in the flannel shirt tried to leap to the right.

But I was ready.

I turned the steering wheel toward him like we were playing bumper cars. There was a crash, a dull thud. I heard a scream. The bushes were caught up in the bumper. I looked for the man in the flannel. Nothing. I had my hand on the door handle, about to open it and go after him, when Rachel said, "No!"

I stopped. She was alive!

Her hand reached up and shifted the car into reverse. "Go back!"

I listened. I don't know what I'd been thinking. The

man was armed. I wasn't. Despite the impact, I didn't know if he was dead or injured or what.

I started back. I noticed that my dark suburban street was lit up now. Shots and shrieking tires are not common noises here on Darby Terrace. People had woken up and turned on the lights. They'd be dialing 911.

Rachel sat up. Relief flooded me. She had a gun in one hand. The other was still over her wound. "It's my ear," she said, and again, the mind working in funny ways, I had already started thinking about what procedure I would use to repair the damage.

"There!" she shouted.

I turned. The man in the flannel was hobbling down the driveway. I turned the wheel and aimed the car lights in his direction. He disappeared around back. I looked over at Rachel.

"Back up," she said. "I'm not sure he's alone."

I did. "Now what?"

Rachel had her gun out, her free hand on the door handle. "You stay."

"Are you out of your mind?"

"You keep revving the engine and moving a little. Let them think we're still in the car. I'll sneak up on them."

Before I could protest any further, she rolled out. With blood still flowing down her side, she darted away. I, per her instructions, revving the engine and feeling like a total dweeb, shifted the car into drive, moved forward, shifted the car into reverse, went back.

A few seconds later, I lost sight of Rachel.

A few seconds after that, I heard two more shots.

Lydia had watched it all from her spot in the backyard.

Pavel had shot too early. It was a mistake on his part. From her vantage point behind a wall of firewood,

Lydia could not see who was in the car. But she'd been impressed. The driver had not only flushed Pavel out but wounded him as well.

Pavel limped into view. Lydia's eyes adjusted enough to see the blood on his face. She raised her arm and waved him toward her. Pavel fell and then started crawling. Lydia kept her eyes on the routes to the backyard. They would have to come from the front. There was a fence behind her. She was near the back neighbor's gate in case she needed to escape.

Pavel kept crawling. Lydia urged him on while keeping watch. She wondered how this ex-fed would play it. The neighbors were awake now. Lights were going on. The cops would be on their way.

Lydia would have to hurry.

Pavel made it to the pile of firewood and rolled next to her. For a moment, he stayed on his back. His breathing was wheezy and wet. Then he forced himself up. He kneeled next to Lydia and looked out into the yard. He winced and said, "Leg broken."

"We'll take care of it," she said. "Where's your gun?"

"Dropped."

Untraceable, she thought. Not a problem. "I have another weapon you can use," she told him. "Keep a lookout."

Pavel nodded. He squinted into the dark.

"What?" Lydia said. She moved a little closer to him.

"Not sure."

As Pavel stared out, Lydia pressed the barrel of her gun against the hollow spot behind his left ear. She squeezed the trigger, firing two shots into his head. Pavel dropped to the ground like a marionette with his strings cut.

Lydia looked down at him. In the end, this might be best. Plan B was probably better than Plan A anyway.

Had Pavel killed the woman—an ex-FBI agent—that would not have ended it. They'd probably search even harder for the mysterious man in flannel. The investigation would have continued. There wouldn't be closure. This way, with Pavel dead—dead by the gun used at the original Seidman crime scene—the police would conclude that either Seidman or this Rachel (or both) was behind it. They'd be arrested. The charges might not stick, but no matter. The police would stop looking for anyone else. They could disappear with the money now.

Case closed.

Lydia suddenly heard the shriek of tire wheels. She tossed the weapon into the neighbor's yard. She didn't want it in plain sight. That would be too obvious. She quickly checked Pavel's pockets. There was money, of course, the wad of bills she'd just given him. She'd let him keep that. One more thing to tie it all up nice and neat.

There was nothing else in his pockets—no wallet, no slip of paper, no identification or anything that could trace back to anything. Pavel had been good about that. More lights in windows now. Not much time. Lydia rose.

"Federal agent! Drop your weapon!"

Damn! A woman's voice. Lydia fired toward where she thought the voice had originated from and ducked back behind the firewood. Shots came back in her direction. She was pinned down. What now? Still behind the firewood, Lydia stretched up behind her and released the gate hatch.

"All right!" Lydia shouted. "I'm surrendering!"

Then she jumped up with the semiautomatic already going. She pulled the trigger as fast as she could. Bullets flew, the sound ringing in her ears. She didn't know if the shots were being returned or not. She didn't think so. There was no hesitation, though. The gate was open. She darted through it.

Lydia ran hard. A hundred yards away, Heshy was waiting in a neighbor's yard. They met up. Keeping low, they followed a trail of recently pruned shrubs. Heshy was good. He always tried to prepare for the worst. His car was hidden in a cul-de-sac two blocks down.

When they were safely on their way, Heshy asked, "You okay?"

"Fine, Pooh Bear." She took a deep breath, closed her eyes, and settled back. "Just fine."

It wasn't until they were near the highway that Lydia wondered what had happened to Pavel's cell phone.

My first reaction, naturally enough, was panic.

I opened the car door to give chase, but my brain finally kicked in and made me pull up. It was one thing to be brave or even foolhardy. It was another to be suicidal. I did not have a gun. Both Rachel and her assailant did. Rushing to her aid unarmed would be, at best, fruitless.

But I couldn't just stay here.

I closed the car door. Once again, my foot stamped down on the accelerator. The car bolted forward. I spun the wheel and veered across my front lawn. The shots had come from the back of the house. I aimed the car there. I tore through the flower beds and shrubs. They had been here so long that I almost cared.

My headlights danced through the dark. I started toward the right, hoping that I could work around the big elm. No go. The tree was too close to the house. The car wouldn't fit. I floored it in reverse. The tires ripped into dewy lawn, taking a second or two to catch. I headed toward the Christies' property line. I took out their new gazebo. Bill Christie would be pissed.

I was in the backyard now. The headlights slipped along the Grossmans' stockade fence. I swung the steering wheel toward the right. And then I saw her. I hit the brake. Rachel stood by the pile of firewood. The wood had been there when we bought the house. We hadn't used any. It was probably rotten and bug infested. The Grossmans had complained that it was so close to their fence that the bugs would start eating into it. I had promised to get rid of it, but I hadn't yet gotten around to it.

Rachel had her gun drawn and pointing down. The man in the flannel was lying at her feet like yesterday's refuse. I didn't have to roll down a window. The windshield was gone from the earlier gunshots. I heard nothing. Rachel lifted her hand. She waved to me, signaling that it was okay. I hurried out of the car.

"You shot him?" I asked, almost rhetorically.

"No," she said.

The man was dead. You didn't have to be a doctor to see that. The back of his skull had been blown off. Brain matter, congealed and pink-white, clung to the firewood. I am not an expert on ballistics but the damage was severe. It was either a very large bullet or from very close range.

"Someone was with him," Rachel said. "They shot him and escaped through that gate."

I stared down at him. The rage boiled up again. "Who is he?"

"I checked his pockets. He has a wad of bills but no ID."

I wanted to kick him. I wanted to shake him and ask what he had done with my daughter. I looked at his face, damaged yet handsome, and wondered what had led him here, why our life paths had crossed. And that was when I noticed something odd.

I tilted my head to the side.

"Marc?"

I dropped to my knees. Brain matter did not bother me. Bone splinters and bloody tissue did not faze me in the least. I had seen worse trauma. I examined his nose. It was practically putty. I remembered that from last time. A boxer, I'd thought. Either that or he'd lived some rough years. His head lolled back at a funny angle. His mouth was open. That was what had drawn my eye.

I put my fingers on his jaw and palate and pulled his mouth farther open.

"What the hell are you doing?" Rachel asked.

"Do you have a flashlight?"

"No."

Didn't matter. I lifted his head up and aimed his mouth toward the car. The headlights did the trick. I could see clearly now.

"Marc?"

"It always bothered me that he let me see his face." I lowered my head toward his mouth, trying to do so without casting too much of a shadow. "They were so careful about everything else. The altered voice, the stolen van sign, the welding together of license plates. Yet he lets me see his face."

"What are you talking about?"

"I thought maybe he'd worn an elaborate disguise the first time I'd seen him. That would make sense. But now we know that's not the case. So why would he let me see him?"

She seemed taken aback that I was asserting myself, but that didn't last long. She joined in. "Because he had no record."

"Maybe. Or . . ."

"Or what? Marc, we don't have time for this."

"His dental work."

"What about it?"

"Look at his crowns. They're tin cans."

"They're what?"

I lifted my head. "On his upper right molar and upper left cuspid. See, our crowns used to be made of gold, though most are now porcelain. Your dentist makes a mold so you can get an exact fitting. But this is just an aluminum, ready-made cap. You put it over the teeth and squeeze it on with pliers. I did two oral rotations overseas, mostly dealing with reconstruction, but I saw lots of mouths with these things in them. They call them tin cans. And they don't do it here in the USA, except maybe as a temporary."

She took a knee next to me. "He's foreign?"

I nodded. "I'd bet he's from the old Soviet bloc, something like that. The Balkans, maybe."

"That would make sense," she said. "Whatever prints they'd find they'd send down to NCIC. Same with any sort of face ID. Our files and computers wouldn't pick him up. Hell, it'll take the police forever to ID him unless someone comes forward."

"Which probably won't happen."

"My God, that's why they killed him. They know that we won't be able to trace him back."

The sirens sounded. Our eyes locked.

"You got a choice to make here, Marc. We stay, we're going to jail. They'll think he was part of our plot and we killed him. My guess is, the kidnappers knew that. Your neighbors will claim it was quiet until we drove up. Suddenly there's shrieking tires and gunfire. I'm not saying that we won't be able to explain it eventually."

"But it will take time," I said.

"Yes."

"And whatever opening we have here, it will close. The cops will pursue it their own way. Even if they can help, even if they believe us, they'll make a lot of noise."

"One more thing," she said.

"What?"

"The kidnappers set us up. They knew about the Q-Logger."

"We figured that out already."

"But now I'm wondering, Marc. How did they find it?"

I looked up, remembering the warning in the ransom note. "A leak?"

"I wouldn't rule it out anymore."

We both started toward the car. I put my hand on her arm. She was still bleeding. Her eye was almost swollen shut now. I looked at her, and again something primitive took over: I wanted to protect her. "If we run, it'll make us look guilty," I said. "I don't mind that—I don't have anything to lose here—but what about you?"

Her voice was soft. "I don't have anything to lose either."

"You need a doctor," I said.

Rachel almost smiled. "Aren't you one?"

"True enough."

There was no time to discuss the pros and cons. We had to act. We got into Zia's car. I swerved it around and headed out the back way, the Woodland Road exit. Thoughts—rational, clear thoughts—were starting to filter in now. When I really considered where we were and what we were doing, the truth nearly crushed me. I almost pulled over. Rachel saw it.

"What?" she said.

"Why are we running?"

"I don't understand."

"We hoped to find my daughter or at least who did this to her. We said there was a small opening."

"Yes."

"But don't you see? The opening, if there ever really was one, is gone. That guy back there is dead. We know he's foreign, but so what? We don't know who he is. We've reached a dead end. We don't have any other clues."

There was suddenly a trace of mischief on Rachel's face. She reached into her pocket and pulled something into view. A cell phone. It wasn't mine. It wasn't hers. "Maybe," she said, "we do."

chapter 34

"**First thing,**" Rachel said, "we need to get rid of this car."

"The car," I said, shaking my head at the damage. "If this search doesn't kill me, Zia will."

Rachel managed another smile. We were in the zone now, so deep in, so far past scared that we had found a little quiet. I debated where we should go, but really there was only one alternative.

"Lenny and Cheryl," I said.

"What about them?"

"They live four blocks from here."

It was five in the morning. Dark had begun to surrender to the inevitable. I dialed Lenny's home number and hoped that he hadn't gone back to the hospital. He answered on the first ring and barked a hello.

"I got a problem," I said.

"I hear sirens."

"That would be part of the problem."

"The police called me," he said. "After you took off."

"I need your help."

"Is Rachel with you?" he asked.

"Yes."

There was an awkward silence. Rachel fiddled with the dead man's cell phone. I had no idea what she was looking for. Then Lenny said, "What are you trying to do here, Marc?"

"Find Tara. Are you going to help me or not?"

Now there was no hesitation. "What do you need?"

"To hide the car we're using and borrow another."

"And then what are you going to do?"

I turned the car to the right. "We'll be there in a minute. I'll try to explain it to you then."

Lenny wore a pair of old gray sweatpants, the kind with the tie waist, a pair of slippers, and a Big Dog T-shirt. He pressed a button and the garage door slid to a smooth close as soon as we entered. Lenny looked exhausted, but then again, I don't think Rachel and I were ready for our close-ups either.

When Lenny saw the blood on Rachel, he took a step back. "What the hell happened?"

"Do you have any bandages?" I asked.

"Cabinet over the kitchen sink."

Rachel still had the cell phone in her hand. "I need to get on the Internet," she said.

"Look," Lenny said, "we have to discuss this."

"Discuss it with him," Rachel said. "I need Web access."

"In my office. You know where it is."

Rachel hurried inside. I followed, staying in the kitchen. She continued on to the den. We both knew this house well. Lenny stayed with me. They had recently renovated the kitchen into something French Farmesque and added a second refrigerator because four kids ate like four kids. The fronts of both fridges were overloaded with artwork and family photos and a brightly colored alphabet. The new one had one of those magnetic poetry sets. The words I STAND ALONE AROUND THE SEA ran down the handle. I started going through the cabinet over the sink.

"You want to tell me what's going on?"

I found Cheryl's first aid kit and pulled it out. "There was a shooting at our house."

I gave him the bare bones, opening the first aid kit and checking the supplies. There'd be enough in here for now. I finally glanced at him. Lenny just gaped at me. "You ran away from a murder scene?"

"If I stayed, what would have happened?"

"The police would have picked you up."

"Exactly."

He shook his head and kept his voice low. "They don't think you did it anymore."

"What do you mean?"

"They think it was Rachel."

I blinked, not sure how to react.

"Has she explained those photos to you?"

"Not yet," I said. Then, "I don't understand. How did they figure it was Rachel?"

Lenny rapidly outlined a theory involving jealousy and rage and my forgetting key moments before the shooting. I stood there too stunned to respond. When I did, I said, "That's nuts."

Lenny did not reply.

"That guy with the flannel shirt just tried to kill us."

"And what ended up happening to him?"

"I told you. Someone else was with him. He was shot."

"You saw someone else?"

"No. Rachel . . ." I saw where he was going. "Come on, Lenny. You know better."

"I want to know about those photos on the CD, Marc."

"Fine, let's go ask her."

When we left the kitchen, I spotted Cheryl on the stairwell. She looked down at me, arms crossed. I don't think I had ever seen that look on her face before. It made me pause. There was some blood on the carpet, probably from Rachel. On the wall was one of those studio photos of all four kids, trying to look casual in matching white turtlenecks against a white background. Children and all that white.

"I'll take care of it," Lenny told her. "You stay upstairs."

We hurried through the den. A DVD case from the latest Disney movie lay splayed on top of the television. I nearly tripped over a Wiffle Ball and plastic bat. A game of Monopoly featuring Pokémon characters was spread across the floor in midgame clutter. Someone, one of the kids I assumed, had scrawled DO NOT TOUCH A THING! on a piece of paper and laid it over the board. As we passed the fireplace mantel, I noticed that they'd recently updated the photographs. The kids were older now, in those images as in real life. But the oldest photograph, the "formal dance" image of the four of us, was gone. I don't know what that meant. Probably nothing. Or maybe Lenny and Cheryl were taking their own advice: It was time to move on.

Rachel sat at Lenny's desk, hovering over the keyboard. The blood had dried down the left side of her neck. Her ear was a mess. She glanced up when she saw us and then went back to typing. I examined her ear. Severe damage. The bullet had scraped along the upper region. It had skimmed the side of her head too. Another inch—hell, another quarter inch—and she'd probably be dead. Rachel ignored me, even when I applied the Bactine and threw on a bandage. It would be good enough for now. I'd fix it for real when we had the chance.

"Bang," Rachel said suddenly. She smiled and hit a key. The printer began to whir. Lenny nodded toward me. I put the finishing touches on the bandage and said, "Rachel?"

She looked up at me.

"We need to talk," I said.

"No," she countered, "we need to get out of here. I just found us a major lead."

Lenny stayed where he was. Cheryl slipped into the room now, her arms still folded. "What lead?" I asked.

"I checked the logs on the cell phone," Rachel said.

"You can do that?"

"They're in plain view, Marc," she said, and I could hear the impatience. "The dialed and received call logs. It's pretty much standard on every phone."

"Right."

"The dial log didn't help. No numbers were listed, which means, if the guy did dial out, it was to a blocked number."

I was trying to stay with her. "Okay."

"But the received log is another story. There was only one incoming call on the list. According to the internal timer, it came in at midnight. I just checked the phone number in the reverse directory at Switchboard-dot-com. It's a residence. One Verne Dayton in Huntersville, New Jersey."

Neither the name nor the city rang any bells. "Where is Huntersville?"

"I MapQuested it. It's near the Pennsylvania border. I zoomed in to within a few hundred yards. The house is all by itself out there. Acres of land in the heart of Nowheresville."

The chill started in my center and spread. I turned to Lenny. "I need to borrow your car."

"Hold up a second," Lenny said. "What we need here are some answers."

Rachel stood. "You want to know about the photos on the CD."

"For starters, yes."

"It's me in the pictures. Yes, I was there. The rest is none of your business. I owe Marc an explanation, not you. What else?"

For once, Lenny didn't know what to say.

"You also want to know if I killed my husband, right?" She looked at Cheryl. "Do you think I killed Jerry?"

"I don't know what to think anymore," Cheryl said. "But I want you both out of here."

"Cheryl," Lenny said.

She shot him a look that could have downed a charging rhino. "They shouldn't have brought this to our doorstep."

"He's our best friend. He's the godfather of our son."

"Which makes it that much worse. He drags this danger into our home? Into the lives of our children?"

"Come on, Cheryl. You're exaggerating."

"No," I said. "She's right. We should get out of here now. Let me have the keys."

Rachel grabbed the sheet out of the printer. "Directions," she explained.

I nodded and looked at Lenny. His head was down. His feet rocked back and forth. Again, I thought of our childhood. "Shouldn't we call Tickner and Regan?" he said.

"And tell them what?"

"I can explain it to them," Lenny said. "If Tara is at this place"—he stopped, shook his head as if he suddenly saw how ridiculous the thought was—"they'll be better equipped to go in."

I moved right up next to him. "They found out about Rachel's tracking device."

"What?"

"The kidnappers. We don't know how. But they found it. Add it up, Lenny. The ransom note warned us that they had an inside source. First time out, they knew I'd told the cops. Second time out, they learn about the tracking device."

"That doesn't prove anything."

"Do you think I have time to look for proof?"

Lenny's face sank.

"You know I can't risk that."

"Yeah," he said. "I know."

Lenny reached into his pocket and handed me the keys. We were off.

chapter 35

When Regan and Tickner got the call about the shooting at the Seidman residence, both men leapt to their feet. They were nearing the elevator when Tickner's cell phone rang.

A stiff, overly formal female voice said, "Special Agent Tickner?"

"Speaking."

"This is Special Agent Claudia Fisher."

Tickner knew the name. He may have even met her once or twice. "What's up?" he asked.

"Where are you right now?" she asked.

"New York Presbyterian Hospital, but I'm heading out to New Jersey."

"No," she said. "Please come down to One Federal Plaza immediately."

Tickner checked the time. It was only five in the morning. "Now?"

"That is what immediately means, yes."

"May I ask what this is about?"

"Assistant Director in Charge Joseph Pistillo would like to see you."

Pistillo? That made him pause. Pistillo was the top agent on the East Coast. He was the boss of Tickner's boss's boss. "But I'm on the way to a crime scene."

"This isn't a request," Fisher said. "Assistant Director Pistillo is waiting. He expects you here within the half hour."

The phone went dead. Tickner lowered his hand.

"What the hell was that about?" Regan asked.

"I gotta go," Tickner said, heading down the corridor.

"Where?"

"My boss wants to see me."

"Now?"

"Right now." Tickner was already halfway down the hall. "Call me when you know something."

"This isn't easy to talk about," Rachel said.

I drove. The unanswered questions had started to gather, weighing us both down, sapping our energy. I kept my eyes on the road and waited.

"Was Lenny with you when you saw the photos?" she asked.

"Yes."

"Was he surprised by them?"

"Looked that way to me."

She settled back. "Cheryl probably wouldn't have been."

"Why's that?"

"When you asked for my number, she called to warn me."

"About what?" I asked.

"About us."

No further explanation required. "She warned me too," I said.

"When Jerry died—that was my husband's name, Jerry Camp—when he died, let's just say it was a very hard time for me."

"I understand."

"No," she said. "Not like that. Jerry and I, we hadn't

worked in a very long time. I don't know if we ever did. When I went for training at Quantico, Jerry was one of my instructors. More than that, he was a legend. One of the best agents ever. You remember that KillRoy case a few years back?"

"He was a serial killer, right?"

Rachel nodded. "That capture was mostly due to Jerry. He had one of the most distinguished records in the bureau. With me . . . I don't know how it happened exactly. Or maybe I do. He was older. Something of a father figure maybe. I loved the FBI. It was my life. Jerry had a crush on me. I was flattered. But I don't know if I ever really loved him."

She stopped. I could feel her eyes on me. I kept mine on the road.

"Did you love Monica?" she asked. "I mean, really love her?"

The muscles in my shoulder bunched. "What the hell kind of a question is that?"

She was still. Then she said, "I'm sorry. That was out of line."

The silence grew. I tried to slow my breathing. "You were telling me about the photos?"

"Yes." Rachel started fidgeting. She only wore one ring. Now she twisted and tugged at it. "When Jerry died—"

"Was shot," I interjected.

Again I could feel her eyes on me. "Was shot, yes."

"Did you shoot him?"

"This isn't good, Marc."

"What isn't?"

"You're already angry."

"I just want to know if you shot your husband."

"Let me tell it my way, okay?"

There was a touch of steel in her voice now. I backed down, gave her a suit-yourself shrug. "When he died, I pretty much lost it. I was forced to resign. Everything I had—my friends, my work, hell, my life—was wrapped in the bureau. Now it was gone. I started drinking. I sank deeper into a funk. I hit bottom. And when you hit bottom, you look for a way to bounce back up. You look for anything. You get desperate."

We slowed at an interchange.

"I'm not saying this right," she said.

I surprised myself then. I reached and put my hand on hers. "Just tell me, okay?"

She nodded, keeping her gaze down, staring at my hand on hers. I kept it there. "One night, when I had too much to drink, I dialed your number."

I remembered what Regan had told me about the phone records. "When was this?"

"A few months before the attack."

"Did Monica answer?" I asked.

"No. Your machine picked up. I—I know how stupid this sounds—I left a message for you."

I slowly took my hand back. "What did you say exactly?"

"I don't remember. I was drunk. I was crying. I think I said that I missed you and hoped you'd call back. I don't think I went further than that."

"I never got the message," I said.

"I realize that now."

Something clicked. "That means," I said, "that Monica listened to it."

A few months before the attack, I thought. When Monica was feeling her most insecure. When we were starting to have serious problems. I remembered other things too. I remembered how often Monica had cried at night. I remembered how Edgar had told me that she'd started seeing a psychiatrist. And there I was, in my oblivious little world, taking her to Lenny and

Cheryl's house, subjecting her to that picture with my old lover in it—my old lover who had called our house late at night and said she missed me.

"My God," I said. "No wonder she hired a private investigator. She wanted to know if I was cheating on her. She probably told him about your call, about our past."

She said nothing.

"You still haven't answered the question, Rachel. What were you doing in front of the hospital?"

"I came to New Jersey to see my mother," she began. There was a hitch in her voice now. "I told you that she has a condo now in West Orange."

"So? Are you trying me to tell me she was a patient there?"

"No." She went quiet again. I drove. I almost flipped on the radio, just out of habit, just to do something. "Do I really have to say this?"

"I think so, yeah," I said. But I knew. I understood exactly.

Her voice was stripped of all passion. "My husband is dead. My job is gone. I've lost everything. I'd been talking to Cheryl a lot. I could tell from what she said that you and your wife were having problems." She turned to me full. "Come on, Marc. You know we never got over each other. So that day I went to the hospital to face you. I don't know what I expected. Was I really naïve enough to think you'd sweep me into your arms? Maybe, I don't know. So I hung around and tried to work up the courage. I even went up to your floor. But in the end, I couldn't go through with it—not because of Monica or Tara. I wish I could say I was that noble. I wasn't."

"So why then?"

"I walked away because I thought you'd reject me and I wasn't sure I could handle that."

We fell into silence then. I had no idea what to say. I don't even know how I felt.

"You're angry," she said.

"I don't know."

We drove some more. I wanted so very much to do the right thing. I thought about it. We both stared straight ahead. The tension pressed against the windows. Finally I said, "It doesn't matter anymore. All that matters is finding Tara."

I glanced at Rachel. I saw a tear on her cheek. The sign was up ahead now—small, discreet, nearly indiscernible. It read simply: HUNTERSVILLE. Rachel brushed the tear away and sat up. "Then let's concentrate on that."

Assistant Director in Charge Joseph Pistillo was at his desk, writing. He was large, barrel chested, big shouldered, and bald, the sort of old-timer that makes you think of dock workers and city-saloon fights—power without the show muscle. Pistillo was probably on the wrong side of sixty. Rumor had it that he'd be retiring soon.

Special Agent Claudia Fisher showed Tickner into the office and closed the door as she left. Tickner took his sunglasses off. He stood with his hands behind his back. He was not invited to sit. There was no greeting, no handshake, no salute, or anything such.

Without looking up, Pistillo said, "I understand you've been asking about the tragic death of Special Agent Jerry Camp."

Alarm bells rang in Tickner's head. Whoa, that was fast. He'd only started his inquiries a few hours ago. "Yes, sir."

More scribbling. "He taught you at Quantico—isn't that right?"

"Yes, sir."

"He was a great teacher."

"One of the best, sir."

"*The* best, Agent."

"Yes, sir."

"Your inquiries into his death," Pistillo went on, "do they have anything to do with your past relationship with Special Agent Camp?"

"No, sir."

Pistillo stopped writing. He put down the pen and folded his rock-breaking hands on his desk. "Then why are you asking about it?"

Tickner looked for the traps and pitfalls he knew lurked in his answer. "His wife's name has arisen in another case I'm working on."

"That would be the Seidman murder-kidnapping case?"

"Yes, sir."

Pistillo frowned. His forehead crinkled. "You think there's a connection between the accidental shooting death of Jerry Camp and the Tara Seidman kidnapping?"

Careful, Tickner thought. Careful. "It's an avenue I need to explore."

"No, Agent Tickner, it is not."

Tickner stayed still.

"If you can tie Rachel Mills to the Seidman murder-kidnapping, do it. Find evidence that connects her to the case. But you don't need Camp's death to do that."

"They could be related," Tickner said.

"No," Pistillo said in a voice that left little room for doubt, "they're not."

"But I need to look—"

"Agent Tickner?"

"Yes, sir."

"I've looked into the file already," Pistillo said. "More than that, I helped investigate the death of Jerry Camp personally. He was my friend. Do you understand?"

Tickner did not reply.

"I am completely satisfied that his shooting was a tragic accident. That means you, Agent Tickner"—Pistillo pointed a meaty finger at Tickner's chest—"are completely satisfied too. Do I make myself clear?"

The two men stared at each other. Tickner was not a foolish man. He liked working for the bureau. He wanted to rise up the ladder. It would not pay to upset someone as powerful as Pistillo. So in the end, Tickner was the first to look away.

"Yes, sir."

Pistillo relaxed. He picked up his pen. "Tara Seidman has been missing for over a year now. Is there any proof she is still alive?"

"No, sir."

"Then the case doesn't belong to us anymore." He started writing now, making no bones about the fact that this was a dismissal. "Let the locals handle it."

New Jersey is our most densely populated state. That doesn't surprise people. New Jersey has cities, suburbs, and plenty of industry. That doesn't surprise people either. New Jersey is called the Garden State and has plenty of rural areas. That surprises people.

Even before we hit the border of Huntersville, signs of life—human life, that is—had already started fading away. There were few houses. We had passed one general store straight out of *Mayberry RFD*, but that was boarded up. During the next three miles we hit six different roads. I saw no houses. I passed no cars.

We were in the thick of the woods. I made my final

turn and the car climbed up the side of a mountain. A deer—the fourth I'd seen by my count—sprinted out of the road, far enough up so I wasn't in any danger of hitting it. I was beginning to suspect that the name Huntersville was to be taken literally.

"It'll be on the left," Rachel said.

A few seconds later, I could see the mailbox. I began to slow, searching for a house or building of some kind. I saw nothing but trees.

"Keep driving," Rachel said.

I understood. We couldn't just pull into the driveway and announce ourselves. I found a small indentation off the road about a quarter of a mile up. I parked and turned off the engine. My heart started to trip-hammer. It was six in the morning. Dawn was here.

"Do you know how to use a gun?" Rachel asked me.

"I used to fire my dad's at the range."

She jammed a weapon into my hand. I stared down at it as if I'd just discovered an extra finger. Rachel had her gun out too. "Where did you get this?" I asked.

"At your house. Off the dead guy."

"Jesus."

She shrugged as if to say, *Hey, you never know.* I looked at the gun again and suddenly a thought hit me: Was this the weapon used to shoot me? To kill Monica? I stopped there. There was no time for this squeamish nonsense. Rachel was already out the door. I followed. We started into the woods. There was no path. We made our own. Rachel took the lead. She tucked her weapon into the back of her pants. For some reason, I didn't do the same. I wanted to hold the gun. Faded orange signs tacked to trees warned trespassers to stay away. They had the word NO in a giant font and a surprising amount of finer print, overexplaining what seemed to me to be pretty obvious.

We angled closer to where we thought the driveway was. When we spotted it, we had our guiding star. We stayed near the unpaved stretch and continued on our way. A few minutes later, Rachel stopped. I nearly bumped into her. She pointed ahead.

A structure.

It looked like a barn of some sort. We were more careful now. We kept low. We darted from tree to tree and tried to stay out of sight. We did not speak. After a bit, I started hearing music. Country, I think, but I'm no expert. Up ahead, I spotted a clearing. There was indeed a barn that appeared to be in middemolition. There was another structure too—a ranch or maybe extended trailer.

We moved a little closer, right to the end of the woods. We pressed ourselves against trees and peeked out. There was a tractor in the yard. I saw an old TransAm up on cement blocks. Directly in front of the ranch was a white, overly sporty car—some might call it a "hot rod," I guess—with a thick black stripe up the hood. It looked like a Camaro.

The woods had ended, but we were still at least fifty feet from the ranch house. The grass was high, knee level. Rachel took out her gun. I still held mine. She dropped to the ground and began to commando-crawl. I did the same. On television commando-crawling looks pretty easy. You simply crawl with your butt down. And for about ten feet, it is pretty easy. Then it gets a lot harder. My elbows ached. The grass kept getting caught up in my nose and mouth. I do not suffer from hay fever or allergies, but we were kicking up something. Gnats and the like rose vengefully as we disturbed their slumber. The music was louder now. The singer—a man hitting nary a note—complained about his poor, poor heart.

Rachel stopped. I crawled to her right and pulled up even. "You okay?" she whispered.

I nodded, but I was panting.

"We may have to do something once we get there," she said. "I can't have you exhausted. We can slow down if you need to."

I shook her off and started moving. I was not going to slow down. Slowing down was simply not on the menu. We were getting closer. I could see the Camaro more clearly now. There were black mud flaps with the silver silhouette of a shapely girl behind the rear tires. There were bumper stickers on the back. One read: GUNS DON'T KILL PEOPLE, BUT THEY SURE MAKE IT EASIER.

Rachel and I were near the end of the grass, almost exposed, when the dog started barking. We both froze.

There are several varieties of dog barks. The yap of an annoying toy dog. The call of a friendly golden retriever. The warning of a basically harmless pet. And then there is that guttural, junkyard, rip-out-the-thorax bark that makes the blood thin.

This bark fit into the last category.

I was not particularly scared of the dog. I had a gun. It'd be easier, I guess, to use it on a dog than a human being. What did frighten me, of course, was that the barking would be heard by the ranch's occupant. So we waited. A minute or two later, the dog stopped. We kept our eyes on the ranch door. I was not sure what we would do if someone came out. Suppose we were spotted. We couldn't shoot. We still didn't know anything. The fact that a call had been made from the residence of Verne Dayton to the cell phone of a dead man did not add up to much. We didn't know if my daughter was here or not.

We knew, in fact, nothing.

There were hubcaps in the yard. The rising sun gleamed off them. I spotted a bunch of green boxes. And something about them held my gaze. Forgetting caution, I started moving closer.

"Wait," Rachel whispered.

But I couldn't. I needed to get a better look at those boxes. Something about them . . . but I couldn't put my finger on it. I crawled to the tractor and then hid behind it. I peered out toward the boxes again. Now I saw it. The boxes were indeed green. They also had a graphic featuring a smiling baby.

Diapers.

Rachel was next to me now. I swallowed. A big box of diapers. The kind you buy in bulk at a price club. Rachel saw it too. She put her hand on my arm, warning me to stay calm. We got back down on the ground. She signaled that we were going to make our way to a side window. I nodded that I understood. There was a long fiddle solo blaring from the stereo now.

We were both on our stomachs when I felt something cold against the back of my neck. I slid my eyes toward Rachel. There was a rifle barrel there too, pressed against the base of her skull.

A voice said, "Drop your weapons!"

It was a man. Rachel's right hand was bent in front of her face. The gun was in it. She let it go. A work boot stepped forward and kicked it away. I tried to discern the odds. One man. I could see that now. One man with two rifles. I could conceivably make a move here. No way I'd make it in time, but it might free up Rachel. I met her eyes and saw panic in them. She knew what I was thinking. The rifle suddenly dug deeper into my skull, pushing my face into the dirt.

"Don't try it, Chief. I can splatter two sets of brains as easy as one."

My mind scurried, but it kept hitting dead ends. So I let the gun drop from my hand and watched this man kick away our hope.

chapter 36

"Stay on your stomachs!"

"I'm an agent with the Federal Bureau of Investigation," Rachel said.

"Shut the hell up."

With our faces still in the dirt, he had us both put our hands on top of our heads, fingers laced. He put a knee in my spine. I grimaced. Using his body for leverage, the man pulled my arms back, nearly popping my shoulders out of their sockets. My wrists were expertly bound together with nylon flex cuffs. They felt like those ridiculously complicated plastic ties they use to package toys so they can't be shoplifted.

"Put your feet together."

Another cuff fastened my ankles together. He pushed down on my back to get up. Then he moved over to Rachel. I was going to say something stupidly chivalric like *Leave her alone!* but I knew that this would be, at best, futile. I kept still.

"I'm a federal agent," Rachel said.

"I heard you the first time."

He put a knee in her back and pulled her hands together. She grunted in pain.

"Hey," I said.

The man ignored me. I turned and took my first real

look at him, and it was like I'd been dropped into a time warp. No doubt about it—the Camaro belonged to him. His hair was eighties-hockey-player long, maybe permed, the color a strange offshoot of orange-blond, tucked back behind his ears and styled into the kind of mullet cut I hadn't seen since a Night Ranger music video. He had a cheesy blond mustache that could have been a milk stain. His T-shirt read UNIVERSITY OF SMITH AND WESSON. His jeans were unnaturally dark blue and looked stiff.

After he bound Rachel's hands, he said, "Get up, missy. You and me are taking a walk."

Rachel tried to make her voice stern. "You're not listening," she said, her hair falling down over her eyes. "I'm Rachel Mills—"

"And I'm Verne Dayton. So what?"

"I'm a federal agent."

"Your ID says retired." Verne Dayton smiled. He wasn't toothless, but he wasn't exactly an orthodontic poster boy either. His right incisor was totally turned in like a door off its hinge. "Kinda young to be retired, don't you think?"

"I still work special cases. They know I'm here."

"Really? Don't tell me. There's a bunch of agents waiting down yonder, and if they don't hear from you in three minutes, they're all gonna come storming in. That about it, Rachel?"

She stopped. He had read her bluff. She had nowhere else to go.

"Get up," he said again, this time pulling on her arms. Rachel stumbled to her feet.

"Where are you taking her?" I asked.

He did not reply. They started walking toward the barn. "Hey!" I called out, my voice booming with impotence. "Hey, come back!" But they kept walking. Rachel struggled, but her hands were tied behind her back. Every time she moved too much, he lifted the hands up, forcing her to bend forward. Eventually she complied and just walked.

Fear lit my nerves. In a frenzy, I looked for something, anything, that would get me free. Our guns? No, he had picked them up already. And even if he hadn't, what would I do? Fire with my teeth? I debated rolling over onto my back, but I wasn't sure how that would help yet. So now what? I started moving inchworm-style toward the tractor. I looked for a blade or anything that I might use to cut myself free.

In the distance, I heard the barn door creak open. My head swerved in time to see them disappear inside. The door closed behind them. The sound echoed into silence. The music—it must have been a CD or tape—had stopped. It was quiet now. And Rachel was gone from sight.

I had to get my hands free.

I started crawling forward, lifting my butt, pushing off with my legs. I made it to the tractor. I searched for some kind of blade or sharp edge. Nothing. My eyes darted to the barn.

"Rachel!" I shouted.

My voice echoed through the stillness. That was the only reply. My heart started doing flip-flops.

Oh God, now what?

I rolled onto my back and sat up. Pushing with my legs, I pressed against the tractor. I had a clear view of the barn. I don't know what the hell that did for me. There was still no movement, no sound. My eyes darted all over the place, desperately hunting for something that could bring salvation. But there was nothing.

I thought about going for the Camaro. A gun nut like this probably had two, three concealed weapons on him at all times. There might be something in there. But again, even if I managed to get there in time, how would I open the door? How would I search for a gun? How would I fire it when I found one?

No, I had to get this cuff off me first.

I looked on the ground for . . . I don't even know. A sharp rock. A broken beer bottle. Something. I wondered how much time had passed since they disappeared. I wondered what he was doing to Rachel. My throat felt as if it might close up.

"Rachel!"

I heard the desperation in the echo. It scared me. But again there was no reply.

What was going on in there?

I looked again for some kind of edge on the tractor, something I could use to break free. There was rust. Lots of rust. Would that work? If I rubbed the cuff against a rusty corner, would it eventually cut through? I doubted it, but there was nothing else.

I managed to get on my knees. I leaned my wrists against the rusted corner and moved up and down like a bear using a tree to scratch his back. My arms slipped. The rust bit into my skin, and the sting ran up my arm. I looked back over at the barn, listened hard, still heard nothing.

I kept going.

The problem was, I was doing this by feel. I turned my head as far as I could, but I couldn't see my wrists. Was this having any effect at all? I had no idea. But it was all I had to work with. So I continued moving up and down, trying to break free by pulling my arms apart like Hercules in a B movie.

I don't know how long I kept it up. Probably no more than two or three minutes, though it felt like a lot longer. The cuff did not break or even loosen. What finally made me stop was a sound. The barn door had opened. For a moment, I saw nothing. Then the Hick with the Hair came out. Alone. He started walking toward me.

"Where is she?"

Without speaking, Verne Dayton bent down and checked my cuffs. I could smell him now. He smelled of dried grass and work sweat. He was studying my hands. I glanced back. There was blood on the ground. My blood, no doubt. An idea suddenly came to me.

I reared back and aimed a head butt in his direction.

I know how devastating a proper head butt can be. I had performed surgeries on faces crushed by such blows.

This would not be the case here.

My body position was awkward. My hands and feet were both bound. I was on my knees. I was twisting behind me. My skull didn't land on the nose or softer part of his face. It caught him on the forehead. There was a hollow *klunk* like something out of a Three Stooges sound track. Verne Dayton rolled back, cursing. I was totally off balance now, in free fall with nothing but my face to cushion my landing. My right cheek took the brunt of it, rattling my teeth. But I was beyond pain. I slid my eyes in his direction. He sat shaking out the cobwebs. There was a small laceration on his forehead.

Now or never.

Still tied up, I flailed toward him. But I was too slow.

Verne Dayton leaned back and raised a work boot. When I was close enough, he stomped my face as if he were beating back a brushfire. I fell back. He backpedaled to a safe distance and grabbed the rifle.

"Don't move!" His fingers checked the gash on his head. He looked at the blood in disbelief. "You out of your mind?"

I was flat on my back, my breaths coming in deep heaves. I didn't think anything was broken, but then again, I wasn't sure it was going to matter. He walked over to me and kicked me hard in the ribs. I rolled over. He grabbed my arms and started dragging me. I tried to get my feet under me. He was strong as hell. The steps to the trailer didn't slow him down. He pulled me up them, shouldered the door open, and tossed me in like a bag of peat moss.

I landed with a thud. Verne Dayton stepped inside and closed the door. My eyes took in the room. It was half what you'd expect, half not. The expected: There were guns mounted on the wall, antique muskets, hunter's rifle. There was the obligatory deer head, a framed NRA membership made out to Verne Dayton, a quilted American flag. The unexpected: The place was spotless and what some might call tastefully furnished. I spotted a playpen in the corner, but it wasn't cluttered. The toys were in one of those fiberglass chests with different-color drawers. The drawers were categorized and labeled.

He sat down and looked at me. I was still on my stomach. Verne Dayton toyed with his hair a little, pushing back the strands, tucking the long sides behind his ears. His face was thin. Everything about him screamed yokel.

"You the one beat her up?" he said.

For a moment I didn't know what he was talking about. Then I remembered that he'd seen Rachel's injuries. "No."

"That get you off, huh? Beating up a woman?"

"What did you do with her?"

He took out a revolver, opened the chamber, slid a bullet into it. He spun it to a close and pointed it at my knee. "Who sent you?"

"No one."

"You want to get capped?"

I'd had enough. I rolled onto my back, waiting to hear him pull the trigger. But he didn't shoot. He let me move, keeping the gun on me. I sat up and stared him down. That seemed to confuse him. He took a step back.

"Where's my daughter?" I said.

"Huh?" He tilted his head. "You trying to be funny?"

I looked into his eyes and I saw it. This was no act. He had no idea what I was talking about.

"You come here with guns," he said, his face reddening. "You want to kill me? My wife? My kids?" Verne raised the gun to my face. "Give me one good reason I don't blow you both away and bury you in the woods?"

Kids. He said kids. Something about this whole setup suddenly wasn't making sense. I decided to take a chance. "Listen to me," I said. "My name is Marc Seidman. Eighteen months ago, my wife was murdered and my daughter abducted."

"What are you babbling about?"

"Please, just let me explain."

"Wait a second." Verne's eyes narrowed. He rubbed his chin. "I remember you. From the television. You were shot too, right?"

"Yes."

"So why do you want to steal my guns?"

I closed my eyes. "I'm not here to steal your guns," I said. "I'm here"—I wasn't sure how to say this—"I'm here to find my daughter."

It took this a second to register. Then his mouth dropped open. "You think I had something to do with that?"

"I don't know."

"You better start explaining."

So I did. I told him all of it. The story sounded insane

in my ears, but Verne listened. He gave me his full attention. Toward the end, I said, "The man who did this. Or was somehow involved. I don't know anymore. We got his cell phone. He only had one incoming call. It came from here."

Verne thought about it. "This man. What's his name?"

"We don't know."

"I call a lot of people, Marc."

"We know the call was made sometime last night."

Verne shook his head. "Nope, no way."

"What do you mean?"

"I wasn't home last night. I was on the road, making a delivery. I only got home about half an hour before you got here. Spotted you when Munch—that's my dog—started the low growl. The bark, that don't mean much. It's the low growl tells me someone's there."

"Wait a second. No one was here last night?"

He shrugged. "Well, my wife and boys. But the boys are six and three. I don't think they were calling anyone. And I know Kat. She wouldn't be making any calls that late either."

"Kat?" I said.

"My wife. Kat. It's short for Katarina. She's from Serbia."

"Get you a beer, Marc?"

I surprised myself by saying, "That would be nice, Verne."

Verne Dayton had cut off the plastic cuffs. I rubbed my wrists. Rachel was next to me. He hadn't harmed her. He'd just wanted us separated, in part, he said, because he thought that I'd beaten her up and forced her to help me. Verne had a valuable gun collection—many of them still in working condition—and people were a little too interested in them. He'd figured that was the case with us.

"A Bud, okay?"

"Sure."

"You, Rachel?"

"No, thanks."

"Soft drink? Some ice water maybe?"

"Water would be great, thanks."

Verne smiled, which wasn't the most pleasant sight. "No problem." I rubbed my wrists again. He spotted it and grinned. "We used those in the Gulf War. Kept them Iraqis under control, I can tell you."

He disappeared into the kitchen. I looked at Rachel. She shrugged. Verne came back with two Buds and a glass of water. He passed out the drinks. He raised the bottle for us to clink. I did. He sat down.

"I got two kids of my own. Boys. Verne Junior and Perry. If something ever happened to them . . ." Verne whistled low and shook his head. "I don't know how you even get out of bed in the morning."

"I think about finding her," I said.

Verne nodded hard at that. "I can relate, I guess. Long as a man ain't fooling himself—you know what I mean?" He looked over at Rachel. "You absolutely sure the phone number is mine?"

Rachel took out the cell phone. She pressed some digits and then showed him the small screen. Using his mouth, Verne extracted a Winston from the pack. He shook his head. "I don't understand it."

"We're hoping your wife can help."

He nodded slowly. "She wrote a note, says she went food shopping. Kat likes to do that early in the morning. At the twenty-four-hour A and P." He stopped. I think Verne was torn here. He wanted to be able to help, but he didn't want to hear that his wife had called a strange man at midnight. He raised his head. "Rachel, how about I get you some fresh bandages?"

"I'm fine."

"You sure?"

"Really, thank you." She held the glass of water with both hands. "Verne, do you mind if I ask you how you and Katarina met?"

"On-line," he said. "You know, one of those Web sites for foreign brides. Cherry Orchid, it's called. They used to call it mail order. I don't think they do that anymore. Anyway, you go to the site. You look at these pictures of women from all over—Eastern Europe, Russia, the Philippines, wherever. They list measurements, a little bio, likes and dislikes, that kinda thing. You see one that strikes your fancy, you can buy her address. They got package deals too, if you want to write to more than one."

Rachel and I gave each other a quick glance. "How long ago was this?"

"Seven years ago. We started sending each other e-mails and stuff. Kat was living on a farm in Serbia. Her parents had nothing. She used to walk four miles to get computer access. I wanted to call too, you know, talk on the phone. But they didn't even have one. She had to call me. Then one day, she says she's coming over. To meet me."

Verne put his hands up, as if to silence an interruption. "Now see, this is where the girls usually hit you up for some money, you know, dollars to buy a plane ticket and stuff. So I was ready for that. But Kat didn't. She came over on her own. I drove up to New York City. We met. We were married three weeks later. Verne Junior came in a year. Perry three years after that."

He took a deep sip of his beer. I did the same. The coldness felt wonderful sliding down my throat.

"Look, I know what you're thinking," Verne said. "But it ain't like that. Kat and me, we're real happy. I was married before to a grade-A American ball-buster. All she did was whine and complain. I wasn't making enough money for her. She wanted to stay at home and do nothing. Ask her to do a load of laundry, she'd go all ballistic on me with that feminazi crap. Always tearing me down, telling me I'm a loser. With Kat, it ain't like that. Do I like the fact that she makes a nice house and home? Sure, okay, that's important to me. If I'm working outside and it's hot, Kat'll fetch me a beer without giving me a *Ms*. magazine lecture. Is there anything wrong with that?"

Neither of us replied.

"Look, I want you to think about it, okay? Why are any two people attracted to each other? Looks maybe? Money? Because you have an important job? We all join up because we want to get something out of it. Give and take—am I right? I wanted a loving wife who'd help me raise children and take care of a home. I wanted a partner too, someone, I don't know, who'd just be nice to me. I get that. Kat, she wanted out of a terrible life. I mean, they were so poor, dirt was a luxury. She and me, we got it good here. In January, we took the kids and went down to Disney World. We like hiking and canoeing. Verne Junior and Perry, they're good kids. Hey, maybe I'm simple. Hell, I'm *definitely* simple. I like my guns, my hunting and fishing—and most of all, my family."

Verne lowered his head. His mullet hair dropped like a curtain blocking his face. He started ripping the label off the beer. "Some places—probably most, I don't know—marriages are arranged. That's the way it's always been. The parents decide. They force them. Well, no one forced Kat and me. She could walk away anytime. Me too. But it's been seven years now. I'm happy. So is she."

Then he shrugged his shoulders. "At least, I thought she was."

We drank in silence.

"Verne?" I said.

"Yeah?"

"You're an interesting man."

He laughed, but I could see the fear. He took a swig of beer to hide it. He'd carved out a life for himself. A nice life. It's funny. I am not a very good judge of people. My initial impressions are usually wrong. I see this gun-toting redneck with his hair and his bumper stickers and his monster-truck-rally 'tude. I hear he has a mail-order bride from Serbia. How can you not judge? But the more I listened to him, the more I liked him. I must be at least as alien to him. I'd crept up on his house with a gun. Yet as soon as I had started telling my story, Verne had acted. He knew that we were telling the truth.

We heard the car pull up. Verne moved to the window and looked out. There was a small, sad smile on his face. His family was pulling into the drive. He cherished them. Intruders had come to his home with guns, and he had done what he could to protect it. And now, maybe, in my attempt to bring my family together, I might tear apart his.

"Look! Daddy's home!"

That had to be Katarina. The accent was unmistakably foreign, something in the Balkan–East European–Russian family. I am not linguist enough to know which. I heard the happy squeals of little children. Verne's smile widened a bit. He stepped out onto the porch. Rachel and I stayed where we were. We could hear running feet on the steps. The greeting lasted a minute or two. I stared at my hands. I heard Verne say something about presents in the truck. The kids sprinted for them.

The door opened. Verne entered with his arm around his wife.

"Marc, Rachel, this here's my wife, Kat."

She was lovely. She wore her long hair straight down. Her yellow sundress left her shoulders exposed. Her skin was pure white, her eyes blue ice. She had that certain bearing so that I could have told, even if I hadn't known, that she was foreign. Or maybe I was projecting. I tried to guess her age. She could pass for mid-twenties, but the age lines around the eyes told me I was probably a decade off.

"Hi," I said.

We both stood and shook her hand. It was dainty, but there was steel in the grip. Katarina held on to the hostess smile, but it wasn't easy. Her eyes stayed on Rachel, on the wounds. The sight, I guess, was rather shocking. I was almost getting used to it.

Still smiling, Katarina turned to Verne as if to ask a question. He said, "I'm trying to help them out."

"Help them?" she repeated.

The children had located the presents and were hooting and hollering. Verne and Katarina didn't seem to hear. They were looking at each other. He held her hand. "That man over there"—he gestured with his chin toward me—"somebody murdered his wife and took away his little girl."

She put a hand to her mouth.

"They're here trying to find his daughter."

Katarina did not move. Verne turned to Rachel and nodded a go-ahead.

"Mrs. Dayton," Rachel began, "did you make a phone call last night?"

Katarina's head jerked as though she'd just been startled. She looked at me first, as if I were some kind of circus oddity. Then she turned her attention to Rachel. "I don't understand."

"We have a phone record," Rachel said. "Last night at midnight, someone placed a call from this house to a certain cell phone. We assume it was you."

"No, that's not possible." Katarina's eyes started shifting as if seeking out an escape route. Verne still held her hand. He tried to meet her gaze, but she kept avoiding it. "Oh wait," she said. "Maybe I know."

We waited.

"Last night, when I was sleeping, the phone rang." She tried the smile again, but it was having trouble staying anchored. "I don't know what time it was. Very late. I thought maybe it was you, Verne." She looked at him and now the smile held. He smiled back. "But when I answered it, there was no one there. So I remembered something I saw on the television. Star, six, nine. You hit those numbers and it dials the number. So I did that. A man answered. It wasn't Verne, so I hung up."

She looked at us expectantly. Rachel and I exchanged a glance. Verne was still smiling, but I saw his shoulders drop. He let go of her hand and half collapsed onto the couch.

Katarina started toward the kitchen. "You need another beer, Verne?"

"No, darling, I don't. I want you to sit here next to me."

She was hesitant but she listened. She sat with her spine still ramrod. Verne, too, sat up tall and again took her hand.

"I want you to listen to me, okay?"

She nodded. The children were wailing with delight outside. Corny to say, but there are few sounds like the unimpeded laughter of children. Katarina looked at Verne with an intensity that almost made me turn away.

"You know how much we love our boys, right?"

She nodded.

"Imagine if someone took them away from us. Imagine if that happened more than a year ago. Think about it. Imagine if someone stole, say, Perry, and for more than a year, we didn't know where he was." He pointed to me. "That man over there. He doesn't know what happened to his little girl."

Her eyes were brimming with tears.

"We have to help him, Kat. Whatever you know. Whatever you done. I don't care. If there are secrets, you tell them now. We wipe the slate clean. I can forgive just about anything. But I don't think I can forgive if you don't help that man and his little girl."

She lowered her head and said nothing.

Rachel ratcheted up a notch. "If you're trying to protect the man you called, don't bother. He's dead. Someone shot him a few hours after you called."

Katarina's head stayed down. I rose and started pacing. From outside, there was another squeal of laughter. I walked over to the window and looked out. Verne Junior—the boy looked to be about six—shouted, "Ready or not, here I come!" It wouldn't be too hard to find him. I couldn't see Perry, but the hiding child's laughter was clearly coming from behind the Camaro. Verne Junior pretended to look elsewhere but not for very long. He sneaked up on the Camaro and yelled, "Boo!"

Perry popped out still laughing and ran. When I saw the boy's face, I felt my world, already teetering, take another hit. See, I recognized Perry.

He was the little boy I'd seen in the car last night.

chapter 37

Tickner parked in front of the Seidman house. They hadn't put up the yellow crime-scene tape yet, but he counted six squad cars and two news vans. He wondered if it'd be a good idea to approach, what with the cameras rolling. Pistillo, his boss's boss, had made it pretty clear where he stood. In the end, Tickner figured that it was safe enough to stay. If he was caught on camera, he could always opt for the truth: He had come to let the locals know that he was off the case.

Tickner found Regan in the backyard with the body. "Who is he?"

"No ID," Regan said. "We'll send in the prints, see what we come up with."

They both looked down.

"He matches that sketch Seidman gave us last year," Tickner said.

"Yup."

"So what does that mean?"

Regan shrugged.

"What have you learned so far?"

"Neighbors heard shots first. That was followed by screeching tires. They saw a BMW Mini driving across the grass. More shots. They spotted Seidman. One neighbor said he might have seen a woman with him."

"Probably Rachel Mills," Tickner said. He looked up in the morning sky. "So what does it mean?"

"Maybe the victim worked for Rachel. She silenced him."

"In front of Seidman?"

Regan shrugged. "The BMW Mini struck a chord though. I remembered that Seidman's partner had one. Zia Leroux."

"That would be who helped him get out of the hospital."

"We have an APB on the car."

"I'm sure they switched vehicles."

"Yeah, probably." Then Regan stopped. "Uh-oh."

"What?"

He pointed at Tickner's face. "You're not wearing your sunglasses."

Tickner smiled. "Bad omen?"

"The way this case is going? Maybe it's a good one."

"I came to tell you I'm off the case. Not just me. The bureau. If you can prove the girl is still alive—"

"—which we both know she ain't—"

"—or that she was transported across state lines, I can probably get back in. But this case is no longer a priority."

"Back to terrorism, Lloyd?"

Tickner nodded. He looked back up in the sky. It felt weird without the sunglasses.

"What did your boss want, anyway?"

"To tell me what I just told you."

"Uh-huh. Anything else?"

Tickner shrugged. "The shooting of Federal Agent Jerry Camp was accidental."

"Your big boss called you into his office before six in the morning to tell you that?"

"Yep."

"Yowza."

"Not only that, he investigated the case personally. He and the victim were friends."

Regan shook his head. "Does this mean Rachel Mills has powerful friends?"

"Not at all. If you can nail her for the Seidman murder or kidnapping, go to it."

"Just don't involve the death of Jerry Camp."

"There you go."

Someone called out. They looked over. A gun had been found in the neighbor's yard. A quick sniff told them that it had been fired recently.

"Convenient," Regan added.

"Yup."

"Any thoughts?"

"Nope." Tickner turned to him. "It's your case, Bob. Always was. Good luck."

"Thanks."

Tickner walked away.

"Hey, Lloyd?" Regan called out.

Tickner stopped. The gun had been bagged. Regan stared at it, then at the body by his feet.

"We still don't know what's going on here, do we?"

Tickner continued toward his car. "Not a clue," he said.

Katarina had her hands in her lap. "Is he really dead?"

"Yes," Rachel said.

Verne stood, fuming, his arms folded over his chest. He had been that way since I told him that Perry had been the child I saw in the Honda Accord.

"His name is Pavel. He was my brother."

We waited for her to say more.

"He was not a good man. I always knew that. He

could be cruel. Kosovo makes you that way. But kidnapping a small child?" She shook her head.

"What happened?" Rachel asked.

But her eyes were on her husband. "Verne?"

He would not look at her.

"I lied to you, Verne. I lied to you about so much."

He tucked his hair behind his ears and blinked. I saw him wet his lip with his tongue. But he would still not look at her.

"I didn't come from a farm," she said. "My father died when I was three. My mother took any job she could. But we couldn't get by. We were too poor. We'd steal rinds out of the garbage. Pavel, he stayed on the streets, begging and stealing. I started working in sex clubs when I was fourteen. You can't imagine what it was like, but there is no way out of that life in Kosovo. I wanted to kill myself. I can't tell you how many times."

She raised her head toward her husband, but Verne still wouldn't meet her gaze. "Look at me," she said to him. When he didn't she leaned forward, "Verne?"

"This ain't about us," he said. "Just tell them what they need to know."

Katarina put her hands in her lap. "After a while, when you live like that, you don't think about escape. You don't think about pretty things or happiness or any of that. You become like an animal. You just hunt and survive. And I don't even know why you do that. But one day, Pavel came to me. He told me he knew a way out."

Katarina stopped. Rachel moved closer to her. I let her handle this. She had experience with interrogation, and at the risk of sounding sexist, I thought that Katarina would have an easier time being drawn out by a fellow female.

"What was the way out?" Rachel asked.

"My brother said he could get us some money—and to America—if I could get pregnant."

I thought—check that: I hoped—I'd heard wrong. Verne whipped his head toward her. This time Katarina was ready. She looked at him steadily.

"I don't understand," Verne said.

"I'm worth something as a prostitute. But a baby is worth more. If I get pregnant, someone can get us to America. They will pay us money."

The room went silent. I could still hear the children outside, but the sound suddenly seemed far away, a distant echo. I was the one who spoke next, reaching through the numb. "They pay you," I said, hearing the horror and disbelief in my own voice, "for the baby?"

"Yes."

Verne said, "Sweet Jesus."

"You can't understand."

"Oh, I understand," Verne said. "Did you go through with it?"

"Yes."

Verne turned away as if he'd been slapped. His hand reached up and took hold of the curtain. He stared out at his own children.

"In my country, if you have a baby, they put it in a horrible orphanage. American parents, they want so much to adopt. But it's hard. It takes a long time. More than a year sometimes. Meanwhile, the baby lives in squalor. The parents, they must pay government officials. The system is so corrupt."

"I see," Verne said. "You were doing it for the good of mankind?"

"No, I did it for me. For me only, okay?"

Verne winced. Rachel put her hand on Katarina's knee. "So you flew over here?"

"Yes. Pavel and I."

"Then what?"

"We stayed at a motel. I would visit a woman with white hair. She would check on me, make sure I was eating okay. She gave me money to buy food and supplies."

Rachel nodded, encouraging. "Where did you have the baby?"

"I don't know. A van with no windows came. The woman with white hair, she was there. She delivered the baby. I remember hearing it cry. Then they took it away. I don't even know if it was a boy or a girl. They drove us back to the motel. The woman with the white hair, she gave us our money."

Katarina shrugged.

It felt as if my circulation had stopped. I tried to think this through, get past the horror. I looked at Rachel and started to ask how, but she shook her head. Now was not the time to make deductions. Now was the time to gather information.

"I loved it here," Katarina said after some time had passed. "You think you have a wonderful country. But you really have no idea. I wanted so much to stay. But the money started running low. I looked for ways. I met a woman who told me about the Web site. You put your name and men write you. They wouldn't want a whore, she told me. So I made up a biography with a farm. When men asked, I gave them an e-mail address. I met Verne three months later."

Verne's face fell even farther. "You mean the whole time we were writing . . . ?"

"I was in America, yes."

He shook his head. "Was anything you told me the truth?"

"Everything that mattered."

Verne made a scoffing sound.

"What about Pavel?" Rachel asked, trying to get us back on topic. "Where did he go?"

"I don't know. He went back home sometimes, I know. He would recruit other girls to bring over. For the finder's fee. Time to time, he would contact me. If he needed a few dollars, I'd give it to him. It was really no big deal. Until yesterday."

Katarina looked up at Verne. "The children, they will be hungry."

"They can wait."

"What happened yesterday?" Rachel asked.

"Pavel called late in the afternoon. He says he needs to see me right away. I don't like that. I ask him what he wants. He says he'll tell me when he gets here, not to worry. I don't know what to say."

"How about no?" Verne snapped.

"I couldn't say no."

"Why not?"

She didn't answer.

"Oh, I see. You were afraid he'd tell me the truth. Isn't that it?"

"I don't know."

"What the hell's that supposed to mean?"

"Yes, I was terrified he'd tell you the truth." Again she looked up at her husband. "And I prayed he would."

Rachel tried to get us back on course. "What happened when your brother got here?"

She started welling up.

"Katarina?"

"He said he needed to take Perry with him."

Verne's eyes widened.

Katarina's chest started hitching, as if it was hard to get air. "I said to him no. I said I wouldn't let him touch my children. He threatened me. He said he'd tell Verne everything. I said I didn't care. I wasn't going to let him

take Perry. Then he punched me in the stomach. I fell
down. He promised me he'd bring Perry back in a few
hours. He promised me no one would get hurt unless I
said something. If I called Verne or the police, he'd kill
Perry."

Verne's hands were balled into tight fists. His face was
scarlet.

"I tried to stop him. I tried to stand up, but Pavel
pushed me back down. And then"—her voice caught—
"then he drove away. With Perry. The next six hours
were the longest of my life." She sneaked a guilty glance
in my direction. I knew what she was thinking. She had
experienced this terror for six hours. I'd been living with
it for a year and half.

"I didn't know what to do. My brother is a bad man.
I know that. But I couldn't believe he'd ever hurt my
children. He was their uncle."

I thought about Stacy then, my sister, my words of
sibling defense echoing in hers.

"For hours, I stayed by the window. I couldn't stand it.
Finally, at midnight, I called his cell phone. He told me
he was on his way back. Perry was fine, he said. Nothing
had happened. He tried to sound light, but there was
something in his voice. I asked him where he was. He
told me he was on Route Eighty near Paterson. I
couldn't just sit in the house and wait. I told him I'd
meet him halfway. I packed Verne Junior and we went.
When we got to the gas station by the Sparta exit. . . ."
She looked at Verne. "He was fine. Perry. I felt such relief, you can't imagine."

Verne was tugging on his bottom lip with his thumb
and index finger. He looked away again.

"Before I left, Pavel grabbed my arm hard. He pulled
me close to him. I could see how scared he was. He said
no matter what, never tell anybody about what hap-

pened. That if they found out about me—if they knew he had a sister—they would kill us all."

"Who is they?" Rachel asked.

"I don't know. Whoever he was working for. The people who bought the babies, I think. He said they were crazy."

"What did you do then?"

Katarina opened her mouth, closed it, tried again. "I went to the supermarket," she said with a sound that might have even been a laugh. "I bought the kids juice boxes. I let them drink while we shopped. I just wanted to do something normal. To, I don't know, to put it all behind me."

Katarina looked up at Verne then. I followed her gaze. I again studied this man with the long hair and the bad teeth. After a moment, he turned to her.

"It's all right," Verne said in the gentlest voice I'd ever heard. "You were scared. You've been scared your whole life."

Katarina started sobbing.

"I don't want you to be scared anymore, okay?"

He moved toward her. He took her in his arms. She settled enough to say, "He said they'd come after us. The whole family."

"Then I'll protect us," Verne said simply. He looked at me over her shoulder. "They took my kid. They threatened my family. You hear what I'm saying?"

I nodded.

"I'm in this now. I'm with you till it's over."

Rachel sat back. I saw her grimace. Her eyes closed. I didn't know how much longer she could go. I moved toward her. She held up her palm. "Katarina, we need you to help us here. Where was your brother staying?"

"I don't know."

"Think. Do you have any of his possessions, something that can lead us to who he worked for?"

She let go of her husband. Verne stroked her hair with a blend of tenderness and strength I envied. I turned to Rachel. I wondered if I had the courage to do the same.

"Pavel just arrived from Kosovo," Katarina said. "And he would not come here empty handed."

Rachel nodded. "You think he brought a pregnant woman with him?"

"He always did before."

"Do you know where she's staying?"

"The women always stay at the same place—the same place I stayed. It's in Union City." Katarina looked up. "You'll want this woman to help you, right?"

"Yes."

"Then I'll have to go with you. She most likely won't speak English."

I looked at Verne. He nodded. "I'll watch the kids."

No one moved for several moments. We needed to gather our strength, adjust as if we'd entered a no-gravity zone. I used the time to step outside and call Zia. She answered on the first ring and started right in.

"The cops might be listening in, so let's not stay on the line too long," Zia said.

"Okay."

"Our friend Detective Regan came to my house. He told me that he thought you used my car to leave the hospital. I called Lenny. Lenny told me to neither confirm nor deny any allegation. You can probably guess the rest."

"Thanks."

"You being careful?"

"Always."

"Sure. By the way, the cops aren't stupid. They figure that if you used one friend's car, maybe they would look for another."

I got her meaning—don't use Lenny's car.

"Better hang up now," she said. "Love you."

The phone went dead. I moved back inside. Verne had unlocked his gun cabinet using a key. He was checking weapons. On the other side of the room, he had a safe with ammunition. It opened by combination. I looked over his shoulder. Verne wiggled his eyebrows at me. He had enough firepower to overthrow a European country.

I told them about my conversation with Zia. Verne did not hesitate. He slapped my back and said, "I have just the vehicle for you."

Ten minutes later, Katarina, Rachel, and I drove off in a white Camaro.

chapter 38

We found the pregnant girl right away.

Before we vroomed off in Verne's ride, Rachel jumped in the shower to rinse off the blood and grime. I quickly changed her bandage. Katarina loaned her a summer dress with a flower print, the kind that fits loose but clings just right. Rachel's hair was wet and kinky, still dripping when we reached the car. Forget the bruises and swelling—I am not sure that I ever saw a more beautiful woman in my life.

We started driving. Katarina insisted on taking the fold-down seat in the back. That left Rachel and me in the front. For a few minutes, nobody spoke. We were, I think, decompressing.

"What Verne said," Rachel began. "About getting the secrets out of the way and wiping the slate clean."

I kept driving.

"I didn't kill my husband, Marc."

She didn't seem to care that Katarina was in the car. Neither did I. "The official word is that it was an accident," I said.

"The official word is a lie." She let out a long breath. She needed time to gather herself. I gave it to her.

"It was Jerry's second marriage. He had two kids from his first. His son, Derrick, has cerebral palsy. The

expenses are ridiculous. Jerry was never good with finances or anything like that, but he did his best there.
He even set up a large life-insurance policy in case
something happened to him."

In my peripheral vision, I could see her hands. They
didn't move or tighten into fists. They just sat primly in
her lap.

"Our marriage fell apart. There were a lot of reasons.
I mentioned some before. I really didn't love him. I
think he sensed that. But most of all, Jerry was a manic-
depressive. When he stopped taking his medication, it
got worse. So I finally filed for divorce."

I peeked over at her. She was biting her lip and blinking.

"On the day they served him papers, Jerry shot himself in the head. I was the one who found him slumped
over our kitchen table. There was an envelope with my
name on it. I recognized Jerry's handwriting right away.
I opened it up. There was just a single sheet of paper
with one word written on it. 'Bitch.' "

Katarina put a comforting hand on Rachel's shoulder. I concentrated hard on the road.

"I think Jerry did it like that on purpose," she said,
"because he knew what I'd have to do."

"What was that?" I asked

"A suicide would mean that the life insurance
wouldn't pay. Derrick would be financially devastated. I
couldn't let that happen. I called one of my old bosses,
a friend of Jerry's named Joseph Pistillo. He's a big deal
in the FBI. He brought down a few of his men, and we
made it look like an accident. The official line was, I mis-
took him for a burglar. The local cops and the insurance
company were both pressured into signing off on it."
She shrugged.

"So why did you leave the bureau?" I asked.

"Because the rank-and-file never bought it. They all thought that I must be sleeping with someone powerful. Pistillo couldn't protect me. It would look bad. I couldn't defend myself, for that matter. I tried to tough it out, but the FBI is not a place for the unwanted."

Her head dropped back against the pad. She looked out the passenger window. I didn't know what to make of the story. I didn't know what to make of any of this yet. I wished that I could say something comforting. I couldn't. I just kept driving until we mercifully arrived at the motel in Union City.

Katarina approached the check-in desk, pretending to speak only Serbian, gesturing like mad, until the clerk, figuring that it was the only way to settle her down, told her the room number of the only other person on the premises who seemed to speak that language. We were in business.

The pregnant girl's room was more a low-end efficiency unit than something you'd find in a normal highway motel. I refer to her as a pregnant "girl" because Tatiana—that was what she said her name was—claimed to be sixteen. I suspected that she was younger. Tatiana had the sunken eyes of a child who'd just stepped out of a war newsreel, which in this situation may have literally been the case.

I stayed back, almost out of the room. So did Rachel. Tatiana did not speak English. We let Katarina handle it. The two of them talked for about ten minutes. After that, there was a brief silence. Tatiana sighed, opened the drawer under the phone, and gave Katarina a piece of paper. Katarina kissed her cheek and then came over to us.

"She's scared," Katarina said. "She only knew Pavel. He left her yesterday and said not to leave the room under any circumstances."

I glanced over at Tatiana. I tried to give her a reassuring smile. It fell, I'm certain, way short.

"What did she say?" Rachel asked.

"She doesn't know anything, of course. Like me. She only knows that her baby will find a good home."

"What was that piece of paper she gave you?"

Katarina lifted the slip of paper into view. "It's a phone number. If there is an emergency, she's supposed to call and dial in four nines."

"A beeper," I said.

"Yes, I believe so."

I looked at Rachel. "Can we trace it?"

"I doubt it will lead anywhere. It's easy to get beepers using a phony name."

"So let's call it," I said. I turned to Katarina. "Has Tatiana met anyone else besides your brother?"

"No."

"Then you make the call," I said to her. "You say you're Tatiana. You tell whoever answers that you're bleeding or in pain or something."

"Whoa," Rachel said. "Slow down a second."

"We need to get someone here," I said.

"And then what?"

"What do you mean, then what? You interrogate them. Isn't that what you do, Rachel?"

"I'm not a fed anymore. And even if I was, we can't just bulldoze them over like that. Pretend you're one of them for a second. You show up and I confront you. What would you do if you were involved in something like this?"

"Cut a deal."

"Maybe. Or maybe you'd just clam up and ask for a lawyer. Then where would we be?"

I thought about that. "If the person asks for a lawyer," I said, "you leave them alone with me."

Rachel stared at me. "Are you serious?"

"We're talking about my daughter's life."

"We're talking about a lot of children now, Marc. These people buy babies. We need to put them out of business."

"So what are you suggesting?"

"We page them. Like you said. But Tatiana will have to do the talking. She'll have to say whatever to get them here. They'll examine her. We check their license plate. We follow them when they leave. We find out who they are."

"I don't understand," I said. "Why can't Katarina make the call?"

"Because whoever comes will want to examine the person they talked to on the phone. Katarina and Tatiana don't sound alike. They'll know what we're up to."

"But why do we need to go through all that? We'll have them here. Why risk following them home?"

Rachel closed her eyes, then opened them again. "Marc, think. If they find out we're on to them, how will they react?"

I stopped.

"And I want to be clear about something else. This isn't about just Tara anymore. We need to bring these guys down."

"And if we just jump them here," I said, seeing her true point now, "they'll be forewarned."

"That's right."

I wasn't sure how much I cared about that. Tara was my priority. If the FBI or cops want to build a legal case against these people, I was all for it. But that sat way off my personal radar.

Katarina talked to Tatiana about our plan. I could see it wasn't taking. The young girl was petrified. She kept shaking her head no. Time passed—time we really didn't have. I snapped and decided to do something fairly stupid. I picked up the phone, dialed the beeper number, and pressed the nine button four times. Tatiana went still.

"You'll do it," I said.

Katarina translated.

No one spoke for the next two minutes. We all just stared at Tatiana. When the phone rang, I did not like what I saw in the young girl's eyes. Katarina said something, her tone urgent. Tatiana shook her head and crossed her arms. The phone rang a third time. Then a fourth.

I took out my gun.

Rachel said, "Marc."

I kept the gun at my side. "Does she know we're talking about my daughter's life?"

Katarina burst off something in Serbian. I looked Tatiana hard in the eyes. There was no reaction. I raised the gun and fired. The lamp exploded, the sound reverberating too loudly in the room. Everyone jumped. Another stupid move. I knew that. I just wasn't sure I cared.

"Marc!"

Rachel put her hand on my arm. I shook it off. I looked at Katarina. "Tell her if the caller hangs up . . ."

I never finished the thought. Katarina started talking quickly. I gripped the gun, but it was back at my side now. Tatiana still had her eyes on me. Sweat popped up on my forehead. I felt my body shake. As Tatiana watched me, something in her face began to soften.

"Please," I said.

On the sixth ring Tatiana snatched up the receiver and started talking.

I glanced over at Katarina. She listened to the conversation and then she nodded at me. I moved back to the other side of the room. I still had the gun in my hand. Rachel stared at me. But I stared back.

Rachel blinked first.

We parked the Camaro in a restaurant lot next door and waited.

There was not a lot of chitchat. The three of us looked everywhere but at each other, as if we were all strangers on an elevator. I wasn't sure what to say. I wasn't sure what I felt. I had fired a gun and come pretty close to threatening a teenage girl. Worse, I don't think I cared very much. The repercussions, if there were any, seemed far away, storm clouds that might gather and then again might disperse.

I flipped on the radio and dialed into the local news station. I half expected someone to say, "We interrupt this program with this special bulletin," and then announce our names and give out descriptions and maybe warn that we were armed and dangerous. But there were no stories on a shooting in Kasselton or a police search for us.

Rachel and I were still in the front while Katarina lay across the fold-down seat in the back. Rachel had her Palm Pilot out. The stylus was in her hand, poised to tap. I debated calling Lenny, but I remembered Zia's warning. They'd be listening in. I had nothing much to report anyway—just that I had threatened a pregnant sixteen-year-old girl with an illegal handgun taken off the corpse of a man who'd been murdered in my backyard. Lenny the Lawyer would certainly not relish the details.

"Do you think she'll cooperate?" I said.

Rachel shrugged.

Tatiana had promised that she was now with us. I didn't know if we could believe her or not. To be on the safe side, I unplugged her phone and took the cord with me. I searched the room for papers and writing material, so she couldn't sneak her visitor a note. I found nothing. Rachel also put her cell phone on the window ledge to be used as a listening device. Katarina had the phone to her ear now. Again she would translate.

Half an hour later, a gold-toned Lexus SC 430 roared into the lot. I whistled low. A colleague at the hospital had just bought the same car. It put him back sixty grand. The woman who emerged sported a short, spiky shock of white hair. She wore a too-tight, hair-matching white shirt and, keeping with the theme, white pants so tight they seemed to be hovering below skin level. Her arms were toned and tan. The woman had that look. You know the one. She brought on memories of the hot mother strutting around the tennis club.

Rachel and I both turned to Katarina. Katarina nodded solemnly. "That's her. That's the woman who delivered my baby."

I saw Rachel begin working her Palm Pilot. "What are you doing?" I asked.

"Putting in the license plate and make. We should know who the car is registered to in a matter of minutes."

"How do you do that?"

"It's not hard," Rachel said. "Every law enforcement officer makes connections. And if you don't, you pay off someone at the DMV. Five hundred bucks usually."

"Are you on-line or something?"

She nodded. "Wireless modem. A friend of mine named Harold Fisher, he's a tech geek who works freelance. He didn't like how the feds pushed me out."

"So he helps you now?"

"Yes."

The white-haired woman leaned back in and pulled out what might have been a medical bag. She threw on a pair of designer sunglasses and hurried toward Tatiana's room. The woman knocked, the door opened, Tatiana let her in.

I turned around in my seat and watched Katarina. She had the phone on mute. "Tatiana is telling her that she feels better now. The woman is annoyed she called for nothing." She paused.

"Have you heard a name yet?"

Katarina shook her head. "The woman is going to examine her."

Rachel stared at her tiny Palm Pilot screen as if it were a magic eight ball. "Bang."

"What?"

"Denise Vanech, Forty-seven Riverview Avenue, Ridgewood, New Jersey. Forty-six years of age. No outstanding parking violations."

"You got it that fast?"

She shrugged. "All Harold has to do is type in the license plate. He's going to see what he can dig up on her." Her stylus started up again. "Meanwhile I'm going to plug the name into Google."

"The search engine?"

"Yup. You'd be surprised what you can find."

I knew about that, actually. I once put my own name in. I don't remember why. Zia and I were drunk and did it for fun. She calls it "ego surfing."

"Not much speaking now." Katarina's face was a mask of concentration. "Maybe she's examining her?"

I looked over at Rachel. "Two hits on Google," she said. "The first is a Web site for the Bergen County planning board. She requested a variance to subdivide her lot. It was rejected. The second, however, is more interesting. It's an alumni site. It lists past graduates that they're trying to locate."

"What school?" I asked.

"University of Philadelphia Family Nurse and Mid-wifery."

That fit.

Katarina said, "They're done."

"Fast," I said.

"Very."

Katarina listened some more. "The woman is telling Tatiana to take care of herself. That she should eat bet-ter, for the baby. That she should call if she feels any fur-ther discomfort."

I turned to Rachel. "Sounds more pleasant than when she arrived."

Rachel nodded. The woman we assumed was Denise Vanech came out. She walked with her head high, her rear end twitching in that cocky way. The stretched white shirt was ribbed and, I couldn't help but notice, rather see-through. She got in her car and took off.

I started up the Camaro, the engine roaring like a life-time smoker with a hacking cough. I followed at a safe distance. I wasn't too worried about losing her. We knew where she lived now.

"I still don't understand," I said to Rachel. "How do they get away with buying babies?"

"They find desperate women. They lure them here with promises of money and a stable, comfortable home for their child."

"But in order to adopt," I said, "there's a whole pro-cedure you have to go through. It's a pain in the ass. I know some children overseas—physically deformed children—people tried to bring over. You can't believe the paperwork. It's impossible."

"I don't have the answer to that, Marc."

Denise Vanech veered onto the New Jersey Turnpike north. That would be the way back to Ridgewood. I let the Camaro drop back another twenty, thirty feet. The right blinker came on, and the Lexus turned off at the Vince Lombardi rest stop. Denise Vanech parked and headed inside. I pulled the car to the side of the ramp and looked at Rachel. She was biting her lip.

"Could be she's using the bathroom," I said.

"She washed up after examining Tatiana. Why didn't she go then?"

"Maybe she's hungry?"

"Does she look like she eats much Burger King to you, Marc?"

"So what do we do?"

There was little hesitation. Rachel gripped the door handle. "Drop me off by the door."

Denise Vanech was pretty sure that Tatiana was faking.

The girl had claimed to be hemorrhaging. Denise checked the sheets. They hadn't been changed, yet there was no blood on them. The tiles on the bathroom floor were clean. The toilet seat was clean. There was no blood anywhere.

That alone, of course, wouldn't mean all that much. There was a chance the girl had cleaned up. But there were other things. The gynecological examination showed no signs of distress. Nothing. Not the slightest red tint. Her vaginal hairs, too, had no traces of blood. Denise checked the shower when she finished up. Dry as a bone. The girl had called less than an hour before. She claimed to be bleeding heavily.

It didn't add up.

Lastly, the girl's demeanor was wrong. The girls are always scared. That goes without saying. Denise had moved out of Yugoslavia when she was nine, during Tito's reign of relative peace, and she knew what a hellhole it was. To this girl, from where she had come, the United States must seem like Mars. But her fear had a different quality to it. Usually the girls stare at Denise as if she were some kind of parent or savior, looking up to her with a mix of trepidation and hope. But this girl averted her gaze. She fidgeted too much. And there was something else. Tatiana had been brought in by Pavel. He was usually good about watching them. But he hadn't been there. Denise was about to ask about that, but she decided to wait and play it out. If nothing was wrong, the girl would certainly raise Pavel's name.

She hadn't.

Yes, something was definitely wrong.

Denise did not want to raise suspicion. She finished the exam and hurried out. Behind her sunglasses, she checked for possible surveillance vans. There were none. She looked for obvious unmarked police cars. Again nothing. Of course, she was no expert. Though she had been working with Steven Bacard for nearly a decade, there had never been any complications. Perhaps that was why she'd let her guard down.

As soon as she got back into her car, Denise reached for her cell phone. She wanted to call Bacard. But no. If they were somehow on to them, they'd be able to trace that back. Denise debated using a pay phone at the nearest gas station. But they'd be expecting that too. When she saw the sign for the rest stop, she remembered that they had a huge bank of pay phones. She could call from there. If she moved fast enough, they wouldn't see her or know what phone she used.

But was that safe either?

She quickly sorted through the possibilities. Suppose she was indeed being followed. Driving to Bacard's office would definitely be the wrong move. She could wait and call him when she got home. But they might have a tap on her phone. This—calling from the large bank of pay phones—seemed the least risky.

Denise grabbed a napkin and used it to keep her fingerprints off the receiver. She was careful not to wipe it off. There were probably dozens of fingerprints already on it. Why make their job any easier?

Steven Bacard picked up. "Hello?"

The obvious strain in his voice made her heart sink. "Where is Pavel?" she asked.

"Denise?"

"Yes."

"Why are you asking?"

"I just visited his girl. Something isn't right."

"Oh God," he moaned. "What happened?"

"The girl called the emergency number. She said she was hemorrhaging, but I think she was lying."

There was silence.

"Steve?"

"Go home. Don't talk to anyone."

"Okay." Denise saw the white Camaro pull up. She frowned. Hadn't she seen it before?

"Are there any records in your house?" Bacard asked.

"No, of course not."

"You're sure?"

"Positive."

"Okay, good."

A woman was getting out of the Camaro. Even from this distance, Denise could see the bandage on the woman's ear.

"Go home," Bacard said.

Before the woman could turn around, Denise hung up the phone and slipped into the bathroom.

Steven Bacard had loved the old *Batman* TV show as a kid. Every episode, he remembered, started out pretty much the same way. A crime would be committed. They would flash to Commissioner Gordon and Chief O'Hara. The two law-enforcement buffoons would be grim faced. They would discuss the situation and realize that there was only one way out. Commissioner Gordon would then pick up the red Batphone. Batman would answer, promise to save the day, turn to Robin and say, "To the Batpoles!"

He stared at the phone with that creepy feeling in the pit of his stomach. This was no hero he was calling. Just the opposite, in fact. But in the end, survival was what mattered. Pretty words and justification were great during times of peace. In times of war, in times of life and death, it was simpler: Us or Them. He picked up the phone and dialed the number.

Lydia answered sweetly. "Hello, Steven."

"I need you again."

"Bad?"

"Very."

"We're on our way," she said.

chapter 39

"When I got in there," Rachel said, "she was in the bathroom. But I have a feeling she made a call first."

"Why?"

"There was a line in the bathroom. She was only three people ahead of me. She should have been more."

"Any way of figuring out who she called?"

"Not in the near future, no. Every phone in that place is taken. Even if I had full FBI access, it would take some time."

"So we keep following."

"Yes." She turned behind her. "Do you have an atlas in the car?"

Katarina smiled. "Many. Verne likes maps. World, country, state?"

"State."

She dug into the pocket behind my seat and handed Rachel the atlas. Rachel uncapped a pen and started marking it up.

"What are you doing?" I asked.

"I'm not sure."

The cell phone rang. I picked it up.

"You guys all right?"

"Yeah, Verne, we're fine."

"Got my sister to watch the kids for me. I'm in the pickup heading east. What's your ten-twenty?"

I told him we were heading to Ridgewood. He knew the town.

"I'm about twenty minutes away," he said. "I'll meet you at the Ridgewood Coffee Company on Van Neste Park."

"We may be at this midwife's house," I said.

"I'll wait."

"Okay."

"Hey, Marc," Verne said, "not to get sentimental or anything, but if somebody needs shooting—"

"I'll let you know."

The Lexus turned off at Linwood Avenue. We dropped farther back. Rachel kept her head down, alternating between the stylus on the Palm Pilot and the marker on the atlas. We hit the suburbs. Denise Vanech turned left on Waltherly Road.

"She's definitely heading home," Rachel said. "Let her go. We need to think this through."

I couldn't believe what she was suggesting. "What do you mean, think this through? We need to approach her."

"Not yet. I'm working on something."

"What?"

"Just give me a few minutes."

I slowed my speed and turned down Van Dien, right near Valley Hospital. I looked back at Katarina. She gave me a small smile. Rachel kept working at whatever. I checked the dashboard clock. Time to meet Verne. I took North Maple to Ridgewood Avenue. A parking spot opened in front of a store named Duxiana. I grabbed it. Verne's pickup truck was parked across the street. It had mag wheels and two bumper stickers, one reading, CHARLTON HESTON FOR PRESIDENT, and the other: DO I LOOK LIKE A HEMORRHOID? THEN GET OFF MY ASS.

Ridgewood's town center was a blend of turn-of-the-century picture-postcard splendor and modern-day extravagant food-court mall. Most of the old mom-n-pop shops were gone now. Sure, the independent bookstore still thrived. There was an upscale mattress store, a cute place that sold sixties paraphernalia, a smattering of boutiques, beauty parlors, and jewelry stores. And, yes, a few of the chains—Gap, Williams-Sonoma, the prerequuisite Starbucks—had gobbled up space. But more than anything, the town center had become a veritable smorgasbord, a potpourri of eateries for too many tastes and budgets. Name a country, they had a bistro here. Throw a stone, even pathetically, in any direction, you would hit three such eateries.

Rachel took the atlas and Palm Pilot with her. She worked as we walked. Verne was already inside the coffee shop, chatting up the burly guy behind the counter. Verne wore a Deere baseball cap with a T-shirt that read: MOOSEHEAD: A GREAT BEER AND A NEW EXPERIENCE FOR A MOOSE.

We grabbed a table.

"So what's the deal?" Verne said.

I let Katarina fill him in. I was watching Rachel. Every time I started to speak, she held up a finger to silence me. I told Verne that he should take Katarina home. We didn't need their help anymore. They should be with their children. Verne was reluctant.

The time was sneaking up on 10:00 A.M. I wasn't really tired. Lack of sleep—even for reasons far less adrenaline generating than this—does not bother me. I credit my medical residency and the many nights on call for that.

"Bang," Rachel said again.

"What?"

With her eyes still on the Palm Pilot, Rachel put out her hand. "Let me use your phone."

"What is it?"

"Just give it to me, okay?"

I handed her the cell phone. She dialed and moved to the corner of the café. Katarina excused herself to use the bathroom. Verne poked me with his elbow and pointed at Rachel.

"You two in love?"

"It's complicated," I said.

"Only if you're a dumb-ass."

I may have shrugged.

"You either love her or you don't," Verne said. "The rest? That's for dumb-asses."

"Is that how you dealt with what you heard this morning?"

He thought about that. "What Kat said. What she did in the past. It don't matter much. There's a core. I've slept with that woman for eight years. I know the core."

"I don't know Rachel that well."

"Yeah, you do. Look at her." I did. And I felt something airy and light travel through me. "She got beaten up. She got shot, for Chrissake." He paused. I wasn't looking, but I bet he shook his mane in disgust. "You let that go, you know what you are?"

"A dumb-ass."

"A *professional* dumb-ass. You give up your amateur status."

Rachel hung up the phone and hurried back over. Maybe it was something Verne said, but I could swear that I saw a bit of fire back in her eyes. In that dress, with her hair mussed, with the confident lick-the-world smile, I was transported back. It didn't last long. No more than a moment or two. But maybe it was enough.

"Bang?" I asked.

"Cannon-fire, Fourth-of-July bang." She started tapping with the stylus again. "I just need to do one more thing. In the meantime, look at this atlas."

I pulled it over. Verne looked over my shoulder. He smelled like motor oil. There were all kinds of markings on the atlas—little stars, crosses, but the thickest line was a circuitous route. I recognized enough of it.

"That's the route the kidnappers took last night," I said. "When we were following them."

"Right."

"What's with all the stars and stuff?"

"Okay, first thing. Look at the actual route they took. Up north over the Tappan Zee. Then west. Then south. Then west again. Then back east and north."

"They were stalling," I said.

"Right. It's like we said. They were setting up that trap for us at your house. But think about it a second. Our theory is that someone from law enforcement warned them about the Q-Logger, right?"

"So?"

"So no one knew about the Q-Logger until you were at the hospital. That means, for at least part of the journey, they wouldn't have known I was tailing them."

I wasn't sure I followed, but I said, "Okay."

"Do you pay your phone bill on-line?" she asked.

The subject change threw me for a moment. "Yes," I said.

"So you get a statement, right? You click on the link, you sign in, you can see all your calls. It probably has a reverse directory link too—so you can click on the number and see who you called."

I nodded. It did.

"Well, I got Denise Vanech's last phone bill." She held up a hand. "Don't worry about how. Again it's fairly easy. Harold could probably do it by hacking, if he had more time, but having a connection or giving a bribe is easier. Now with the Internet billing, it's easier than ever."

"Harold sent you her bill on-line?"

"Yep. Anyway, Ms. Vanech makes a fair amount of calls. That's what took me so long. We've been sorting through them, finding the names, then the addresses."

"And a name popped out?"

"No, an address did. I wanted to see if she called anybody on the kidnapper's route."

Now I saw where she was going. "And I assume the answer is yes?"

"Better than yes. Remember when they stopped at the MetroVista office complex?"

"Sure."

"Over the past month, Denise Vanech placed six calls to the law office of a Steven Bacard." Rachel pointed to the star she'd drawn on the map. "At MetroVista."

"A lawyer?"

"Harold is going to see what he can dig up, but again I just used Google. The name Steven Bacard pops up frequently."

"In what context?"

Rachel smiled again. "His expertise is adoption."

Verne said, "Sweet mother of God."

I sat back and tried to digest it all. Warning lights flashed, but I wasn't sure what they meant. Katarina came back to the table. Verne told her what we'd found. We were getting close. I knew that. But I felt adrift. My cell phone—or should I say, Zia's—rang. I looked down at the Caller ID. It was Lenny. I debated not answering, remembering what Zia had said. But of course, Lenny would know about the possibility of a tap. He had been the one who warned Zia.

I hit the ANSWER button.

"Let me talk first," Lenny said before I could even utter a hello. "For the record, if this is being taped, this conversation is between an attorney and his client. It is thus protected. Marc, don't tell me where you are. Don't tell me anything that would force me to lie. You understand?"

"Yes."

"Did your trip bear fruit?" he asked.

"Not the fruit we wanted. Not yet anyway. But we're getting very close."

"Any way I can help?"

"I don't think so." Then, "Wait." I remembered that Lenny had handled my sister's arrests. He had been her main legal advisor. "Did Stacy ever say anything to you about adoption?"

"I'm not following."

"Did she ever think about giving up a baby for adoption, or in any way mention adoption to you?"

"No. Is this somehow connected with the kidnapping?"

"Could be."

"I don't remember anything like that. Look, they might be taping us, so let me tell you why I called. They found a dead body at your house—a man shot twice in the head." Lenny knew that I was already aware of this. I assumed that he was saying this for the benefit of whoever might be eavesdropping. "They haven't made an ID, but they did locate the murder weapon in the Christies' backyard."

I was not surprised. Rachel had figured that they'd plant the gun somewhere.

"The thing is, Marc, the murder weapon is your old gun, the one that's been missing since the shooting at your house. They already ran a ballistics test. You and

Monica were shot with two different thirty-eights, re-member?"

"Yes."

"Well, that gun—*your* gun—was one of the two used that morning."

I closed my eyes. Rachel mouthed a "What?" at me.

"I better go," Lenny said. "I'll look into Stacy and an adoption angle, if you want. See what I can dig up."

"Thanks."

"Stay safe."

He hung up. I turned to Rachel and told her about the gun discovery and the ballistics test. She leaned back and bit down on her lower lip, another familiar habit from our dating days. "So that means," she said, "that Pavel and the rest of these people are definitely linked to the first attack."

"You still had doubts?"

"A few hours ago, we thought it was a total hoax, re-member? We thought that maybe these guys knew enough to fake like they had Tara, just to con some ran-som money out of your father-in-law. But now we know different. These people were there that morning. They were part of the original abduction."

It made sense, but something about it still felt wrong. "Where do we go from here?" I asked.

"The logical step is to visit this lawyer, Steven Bac-ard," Rachel said. "The problem is, we don't know if he's the boss or just another employee. For all we know, Denise Vanech is the mastermind and he works for her. Or they both work for a third party. And if we go bust-ing in there, Bacard is just going to clam up. He's a lawyer. He's too smart to talk to us."

"So what do you suggest?"

"I'm not sure," she said. "It might be time to call in the feds. Maybe they can raid his office."

I shook my head. "That'll take too long."

"We might be able to get them to move fast."

"Assuming they believe us—which is a big assumption—how fast?"

"I don't know, Marc."

I didn't like it. "Suppose Denise Vanech was suspicious back there. Suppose Tatiana gets scared and calls her again. Suppose there is indeed a leak. There are too many variables here, Rachel."

"So what do you think we should do?"

"A two-prong attack," I said, the words coming out without much thought. There was a problem. I suddenly had a solution. "You take Denise Vanech. I take Steven Bacard. We coordinate it so that we hit them at the same time."

"Marc, he's a lawyer. He's not going to open up to you."

I looked at her. She saw it. Verne sat up a little and made a small *woo-ee* noise.

"You're going to threaten him?" Rachel asked.

"We're talking about my child's life."

"And you're talking about taking the law into your own hands." Then she added, "Again."

"So?"

"You threatened a teenage girl with a gun."

"I was trying to intimidate, that's all. I would have never really hurt her."

"The law—"

"The law hasn't done squat to help my daughter," I said, trying not to shout. In the corner of my eye, I saw Verne nodding along with my outrage. "They're too busy wasting time on you."

That made her straighten up. "Me?"

"Lenny told me at the house. They think you did it. Without me. That you were obsessed with having me back or something."

"What?"

I rose from the table. "Look, I'm going to see this Bacard guy. I don't plan on hurting anyone, but if he knows something about my daughter, I'm going to find out what it is."

Verne raised his fist. "Right on."

I asked Verne if I could keep borrowing the Camaro. He reminded me that he was behind me all the way. I expected Rachel to argue some more. She didn't. Maybe she knew that I would not change my mind. Maybe she knew I was right. Or maybe—perhaps most likely—she had been stunned to learn that her old colleagues had zeroed in on her as the sole serious suspect.

"I'll come with you," Rachel said.

"No." My voice left no wiggle room. I had no idea what I would do when I got there, but I knew that I was capable of plenty. "What I said before makes sense." I could hear my familiar surgeon tone taking over. "I'll call you when I get to Bacard's office. We hit him and Denise Vanech at the same time."

I didn't wait for a response. I got back in the Camaro and started toward the MetroVista office complex.

chapter 40

Lydia checked her surroundings. She was a little more in the open than she liked to be, but that couldn't be helped. She had on the spiky blond wig—the one not unlike Steven Bacard's description of Denise Vanech. She knocked on the door of the efficiency.

The curtain next to the door moved. Lydia smiled. "Tatiana?"

No reply.

She had been warned that Tatiana spoke very little English. Lydia had debated how to play this. Time was critical. Everything and everyone needed to be shut down. When someone who dislikes blood as much as Bacard says that, you immediately understand the ramifications. Lydia and Heshy had split up. She had come down here. They would meet up afterward.

"It's okay, Tatiana," she said through the door. "I'm here to help."

There was no movement.

"I'm a friend of Pavel's," she tried. "You know Pavel?"

The curtain moved. A young woman's face appeared for a brief moment, gaunt and childlike. Lydia nodded at her. The woman still did not open the door. Lydia scanned her surroundings. Nobody looking, but she still felt too exposed. This had to end fast.

"Wait," Lydia said. Then, looking at the curtain, she reached into her purse. She pulled out a piece of paper and pen. She wrote something down, making sure that if someone was still at the window, they would see exactly what she was doing. She capped the pen and stepped close to the window. Lydia held the piece of paper up to the pane of glass so Tatiana could read it.

It was like drawing a scared cat out from under the sofa. Tatiana moved slowly. She came toward the window. Lydia stayed still, so as not to startle her. Tatiana leaned closer. Here, kitty, kitty. Lydia could see the girl's face now. She was squinting, trying to see what was on the piece of paper.

When Tatiana came close enough, Lydia pressed the barrel of the gun against the glass and aimed between the young girl's eyes. At the last second, Tatiana tried to veer away. Too little, too late. The bullet went clean through the glass and into Tatiana's right eye. Blood appeared. Lydia fired again, automatically tilting the gun downward. It caught the falling Tatiana in the top of the forehead. But the second bullet had been superfluous. The first shot, the one in the eye, had ripped into the brain and killed the young girl instantly.

Lydia hurried away. She risked a glance behind her. No one. When she reached the neighboring mall, she dumped the wig and the white coat. She found her car in a lot another half mile away.

I called Rachel when I arrived at MetroVista. She was parked down the street from Denise Vanech's house. We were both ready to go.

I'm not sure what I expected to happen here. I guess I figured that I would explode into Bacard's office, stick my gun in his face, and demand answers. What I hadn't foreseen was a regular, state-of-the-art office setup—

that is, Steven Bacard had a well-appointed reception area. There were two people waiting—a married couple, by all appearances. The husband had his face stuck in a laminated *Sports Illustrated*. The wife looked to be in pain. She tried to smile at me, but it was as if the effort would wound her.

I realized how shoddy I must look. I was still in my hospital scrubs. I was unshaven. My eyes were undoubtedly red from lack of sleep. My hair, I imagined, was probably sticking up in a textbook case of bedhead.

The receptionist was behind one of those sliding glass windows I usually associate with a dental practice. The woman—a small nameplate read AGNES WEISS—smiled at me sweetly.

"May I help you?"

"I'm here to see Mr. Bacard."

"Do you have an appointment?" She kept the tone sweet, but there was a rhetorical twang there too. She already knew the answer.

"This is an emergency," I said.

"I see. Are you a client of ours, Mr. . . . ?"

"Doctor," I snapped back automatically. "Tell him Dr. Marc Seidman needs to see him immediately. Tell him it's an emergency."

The young couple was watching us now. The receptionist's sweet smile began to falter. "Mr. Bacard's schedule is very full today." She opened her appointment ledger. "Let me see when we have something available, okay?"

"Agnes, look at me."

She did.

I gave her my gravest, you-might-die-if-I-don't-operate-right-away expression. "Tell him Dr. Seidman is here. Tell him it's an emergency. Tell him if he doesn't see me now, I will go to the police."

The young couple exchanged a glance.

Agnes adjusted herself in the chair. "If you'll just have a seat—"

"Tell him."

"Sir, if you don't step back, I'll call security."

So I stepped back. I could always step forward again. Agnes did not pick up the phone. I moved to a non-threatening distance. She slid the little window closed. The couple looked at me. The husband said, "She's covering for him."

The wife said, "Jack!"

Jack ignored her. "Bacard ran out of here half an hour ago. That receptionist keeps telling us he'll be right back."

I noticed a wall of photographs. Now I took a closer look. The same man was in all of them with a potpourri of politicos, quasicelebrities, gone-to-flab athletes. Steven Bacard, I assumed. I stared at the man's face—pudgy, weak chinned, country-club shiny.

I thanked the man named Jack and started for the door. Bacard's office was on the first floor, so I decided to wait by the entrance. This way, I could catch him un-awares on neutral ground and before Agnes had a chance to warn him. Five minutes passed. Several suits came and went, all harried from their days of printer toner and paperweights, dragged down by briefcases the size of car trunks. I paced the corridor.

Another couple entered. I could tell right away by their tentative steps and shattered eyes that they, too, were heading for Bacard's office. I watched them and wondered what path they had taken here. I saw them getting married, holding hands, kissing freely, making love in the morning. I saw their careers begin to thrive. I saw them feel the pang and segue toward the initial at-tempts at conceiving, the wait-till-next-month shrug when the home tests were negative, the slowly blossoming worry. A year passes. Still nothing. Their friends are starting to have children now and talk about them incessantly. Their parents are wondering when they'll have grandkids. I see them visiting the doctor—"a specialist"—the endless probing for the woman, the humiliation of masturbating into a beaker for the man, the personal questions, the blood and urine samples. More years pass. Their friends drift away. Making love is now strictly about procreation. It is calculated. It is always tinged with sadness. He stops holding her hand. She rolls over at night unless it's the right time in her cycle. I see the drugs, the Pergonal, the ridiculously expensive in-vitro fertilization, the time off from work, the checking of calendars, the same home tests, the crushing disappointments.

And now they were here.

No, I didn't know if any of this was really the case. But somehow I suspected that I was close. How far, I wondered, would they go to end this pain? How much would they pay?

"Oh my God! Oh my God!"

I jerked my head toward the scream. A man banged through the door.

"Call nine-one-one!"

I ran toward him. "What is it?"

I heard another scream. I ran through the door and outside. Yet another scream, this one more high pitched. I turned to my right. Two women were running out of the lower-level parking garage. I sprinted down the ramp. I slipped past the gate where you pick up your parking ticket. Someone else was calling for help, begging people to call 911.

Up ahead, I saw a security guard shouting into a walkie-talkie of some sort. He broke into a full gallop too. I followed him. When we turned the corner, the security guard pulled up. There was a woman next to him. She had her hands on her cheeks and was screaming. I ran next to them and looked down.

The body was jammed between two cars. His eyes stared open at nothing. His face was still pudgy, weak chinned, country-club shiny. The blood flowed from the wound in his head. The world teetered again.

Steven Bacard, maybe my last hope, was dead.

chapter 41

Rachel rang the doorbell. Denise Vanech had one of those pretentious chimes that ring up and then down the scale. The sun was all the way up now. The sky was blue and clear. On the street, two women power-walked carrying tiny mauve dumbbells. They nodded at Rachel, never missing a step. Rachel nodded back.

The intercom sounded. "Yes?"

"Denise Vanech?"

"Who is this please?"

"My name is Rachel Mills. I used to work with the FBI."

"Did you say, used to?"

"Yes."

"What do you want?"

"We need to talk, Ms. Vanech."

"About what?"

Rachel sighed. "Could you please just open the door?"

"Not until I know what this is about."

"The young girl you just visited in Union City. It's about her. For starters."

"I'm sorry. I don't discuss my patients."

"I said, for starters."

"Why would a former FBI agent be interested in any of this anyway?"

"Would you prefer I call a current agent?"

"I don't care what you do, Ms. Mills. I have nothing else to say to you. If the FBI has questions, they can call my lawyer."

"I see," Rachel said. "And would your lawyer be Steven Bacard?"

There was a brief silence. Rachel glanced back at the car.

"Ms. Vanech?"

"I don't have to talk to you."

"No, that's true. I'll start going door-to-door maybe. Talk to your neighbors."

"And say what?"

"I'll ask them if they know anything about a baby-smuggling operation that runs out of this house."

The door opened quickly. Denise Vanech with her tan skin and white hair pushed her head through the door. "I'll sue you for libel."

"Slander," Rachel said.

"What?"

"Slander. Libel is for the printed word. Slander is for the spoken. You mean slander. But either way, you'd have to prove what I'm saying is untrue. And we both know better."

"You have no evidence I've done anything wrong."

"Sure I do."

"I was treating a woman who claimed to be ill. That's all."

Rachel pointed up the lawn. Katarina stepped out of the car. "And what about this former patient?"

Denise Vanech put a hand to her mouth.

"She'll testify that you paid her money for her baby."

"No, she won't. They'll arrest her."

"Oh sure, right, the FBI would much rather crack down on a poor Serbian woman than break up a baby-smuggling ring. That's rich."

When Denise Vanech paused, Rachel pushed open the door. "Mind if I come in?"

"You have it wrong," she said quietly.

"Cool." Rachel was inside now. "You can correct me on all my misgivings."

Denise Vanech seemed suddenly unsure what to do. With one more look at Katarina, she slowly closed the front door. Rachel was already heading into the den. It was white. Totally white. White sectional couches against a white carpet. White porcelain statues of naked women riding horses. White coffee table, white side tables, and two of those white ergonomic-looking chairs with no backs. Denise followed her in. Her white clothes blended into the background, camouflagelike, making it look like her head and arms were floating.

"What do you want?"

"I'm looking for a specific child."

Denise let her eyes wander toward the door. "Hers?" She was talking about Katarina.

"No."

"It wouldn't matter. I don't know anything about placement."

"You're a midwife, correct?"

She folded the smooth, muscular arms under her bosom. "I'm not answering any of your questions."

"See, Denise, I know most of it. I just need you to fill in a few blanks." Rachel sat on the vinyl couch. Denise Vanech didn't move. "You have people in a foreign country. Maybe more than one country, I don't know. But I know about Serbia. So let's start there. You have people there who recruit girls. The girls come over pregnant, but they don't mention that at customs. You deliver the baby. Maybe here, maybe you have another spot, I don't know."

"You don't know a lot."

Rachel smiled. "I know enough."

Denise put her hands on her hips now. Her poses all seemed unnatural, as if she practiced them in front of a mirror.

"Anyway, the women have the babies. You pay them. You turn the baby over to Steven Bacard. He works for desperate couples who might be willing to bend the rules. They adopt the child."

"That's a nice story."

"Are you saying it's fiction?"

Denise grinned. "Total fiction."

"Cool, fine." She took out her cell phone. "Then let me call the feds. I'll introduce them to Katarina. They can go down to Union City and grill Tatiana. They can start going through your phone records, your finances—"

Denise started waving her hands. "Okay, okay, tell me what you want. I mean, you said you're not an FBI agent anymore. So what do you want with me?"

"I want to know how it works."

"You trying to cut yourself in?"

"No."

Denise waited a beat. "You said before that you're looking for a specific kid."

"Yes."

"You're working for someone, then?"

Rachel shook her head. "Look, Denise, you don't have a lot of options here. You either tell me the truth or you do serious jail time."

"And if I do tell you what I know?"

"Then I'll leave you out of it," Rachel said. It was a lie. But it was an easy one. This woman was involved in baby selling. There was no way Rachel was just going to let that go.

Denise sat. The tan seemed to be leaving her face. She

looked suddenly older. The lines around her mouth and eyes deepened. "It's not what you think," she began.

Rachel waited.

"We aren't hurting anyone. The truth is, we're helping."

Denise Vanech picked up her purse—white, of course—and dug out a cigarette. She offered one to Rachel. Rachel shook her off.

"Do you know anything about orphanages in poor countries?" Denise asked.

"Just what I see on PBS documentaries."

Denise lit the cigarette and drew a deep breath. "They are beyond awful. They may house forty babies to one nurse. The nurse is uneducated. The job is often a political favor. Some of the children are abused. Many are born drug dependent. The medical care—"

"I get the picture," Rachel said. "It's bad."

"Yes."

"And?"

"And we've found a way to save some of these children."

Rachel sat back and crossed her legs. She could see where this was going. "You pay pregnant women to fly over and sell you their babies?"

"That's hyperbole," she said.

Rachel shrugged. "How would you put it?"

"Put yourself in their position. You are a poor woman—and I mean poor—maybe a prostitute or somehow involved in white slavery. You are dirt. You have nothing. Some man knocks you up. You can abort or, if your religion forbids that, you can stick the kid in a godforsaken orphanage."

"Or," Rachel added, "if they're lucky, they end up with you?"

"Yes. We will give them adequate medical care. We

will offer financial restitution. And most importantly, we will make sure that their baby is placed in a loving home with caring, financially stable parents."

"Financially stable," Rachel repeated. "As in wealthy?"

"The service is expensive," she admitted. "But let me ask you something now. Take your friend out there. Katarina you said her name was?"

Rachel kept still.

"What would her life be like right now if we hadn't brought her here? What would her child's life be like?"

"I don't know. I don't know what you did with her child."

Denise smiled. "Fine, be argumentative. But you know what I mean. Do you think the baby would be better off with a dirt-poor prostitute in a war-torn hell-hole—or with a caring family here in the United States?"

"I see," Rachel said, trying not to squirm. "So you're sort of like the world's most wonderful social worker. This is charity work you're doing?"

Denise chuckled. "Look around you. I have expensive taste. I live in a ritzy neighborhood. I have a kid in college. I like to vacation in Europe. We have a house in the Hamptons. I do this because it's incredibly profitable. But so what? Who cares about my motives? My motives don't change the conditions in those orphanages."

"I still don't understand," Rachel said. "The women sell you their babies."

"They give us their babies," she corrected. "In return, we offer financial restitution—"

"Yeah, yeah, whatever. You get the baby. They get money. But then what? There has to be paperwork on the child; otherwise the government would step in. They wouldn't just let Bacard keep running adoptions like this."

"True."

"So how do you work it?"

She smiled. "You plan on busting me, don't you?"

"I don't know what I'm going to do."

She was still smiling. "You'll remember I cooperated, right?"

"Yes."

Denise Vanech pressed her palms together and closed her eyes. It looked as if she might be praying. "We hire American mothers."

Rachel made a face. "Excuse me?"

"For example, let's say Tatiana is about to have the baby. We might hire you, Rachel, to pose as the mother. You'd go to vital records at your town hall. You'd tell them you're pregnant and going to have a home birth, so there won't be a hospital record. They give you forms to fill out. They never check to see if you're really pregnant. How would they? It's not like they can give you a gynecological exam."

Rachel sat back. "Jesus."

"It's pretty simple when you think about it. There is no record that Tatiana is going to have a baby. There is a record that you are. I deliver the baby. I sign as the attending witness to your child being born. You become the mother. Bacard has you fill in the paperwork for adoption. . . ." She shrugged.

"So the adopting parents never learn the truth?"

"No, but they don't look too hard either. They're desperate. They don't want to know."

Rachel suddenly felt drained.

"And before you turn us in," Denise went on, "consider something else. We've been doing this for almost ten years now. That means there are children who've been happily placed with families that long. Dozens. All of those adoptions will be considered null and void. The birth mothers can come over here and demand their children back. Or take a payoff. You'd be ripping apart a lot of lives."

Rachel shook her head. It was too much to consider right now. Another time. She was getting off track. Had to keep her eye on the prize. She turned and squared her shoulders. She looked Denise deep in the eye.

"So how does Tara Seidman fit into all this?"

"Who?"

"Tara Seidman."

Now it was Denise's turn to look confused. "Wait a second. Wasn't that the little girl kidnapped in Kasselton?"

Rachel's cell phone rang. She checked the Caller ID and saw it was Marc. She was just about to press the answer button when a man stepped into view. Her breath stopped. Sensing something, Denise turned around. She jumped back at the sight.

It was the man from the park.

His hands were huge, making the gun he now pointed at Rachel look like a child's toy. He wiggled his fingers in her direction. "Give me the phone."

Rachel handed it to him, trying her best to avoid his touch. The man put the barrel of the gun against her head. "Now give me your gun."

Rachel reached into her handbag. He told her to lift it into view with two fingers. She complied. The phone rang for the fourth time.

The man hit the ANSWER button and said, "Dr. Seidman?"

Even Rachel could hear the reply. "Who is this?"

"We're all at Denise Vanech's house now. You will come here unarmed and alone. I will tell you all about your daughter then."

"Where's Rachel?"

"She's right here. You have thirty minutes. I will tell you what you need to know. You have a tendency to try to be cute in these situations. But not this time or your friend Ms. Mills dies first. Do you understand?"

"I understand."

The man hung up the phone. He looked down at Rachel. His eyes were brown with a gold center. They looked almost gentle, the eyes of a doe. Then the big man swung his gaze toward Denise Vanech. She flinched. A smile came to the man's lips.

Rachel saw what he was about to do.

She shouted, "No!" as the big man aimed the gun at Denise Vanech's chest and fired three shots. All three hit dead center. Denise's body went slack. She slid off the couch and onto the floor. Rachel started to stand, but now the gun was pointed at her.

"Stay put."

Rachel obeyed. Denise Vanech was clearly dead. Her eyes were open. Her blood streamed down, the color startlingly red against a sea of white.

chapter 42

Now what do I do?

I had been calling to tell Rachel about the shooting death of Steven Bacard. Now this man was holding her hostage. Okay, so what's my next step? I tried to think it through, to analyze the data carefully, but there was not enough time. The man on the phone had been right. I had been "cute" in the past. During the first ransom drop, I had let the police and FBI in on it. During the second, I'd enlisted the aid of an ex–federal agent. For a long time, I blamed the first drop-gone-wrong on my decision. Not anymore. I had played the odds both times, but now I think the game was fixed from the get-go. They had never intended to give me back my daughter. Not eighteen months ago. Not last night.

And not now.

Maybe I had been on a search for an answer that I knew all along. Verne had understood my quest with one caveat: "Long as a man ain't fooling himself." But maybe I had been. Even now, even as we were uncovering this baby-smuggling scam, I had allowed myself fresh hope. Perhaps my daughter was alive. Perhaps she had gotten ensnared in this adoption con. Would that be horrible? Yes. But the obvious alternative—that Tara is dead—was a hell of a lot worse.

I no longer knew what to believe.

I checked my watch. Twenty minutes had passed. I wondered about how to play it. First things first. I called Lenny on the private line at his office.

"A man named Steven Bacard was just murdered in East Rutherford," I said.

"Bacard the lawyer?"

"You know him?"

"I worked a case with him a few years ago," Lenny said. Then: "Oh damn."

"What?"

"You asked before about Stacy and an adoption. I didn't see a connection. But now that you say Bacard's name . . . Stacy asked me about him, what, three, four years ago."

"What about him?"

"I don't remember anymore. Something about being a mother."

"What does that mean?"

"I don't know. I really didn't pay that much attention. I just told her not to sign anything without showing it to me." Then Lenny asked, "How do you know he's been murdered?"

"I just saw his body."

"Whoa, don't say anything else. This line might not be secure."

"I need your help. Call the cops. They need to get Bacard's records. He ran an adoption scam. There's a possibility that he had something to do with Tara's kidnapping."

"How?"

"I don't have time to explain."

"Yeah, okay, I'll call Tickner and Regan. Regan's been searching for you pretty much nonstop, you know."

"I figured."

I hung up before he could ask more. I am not really sure what I expected them to find. I couldn't make myself believe that the answer to Tara's fate lay in some file cabinet in a law office. But maybe. And if something went wrong here—and there was certainly a decent chance of that happening—I wanted someone to be able to follow up.

I was in Ridgewood now. I did not believe for a second that the man on the phone was telling the truth. They were not in the trade-information business. They were here to clean house. Rachel and I knew too much. They were drawing me there so that they could kill us.

So what do I do?

There was very little time. If I stalled—if it took me much longer than a half an hour—the man on the phone would start getting antsy. That would be bad. I thought again about calling the police, but I remembered his warning about being "cute" and I still worried about a leak. I had a gun. I knew how to use it. I was a pretty good shot, but that was at a range. Shooting at people would, I assumed, be different. Or maybe not. I no longer had qualms about killing these people. I'm not sure I ever had.

A block away from Denise Vanech's house, I parked the car, grabbed the gun, and started down the street.

He called her Lydia. She called him Heshy.

The woman had arrived five minutes ago. She was petite and pretty, her baby-doll eyes wide with excitement. She stood in front of Denise Vanech's corpse and watched the blood still trickling out. Rachel sat still. Her hands had been bound behind her back with duct tape. The woman named Lydia turned to Rachel.

"That stain is going to be a bitch to get out."

Rachel stared at her. Lydia smiled.

"You don't think that's funny?"

"Inside," Rachel said. "Inside I'm cracking up."

"You visited a young girl named Tatiana today, yes?"

Rachel said nothing. The big man named Heshy began to pull down the shades.

"She's dead. Just thought you'd like to know." Lydia sat next to Rachel. "Do you remember the TV show *Family Laughs*?"

Rachel wondered how to play this. This Lydia was insane, no doubt about it. Tentatively she said, "Yes."

"Were you a fan?"

"The show was puerile nonsense."

Lydia threw back her head and laughed. "I played Trixie."

She smiled at Rachel. Rachel said, "You must be very proud."

"Oh I am. I am." Lydia stopped, tilted her face, moved it closer to Rachel's. "You know, of course, that you're going to die soon."

Rachel did not blink. "Then how about telling me what you did with Tara Seidman?"

"Oh please." Lydia stood. "I was an actress, remember? I was on television. So, what, is this the part of the show where we tell all so that the audience can catch up and your hero can sneak up on us? Sorry, sweetie." She turned to Heshy. "Gag her, Pooh Bear."

Heshy used the duct tape and wrapped it around Rachel's mouth and the back of her head. He moved back toward the window. Lydia bent close to Rachel's ear. Rachel could feel the woman's breath.

"I will tell you this," she whispered, "because it's funny." Lydia bent in a little closer. "I have no idea what happened to Tara Seidman."

Okay, I wasn't about to drive up and knock on the door.

Let's face it. They were out to kill us. My only chance was to surprise them. I didn't know the layout of the house, but I figured that I could find a side window and try to sneak in. I was armed. I was confident I could shoot without hesitation. I really wished that I had a better plan, but even if I had more time, I doubt that I'd come up with anything.

Zia had mentioned my surgeon's ego. I admit that it scared me. I actually felt confident that I could pull this off. I was smart. I knew how to be careful. I would look for an opening. If I didn't see one, I would offer them a trade—me for Rachel. I would not be sucked in by talk of Tara. Yes, I wanted to believe that she was still alive. Yes, I wanted to believe that they knew where she was. But I would no longer risk Rachel's life for a pipe dream. My life? Sure. But not Rachel's.

I moved closer to Denise Vanech's house, trying to duck behind trees while not looking conspicuous. In an upscale suburban neighborhood, this was impossible. People don't skulk. I imagined the neighbors watching me from behind the blinds, their fingers on the auto-911 dial button. I couldn't worry about it. Whatever was going to happen, one way or the other, would happen before any police could get here.

When my cell phone rang, I nearly jumped out my skin. I was three houses away now. I cursed under my breath. Dr. Cool—Dr. Confident—had forgotten to put his phone on vibrate. I realized with a sinking certainty that I was deluding myself. I was out of my element here. Suppose, for example, the phone had rung when I was right up against the house. What then?

I leapt behind a shrub and answered it with a snap of my wrist.

"You got a lot to learn about sneaking up on places," Verne whispered. "I mean, you're god-awful at it."

"Where are you?"

"Check out the second-floor window, far back."

I peeked out at Denise Vanech's house. Verne was in the window. He waved to me.

"Back door was unlocked," Verne whispered. "I let myself in."

"What's going on in there?"

"Stone-cold killing. I heard them say they killed that girl at the motel. They blew away that Denise woman. She's lying dead not three feet from Rachel."

I closed my eyes.

"This is a trap, Marc."

"Yeah, I figured that."

"There's two of them—one man, one woman. I want you to hustle back to your car. I want you to drive and park on the street. You'll be far enough away so that they won't get a clear shot at you. Stay there. Don't get any closer. I just want you to draw their attention—you got me?"

"Yes."

"I'll try to keep one alive, but I can't make any promises."

He hung up. I hurried back to the car and did as he said. I could feel my heart pounding against my chest. But there was hope now. Verne was there. He was inside the house and armed. I pulled up to the front of Denise Vanech's house. The blinds and curtains were drawn. I took a deep breath. I opened the car door and stood.

Silence.

I expected to hear shots. But that was not what came first. The first sound was shattering glass. And then I saw Rachel fall out the window.

"His car just pulled up," Heshy said.

Rachel's hands were still bound behind her back, the

duct tape over her mouth. She knew that this was it. Marc would come to the door. They would let him in, this mutant version of Bonnie and Clyde, and then they would shoot them both.

Tatiana was already dead. Denise Vanech was already dead. There was no other way to play this. Heshy and Lydia could not let them survive. Rachel had hoped that Marc would realize this and go to the police. She hoped that he wouldn't show up, but of course, that would not be an option for him. So he was here. He would probably try something foolhardy or maybe he was still so blinded by hope that he would simply walk into the trap.

Either way, Rachel had to stop him.

Her only chance was to surprise them. Even then, even if everything fell into place, the best she could realistically hope for was to save Marc. The rest was fool's gold.

Time to act.

They hadn't bothered to tie her feet. With her hands behind her back and her mouth taped shut, what harm could she do? Trying to run at them would be suicide. She'd make an easy target.

And that was what she was counting on.

Rachel got to her feet. Lydia turned around and pointed the gun at her. "Sit down."

She didn't. And now Lydia had a dilemma. If she fired the gun, Marc would hear it. He would know something was wrong. A stalemate. But it wouldn't last. An idea—a pretty lame idea—came to Rachel. She broke into a run. Lydia would either have to shoot or give chase or . . .

The window.

Lydia saw what Rachel was doing, but there was no way to stop her. Rachel lowered her head like a battering ram and dived straight toward the picture window.

Lydia raised her gun to shoot. Rachel braced herself. She knew that this would hurt. The glass broke with surprising ease. Rachel flew through it, but what she hadn't counted on was how far off the ground she was. Her hands were still tied behind her back. There was no way to break the fall.

She turned to the side and took the impact on her shoulder. Something popped. She felt a stabbing pain run down her leg. A shard of glass stuck out of her thigh. The sound would warn Marc, no question about it. He could be saved. But as Rachel rolled over, dread—deep, heavy dread—hit her next. Yes, she had warned Marc. He had seen her fall out the window.

But now, without thinking of the danger, Marc was running toward her.

Verne was crouched on the stairs.

He'd been about to make his move when Rachel suddenly stood up. Was she crazy? But no, he realized, she was just a brave lady. After all, she had no idea that he was hiding upstairs. She couldn't just sit there and let Marc walk in on this setup. She wasn't built that way.

"Sit down."

The woman's voice. The pert thing named Lydia. She started to swing her gun up. Verne panicked. He wasn't in position yet. He wouldn't have a clear shot. But Lydia didn't pull the trigger. Verne watched in amazement as Rachel ran and jumped through the window.

Talk about a distraction.

Verne moved now. He had heard countless times about how time stands still in moments of extreme violence, that brief seconds can drag so that you can see everything clearly. In reality, that was total bull. When you looked back, when you ran it through your mind in safety and comfort, that's when you imagine it went by slowly. But in the heat of the moment, when he and three buddies had gotten into a firefight with some of Saddam's "elite" soldiers, time had actually sped up. That was what was happening here.

Verne spun around the corner. "Drop it!"

The big man had his gun aimed at the window, where Rachel had fallen out. There was no time to call out another warning. Verne fired twice. Heshy went down. Lydia screamed. Verne ducked into a roll and disappeared behind the couch. Lydia screamed again.

"Heshy!"

Verne peered out, expecting to see Lydia aiming the gun at him. But that wasn't the case. She ditched the weapon. Still crying out, Lydia dropped to her knees and gently cradled Heshy's head.

"No! Don't die. Please, Heshy, please don't leave me!"

Verne kicked her gun away. He kept his pointed at Lydia.

Her voice was low now, soft and motherly. "Please, Heshy. Please don't die. Oh God, please don't leave me."

Heshy said, "I never will."

Lydia looked at Verne, her eyes pleading. He didn't bother calling 911. He could hear the sirens now. Heshy grabbed Lydia's hand. "You know what you have to do," he said.

"No," she said, her voice small.

"Lydia, we planned for this."

"You're not going to die."

Heshy closed his eyes. His breathing was labored.

"The world will think you were a monster," she said.

"I only care what you think. Promise me, Lydia."

"You're going to be fine."

"Promise me."

Lydia shook her head. The tears were flowing freely now. "I can't do it."

"You can." Heshy managed a final smile. "You're a great actress, remember?"

"I love you," she said.

But his eyes were closed. Lydia kept sobbing. She kept pleading with him not to leave her. The sirens came closer. Verne stepped back. The police arrived. When they came inside, they stood around her in a circle. Lydia suddenly lifted her head off Heshy's chest.

"Thank God," she said to them—and the tears started rolling again. "My nightmare is finally over."

Rachel was rushed to the hospital. I wanted to follow, but the police had other ideas. I spoke to Zia. I asked her to look in on Rachel for me.

The police questioned us for hours. They questioned Verne, Katarina, and me separately and then together. I think they believed us. Lenny was there. Regan and Tickner showed up, but it took some time. They'd been going through Bacard's files per Lenny's phone call.

Regan took the lead with me. "Long day, huh, Marc?"

I sat across from him. "Do I look in the mood for chitchat, Detective?"

"The woman goes by the name Lydia Davis. Her real name is Larissa Dane."

I made a face. "Why does that name sound familiar?"

"She was a child actor."

"Trixie," I said, remembering. "On *Family Laughs*."

"Yep, that's her. Or at least, that's what she says. Anyway, she claims this guy—we only know him as Heshy—kept her locked up and abused her. She said he forced her to do things. Your friend Verne thinks it's all a scam. But that's not important right now. She claims that she doesn't know anything about your daughter."

"How can that be?"

"She says they were just hired hands. That Bacard came to Heshy with this scheme about asking for ransom for a kid they hadn't kidnapped. Heshy loved the idea. Lot of money—and since they didn't really have the kid, there was almost no risk."

"She says they had nothing to do with the shooting at my house?"

"That's right."

I looked at Lenny. He saw the problem too. "But they had my gun. The one they used on Katarina's brother."

"Yeah, we know. She claims that Bacard gave it to Heshy. To set you up. Heshy shot Pavel and planted the gun so you and Rachel would take the fall."

"How did they get Tara's hair for the ransom drop? How did they get her clothes?"

"According to Ms. Dane, Bacard provided them."

I shook my head. "So Bacard was the one who kidnapped Tara?"

"She claims not to know."

"How about my sister? How did she get involved?"

"Again she claims it was Bacard. He gave them Stacy's name as a fall guy. Heshy gave Stacy the money and told her to cash it at a bank. Then he killed her."

I looked over at Tickner, then back at Regan. "It doesn't add up."

"We're still working on it."

Lenny said, "I have a question. Why did they come back after a year and a half and try it again?"

"Ms. Dane claims not to know for sure, but she suspects it was simple greed. She says Bacard called and asked if Heshy would want to make another million. He said yes. Going through Bacard's records, he was clearly in financial trouble. We think she's right. Bacard simply decided to take another bite of the apple."

I rubbed my face. My ribs began to ache. "Did you find Bacard's adoption records?"

Regan glanced at Tickner. "Not yet."

"How can that be?"

"Look, we just got on this. We'll find them. We're going to check every adoption he's ever made, especially anything involving a female eighteen months ago. If Bacard had Tara adopted, we'll find out."

I shook my head again.

"What is it, Marc?"

"That doesn't make any sense. The guy has a decent thing going with this adoption scam. Why shoot me and Monica and up the ante to kidnapping and murder?"

"We don't know," Regan said. "I think we can all agree that there's more to the story. But the truth is, the most likely scenario right now is that your sister and an accomplice shot you and Monica and took the baby. She then brought it to Bacard."

I closed my eyes and replayed it in my head. Could Stacy have really done that? Could she have broken into my house and shot me? I still couldn't make myself believe. And then I thought of something.

Why hadn't I heard the window break?

More than that, before I was shot, why hadn't I heard *anything*? A window break, a doorbell, heck, a door opening. Why hadn't I heard any of that? The answer, according to Regan, had been that I was blocking. But now I saw that wasn't it.

"The granola bar," I said.

"Pardon me?"

I turned to him. "Your theory is that I'm forgetting something, right? Stacy and her accomplice either broke the window or, I don't know, rang the doorbell. I would have heard either one of those. But I didn't. I remember eating my granola bar and then going down."

"Right."

"But see, I was pretty specific. I had the granola bar in my hand. When you found me, it was on the floor. How much had been eaten?"

"Maybe a bite or two," Tickner said.

"Then your amnesia theory is wrong. I was standing over the sink eating the granola bar. I remember that. When you found me, that's what I was doing. There is no time unaccounted for. And if it was my sister, why would she strip Monica, for Chrissake . . . ?" I stopped.

Lenny said, "Marc?"

Did you love her?

I stared straight ahead.

You know who shot you, don't you, Marc?

Dina Levinsky. I thought about her bizarre visits to the house she'd grown up in. I thought about the two guns—one being mine. I thought about the CD-ROM hidden in the basement, in the spot Dina had told me about. I thought about those pictures taken in front of the hospital. I thought about what Edgar said about Monica seeing a psychiatrist.

And then an awful thought, one so terrible I might indeed have suppressed it, began to surface.

chapter 43

I feigned illness and excused myself. I went to the bathroom and dialed Edgar's phone number. My father-in-law himself answered. "Hello?"

"You said Monica was seeing a psychiatrist?"

"Marc? Is that you?" Edgar cleared his throat. "I just heard from the police. Those pissant fools had me convinced that you were behind all this—"

"I don't have time for that now. I'm still trying to find Tara."

"What do you need?" Edgar asked.

"Did you ever find out the name of her psychiatrist?"

"No."

I thought about it. "Is Carson there?"

"Yes."

"Put him on."

There was a brief pause. I tapped my foot. Uncle Carson's rich voice came over the line. "Marc?"

"You knew about those pictures, didn't you?"

He didn't reply.

"I checked our accounts. The money didn't come from us. You paid for the private detective."

"It had nothing to do with the shooting or kidnapping," Carson said.

"I think it did. Monica told you the name of her psychiatrist, didn't she? What was it?"

Again he did not reply.

"I'm trying to find out what happened to Tara."

"She only saw him twice," Carson said. "How can he help you?"

"He can't. His name can."

"What?"

"Just tell me, yes or no. Was his name Stanley Radio?"

I could hear him breathing.

"Carson?"

"I already spoke to him. He knows nothing—"

But I had already hung up. Carson wouldn't say any more.

But Dina Levinsky might.

I asked Regan and Tickner if I was under arrest. They said no. I asked Verne if I could still borrow the Camaro.

"No problemo," Verne said. Then squinting, he added, "Do you need my help?"

I shook my head. "You and Katarina are out of this now. It's over for you."

"I'm still here, if you need me."

"I don't. Go home, Verne."

He surprised me with a big hug then. Katarina kissed my cheek. I let go and watched them drive off in the pickup. I headed toward the city. There was heavy traffic at the Lincoln Tunnel. It took me over an hour to get through the tolls. That gave me time to make some phone calls. I learned that Dina Levinsky shared an apartment in Greenwich Village with a friend.

Twenty minutes later, I knocked on her door.

*   *   *

When Eleanor Russell returned from lunch, there was a plain manila envelope on her chair. It was addressed to her boss, Lenny Marcus, and marked PERSONAL AND CONFIDENTIAL.

Eleanor had worked with Lenny for eight years. She loved him dearly. Having no family of her own—she and her husband, Saul, who had died three years before, had never been blessed with children—she had become something of a surrogate grandmother to the Marcuses. Eleanor even had photographs of Lenny's wife, Cheryl, and their four children on her desk.

She studied the envelope and frowned. How had it gotten here? She peeked into Lenny's office. He looked so harried. That was because Lenny had just returned from a homicide scene. The case involving his best friend, Dr. Marc Seidman, had exploded back into the headlines. Normally Eleanor would not bother Lenny at a time like this. But the return address ... well, she thought he should see it for himself.

Lenny was on the phone. He saw her enter and put his hand over the receiver. "I'm kinda busy," he said.

"This came for you."

Eleanor handed him the envelope. Lenny almost ignored it. Then Eleanor watched as he spotted the return address. He turned it over, then back again.

The return address simply read, *From a friend of Stacy Seidman.*

Lenny put down the phone and tore open the envelope.

I don't think Dina Levinsky was surprised to see me.

She let me in without a word. The walls were blanketed with her paintings, many hung at odd angles. The effect was dizzying, giving the entire apartment a Salvador Dalí feel. We sat in the kitchen. Dina offered to make tea. I said no. She put her hands on the table. I could see that her fingernails were bitten down past the cuticle. Had they been that way at my house? She seemed different now, sadder somehow. Her hair was straighter. Her eyes were downcast. It was as if she was transforming back to the pitiful girl I had known in elementary school.

"You found the pictures?" she asked.

"Yes."

Dina closed her eyes. "I should have never led you to them."

"Why did you?"

"I lied to you before."

I nodded.

"I'm not married. I don't enjoy sex. I do have troubles with relationships." She shrugged. "I even have problems with telling the truth."

Dina tried to smile. I tried to smile back.

"In therapy we're taught to confront our fears. The only way to do that is to let the truth in, no matter how much it hurts. But see, I wasn't even sure what the truth was. So I tried to lead you there."

"You were back in the house before the night I saw you, weren't you?"

She nodded.

"And that's how you met Monica?"

"Yes."

I kept going. "You two became friends?"

"We had something in common."

"That being?"

Dina looked up at me, and I saw the pain.

"Abuse?" I said.

She nodded.

"Edgar sexually abused her?"

"No, not Edgar. Her mother. And it wasn't sexual. It

was more physical and emotional. The woman was very ill. You knew that, right?"

"I guess I did," I said.

"Monica needed help."

"So you introduced her to your therapist?"

"I tried. I mean, I set up an appointment for her with Dr. Radio. But it didn't work out."

"How come?"

"Monica was not the sort of woman who believed in therapy. She thought that she could best handle her own problems."

I nodded. I knew. "At the house," I said, "you asked me if I loved Monica."

"Yes."

"Why?"

"She thought you didn't." Dina put her finger in her mouth, searching for a sliver of nail to bite. There was none. "Of course, she thought herself unworthy of love. Like me. But there was a difference."

"What was that?"

"Monica felt that there was one person who could love her forever."

I knew the answer here. "Tara."

"Yes. She trapped you, Marc. You probably realize that. It wasn't an accident. She wanted to get pregnant."

Sadly, I was not surprised. Again I tried, as in surgery, to put the pieces together. "So Monica believed that I no longer loved her. She was afraid I wanted a divorce. She was troubled. She was crying at night." I paused. I was saying this as much for my benefit as Dina's. I didn't want to keep following this train of thought, but there was no way to stop me. "She's fragile. Her mind is frayed. And then she hears that phone message from Rachel."

"That's your ex-girlfriend?"

"Yes."

"You still keep her picture in your desk drawer. Monica knew about that too. You keep mementos of her."

I closed my eyes, remembering the Steely Dan CD in Monica's car. College music. Music I had listened to with Rachel. I said, "So she hired a private detective to see if I was having an affair. He took those photographs."

Dina nodded.

"So now she has proof. I'm going to leave her for another woman. I'm going to claim she's unstable. I'll say she's an unfit mother. I'm a well-respected doctor, and Rachel has connections with law enforcement. We'd end up with custody of the only thing that really mattered to Monica. Tara."

Dina rose from the table. She washed out a glass in the sink and then filled it with water. I thought again about what had happened that morning. Why hadn't I heard the window break? Why hadn't I heard the doorbell ring? Why hadn't I heard the intruder enter?

Simple. Because there was no intruder.

Tears filled my eyes. "So what did she do, Dina?"

"You know, Marc."

I squeezed my eyes shut.

"I didn't think she'd really do it," Dina said. "I thought she was just acting out, you know? Monica was so despondent. When she asked me if I knew how to get a gun, I thought she wanted to kill herself. I never thought . . ."

"She would shoot me?"

The air was suddenly heavy. Exhaustion overwhelmed me. I was too tired to cry anymore. But there was still more to unearth here. "You said she asked you to help her get a gun?"

Dina wiped her eyes and nodded.

"Did you?"

"No. I wouldn't know how to get one. She said you had a gun at home, but she didn't want something that could be traced back. So she went to the only person she knew with seedy enough contacts to help."

I saw it now. "My sister."

"Yes."

"Did Stacy get her a gun?"

"No, I don't think so."

"What makes you say that?"

"The morning you were both shot, Stacy came to see me. See, Monica and I had come up with the idea of going to Stacy together. So Monica mentioned me to her. She came and asked what Monica needed a gun for. I didn't tell her because, well, I really wasn't all that sure. Stacy ran out. I was in a panic. I wanted to ask Dr. Radio what to do, but my next session was that afternoon. I figured it could wait."

"And then?"

"I still don't know what happened, Marc. That's the truth. But I know Monica shot you."

"How?"

"I got scared. So I called your house. Monica answered. She was crying. She told me you were dead. She kept saying, 'What have I done, what have I done?' And then suddenly she hung up. I called back. But no one answered. I really didn't know what to do. Then the TV had the story. When they said your daughter was missing ... I didn't understand. I thought they'd find her right away. But they never did. And I never heard anything about those pictures either. I hoped, I don't know, I hoped leading you to those photographs might shed some light on what really happened. Not so much for the two of you. But for your daughter."

"Why did you wait so long?"

Her eyes closed, and for a moment, I thought that she might be praying. "I had a bad spell, Marc. Two weeks after you were shot, I was hospitalized with a breakdown. The truth is, I was so far gone I forgot about it. Or maybe I wanted to forget. I don't know."

My cell phone rang. It was Lenny. I picked it up.

"Where are you?" he asked.

"With Dina Levinsky."

"Get over to Newark Airport. Terminal C. Now."

"What's going on?"

"I think," Lenny said. Then he slowed down, caught his breath. "I think I may know where we can find Tara."

chapter 44

By the time I arrived at Terminal C, Lenny was already standing by the Continental check-in desk. It was six o'clock at night now. The airport was jammed with the weary. He handed me the anonymous note that had been found in his office. It read:

Abe and Lorraine Tansmore
26 Marsh Lane
Hanley Hills, MO

That was it. Just the name and address. Nothing else.

"It's a suburb near St. Louis," Lenny explained. "I did some research already."

I just kept staring down at the name and address.

"Marc?"

I looked up at him.

"The Tansmores adopted a daughter eighteen months ago. She was six months old when they got her."

Behind him, a Continental service rep said, "Next please." A woman pushed past me. She might have said, "Excuse me," but I'm not sure.

"I have us booked on the next flight to St. Louis. We're leaving in an hour."

*   *   *

When we reached the departure gate, I told him about my meeting with Dina Levinsky. We sat, as we often do, next to each other, facing out. When I finished, he said, "You have a theory now."

"I do."

We watched a plane take off. An old couple sitting across from us shared a tin of Pringles. "I'm a cynic. I know that. I hold no illusions about drug addicts. If anything, I overestimate their depravity. And that, I think, is what I did here."

"How do you figure?"

"Stacy wouldn't shoot me. And she would never hurt her niece. She was an addict. But she still loved me."

"I think," Lenny said, "that you're right."

"I look back. I was so wrapped up in my own world that I never saw . . ." I shook my head. Now was not the time for this. "Monica was desperate," I said. "She couldn't get a gun and maybe, she decided, she didn't have to."

"She used yours," Lenny said.

"Yes."

"And then?"

"Stacy must have guessed what was up. She ran to the house. She saw what Monica had done. I don't know how it played exactly. Maybe Monica tried to shoot her too—that could explain the bullet hole near the stairs. Or maybe Stacy just reacted. She loved me. I was lying there. She probably thought I was dead. So I don't know, but either way Stacy came armed. And she shot Monica."

The gate attendant announced that the flight would soon be boarding but those with special needs or One Pass Gold and Platinum members could board now.

"You said on the phone that Stacy knew Bacard?"

Lenny nodded. "She mentioned him, yeah."

"Again I'm not sure how it played out exactly. But think about it. I'm dead. Monica is dead. And Stacy is probably freaking out. Tara is crying. Stacy can't just leave her. So she takes Tara with her. Later she realizes that she can't raise a kid on her own. She's too messed up. So she turns her over to Bacard and tells him to find her a good family. Or, if I want to be cynical, maybe she gives Tara over for the money. We'll never know."

Lenny was nodding.

"From there, well, we just follow what we already learned. Bacard decides to rake in extra money by pretending it was a kidnapping. He hires those two lunatics. Bacard would be able to get hair samples, for example. He double-crossed Stacy. He set her up to take the fall."

I saw something cross Lenny's face.

"What?"

"Nothing," he said.

They called our row.

Lenny stood. "Let's board."

The flight was delayed. We didn't arrive in St. Louis until past midnight local time. It was too late to do anything tonight. Lenny booked us a room at the Airport Marriott. I bought clothes at their all-night boutique. When we got to the room, I took a very long, very hot shower. We settled in and stared at the ceiling.

In the morning, I called the hospital to check on Rachel. She was still sleeping. Zia was in her room. She assured me that Rachel was doing fine. Lenny and I tried to eat the hotel's buffet breakfast. Nothing would stay down. Our rental car was waiting for us. Lenny had gotten directions to Hanley Hills from the desk clerk.

I don't remember what we saw on the drive. Aside from the Arch in the distance, there was nothing distinct. The United States has a strip-mall sameness about it now. It's easy to criticize that—I often do—but maybe the appeal is that we all like what we already know. We claim to embrace change. But in the end, especially in these times, what truly draws us is the familiar.

When we reached the town limits, I felt a tingling in my legs. "What do we do here, Lenny?"

He had no answer.

"Do I just knock on the door and say, 'Excuse me, I think that's my daughter?' "

"We could call the police," he said. "Let them handle it."

But I didn't know how that would play out. We were so close now. I told him to keep on driving. We made a right onto Marsh Lane. I was shaking now. Lenny tried to give me a buck-up look, but his face was pale too. The street was more modest than I'd expected. I had assumed that all of Bacard's clients were wealthy. That was clearly not the case with this couple.

"Abe Tansmore works as a schoolteacher," Lenny said, reading my thoughts as usual. "Sixth grade. Lorraine Tansmore works for a day-care center three days a week. They're both thirty-nine years old. They've been married for seventeen years."

Up ahead, I saw a house with a cherry-wood sign that read 26—THE TANSMORES. It was a small one-level, what I think they called "bungalow" style. The rest of the houses on the block seemed tired. This one did not. The paint glistened like a smile. There were lots of clusters of color, of flowers and shrubs, all trimly laid out and perfectly pruned. I could see a welcome mat. A low picket fence encircled the front yard. A station wagon, a Volvo model from several years back, sat in the driveway. There was a tricycle, too, and one of those bright-hued plastic Big Wheels.

And there was a woman outside.

Lenny pulled over in front of an empty lot. I barely noticed. The woman was in the flower beds, on her knees. She was working a small digging spade. Her hair was tied back with a red bandanna. Every few digs she would wipe her forehead with her sleeve.

"You say she works at a day-care center?"

"Three days a week. The daughter goes with her."

"What do they call the daughter?"

"Natasha."

I nodded. I don't know why. We waited. The woman, this Lorraine, worked hard, but I could see she enjoyed it. There was a serenity about her. I opened the car window. I could hear her whistling to herself. I don't know how many minutes passed. A neighbor walked by. Lorraine rose and greeted her. The neighbor gestured toward the garden. Lorraine smiled. She wasn't a beautiful woman, but she had a great smile. The neighbor left. Lorraine waved good-bye and turned back to her garden.

The front door opened.

I saw Abe. He was a tall man, thin and wiry, slightly balding. He had a neatly trimmed beard. Lorraine stood and looked over at him. She gave him a small wave.

And then Tara ran outside.

The air around us stopped. I felt my insides shut down. Next to me, Lenny stiffened and muttered, "Oh my God."

For the last eighteen months, I had never really believed that this moment was possible. What I had done instead was convince myself—no, trick myself—into believing that maybe, somehow, Tara was still alive and okay. But my subconscious knew it was only a self-delusion. It winked at me. It nudged me in my sleep. It whispered the obvious truth: that I would never see my daughter again.

But it was my daughter. She was alive.

I was surprised at how little Tara had changed. Oh she'd grown, of course. She was able to stand. She was even able, as I now saw, to run. But her face . . . there was no mistake. No being blinded by hope. It was Tara. It was my little girl.

With a huge smile, Tara ran with total abandon toward Lorraine. Lorraine bent low, her face lighting up in that celestial way only a mother's can. She swept my child into her arms. Now I could hear the melodious sound of Tara's laughter. The sound pierced my heart. Tears streamed down my face. Lenny put a hand on my arm. I could hear him sniffling. I saw the husband, this Abe, walk toward them. He was smiling too.

For several hours, I watched them in their small, perfect yard. I saw Lorraine patiently point out the flowers, explaining what each one was. I saw Abe give her a horsey ride on his back. I saw Lorraine teach her how to pat the dirt down with her hand. Another couple dropped by. They had a little girl about Tara's age. Abe and the other father pushed the girls on the metal swing-set in the backyard. Their giggles pounded in my ears. Eventually they all went inside. Abe and Lorraine were the last to disappear. They walked through the door with their arms around each other.

Lenny turned to me. I let my head drop back. I had hoped that today would be the end of my journey. But it wasn't.

After a while, I said, "Let's go."

chapter 45

When we got back to the Airport Marriott, I told Lenny to go home. He said he would stay. I told him that I could handle this on my own—that I *wanted* to handle this on my own. He reluctantly agreed.

I called Rachel. She was doing well. I told her what had happened. "Call Harold Fisher," I said. "Ask him to do a thorough background check on Abe and Lorraine Tansmore. I want to know if there's something there."

"Okay," she said softly. "I wish I could be there."

"Me too."

I sat on my bed. My head dropped into my hands. I don't think I cried. I don't know what I felt anymore. It was over. I had learned as much as I would. When Rachel called back two hours later, nothing she told me was a surprise. Abe and Lorraine were solid citizens. Abe was the first person in his family to graduate college. He had two younger sisters who lived in the area. Both had three children. He had met Lorraine during their freshman year at Washington University in St. Louis.

Night fell. I stood and looked in the mirror. My wife had tried to kill me. Yes, she was unstable. I knew that now. Hell, I probably knew it then. I didn't much care, I guess. When a child's face breaks, I put it back together.

I can do miracles in the surgical room. But my own family fell apart and I did nothing but watch.

I thought now about what it meant to be a father. I loved my daughter. I know that. But when I saw Abe today, when I see Lenny coaching soccer, I wonder. I wonder about my fitness. I wonder about my commitment. And I wonder if I am worthy.

Or do I already know the answer?

I wanted so badly to have my little girl back with me. I also wanted so badly for this not to be about me or my wants.

Tara had looked so damn happy.

It was midnight now. I looked at myself in the mirror again. What if leaving this alone—letting her stay with Abe and Lorraine—was the right thing? Was I really brave enough, strong enough, to walk away? I kept staring in the mirror, challenging myself. Was I?

I lay back. I think I fell asleep. A knock on the door startled me awake. I glanced at the digital clock next to my bed. It read 5:19 A.M.

"I'm sleeping," I said.

"Dr. Seidman?"

It was a male voice.

"Dr. Seidman, my name is Abe Tansmore."

I opened the door. He was handsome up close, in a sort of James Taylor way. He wore jeans and a tan shirt. I looked at his eyes. They were blue but tinged with red. So, I knew, were mine. For a long time, we just stared at one another. I tried to speak, but I couldn't. I stepped back and let him in.

"Your lawyer stopped by. He"—Abe stopped, swallowed hard—"he told us the whole story. Lorraine and I stayed up all night. We talked it out. We cried a lot. But I think we knew right from the get-go that there was only one decision here." Abe Tansmore was trying to hold on, but he was losing it now. He closed his eyes. "We have to give you your daughter back."

I didn't know what to say. I shook my head. "We have to do what's best for her."

"That's what I'm doing, Dr. Seidman."

"Call me Marc. Please." It was a dumb thing to say. I know that. But I wasn't ready for this. "If you're worried about a long, drawn-out court case, Lenny shouldn't have—"

"No, that's not it."

We stood there a little longer. I pointed toward the chair in the room. He shook his head. Then he looked at me. "All night, I've been trying to imagine your pain. I don't think I can. I think there are places a man just can't get to without experience. Maybe this is one of them. But your pain, awful as it must be, that's not why Lorraine and I came to this decision. And it's not because we blame ourselves either. In hindsight, maybe we should have wondered what was going on. We went to Mr. Bacard. But the fees would have added up to over a hundred thousand dollars. I'm not a rich man. I couldn't afford that. Then a few weeks later, Mr. Bacard calls us. He said he had a baby that needed immediate placing. She wasn't a newborn, he said. The mother had just abandoned her. We knew something was not quite right, but he said that if we wanted this, we'd have to go in no questions asked."

He looked off then. I watched his face. "I think deep down, maybe we always knew. We just couldn't face it. But that's not the reason we came to this decision either."

I swallowed. "What then?"

His eyes drifted toward mine. "You can't do the wrong thing for the right reason." I must have looked confused. "If Lorraine and I don't do this, we're not fit

to raise her. We want Natasha to be happy. We want her
to be a good person."

"You might be the best ones to make that happen."

He shook his head. "That's not how it works. We don't
give children to whatever parents would be best to raise
them. You and I can't make that judgment. You don't
know how hard this is for us. Or maybe you do."

I turned away. I caught my reflection in the mirror.
Just for a second. Less maybe. But it was enough. I saw
the man I was. I saw the man I wanted to be. I turned to
him and said, "I want us both to raise her."

He was stunned. So was I. "I'm not sure I understand," he said.

"Neither do I. But that's what we're going to do."

"How?"

"I don't know."

Abe shook his head. "It can't work. You know that."

"No, Abe, I don't know that. I came here to bring my
daughter home—and I find that maybe she already is. Is
it right for me to rip her away from that? I want you
both in her life. I'm not saying it'll be easy. But kids are
raised by single parents, by stepparents, in foster homes.
There are divorces and separations and who-knows-
what. We all love this little girl. We'll make it work."

I saw the hope return to the man's thin face. He
couldn't speak for a few seconds. Then he said, "Lorraine is in the lobby. Can I go talk to her?"

"Of course."

They didn't take long. There was a knock on my door.
When I opened it, Lorraine threw her arms around me.
I hugged her back, this woman I had never met. Her
hair smelled of strawberry. Behind her, Abe came into
the room. Tara was sleeping in his arms. Lorraine let go
of me and moved away. Abe stepped closer. He handed
me my daughter carefully. I held her, and my heart burst

into flame. Tara began to stir. She started to fuss. I still held her. I rocked her back and forth and made shushing sounds.

And soon she settled on me and fell back to sleep.

chapter 46

It started to all go wrong again when I looked at the calendar.

The human brain is amazing. It is a curious mix of electricity and chemicals. It is, in effect, pure science. We understand more about the workings of the great cosmos than we do about the curious circuitry of the cerebrum, cerebellum, hypothalamus, medulla oblongata, and all the rest. And like any tricky compound, we are never sure how it will react to a certain catalyst.

There were several things that gave me reason to pause. There was the question of leaks. Rachel and I had thought that someone in either the FBI or police department had told Bacard and his people what was happening. But that never fit in with my theory about Stacy shooting Monica. There was the fact that Monica was found with no clothes on. I think I understood why now, but the thing is, Stacy wouldn't have.

But the main catalyst occurred, I think, when I looked at the calendar and realized that today was Wednesday.

The shootings and original abduction had taken place on a Wednesday. Of course, there had been plenty of Wednesdays in the past eighteen months. The day of the week was a pretty innocuous thing. But this time, after we had learned so much, after my brain had digested all the fresh data, something meshed. All those little questions and doubts, all those idiosyncrasies, all those moments I took for granted and never really examined . . . they all shifted a little. And what I saw was even worse than what I had originally imagined.

I was back in Kasselton now—at my house where it had all started. I called Tickner for confirmation.

I said, "My wife and I were shot with thirty-eights, right?"

"Yes."

"And you're sure they were two different guns?"

"Positive."

"And my Smith and Wesson was one of them?"

"You know all this, Marc."

"Did you get all the ballistic reports back yet?"

"Most of them."

I licked my lips and readied myself. I hoped to hell that I was wrong. "Who was shot with my gun—me or Monica?"

He turned coy on me. "Why are you asking me this now?"

"Curiosity."

"Yeah, right. Hold on a second." I could hear him shuffling papers. I felt my throat constrict. I almost hung up. "Your wife was."

When I heard the car pull up outside, I put the receiver back in the cradle. Lenny turned the knob and opened the door. He didn't knock. After all, Lenny never knocked, right?

I was sitting on the couch. The house was still, all the ghosts sleeping now. He had a Slurpee in either hand and a broad smile. I wondered how many times I had seen that smile. I remembered it more crooked. I remembered it jammed to overflowing with braces. I remembered it bleeding after he hit a tree when we went sledding down the Gorets' backyard. I thought again about when big Tony Merruno picked a fight with me in third grade, how Lenny jumped on his back. I remembered now that Tony Merruno broke Lenny's glasses. I don't think Lenny cared.

I knew him so well. Or maybe I hadn't known him at all.

When Lenny saw my face, his smile faded away.

"We were supposed to play racquetball that morning, Lenny. Remember?"

He lowered the cups and put them on the end table.

"You never knock. You always just open the door. Like today. So what happened, Lenny? You came to pick me up. You opened the door."

He started shaking his head, but I knew now.

"The two guns, Lenny. That's what gave it away."

"I don't know what you're talking about." But there was no conviction in his voice.

"We figured that Stacy didn't get Monica a gun—that Monica used mine. But you see, she didn't. I just checked with ballistics. It's funny. You never told me that Monica was shot with my gun. I was shot with the other weapon."

"So?" Lenny said, suddenly the attorney again. "That doesn't mean anything. Maybe Stacy got her a gun, after all."

"She did," I said.

"So fine, okay, it still adds up."

"Tell me how."

He shifted his feet. "Maybe Stacy helped Monica get a gun. Monica shot you with it. When Stacy arrived a few minutes later, Monica tried to shoot her." Lenny moved over to the staircase as if to demonstrate. "Stacy ran upstairs. Monica fired—that would explain the bullet hole." He pointed to the spackled area by the stairs. "Stacy grabbed your gun out of the bedroom, came downstairs, and shot Monica."

I looked at him. "Is that how it happened, Lenny?"

"I don't know. I mean, it could be."

I waited a beat. He turned away. "One problem," I said.

"What?"

"Stacy didn't know where I hid the gun. She didn't know the lockbox's combination either." I took a step closer. "But you did, Lenny. I kept all my legal documents there. I trusted you with everything. So now I want the truth. Monica shot me. You came in. You saw me lying on the floor. Did you think I was dead?"

Lenny closed his eyes.

"Make me understand, Lenny."

He shook his head slowly. "You think you love your daughter," he said. "But you have no idea. What you feel, it grows every day. The longer you have a child, the more attached you get. The other night I came home from work. Marianne was crying because some girls were teasing her in school. I went to bed feeling sick, and I realized something. I can only be as happy as my saddest child. Do you understand what I'm saying?"

"Tell me what happened," I said.

"You have it pretty much right. I came to your house that morning. I opened the door. Monica was on the phone. She was still holding the gun in her hand. I ran over to you. I couldn't believe it. I felt for a pulse but . . ." He shook his head. "Monica started screaming at me, about how she wouldn't let anyone take away her baby. She pointed the gun at me. I mean, Jesus Christ. I thought for sure I was going to die. I rolled away and then I ran for the stairs. I remembered you had a gun up there. She fired at me." He pointed again. "That's the bullet hole."

He stopped. He took a few breaths. I waited.

"I grabbed your gun."

"Did Monica follow you up the stairs?"

His voice was soft. "No." He started blinking. "Maybe I should have tried to use the phone. Maybe I should have sneaked out. I don't know. I've gone through it hundreds of times. I try to imagine how I should have played it. But you were lying there, my best friend, dead. That crazy bitch was shouting about running away with your daughter—my godchild. She had already taken a shot at me. I didn't know what she would do next."

He looked away.

"Lenny?"

"I don't know what happened, Marc. I really don't. I sneaked back down the stairs. She still had the gun. . . ." His voice tailed.

"So you shot her."

He nodded. "I didn't mean to kill her. At least, I don't think I did. But suddenly you were both lying there, dead. I was going to call the police. But now I wasn't sure how it would look. I had shot Monica at a funny angle. They could claim her back was turned."

"You thought maybe they'd arrest you?"

"Of course. The cops hate me. I'm a successful defense attorney. What do you think would have happened?"

I didn't reply. "You broke the window?"

"From the outside," he said. "So it would look like an intruder."

"And you took Monica's clothes off?"

"Yes."

"Same reason?"

"I knew that there would be gunpowder residue on the clothes. They'd realize she fired a gun. I was trying to make it look like a random attacker. So I got rid of her clothes. I used a baby wipe to clean off her hand."

That was another thing that had bothered me. Monica being stripped down. There had been the possibility that Stacy would have done it to throw off the police, but I couldn't imagine her thinking of that. Lenny was the defense attorney—him I could see.

We were getting to the heart of it now. We both knew that. I crossed my arms. "Tell me about Tara."

"She was my godchild. It was my job to protect her."

"I don't understand."

Lenny spread his hands. "How many times did I beg you to write a will?"

I was confused. "What does that have to do with anything?"

"Think it through for a second. During all this, when you were in trouble, you resorted to your surgical training, right?"

"I guess."

"I'm an attorney, Marc. I did the same. You were both dead. Tara was wailing in the other room. And I, Lenny the Lawyer, realized instantly what would happen."

"What?"

"You hadn't made out a will. You hadn't named guardians. Don't you see? That meant Edgar would get your daughter."

I looked at his face. I hadn't thought of that.

"Your mother might contest, but she wouldn't stand a chance against his finances. She had your father to worry about. She had a drunk driving conviction six years ago. Edgar would get custody."

I saw it now. "And you couldn't allow that."

"I'm Tara's godfather. It was my job to protect her."

"And you hated Edgar."

He shook his head. "Was I clouded by what he did to

my dad? Yeah, maybe subconsciously, a little. But Edgar Portman is evil. You know that. Look at how Monica turned out. I couldn't let him destroy your daughter like he did his own."

"So you took her."

He nodded.

"You brought her to Bacard."

"He had been a client. I knew some of what he did, though not to what extent. I also knew that he would keep it confidential. I told him I wanted the best family he had. Forget money, forget power. I wanted good people."

"So he placed her with the Tansmores."

"Yes. You have to understand. I thought you were dead. Everyone did. And then it looked like you might end up a vegetable. By the time you were okay, it was too late. I couldn't tell anybody. I would go to prison for sure. Do you know what that would do to my family?"

"Gee, I can't imagine," I said.

"That's not fair, Marc."

"I don't have to be fair here."

"Hey, I didn't ask for any of this." He was shouting now. "I walked in on a terrible situation. I did what I thought best—for your daughter. But you can't expect me to sacrifice my family."

"Better to sacrifice mine?"

"The truth? Yes, of course. I'd give up anything to protect my children. Anything. Wouldn't you?"

Now I was the one who stayed silent. I had said it before: I would lay down my life in a second for my daughter. And truth be told, if push came to shove, I would lay down yours too.

"Believe it or not, I tried to think through this coldly," Lenny said. "A cost-benefit analysis. If I come forward with the truth, I destroy my wife and four children and you take your daughter from a loving home. If I keep quiet . . ." He shrugged. "Yeah, you suffered. I didn't want to do that. It hurt me to watch you. But what would you have done?"

I didn't want to think about it. "You're leaving something out," I said.

He closed his eyes and muttered something unintelligible.

"What happened to Stacy?"

"She wasn't supposed to be hurt. It was like you said. She had sold Monica the gun, and when she realized why, she rushed to stop her."

"But she arrived too late?"

"Yes."

"She saw you?"

He nodded. "Look, I told her everything. She wanted to help, Marc. She wanted to do the right thing. But in the end, the habit was too strong."

"She blackmailed you?"

"She asked for money. I gave it to her. That wasn't important. But she was there. And when I went to Bacard, I told him everything that had happened. You have to understand. I thought you were going to die. When you didn't, I knew that you'd go nuts without closure. Your daughter was gone. I talked to Bacard about it. He came up with the idea of a fake kidnapping. We'd all make a lot of money."

"You took money for this?"

Lenny leaned back as if I'd just slapped him. "Of course not. I put my share into a trust fund for Tara's college. But the idea of this fake kidnapping appealed to me. They'd set it up so in the end, it would look like Tara was dead. You'd have closure. We'd also be taking money from Edgar and funneling at least some of it to Tara. It seemed like a win-win."

"Except?"

"Except when they heard about Stacy, they decided that they couldn't depend on a drug addict to keep quiet. The rest you know. They lured her with money. They made sure she got caught on tape. And then, without telling me, they killed her."

I thought about that. I thought about Stacy's last minutes in the cabin. Did she know that she was going to die? Or did she just drift off, thinking she was merely getting yet another fix?

"You were the leak, weren't you?"

He didn't reply.

"You told them about the police being involved."

"Don't you see? It made no difference. They never intended to give Tara back. She was already with the Tansmores. After the ransom drop, I thought it was over. We all tried to move on."

"So what happened?"

"Bacard decided to run the ransom again."

"Were you in on it?" I asked.

"No, he kept me out of the loop."

"When did you learn about it?"

"When you told me in the hospital. I was furious. I called him. He told me to relax, that there was no way it could be traced back to us."

"But we did trace it back."

He nodded.

"And you knew that I was getting close to Bacard. I told you on the phone."

"Yes."

"Wait a minute." A fresh chill ran up my neck. "In the end, Bacard wanted to clean house. He called those two lunatics. The woman, that Lydia, she went out and killed Tatiana. Heshy was sent to take care of Denise Vanech. But"—I thought it through—"but when I saw Steven

Bacard, he had just been shot. He was still bleeding. There was no way either of them could have done it."

I looked up. "You killed him, Lenny."

Rage seeped into his voice. "You think I wanted to?"

"Then why?"

"What do you mean, why? I was Bacard's get-out-of-jail-free card. When it all started to go wrong, he said he would turn state's evidence against me. He'd claim I shot you and Monica and brought him Tara. Like I said before, the cops hate me. I've gotten too many bad guys off. They'd go for the deal in a second."

"You'd have gone to jail?"

Lenny looked near tears.

"Your kids would have suffered?"

He nodded.

"So you killed a man in cold blood."

"What else could I do? You're looking at me like that, but deep down, you know the truth. This was your mess. I got stuck cleaning it up. Because I cared about you. I wanted to help your child." He stopped, closed his eyes, and added, "And I knew that if I killed Bacard, maybe I could save you too."

"Me?"

"Another cost-benefit analysis, Marc."

"What are you talking about?"

"It was over. Once Bacard was dead, he could take the fall. For everything. I was in the clear." Lenny came over and stood in front of me. For a moment I thought he was going to try to hug me. But he just stood there.

"I wanted you to have peace, Marc. But that would never be. I knew that now. Not until you found your daughter. With Bacard dead, my family was safe. I could let you know the truth."

"So you wrote up that anonymous note and left it on Eleanor's desk."

"Yes."

I nodded and Abe's words came back to me. "You did the wrong thing for the right reason."

"Put yourself in my place. What would you have done?"

"I don't know," I said.

"I did it for you."

And the saddest part was, he was telling the truth. I looked at him.

"You were the best friend I ever had, Lenny. I love you. I love your wife. I love your children."

"What are you going to do?"

"If I say I'm going to talk, will you kill me too?"

"Never," he said.

But I wasn't sure, much as I loved him, much as he loved me, that I believed him.

epilogue

A year has passed.

During the first two months, I racked up the frequent flier miles coming out to St. Louis every week, trying to figure out with Abe and Lorraine what we were going to do. We started slowly. For the first few visits, I asked Abe and Lorraine to stay in the room. Eventually, Tara and I started going places alone—the park, the zoo, the merry-go-round at the mall—but she looked over her shoulder a lot. It took some time for my daughter to get comfortable with me. I understood that.

My father passed away in his sleep ten months ago. After his funeral, I bought a house on Marsh Lane, two down from Abe and Lorraine, and moved out here permanently. Abe and Lorraine are remarkable people. Get this: We call "our" daughter Tasha. Think about it. It's short for Natasha and close to Tara. The reconstructive surgeon in me likes that. I keep waiting for things to go wrong. They haven't. It's weird, but I don't question it much.

My mother bought a condo and moved out here too. With Dad gone, there was no reason for her to stay in Kasselton anymore. After all the tragedies—my father's poor health, Stacy, Monica, the attack, the abduction—we both needed a second act. I'm glad she's near us.

Mom has a new boyfriend, a guy named Cy. She's happy. I like him, and not just because he has season tickets to the Rams. They laugh a lot. I almost forgot how hard my mom could laugh.

I talk to Verne a fair amount. He and Katarina brought Verne Junior and Perry out in an RV during the spring. We had a great week together. Verne took me fishing, a first for me. I liked it. Next time he wants to hunt. I told him no way, but Verne can be pretty persuasive.

I don't talk much to Edgar Portman. He sends presents on Tasha's birthday. He's called twice. I'm hoping he'll come out and see his granddaughter soon. But there is simply too much guilt there for both of us. It's like I said before. Maybe Monica was unstable. Maybe it was just a chemical thing. I know that a great deal of psychiatry problems stem more from the physical, from hormonal imbalances, than life experiences. Chances are there was nothing we could have done. But in the end, whatever may have been the origin, we both let Monica down.

Zia was initially hit hard by my leaving, but then she saw it as an opportunity. She has a new doctor in the practice. I hear he's pretty good. I've opened up a One World WrapAid branch office in St. Louis. So far, it seems to be going well.

Lydia—or Larissa Dane, if you prefer—is going to get off. She did a double-flip off a murder rap and stuck the "I was abused" landing with both feet. She is a celebrity again, what with the mysterious return of the Pixie named Trixie. Lydia appeared on *Oprah*, crying on cue about the years of torment at the hands of Heshy. They flashed his picture up on the screen. The audience gasped. Heshy is hideous. Lydia is beautiful. So the world believes. Rumor has it she is set to appear in a TV movie based on her life story.

As for the baby-smuggling case, the FBI decided to "enforce the law," which meant bringing the bad guys to justice. Steven Bacard and Denise Vanech were the bad guys here. They're both dead. Officially, authorities are still searching for the records, but nobody wants to look too closely at what child ended up where. I think that's best.

Rachel fully recovered from her injuries. I ended up doing the reconstructive work on her ear myself. Her bravery got major play in the press. She received credit for smashing the baby-smuggling ring. The FBI rehired her. She requested and received a post in St. Louis. We live together. I love her. I love her more than you can imagine. But if you are expecting a totally happy ending, I'm not sure I can give you one.

As of now, Rachel and I are still together. I cannot imagine living without her. I think about losing her and it makes me physically ill. Yet I'm not sure that's enough. There is a lot of baggage here. It confuses things. I understand about her making that late-night call and showing up outside the hospital—and yet, I know those acts eventually led to death and destruction. I don't blame Rachel, of course. But there is something there. Monica's death has given our relationship a second chance. That feels strange. I tried explaining all of this to Verne when he visited. He told me that I'm a dumb-ass. I think he's probably right.

The doorbell rings. There is a tug on my leg. Yes, it's Tasha. She is fully acclimated to having me in her life now. Children, after all, adapt better than adults. Across the room, Rachel is on the couch. She is sitting with her legs curled under her. I look at her, then at Tasha, and I feel the wondrous blend of bliss and fear. They—bliss and fear—are constant companions. Rarely does one venture out without the other.

"One second, pumpkin," I say to her. "Let's go answer the door, okay?"

"Okay."

The UPS man is there. He has packages. I bring them inside. When I look at the return address, I feel the familiar ache. The little sticker tells me that they are from Lenny and Cheryl Marcus of Kasselton, New Jersey.

Tasha looks up at me. "My present?"

I never told the police about Lenny. There was no evidence anyway—only his confession to me. That wouldn't stand up in court. But that's not why I decided not to say anything.

I suspect Cheryl knows the truth. I think maybe she knew from the beginning. I flash back to her face on the stairs, the way she snapped when Rachel and I arrived at their house that night, and now I wonder if it was out of anger or fear. I suspect the latter.

The fact is, Lenny was right. He did do it for me. What would have happened if he had just left the house? I don't know. It might have been even worse. Lenny asked me if I would have done the same in his place. Back then, probably not. Because maybe I wasn't that good a man. Verne, I bet, would have. Lenny was trying to protect my daughter without sacrificing his own family. He just messed up.

But man, I miss him. I think about how big a part of my life he was. There are times I reach for the phone and begin dialing his number. But I never finish the call. I won't speak to Lenny again. Not ever. I know that. And it hurts like hell.

But I also think about little Conner's inquisitive face at the soccer game. I think about Kevin playing soccer and Marianne's hair smelling of chlorine from her morning swim practice. I think about how beautiful Cheryl had become since she had the children.

I look down at my daughter now, safe and with me. Tasha is still gazing up. It is indeed a present for her from her godfather. I remember the first time I met Abe, that strange day at the Airport Marriott. He told me that you shouldn't do the wrong thing for the right reason. I thought about that a lot before deciding what to do about Lenny.

In the end, well, chalk it up as "too close to call."

I mix it up sometimes. Is it the wrong thing for the right reason or the right thing for the wrong reason? Or are they same? Monica needed to feel love, so she deceived me and got pregnant. That was how it all started. But if she hadn't done that, I wouldn't be staring down at the most wonderful creation I would ever know. Right reason? Wrong reason? Who's to say?

Tasha tilts her head and twitches her nose at me. "Daddy?"

"It's nothing, sweetheart," I say softly.

Tasha gives me a big, elaborate kid shrug. Rachel looks up. I see the concern on her face. I take the package and place it high up in the closet. Then I close that door and pick up my daughter.

acknowledgments

The author—man, I love referring to myself in the third person—would like to thank the following for their technical expertise: Steven Miller, M.D., Director of Pediatric Emergency Medicine, Children's Hospital of New York Presbyterian, Columbia University; Christopher J. Christie, United States Attorney for the state of New Jersey; Anne Armstrong-Coben, M.D., Medical Director of Covenant House Newark; Lois Foster Hirt, R.D.H.; Jeffrey Bedford, FBI; Gene Riehl, FBI (retired); Andrew McDade, brother-in-law extraordinaire and Renaissance man. Any mistakes are theirs and theirs alone. After all, they're the experts, right? Why should I take the heat?

I also want to acknowledge Carole Baron, Mitch Hoffman, Lisa Johnson, and everyone at Dutton and Penguin Group (USA); Jon Wood, Susan Lamb, Malcolm Edwards, Anthony Cheetham, Juliet Ewers, Emily Furniss, and everyone at Orion; and the always reliable Aaron Priest, Lisa Erbach Vance, Maggie Griffin, and Linda Fairstein.

Oh, and of course, a big thanks to Katharine Foote and Rachel Cooke for freeing me up so I could get over that final hurdle.

New York Times bestselling author
Harlan Coben is back
with a riveting thriller.
Turn the page for a preview of

JUST ONE LOOK

Available now from Signet.

Scott Duncan sat across from the killer.

The windowless room of thunder-cloud gray was awkward and still, stuck in that lull when the music first starts and neither stranger is sure how to begin the dance. Scott tried a noncommittal nod. The killer, decked out in prison-issue orange, simply stared. Scott folded his hands and put them on the metal table. The killer—his file said he was Monte Scanlon, but there was no way that was his real name—might have done likewise had his hands not been cuffed.

Why, Scott wondered yet again, am I here?

His specialty was prosecuting corrupt politicians—something of a vigorous cottage industry in his home state of New Jersey—but three hours ago, Monte Scanlon, a mass executioner by any standards, had finally broken his silence to make a demand.

That demand?

A private meeting with assistant U.S. Attorney Scott Duncan.

This was strange for a large variety of reasons, but here were two: One, a killer should not be in a position to make demands. Two, Scott had never met or even heard of Monte Scanlon.

Scott broke the silence. "You asked to see me?"

"Yes."

Scott nodded, waited for him to say more. He didn't. "So what can I do for you?"

Monte Scanlon maintained the stare. "Do you know why I'm here?"

Scott glanced around the room. Besides Scanlon and himself, four people were present. Linda Morgan, the United States attorney, leaned against the back wall trying to give off the ease of Sinatra against a lamppost. Standing behind the prisoner were two beefy, nearly identical prison guards with tree-stump arms and chests like antique armoires. Scott had met the two cocky agents before, had seen them go about their tasks with the sereneness of yoga instructors. But today, with this well-shackled prisoner, even these guys were on edge. Scanlon's lawyer, a ferret reeking of checkout-counter cologne, brought the total to six. All eyes were on Scott.

"You killed people," Scott answered. "Lots of them."

"I was what is commonly called a hit man. I was"— Scanlon paused—"an assassin for hire."

"On cases that don't involve me."

"True."

Scott's morning had started off normal enough. He'd been drafting a subpoena on a waste-disposal executive who was paying off a small-town mayor. Routine matter. Everyday graft in the Garden State of New Jersey. That had been, what, an hour, an hour and a half ago? Now he sat across the bolted-down table from a man who had murdered—according to Linda Morgan's rough estimate—one hundred people.

"So why did you ask for me?"

Scanlon looked like an aging playboy who might have squired a Gabor sister in the fifties. He was small, wizened even. His graying hair was slicked back, his teeth cigarette yellow, his skin leathery from the midday sun and too many long nights in too many dark clubs. No one in the room knew his real name. When he'd been captured, his passport read Monte Scanlon, an Argentine national, age fifty-one. The age seemed about right, but that would be about it. His fingerprints had not popped up in the NCIC computer banks. Facial recognition software had come up with a big goose egg.

"We need to speak alone," Scanlon said.

"This is not my case," Scott said again. "There's a U.S. attorney assigned to you."

"This has nothing to do with her."

"And it does with me?"

Scanlon leaned forward. "What I'm about to tell you," he said, "will change your entire life."

Part of Scott wanted to wiggle his fingers in Scanlon's face and say, "*Ooooo.*" He was used to the captured criminal mind-set—their serpentine maneuverings, their quest for an edge, their search for a way out, their overblown sense of importance. Linda Morgan, perhaps sensing his thoughts, shot a warning glare across his bow. Monte Scanlon, she'd told him, had worked for various connected families for the better part of thirty years. RICO hungered for his cooperation in a starving-man-near-a-buffet way. Since his capture, Scanlon had refused to talk. Until this morning.

So here Scott was.

"Your boss," Scanlon said, gesturing with his chin at Linda Morgan, "she hopes for my cooperation."

"You're going to get the needle," Morgan responded, still trying to give off the scent of nonchalance. "Nothing you say or do will change that."

Scanlon smiled. "Please. You fear losing what I have to say much greater than I fear death."

"Right. Another tough guy who doesn't fear death." She peeled herself off the wall. "Know what, Monte? The tough guys are always the ones who soil their pants when we strap them to the gurney."

Again Scott fought off the desire to wiggle his fingers—this time at his boss. Scanlon kept smiling. His eyes never left Scott's. Scott didn't like what he saw. Scanlon's eyes were, as one would expect, black and shiny and cruel. But—and Scott might be imagining things—maybe he saw something else there. Something beyond the standard vacancy. There seemed to be a pleading in the eyes; Scott couldn't turn away from them. There was regret there maybe.

Remorse even.

Scott looked up at Linda and nodded. She frowned, but Scanlon had called her bluff. She touched one of the beefy guards on the shoulder and gestured for him and the other to leave. Rising from his seat, Scanlon's lawyer spoke for the first time. "Anything he says is off the record."

"Stay with them," Scanlon ordered. "I want you to make sure that they don't listen in."

The lawyer picked up his briefcase and followed Linda Morgan to the door. Soon Scott and Scanlon were alone. In the movies, killers are omnipotent. In real life, they are not. They don't escape from handcuffs in the middle of a high security federal penitentiary. The Beef Brothers, Scott knew, would be behind the one-way glass. The intercom, per Scanlon's instructions, would be off. But they'd all be watching.

Scott shrugged a "Well?" at him.

"I am not your typical assassin for hire."

"Uh-huh."

"I have rules."

Scott waited.

"For example, I only kill men."

"Wow," Scott said. "You're a prince."

Scanlon ignored the sarcasm. "That is my first rule. I kill only men. No women."

"Er, right. Tell me, does rule two have anything to do with not putting out until the third date?"

"You think I'm a monster?"

Scott shrugged as if the answer was obvious.

"You don't respect my rules?"

"What rules? You kill people. You make up these so-called rules because you need the illusion of being human."

Scanlon seemed to consider that. "Perhaps," he allowed, "but the men I've killed were scum. I was hired by scum to kill scum. I am no more than a weapon."

"A weapon?" Scott repeated.

"Yes."

"A weapon doesn't care who it kills, Monte. Men, women, grannies, little kids. A weapon doesn't differentiate."

Scanlon smiled. "Touché."

Scott rubbed his palms on his pants legs. "You didn't call me here for an ethics class. What do you want?"

"You're divorced, aren't you, Scott?"

Scott said nothing.

"No children, amicable split, still friendly with the ex."

"What do you want?"

"To explain."

"To explain what?"

He lowered his eyes but only for a moment. "What I did to you."

"I don't even know you."

"But I know you. I've known you for a long time."

Scott let the silence in. He glanced at the mirror.

Linda Morgan would be behind the glass, wondering what they were talking about. She wanted information. He wondered if they had the room bugged. Probably. Either way, it would pay to keep Scanlon talking.

"You are Scott Duncan. Thirty-nine years old. You graduated from Columbia Law School. You could be making a great deal more money in private practice, but that bores you. You've been with the U.S. Attorney's office six months. Your mother and father moved to Miami last year. You had a sister, but she died in college."

Scott shifted in his seat. Scanlon studied him.

"You finished?" Scott asked.

"Do you know how my business operates?"

Change of subject. Scott waited a beat. Scanlon was playing a head game, trying to keep Scott off-balance or some such nonsense. Scott was not about to fall for it. Nothing Scanlon had "revealed" about Scott's family was surprising. A person could pick up most of that info with a few well-placed keystrokes and phone calls.

"Why don't you tell me?" Scott said.

"Let's pretend," Scanlon began, "that you wanted someone dead."

"Okay."

"You would contact a friend who knows a friend who knows a friend who can reach me."

"And only that last friend would know you?"

"Something like that. I had only one go-between man, but I was careful even with him. We never met face-to-face. We used code names. The payments always went to offshore accounts. I would open a new account for every—shall we say, transaction?—and I closed it as soon as the transaction was completed. You still with me?"

"It's not that complicated," Scott said.

"No, I guess not. But you see, nowadays we communicate by e-mail. I'll set up a temporary e-mail account with Hotmail or Yahoo! or whatever with fake names. Nothing that can be traced back. But even if it could, even if you could find out who sent it, where would it lead you? All e-mails were sent and read at libraries or public places. We were totally covered."

Scott was about to mention that this total coverage had eventually landed Scanlon's ass in jail, but he decided to save his breath. "What does this have to do with me?"

"I'm getting to that." Scott could see that Scanlon was warming up to his own tale. "In the old days—when I say old days, I mean eight, ten years ago—we did it mostly with pay phones. I'd never see the name written. The guy would just tell me over the phone."

Scanlon stopped and made sure that he had Scott's full attention. His tone softened a bit, became less matter-of-fact. "That's the key, Scott. It was by phone. I'd only hear the name on the phone, not see it."

He looked at Scott expectantly. Scott had no idea what he was trying to say, so he went, "Uh-huh."

"Do you understand why I'm stressing that it was done by phone?"

"No."

"Because a person like me, a person with rules, could make a mistake with the phone."

Scott thought about that. "I still don't get it."

"I never kill women. That was rule number one."

"So you said."

"So if you wanted to put a hit on someone named Billy Smith, I'd figure Billy was a man. You know with a 'y.' I'd never think Billy would be a woman. With an 'ie' at the end. You understand?"

Scott went very still. Scanlon saw it. He dropped the smile. His voice was very soft. "We talked before about your sister, didn't we, Scott?"

Scott did not respond.

"Her name was Geri—am I right?"

Silence.

"You see the problem, Scott? Geri is one of those names. If you heard it on the phone, you'd assume it would be with a 'j' in the front and a 'y' at the end. So fifteen years ago, I got a phone call. From that go-between man I told you about."

Scott shook his head.

"I was given an address. I was told exactly what time 'Jerry' "—Scanlon made quote marks with his fingers—"would be home."

Scott's own voice seemed to come from very far away. "It was ruled an accident."

"Most arsons are, if you know what you're doing."

"I don't believe you."

But Scott looked at the eyes again and felt his world teeter. The images flood in: Geri's contagious smile, the unruly hair, the braces, the way she stuck her tongue out at him during family gatherings. He remembered her first real boyfriend (a dork named Brad), her not getting a date to the junior prom, the gung-ho speech she made when she ran for student council treasurer, her first rock band (they were awful), her college acceptance letter.

Scott felt his eyes well up. "She was only twenty-one."

No response.

"Why?"

"I don't get into the whys, Scott. I'm just a hired hand—"

"No, not that." Scott looked up. "Why are you telling me this now?"

Scanlon studied his reflection the mirror. His voice was very quiet. "Maybe you were right."

"Right about what?"

"What you said before." His head turned back toward Scott. "Maybe after all is said and done, I need the illusion of being human."

about the author

Harlan Coben is the winner of the Edgar, Shamus, and Anthony Awards, the first writer to win all three. He is the author of nine previous novels, including *Tell No One,* an international bestseller, as well as the recent blockbuster *Gone for Good,* a main selection of the Book-of-the-Month Club. He lives with his family in New Jersey.

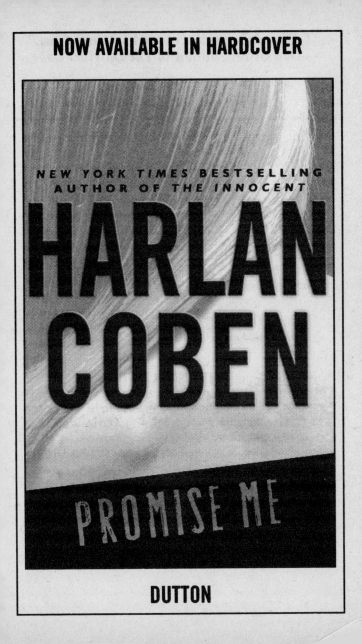

NOW AVAILABLE IN HARDCOVER

NEW YORK TIMES BESTSELLING
AUTHOR OF *THE INNOCENT*

HARLAN COBEN

PROMISE ME

DUTTON

> "The modern master of the hook-and-twist."
> —Dan Brown, author of *The Da Vinci Code*

NEW YORK TIMES BESTSELLING AUTHOR
HARLAN COBEN

JUST ONE LOOK

When Grace Lawson picks up a newly developed set of family photographs, there is a picture that doesn't belong—a photo from at least 20 years ago with a man in it who looks strikingly like her husband, Jack. And though Jack denies it, he disappears that night, taking the photo with him. Now, to save her family from a fierce, silent killer who will stop at nothing to get the photo, Grace must confront the dark corners of her own tragic past.

0-451-21320-3

THE INNOCENT

One night, Matt Hunter innocently tried to break up a fight—and ended up a killer. Now, nine years later, he's an ex-con who takes nothing for granted. His wife, Olivia, is pregnant, and the two of them are closing on their dream house. But all it will take is one shocking, inexplicable call from Olivia's phone to shatter his life—a second time...

0-451-21577-X

**Available wherever books are sold or at
penguin.com**